FOR THE GOOD OF ALL

ENDORSEMENTS

Part *Hunger Games*, part *Divergent*, part *1984*, *For the Good of All* weaves a world at once intriguing and terrifying. Dahl's imagination is on full display as she crafts a heartfelt story of a common struggle—being different. Ren's journey and growth through the novel is one readers can both relate to and learn from. From the opening chapter, to the close of the book, the action and intrigue will keep readers engrossed in Dahl's immersive storytelling
—**Aaron Gansky**, author of the Hand of Adonai series, *Heart's Song*, *The Bargain*, and *Who is Harrison Sawyer*

Sometimes a book grabs you and won't let go until it etches a mark on your soul. From the first chapter of *For The Good Of All*, I felt as if I knew Ren. Her dystopian world with its upside down form of justice was both thrilling to explore and easy to become immersed in. By the middle of the book, Ren's friends had become mine, and I wanted to fight for her and with her against her enemies. So by the end of the book ... I won't spoil it, but I will say grab the tissues. If you're looking for a book to get lost and found in—THIS is the one to read.
—**Annette Marie Griffin**, award-winning author of *What is a Family?*

FOR THE GOOD OF ALL

MB DAHL

Young Adult Speculative Fiction

PUBLISHING THE POSITIVE
Plymouth, Massachusetts

Copyright Notice

For the Good of All

Cover and Interior Design: Derinda Babcock

Editor(s): René Holt, Deb Haggerty

PUBLISHED BY: Elk Lake Publishing, Inc., 35 Dogwood Drive, Plymouth, MA 02360, 2021

Library Cataloging Data

Names: Dahl, MB (MB Dahl)

For the Good of All / MB Dahl

334 p. 23cm × 15cm (9in × 6 in.)

ISBN-13: 978-1-64949-348-4 (paperback) | 978-1-64949-349-1 (trade paperback) | 978-1-64949-350-7 (e-book)

Key Words: speculative fiction, good vs. evil, values & virtues, magical gifts, coming of age, Christian world view, romance

Library of Congress Control Number: 2021943772 Fiction

DEDICATION

This book is dedicated to my mom, Mary Owen Minton, who stepped into heaven on June 11, 2021. She was a true warrior and friend, and I'll forever be grateful for her presence in my life. An unlikely hero, my mom held on to Truth even through hardship, and she taught me how all good stories have conflict. As a matter of fact, I modeled a character in this story after her. She loved much, worked hard, and knew the price of perseverance. She would never think herself a hero, but sometimes heroes have scars and struggle. Their victory is greater because of the battle. Mom understood the fight to let go of the past and embrace the future. She knew that with Jesus, the darkness doesn't win, there's more to life, and good triumphs over evil. Thank you, Mom, for showing me there's always hope.

ACKNOWLEDGMENTS

So many incredible people have played a part in making this story a reality.

My first note of thanks goes to Elk Lake Publishing for giving me this incredible opportunity and for believing in Ren's story. Thank you a thousand times for inviting me into the Elk Lake family.

Some other dear folks to thank are the treasured Light Brigade (Lori, Cathy, Marcia, Lynn, Edie, Deb, Felicia, Tammie, Dee Dee, Jacquelyn, Colleen, Bethany, and Cynthia). Your prayers, encouragement, and example have strengthened me. I love that we've journeyed together for so many years.

Thanks also to my Word Weavers Page 18 crew (Annette, Denise, Franella, and Michele). Thank you for finding the story flaws and lovingly guiding me to a better place. And for your dear friendship. I treasure each of you.

A special thanks goes out to my super wonderful beta readers (Annette, Carole, Esther, Matthew, Tammy, and HmiChaye). Your insights and observations have strengthened this story. You helped make the characters lovable, the love story believable, and the twists unexpected.

A huge thank you also needs to be said to Vie Herlocker whose encouragement and guidance through the years has blessed me beyond measure. And I'll forever be grateful to Tammy Van Gils for being my writing buddy and dreaming that we might make a difference with our stories.

I also owe a deep debt of gratitude to my sweet family. Thank you, Mom Fran and Dad Ron, for always being interested in my writing. Thank you to my dad and stepmom Belle for your constant encouragement and for believing in me. Thank you to my mom for sparking in me the love of crafting a story and creating something new. Thank you, Julia, for reading my pages and giving me solid critique. Some of your spunk and verve has spilled out onto the pages. Thank you, Elizabeth, for the hundreds of conversations as I unpacked the plot and shaped the characters. Your feedback and willingness to come alongside me kept me going. And your creative touch is woven within the lines. And a thousand thank yous to my best fan and loving husband, Cameron. You made this possible. I might have given up long ago if you hadn't picked me up, set me on my feet, and pointed me toward the computer. You're the Owen to my Ren.

And finally, thankful acknowledgment must be given to the Lord God Almighty who walked me through every inch of this story. He gave me strength to start over when what I'd written was rubbish, and he helped me persevere until the characters came to life, and the climax became clear. He is the master storyteller. May this book and the ones to come in the Silver Rim Series glorify him.

CHAPTER 1

THE PROTECTORATE

Figuring out who you are should happen before you die. Ren hoped her self-discovery wouldn't take that long, but judging from her classmates' smiling faces, she was already behind the curve. Of course, they didn't have something to hide like she did.

The thought pulled the corner of her mouth into a sneaky grin. Here she sat amid fellow graduates, nannies, and guardians, and none had found her out. Seventeen years, one close call, and a thousand lies made the fake Ren the only Ren any of them knew.

Her teachers called her average, if not slightly challenged. They didn't see her breeze through assignments, feign shyness, or ace Bala's special training. Her classmates didn't see her either. They kept their distance. Ren glanced at the expectant faces around her.

She knew each name, their number, and the details of when she met each one. They didn't know her, though. To them, she was a lower level. A five station at best, not someone of consequence, a ghost in society—a cog in the machine.

The guardians were another story. They knew her. All twenty had interviewed her, tested her mind, and analyzed her body for the last five years. It was almost like they wanted her to mess up—like they wanted to discover she was broken somehow. But they didn't.

Bala helped with that. Ren searched the audience for her mentor. Bala sat three rows from the front, beaming and looking stronger than ever. The fierce nanny carried herself like a sentry guard. The defiant look in her eyes and disregard for the guardians made her unique.

And today, their fight to hide the aberration would be over. No one makes it through the raising home without being exposed. It's impossible. Nannies are everywhere, examining everything you do. Tons of tests. No one makes it above ground with an affliction, difference, or any other label they put on it.

But she and Bala had beaten them all.

And now, with every tick of the underground auditorium's oversized clock, Ren moved closer to her new life. She was more ready than ever, except for that nagging question of personal identity.

The clapping died down, and the Guardian Master took his place at the lectern. He nodded to the seventeen plebe graduates, dressed in their rusty plebe orange tops and seated center stage. Then, he bowed to the twenty guardians in red and black, gracing stage right.

The time had come. Ren would graduate. And sure, she was two years late, but in the Viand Village, no one would know her age or her struggle. They would only know her number and her name. She would have a clean slate.

A ripple of tingles flitted across her head, and the grin came back. Hours of training. Days, weeks, years of practice had brought them to this moment. Freedom awaited.

Without fear, Ren summoned the ability just enough to see the room. Her eyes wouldn't sparkle and give her away if she took a quick peek.

The gym lit up as if actual sunlight streamed through the fake windows. The vision moved to the catwalk, the rafters, and the banners she'd planted for a little surprise. She'd liberated them from a closet in the archive where she and Bala trained and chatted about everything from the formation of the Silver Rim to how baking soda and water make a good face mask.

It seemed fitting to unfurl two banners with the words Freedom and Truth spelled out in sparkling letters as the Guardian Master announced her assignment. No one would ever think her capable of the prank. Not someone assigned to the Viand, delayed for slow progress.

She ran her hand over the signal box in her pocket.

The green light on the receiver of the rolled-up banner blinked. Bala wouldn't have approved, but afterward, she would like it.

The vision blinked, and the banners gave way to black. Ren's attention swirled to the main doorway. Two sentry guards pushed through the doors, looking from their plateau-issued clip-pads to the audience.

Ren leaned forward, unsure if her aberration had taken a weird turn or if this was actually happening. She closed her eyes, then eased them back open. The sentries remained. They had their sights set on a nanny five rows back from Bala. The poor girl sat stone-faced, looking at the stage. She'd seen the guards too.

So had Bala. A glare replaced the nanny's smile. Two things the nanny hated more than guardians were sentries and people who did stupid things to get themselves into trouble.

The air conductor kicked on, and a rush of cool air washed across Ren's face. With it came an unbidden vision—a scene of the targeted nanny standing before the Guardian Master, pleading her cause. The picture flooded in and out in a few seconds, but it was clear. The nanny faced the Guardian Master while a child cried on the floor between them, a moment from the past.

"This little one has done nothing to merit an adjustment." The nanny knelt by the child.

"Nanny Reece, step back. You are not qualified to identify an aberration." A sentry grabbed the nanny while another guard scooped the crying child away.

The vision dissolved, and applause filled the room. The oblivious crowd cheered for the Guardian Master. He finished his speech and handed the ceremony over to Nanny Skelt. Ren's stomach tightened.

Bala didn't clap, and neither did Reece. Seventeen plebes might graduate, but the Castle Raising home would lose eighteen. The guardians wouldn't let Nanny Reece off with a reprimand. No, that kind of defiance demanded immediate action, the price paid for defiance to the mandates of the machine.

History lessons called it an evolution to utopia, but Ren felt the flip side of that message. The side where not fitting into a definition demanded a personal sacrifice. Where *goodness* called for surrendering to the needs of society for the good of all.

Ren closed her eyes and tried not to think about it. A pang of guilt swept through her. She hadn't surrendered. If anything, she and Bala had defied everything their world promoted. Her aberration remained hidden. She would graduate, and their victory would somehow weaken society. While a kind nanny would be accomplished and never seen again, for the good of all.

It made Ren sick. Bala didn't share the same confusion on hiding abnormalities and disregarding guidelines. To the nanny, defiance was a good thing, and *for the good of all* meant taking care of yourself.

"The Viand Village ..." Nanny Skelt tapped the microphone. "Is this on?" She poked it again, then continued. "Okay, I thought it wasn't on. Now, I'd like to introduce the ten plebes assigned to the Viand Village."

Ren sat straight and forced a happy face. She'd made it, and she needed to enjoy this moment. Tomorrow she would leave. She'd hug Bala, climb on the transport, and say goodbye to this hole of a raising home buried beneath the real world. Except for Bala, she wouldn't miss a thing. And she'd see Bala after a month, when it wouldn't seem out of the norm.

Skelt paused after reading each name for the smattering of pity applause. Going to the Viand Village ranked right next to making your bed or washing the dishes or a thousand other labor jobs that anybody and everybody could do.

Ren didn't care. She would cheer. She'd whoop and holler and push the buttons to release the banners. She and Bala knew what this day meant, even if no one else ever would.

"And Candler-42557R1." Skelt finished the list and waved her hand toward the ten standing Viand Villagers. Ren looked around. Skelt hadn't called her name. Bala looked confused too, which did nothing to calm Ren's pounding heart.

"Now, for the four placements in the Wall Lot." Skelt kept talking, but Ren couldn't compute anything. There had to be some mistake. Four large boys stood up behind her, and Skelt jumped on to the next list. "And now, the three prized placements to the Protectorate. We are proud of these three. Represent Castle Raising Home with your best. Please stand as I say your name."

"Ren-423B7."

Ren didn't move. Skelt repeated her name and number. The room was the quietest it had been all evening. Bala motioned for Ren to stand, but the mentor didn't look happy. Of course, she didn't look happy. The Protectorate was the last place Ren should go.

Taking a deep breath, Ren pushed up from her seat and felt Skelt's relief at not having to repeat herself. Bala exited the gym, passing the sentries who still waited at the doorway for their prey. Something was terribly wrong.

This wasn't how it should go. They had a plan. Bala had arranged it. The Viand Village, not the Protectorate.

Ren felt as if she were on the outside looking in. As she took her seat, her hand landed on the signal for the banners, causing the bright blue and purple swaths of velvet to unroll from the rafters. The crowd gasped and then cheered. Ren sat motionless. Freedom and truth were the last things she'd be experiencing. Tomorrow, she would go. She would leave for the Protectorate, and most likely before the first month ended, she would be the one with sentries waiting for her.

CHAPTER 2

THE ORDER

Owen shifted in his leather chair and scrolled through the pictorial list of plebes on his electronic clip-pad. None of the faces were friends, but a tinge of guilt shadowed his scanning, anyway. The elimination of one of them from his team would be hard.

His assistant, Nil, patrolled the aisles between the desks of their fifth-level office. The view from the large windows always drew Owen's gaze to the sky and to the faint shimmer of the Silver Rim in the distance. Usually, the view gave him a sense of all being right with the world, but not today.

The plebes—his little worker bees—chewed away at their assignments without a peep. Most of them didn't like him, but they followed his orders, and the relationship worked.

Two of the girls closest to the windows tapped on their clip-pad as Nil passed. Their messages popped up on Owen's device. Without reviewing them, he swiped away the alert from his screen. Why it never occurred to the plebes that the compliance regulators also monitored their clip-pads baffled him. The fragile world within the rim required balance, and balance demanded observation. Clip-pads were no different. It never failed, though. Someone would ignore traveling restrictions, or two unmatched lovers would message a little too much.

Owen shook his head and pulled up Whitler's order again.

J-This came down from the Plateau late yesterday.
New plebe arriving on the 3rd. Only twelve plebes

allowed per department. Send recommendation for transfer or accomplishment by the 20th. This is your department. See that it's done.—Overseer Whitler

See that it's done. Like eliminating a member of his team happened every day. The whole situation felt impossible. This wasn't like in the raising home when he had to decide who would be on his advanced team and who would stay back in the basics. At least then, the people left behind didn't become targets for accomplishment. They just had to wait another six months or settle on a lower tier.

Owen swallowed and realized his mouth was dry. He'd never intentionally sent anyone away for accomplishment. As much as he wanted the power and respect of a guardian, he didn't want to be the one to decide how much longer someone got to exist.

Not that there hadn't been a rival or two whose accomplishment would have been helpful. This was different. No matter how much the guardians preached that accomplishment of the few was for the good of all, something about it left him feeling empty.

His eyes cut to the large window of Whitler's office. The overseer typed away, oblivious to the team. Owen shook his head, if only he could transfer Whitler, that would solve everything.

The clip-pad pinged, and a message popped up. "Get in here." Whitler pushed all of Owen's buttons. The man lacked the capacity to care for anything but the appearance of excellence. Not actual excellence, mind you. Just ticking the boxes that made it look like you had done a good job. Anything deeper than that was beyond him.

Owen perused the room again and pushed up from his desk. The buzz of work and the innocence on the plebes' faces lifted him. There had to be a way around this. Maybe the new person wouldn't work out. It would be much easier to eliminate a newbie than one of his team.

Whitler kept typing as Owen shut the door. The rich smell of leather mixed with aftershave greeted the guide. As offices go, Whitler's was one of the best in the Sharp Complex. Enormous windows, handmade furniture, and the latest technology. The next step from here would be the Plateau—the guardians.

Whitler motioned to one of the large brown seats in front of the desk. "Please, sit." Owen complied without a word, and Whitler continued, "Did you get my message about the new plebe?"

"Yes, sir."

"What do you think?"

"Sir?"

"Do you have an opinion on who to transfer?" The overseer's face conveyed no emotion, just a matter-of-fact simplicity.

Owen rubbed his palms on his navy pants and tried not to sound dismissive. "Don't you think it's a little early to decide? The new plebe hasn't even arrived yet."

"Yes, I know. But I also understand these decisions aren't the easiest to make." He leaned back in his chair. "And we don't want to eliminate anyone who could serve a purpose down the road."

It seemed weird to talk about the dismissal of a plebe so lightly. Owen managed a weak nod.

Whitler noticed. "I see what's going on here."

"What, sir?" The room felt warmer.

"You're hesitant. I suspected this might be the case." The overseer glided up from the desk and stood. He had that fake let-me-be-your-buddy look on his face.

Owen wanted to refute him, but it was true. He didn't want to get rid of anyone, especially not for someone they didn't ask for or need. He nodded and swallowed the lump in his throat. Perhaps the overseer could step outside his narcissism and figure out a way around sentencing someone to nothingness.

"I've been where you are." Whitler moved to the long window facing the park near the river. Afternoon light silhouetted him. "I get how hard it is to judge someone else's merits and then decide their fate. This is a different playing field than the raising home."

Owen understood the differences very well. Two years out of the home, and he'd made plenty of hard calls, just none like this.

"It is what it is, though. We live in a small world surrounded by a wall. We do what we must." The overseer settled back at his desk. "After all, the choices we make are for the good of all."

"We give ourselves." Owen responded as he should but kept his eyes on the wooden desk in front of him.

"That's right. We give ourselves. And part of the giving is making the tough choices. Think about it. For the good of all, we give ourselves. It's not just our mantra. It's the fundamental rule for survival—putting aside our own needs to seek the good of the whole."

A charged quiet gathered in the room. Owen filed through his objections but knew better than to voice them. How could he argue with the sacrificial premise upon which their society survived? Master Tatief had created a utopia on the ashes of bygone worlds steeped in the idolization of the individual instead of the perfection of the mass. Still, sacrificing one of his team for the betterment of society felt wrong on a deeper level.

"I didn't call you in here to tell you what you already know." Whitler pecked his keyboard, and an image and bio flashed onto the wall screen to his right. A girl with dark brown hair, creamy caftewater-colored skin, and light blue eyes filled the left side of the wall. "Her name is Ren-423B7." Whitler leaned back. "She's from the Castle Raising Home, and she's seventeen years."

"Seventeen?" Owen took a closer look. "What's wrong with her?"

"Nothing. Seems the nanny assigned to her felt she wasn't ready until now."

"Isn't it odd? I mean, two whole years beyond the norm?" Owen read over the girl's file on the screen. Good marks in writing, math, and all the basics, but she had a few demerits for social issues. "What's the A with a circle around it at the bottom mean?"

Whitler tapped his keypad. "Looks like someone recommended her for adjustment."

"What?" Hope took a running leap into Owen's churning insides. "Why are we even having this conversation then? How is she at all fit for the Protectorate?"

"Let's see." Whitler examined the screen at his desk. "She went for an adjustment back when she was a little one. One of her classmates turned her in."

The scenario sounded familiar, and the exchange with Tylon flooded Owen's mind with guilt. He forced the memory back into a closet and focused on the current situation. "Why? What happened?" His voice shook. Residual guilt weakened his confidence.

Whitler's eyebrows went up. "You know how it is, Owen, don't you?" The overseer knew the history. Of course, he knew. He had everyone's file. "This time a classmate and a nanny reported her for adjustment, but the evaluation found her possibilities at contribution to be high with no abnormalities present."

"Well, I suppose that's something." Owen tried to move on. "She will have a lot to prove. Perhaps the order of dismissal won't be so hard to decide after all."

The overseer flashed him a look. "It won't be that simple." With a swipe of his finger in the air, the screen on the wall scrolled up to show the assignment orders at the bottom of the page.

Assigned to the Protectorate by special order of the Superintendre.

Owen felt the last drop of hope crash into the sea of his churning stomach acid, and Whitler's face confirmed the need to worry. The Superintendre wasn't someone to cross. This new plebe would not be the one to go.

CHAPTER 3

THE SUPERINTENDRE

Ren's hands shook like a guardian with a wagging finger and a guideline to prove. What had just happened? She couldn't go to the Protectorate. She would be a bunny thrown into a den of foxes.

A door creaked open in the old tunnel, and Bala hurried out. Ren ran to her in the dim light.

The nanny grabbed Ren's shoulders. "It will be okay. You can do this."

"No, no, it won't." Two levels below the main floor of the Castle, and Ren didn't bother lowering her voice. "There is nothing remotely okay about this."

"You are ready." Bala's dark eyes softened. "You can do it."

A cobwebbed globe dimmed and brightened on the cracked wall, silhouetting the nanny with an amber glow. Ren stood in her shadow, the knot choking her throat thudded to her stomach. "I'm not so sure."

"Oh, zounds. You're ready. You are more than ready. And you ought to be."

Tears perched on the rims of Ren's eyes. "Ready for the Viand or the Progenate or anywhere besides the Protectorate."

"Oh, stop it. The Protectorate's just another village filled with people who are all trying to do the same thing you'll be doing. Survive."

"The Protectorate's not safe." Five villages for assignment, and the Protectorate was the worst of all.

"Safety, smafety." Bala waved her hand. "There's no place that's really safe, and you've seen the worst of it here. We saw that today, with poor nanny Reece."

"That doesn't make me feel any better." Ren hunkered down. "At least in the Viand, I wouldn't be around people trained to identify aberrations and people of difference."

Cupping Ren's face with her hands, Bala gave her a look—the I'm-not-going-to-feel-sorry-for-you look. Then, she nodded toward a skinny tunnel on their left and headed toward the archive. The book-laden chamber served as their hideaway from the guideline-laced instruction going on above.

Bala waved on the orbs. "It's been a few weeks since we've been down here?"

The door to the closet where Ren found the banners sat slightly ajar. "Yeah, sure." Leather chairs, a large circular table, plus shelves of old-timey books filled the room. It was a forgotten place from a time when stories left you better than when you started them.

Ren latched onto Bala's strong arm. "Can't you just hide me here or something? There's got to be another way."

The nanny took Ren's hand in hers. "We're way beyond you staying now." The warmth in Bala's face melted into more worry than Ren had ever seen there. A spray of tingles washed up Ren's back.

Bala's hands were freezing. "I need to tell you something." More tingles, and now the knot in Ren's stomach turned to ice.

"The order for you to go to the Protectorate came from the Superintendre." She said the words like a big announcement.

"Yeah, so?"

"I've never heard of the Superintendre getting involved with a placement." Ren shrugged, and Bala gripped her hands tighter. "It's like the Guardian Master deciding what the motif for the new laundry room will be. It just doesn't happen."

She released Ren's hands. "I'd always thought getting you placed anywhere besides the Protectorate might be a challenge. You're too smart for your own good. Evidently, I fooled no one by holding you back two years."

Any other time the compliment might have been encouraging.

"I went to the registrar's office just now. The lady there didn't say much. She was terrified, and I guess she should be." The air kicked off, and the lights brightened. Bala leaned forward. "I know you don't get it, but the last thing we want is for the Superintendre to watch you."

"Why would he be watching me? I'm no one."

"She."

"What?"

"The Superintendre is a *she*, not a *he*, and the only thing I can come up with is she either knows something about you, or she's figured out who I am."

Another shower of tingles spread across Ren's head; a vision would come soon. "My aberration?"

"I don't think so."

"And what do you mean, *who you are*?" Numbing tingles grew in Ren's neck and shoulders as she watched the face of her dearest friend.

Bala had been there for everything. Ren knew it was a gift. Nannies didn't stay with a child for their entire life. Familial connections weaken the mind or something like that. Knowing Bala hadn't been a weakness, though. It had saved Ren.

"We need to talk." Bala pulled Ren to the chairs. "There are things I've hidden from you—things I'd planned to tell you once you got settled in the Viand."

"What are you talking about?" Ren wrung her hands. The tingles had moved to her arms now.

"I wasn't always a nanny."

Those were not the words Ren expected to hear.

"I once served as a sentry guard."

And neither were those. "What?" The confession registered in slow motion. More tingles and a wave of disbelief. "I thought you hated them."

A thin crescent smile lined Bala's pale face. "I was good too. My assignment with Master Tatief's personal guard meant everything to me."

The mention of Tatief stopped every tingle, thought, and feeling.

"I know." Bala looked like the same person, but she wasn't. "It's a very long story."

Ren couldn't look at her. "How could you?" A thousand conversations about the Master and the guardians crowded her mind. "How could you have never told me this?"

Bala stiffened. "I made a mistake back then, and now I'm bearing the consequences of that mistake. That's mine. It has very little to do with you except where our paths intersected."

"It has a lot to do with how much I believe you. How could it never have crossed your mind to mention this? All those talks about how the guardians don't live for anyone's good, how *they're* hypocrites, and how Master Tatief is the worst of all? You didn't think to tell me you were practically one of them?"

"I thought you'd be safer not knowing, but now it seems..." Her voice trailed off.

The threat of a vision populated Ren's senses again, sending a thousand prickles of energy through her body. This would be an unstoppable vision. Taking a deep breath, she focused and pushed the aberration back. Not yet.

The nanny touched Ren's knee. "Stay with me."

Ren swallowed and nodded, keeping the rest of her body still.

Bala eased back. She looked lost. If Ren hadn't been concentrating against the vision and already facing life-altering doom, she would've been worried.

"I'm sorry I never told you."

A threat of tears accompanied the tingles. So many things were changing.

"I wanted to protect you." Bala's eyes glistened. "I guess I'm not as good at saving a life as I'd hoped."

"I...." The invading vision made it hard to speak. "Hide me." Ren took a deep breath. *Focus.* "There's still time." Until the transport pulled away, there was still time.

"Most people only see their genetic donors once." Bala stroked Ren's hand. "That's Tatief's imperative. He creates life, and he takes it away." The scars on the nanny's face and hands took on a different hue. "Maybe this isn't about you or me or your mother."

"Mother?" That wasn't a term anyone used for anything.

Bala plucked a piece of brown cloth from her pocket. "I was going to give you this when we visited in the Viand.

I had planned to tell you more then, but you might need it now." Her icy hand slipped the cloth into Ren's. "It's a map of a place beyond the boundary. I got it from your father."

Ren pushed the cloth back to Bala. "Let me stay here. Please don't make me go."

Sprinkles of light now cascaded around Bala's face. She reached up and stroked Ren's cheek. "I would. You know I would. But now, you must go, and you have to blend in and not draw attention to yourself." The glow from Ren's eyes glimmered in Bala's.

"Take the map. If anything happens, if you need to get away, go to the cabin. I marked it. Your father's people will help you." Bala didn't sound like herself.

"The guidelines?" Ren screamed in her head. She hated the visions, what they stole from her. A thousand questions needed asking. Hugs needed to be given. Bala needed to hear how much she meant, but none of it would come. Everything Ren wanted was crammed into a basket and pulled back by the aberration, catapulted away. Instead of sharing her heart, she could only manage two words about breaking the rules.

Bala pulled her into a hug. "A guideline is only as good as the person who made it, dear one. Don't forget that." When she sat back, her tears left their perches. "If she comes for you, there will be no safer place for you than beyond the boundary. Keep the map, and trust no one."

Ren couldn't respond. The aberration had her now.

"You're going to be okay." The words sounded far away. "I'm so proud of you." Bala looked fierce again. "You deserve so much more than this. We've spent the last seventeen years hiding part of you, but the aberration isn't the enemy. This crummy world that doesn't see you for who you are—that's the enemy."

The flare in Bala's cheeks yielded to the vision, and the archive filled with blinding light. The aberration carried Ren away. She pulled her knees into the chair and watched the strange scenes unfold before her eyes. Faces she'd never seen. Places she'd never been. A world she wasn't ready for.

CHAPTER 4

THE SECRET

Dart ran past the line of old shanties without worrying. Most of the exiled had moved on, and she hadn't seen a sentry since before Altrist had found her.

The early-roll sun still hid behind the treetops. Morning dew dampened her boots. Slowing, she listened for a sign of Altrist in the thick woods in front of her. Nothing but happy birds and rustling leaves.

"Where'd you go?" She eyed the road into the woods. The dirt trail would end at a crossroads. One way led to the Protectorate and the other to the Silver Rim. Neither a happy destination. The last time she'd been to the Protectorate, she'd stolen a skeer and used it on the sentry she'd liberated it from. That was four years ago. She was twelve, and the sentry never saw her coming.

Dart left the road and climbed ten meters up a pine. A misty haze hung over the trees near the river behind her. Her new friends were back there, probably still getting ready for the roll and divvying up the long list of tasks for their big reunion.

To the east, an orangey strip of sky escorted the sun from the horizon, and in front of her lay the valley to the Protectorate with the tracks for the transport peeking between green hills. The rail curved closer to the forest farther up. Scrambling down, she aimed for a section of the woods where she could see the tracks better.

Her gut told her the transport had something to do with Altrist's running off. His secrecy about why he snuck away every morning didn't bother the others, but they hadn't faced the scariest parts of life like she had. They'd not lived with someone like Sully. They didn't understand how dangerous secrets could be.

Plopping down on a dry patch, Dart let out a heavy sigh. If Altrist showed, she'd see him. And maybe she'd get some answers and shake the feeling of dread that had been plaguing her.

A ray of sunshine filtered through the trees and fell across her knees. The thin material in her leggings needed a patch, and threads hung from the seams around the cuff of her brown coverup. Her mama would not have stood for such disarray. They might have been homeless, living in the woods, but they were the best dressed ones out there. Mama got her style from the villages and her days as a seamstress in the Viand. Dart knew early the importance of at least looking like you meant business, even if you didn't have a clue what you were doing.

Of course, that advice only went so far. Looking good didn't help either of them when a scinter was put to their throats. Dart forced the thoughts of Mama away, except for one. Mama would have liked it here with Altrist and the others. She always said there had to be a better way—something else besides Tatief's lies and the cruelty of the packs in the woods. She would've embraced these people and their mysterious leader.

Dart unfolded her hand in the light and traced her finger over the near faded image on her palm, a remnant of the leader's touch. The lines of the sunburst glistened in the light.

The body art had appeared the day she shared her story with the community at Snowshoe Falls. No body artist in the villages could have drawn it better. Altrist said the leader put it there.

They'd cried for her when she told them how the sentry had killed Mama, and they offered knowing, compassionate looks when she explained how she had no choice but to join a pack. A few of them had come from packs, though none of them were wild born. All came from the villages, refuse thrown to the side by a society primed to make the world a better place.

The sunburst was supposed to be a sign of the leader's care for her. A bright light shining in a dark place, and the forerunner to the gift she would get—a special ability picked just for her from the leader. But the gift hadn't come, and now the art looked more like a smudge than a promise.

A sudden rustle in the bushes interrupted her thoughts. Dart jumped to a crouched position and reached for her knife. It wouldn't be someone from a pack. They never made it out of their camps until later in the roll, and a sentry wouldn't be worried about being seen.

The sound of a struggle came from the thick bush. "Ouch. You have got to be kidding me."

Dart knew the voice. *Great.* Putting her knife away, she strolled up to the bush. Liza sat in the middle of a briar patch; her shiny black hair caught on both sides by thorns. Dart pulled the knife out again. "You're lucky you didn't land in a taxar bush."

Liza's head popped up. "Dart, what a wonderful surprise. I wasn't sure what was going on. One flash, I'm fixing my caftewater, and the next I'm being attacked by a bush. Can you help me?"

Dart cut Liza loose and helped her out into the clearing. "You'd think the leader would take care with where he deposits you when he whisks you away with that special gift of yours."

Liza gave her a look and didn't respond to the jab. No one thought controlling the gift was possible. Some gifts work that way, they said. You don't get to control them. It's total dependence on the hand of the giver of the gift.

None of it made sense. Who would give a gift that could land you in the middle of some place you did not need to be? Of course, any gift would be nice at this point. She wouldn't be choosy.

Liza hugged her and then spun around. "What a beautiful roll."

"Peachy." Dart breezed past her and returned to the dry patch of grass. Her happy-go-teleporting buddy followed.

"Oh, look. You can see the transport tracks."

"Can you?"

"Hey, a transport. Look, way over there." Liza pointed off to their left. A silver car hovered along the tracks.

Out of the corner of her eye, Dart caught a flash of white and Altrist stepping out of a wide circle of light. *Finally.* She started toward him, but Liza caught her wrist.

FOR THE GOOD OF ALL

"Oh, dear. I guess you're the reason I came here." White energy swirled around Liza and engulfed Dart. "Here we go."

Dart pulled, but it was too late. Liza's crazy gift consumed her and tore her away from the woods. The last thing she saw as the trees disappeared was Altrist's smiling face as he waved goodbye.

CHAPTER 5

THE BOY

The repetitive hum of the transport over the tracks steadied Ren's nerves. *It's okay. It's okay. It's okay.* At least that's what she kept telling herself. After Bala's huge confession last night, nothing would ever be *okay* again.

Someone laughed from the back of the car, and Ren slumped farther down in her seat. They'd been travelling for about an hour—she and thirty other graduates from Castle and nearby raising homes. This journey topside should have her smiling and laughing like everyone else, but all Ren could think about was last night.

Out of everything Bala had confessed, the nanny's working for Tatief hurt the most. The Superintendre didn't matter and neither did the mother/father stuff. But seeing her closest friend as a sentry fractured Ren's worldview. She heavy sighed.

The dark tunnel behind the window glass offered no sign of where they were. Just traveling upward, leaving the world of raising homes and progenates behind. Leaving Bala behind. So much of their insulated world was dark. Only knowing what you're told. Only doing what they say you can do.

A sparkle of light glittered in Ren's reflection, and she breathed in and forced it away. Bala had trained her for this—to hide in plain sight. Her focus needed to be on that right now.

She pulled the shade down and stared at the red leather seat in front of her. So far, the not-getting-noticed thing hadn't been hard. The other graduates ignored her like most people did.

Two Protectorate sentries, tall, lean, and focused, watched from the front of the transport. That's what she had to look forward to. A life of hiding under the watchful eyes of people trained to detect weakness and differences that weren't *for the good of all.*

How could Bala have ever been one of them? She was nothing like them. But the more Ren rolled it around in her head, the more she could see it—the way Bala moved, how she stayed alert, how she skipped cooking lessons for Aikido training.

It made sense, but it also hurt. Ren leaned her head against the metal window shade and closed her eyes. Last week she had lugged banners across the catwalk and planned to decorate her shanty in the Viand. And now look at her. Lied to, forced to the Protectorate, and hoping her head wouldn't start tingling.

Still, some place deep inside pulsed with hope as the transport snaked farther and farther from home. If those Protectorate sentries accomplished her, at least she would have seen the beautiful sky, felt a real breeze on her face, and walked barefoot under the moon. Those thoughts filled in the gaping hole more than she thought they could.

"May I have your attention, please?" The transport master's voice snapped through the speaker as he squeezed in between the two sentries. "The time has come, young plebes, to push your window shades up, if you haven't already."

Ren and the surrounding plebes didn't move.

He cleared his throat. "Now, please. Everyone needs to experience this at the same time. I'll wait."

The sound of window shades sliding up filled the cabin. Ren's hand trembled as she pushed hers up. A hazy gray tunnel greeted her, and she couldn't help but lean closer.

"This is the day you will see the topside world for the first time." He strolled down the aisle. "Oh yes, you've seen pictures and been in simulators, but there's nothing like a sunny day in the fresh air."

He kept talking, but Ren hugged the window. The gray tunnel lightened, revealing cement walls. She held her breath as a flood of whiteness poured through the transport. It felt like a dream—like there should be a crescendo of music somewhere and a choir singing.

"Take a minute to get used to it. It's overwhelming at first, I know." The TM's nasally voice detracted from the miracle unfolding.

A colorful world burst into view as the transport emerged from the tunnel. Trees and blue sky—Ren practically kissed the glass. Its perfection was too much. Her eyes watered.

"I've asked the engineer to slow down." The TM hushed his voice. "The area you see is unprotected and wild. Remember, the boundaries are for your protection. Don't be deceived by the bucolic beauty. Our Master put up the Silver Rim to keep us safe from destruction on the outside, and the boundaries around the villages do the same just like your raising homes kept you protected underground."

A stream flowed through the forest and crept away. Green leaves and pink blossoms colored the thick trees. Hills gave way to mountains, and the world went on and on.

Ren's body tingled, but not from her aberration. Beauty had awakened and taken on the form of pristine fields and puffy clouds. The guardians could make their guidelines, lay down their rules, and demand the unproductive in society be accomplished, but they couldn't stifle beauty. She was fierce and untamed. Alive, well, and present for everyone—weak, strong, aberrant, or flawless.

A tear slid down her cheek. "It's perfect." For a second, all her fears about what lie ahead vanished.

The other plebes shouted out everything they saw. "A squirrel."

"Look, the wind is blowing the branches," called the girl across from Ren.

"It's so big." the boy behind her said.

A flash of white pulled Ren's attention to a clump of trees deep in the woods. Wiping her breath from the window, she scanned the area. Something fluttered. A person stood among the trees, but she couldn't make them out. They were too far away.

Taking a breath, she focused, then hesitated. Using the aberration when she was already weakened with stress might not be good. Still, having another vision like last night's wasn't likely.

Another breath sent a soft spray of tingles through her head, and she willed the aberrant ability to guide her into the woods. A boy with prickly white hair capping his pale skin stood right in front of her. His puzzled face broke into a wide grin. He could see her. How could he see her?

She slid back in her seat. "A boy." The words popped out. The stranger waved, and then the transport curved away. Ren couldn't hold the scene.

"What in the world?" The plebe behind her hung over the seat. "What was that?"

Ren kept her eyes closed and concentrated on being normal.

"Did you see that?" The plebe asked again.

Ren lowered her voice. "Yes. Sit down and stop talking."

He leaned so close she could smell his soap. "Did you say it was a boy? It was kinda far away. All I saw was something white."

"What's going on here?" The transport master jumped in.

Ren eased her eyes open.

The plebe stood at attention. "Sir, this girl said she saw a boy in the woods."

Ren shot the kid a look.

"Oh, my dear, you are mistaken." The transport master smiled, but there was some worry in his dark eyes. "Back to your seats, everyone."

Without meeting the challenge, Ren cleared her throat. "I'm sorry for the disruption, sir. It won't happen again." What was Bala's first rule? Don't draw attention to yourself. *No attention needed here. Keep moving.*

The transport master didn't budge. "People don't live this far out. It's too dangerous."

It didn't look very dangerous. Ren nodded. "Yes, sir." Five more seconds passed before the master returned to the front of the car.

The guy behind her snickered. *Big mouth.*

The beautiful world looked less beautiful now. It took Ren a good ten minutes to shake the fear off and settle back into marveling at the countryside.

A flock of geese helped. The woods opened to yellow-flowered fields, and in the distance, smoke trickled into the sky from the rooves of shanties.

This would be it. Soon, she would step off the transport and start her new life, something thousands of others before her had done successfully. Maybe she could do it.

A burst of cool air flooded the transport as it lurched toward the station. Ren ran her fingers through her thick brown hair and slipped her shoes on. First, orientation, and then she'd go to her new housing. Tomorrow, she'd start at the Sharp Complex. It didn't sound too difficult.

Keeping her head down and doing her work shouldn't be hard. She'd done that before. The Superintendre's assignment could be met by a loyal plebe, doing her best for the good of all. Nothing strange and nothing out of the ordinary.

The inward pep talk lifted Ren's spirits, though her mouth felt like a sauna on steroids. Maybe the orientation would have refreshments.

By the time the transport finally stopped, her heart had practically beat its way to her mouth. She grabbed her bag, took one last look at her classmates, and headed toward the sentries in the front. The grouchiest sentry left his post and opened the side door. Ren followed him onto the platform.

Freedom. Topside freedom. The sun smooched her a warm welcome, and the lack of a ceiling and walls didn't bother her at all. No matter everything else, this had to be one of the most amazing moments of her life.

Before she could take another step, a guard came up with the transport master trailing behind. "423B7?"

A slight tingling flickered up her neck. "I'm Ren." She spoke through clinched teeth, more to maintain focus than to be temperamental, though she hated it when they used the number and not her name.

"Is this the one?" The sentry guard addressed the transport master.

"Yes, I believe it is." The master's voice quivered.

The sentry smelled like he had substituted cologne for deodorant. "Come with me, plebe. We have a few questions for you."

A happy-looking woman, wearing a blue coverup and white leggings, met the other two plebes. The woman shot a worried look Ren's way and then ushered the others through bright doors to their orientation meeting.

Ren stepped toward the woman. "But I have to go to orientation."

The sentry grabbed Ren's arm. She jerked away out of reflex and caught surprise in the sentry's eyes. Bala had taught her well.

"Sir." Ren recovered. "I'm happy to answer all your questions, but there will be only one orientation." She held up her clip-pad as if she had the guideline showing on the screen. "I will come directly to see you after orientation."

A smirk darkened the sentry's face. "Oh, really." He grabbed her arm again, harder this time. "You will come with me now, or not making it to your orientation will be the last of your problems." Jerking her away from the transport, he lowered his voice. "Try me again, and I'll ship you to the center."

Ren acquiesced and followed the guard. So much for not drawing attention to herself.

CHAPTER 6

The Opportunity

Late day sun shot amber rays across the line of fidgeting plebes. Owen had lined them up outside the Sharp building thirty minutes ago to welcome the new plebe.

He checked the placement orders again.

> *423B7 arrives mid-day for orientation; to the Sharp Complex by late afternoon.*

She should be here. He clicked the empty square at the top of the clip-pad. No new messages. How annoying.

He caught two of the plebes whispering. "Okay, okay, you can go."

With a collective sigh, the group dispersed. Owen leaned against the thick glass by the revolving door. He still had not figured out who to remove from his team. Petitioning for an exception might be an option, but he wasn't sure who to ask. Guardians didn't make change easy.

"Master Owen?" A blonde orientator climbed the steps of the Sharp Complex. The blank look on her face reminded Owen of someone returning from adjustment. "Your plebe was detained by the guard."

Owen glanced toward where his team had stood. They had just left him. How could they be in trouble so fast? Then he realized she meant the new plebe.

The orientator continued. "She's being questioned and should be released before all-in. Here." She handed him the detainment order, then marched off.

Owen brightened. This could settle having to eliminate someone. The Superintendre couldn't overlook a major infraction.

He jogged down the steps and caught a tier-three cart ride. The inner village square blurred by, giving way to shops, then to tier-five flats, and then opening to the tier-four shanty block.

"Halt." He called and stepped off the slowed cart. The hundred steps to the Transport Post would give him time to think. Adding an unwanted plebe to the team made little sense, especially if the new plebe had already committed an infraction.

Shadows draped the transport station, as pink and orange lit the warm evening sky. By the door, a huge plasma screen polluted the scene with messages. The words *You can make it happen* faded into an advertisement for the Transitory Matchmaker Service. Happy couples flashed by, and then the screen dissolved to black before coming back to life.

Owen pressed his palm to the screen. It flashed to white, then popped with the face of a sentry.

"Owen-427M8? What is your business at the Transport Post?"

"My plebe, sir. I got word of a detainment. I've come for a briefing."

"Your orders?"

Owen held up the detainment order. His hand shook a little. The sentry reviewed it, and then the doorway opened, revealing two armed patrolmen.

The guards walked fast on the slick black tiles, and Owen tried not to look like a little one running alongside his nanny. A female guardian, decked in full black, met them with a clip-pad in hand and a friendly face.

"Guide Owen, how good of you to make the effort. For the good of all."

"We give ourselves," Owen replied, a little too loud. Two years in the Protectorate, and he'd never been inside the Transport Post except for orientation and the paid tour.

The guardian led him down a darkened hallway to an even darker room. "The observation cube." She deposited him into a room with colorful buttons flashing and officers manning their stations.

A golden-barred sentry with poster arms for a workout vid looked Owen's direction, but then returned his gaze to the glass wall. Behind the glass, a girl in raising-home orange traced the decorative seam of the table with her finger.

Another guardian zipped into the room. "Sir, the report. The patrol in the woods turned up empty." He offered a thin clip-pad to the golden-barred sentry.

The sentry scanned the pad, grunting a few times before blindly handing it back. "Let's do this one more time, then I'll take a turn."

On the other side of the glass, a door opened, and a brunette in Protectorate blue slid into the chair opposite the girl. 423B7 sat up and clasped her hands.

"Ren." The woman leaned forward. "I need to ask you a few more questions."

"I've told you everything I know." A slight tremor in the girl's voice detracted from her look of confidence.

"I know you're tired, dear. We've been here longer than necessary." A threat outlined the words. "Let's go through this one more time. Can you tell me what you saw?"

Ren looked down, as if she were holding back a sneeze. Pink flushed her tan skin, and she started with a whisper.

"I was on the transport. We'd just gotten into the open, and I saw something white flutter in the trees."

"White?"

"Maybe." Ren flashed her icy blue eyes. "I don't know. It all happened fast."

"And then?"

"I thought I saw a person. It was so far away, though. I'm not sure what it was."

"A person? A boy?" The interrogator looked like she might pounce.

Ren shrugged.

The woman leaned back. "And there's nothing more you can offer?" An edge to her voice.

"No."

She went to Ren's side. "I hope you will trust us soon." She patted the plebe's shoulder, then left.

A door opened, and the woman entered the observation room. "Who's he?"

"This is 423B7's new employer." The golden-barred sentry smirked.

The woman offered her hand. "Oh, Overseer Whitler. It's good to meet you. We've been hearing great things about the Sharp Complex."

Owen shook her hand and shot through his options for correcting the first guardian interrogator he'd ever met. "It's actually Owen, ma'am. I am 423B7's guide."

"Oh, forgive me. A guide—" She caught the Master Sentry's eye. "How ambitious of you. It's good you're taking an interest in this recruit. She will need monitoring."

Gold-barred guy grouched at them. "I think it's my turn to *talk* to her."

The guardian held up her hand. "Not so fast, Jasper. The Superintendre doesn't want to draw attention or use force—yet. You're to stand down for now."

The tension between them quieted the room. "Your boss should let me do what I do best." Jasper eased off.

"Well, I don't think your methods will work with her. This is going to be a long play, and she will need a confidante." The guardian's gaze drifted to Owen. "She needs to believe someone actually cares about her— someone she will see every day. Someone ambitious and ready to do what's best for the good of all."

"We give ourselves." Owen chimed the mantra with the others.

The guardian huddled up to Owen. "Look at her." Ren had turned her chair from the glass and faced the opposite wall. "We believe she's a target for contact from a dissenter. Do you think you have what it takes to endear yourself to her?"

"Yes." Owen swallowed. "I think I can." Not exactly a genius reply, but it worked. The guardian returned the smile, though hers seemed a little wary.

Owen regrouped. "You know, new plebes often fall for their guides or overseers. It's quite common."

"Yes, I've heard of Master Whitler's charming ways." She hesitated. "But I've not heard of you."

Owen reached for a plausible explanation for his inability to have any type of relationship. "I'm just a mystery." That sounded better than an introvert who's happy to spend his evenings alone. "But ..." He turned up the spin. "... that makes me quite the catch, doesn't it?"

The guardian didn't buy it. "No, that will make you stand out more when you fawn all over her. What about Whitler? Perhaps he would be the better choice. He has a reputation for leading them on. It wouldn't be unordinary for him to take a special interest—"

"No," Owen interrupted. The tapping of buttons around him slowed, and the heat in the room quadrupled. Did he really just interrupt a guardian? Ignoring her icy look, he plunged on. "I can handle this. I'm quite adept at reading people, and as you've noticed, I'm highly motivated."

She softened. "All right then. I'm Maxey. You report to me. And remember, don't draw attention. Keep it natural. Your mission is to find the boy. He's the real prize. The girl's just a means to an end."

Owen nodded and met her charge with shaky legs and more volume than he needed. "You can count on me."

"Good. I'll forward my report to your clip-pad with more details." She motioned to a guard by the door. "You can escort her to her shanty."

Jasper joined them. "You know what this means, don't you?" He looked like he might take a bite out of them.

"What?" Maxey glared.

"It means instead of one, I might get two." He looked at Owen. "Or even three …" His eyes landed back on Maxey. "because no matter what favor you have with the Superintendre, if you fail the Master, you'll have me to face."

Owen stepped away. "If you'll excuse me, I'll go then." He hesitated for Maxey's assent.

The guardian skirted around Jasper and took Owen by the arm. "You may go. And ignore Jasper. It won't come to him, because you're going to succeed. Aren't you?"

"Yes, ma'am." Better platitudes of assurance eluded him.

"You have a month." Maxey walked with him to the exit. "Bring us some good intel, or I'll drag you to the sentry guard myself."

Ren tuned out her chatty guide. Her body ached from sitting in a chair for five hours, and the hints of her aberration peeked around the corners of her mind.

She'd kept the visions away throughout the interrogation. The constant testing by the nanny progenators in the raising home had prepared her well. Plus, Bala's training had come into play. Now, she just wanted to put it behind her, be alone, close her eyes, and wish herself back to a tunnel with Bala.

"It's important to contribute to the whole. Everyone does their part, and we all benefit." Guide Owen sounded like he had it all figured out. Just one happy world where beautiful people live on the bones of those who lacked a proper contribution.

Ren couldn't listen anymore. "We *all* benefit?"

Guide Owen didn't answer. The silence was nice, but Ren regretted her snark.

Owen slowed his pace. "You have every reason to not feel like the sentries are working for your good, but sometimes what appears to hinder our progress is actually very good for all."

"We give ourselves." Ren mumbled the words. If she weren't so tired, she would have tried harder at compliance.

"You need to be careful," Owen whispered. "I'm safe, but copping an attitude won't do you any favors."

"Not to mention, they're always listening, right?" She met his brown eyes.

"No, not at all. You're free now."

She shook her head and picked up her step.

Owen caught up and lowered his voice. "Okay, you're right. You'll need to be careful." He pointed to a tiny shanty nestled at the end of a narrow path. "They'll have a listening bean and cameras in your cabin."

"That's it? That's my new home." Her sanctuary. Another minute and she'd be pecking out a secret message to Bala, looping the cameras, and jamming the bean.

"Yes, that's it." He held out her bag.

A yellow light lit the square porch. "It's perfect."

"If you do well, you can move up." He took a step on the lane, but she cut him off.

"I like this just fine. And thanks for the tip about the camera and bean" He nodded like he'd schooled her, and she couldn't resist. "Oh, and by the way, they're watching this conversation too." She pointed to a fake nest in the tree behind Owen. "Keeping us all safe, no doubt."

Surprise flittered across Owen's face.

"See you tomorrow." She grabbed her bag and left him there to ponder how many more cameras and beans he'd missed.

CHAPTER 7

THE CHALLENGE

Ren held the clip-pad out for Lidya. The new friend snatched the device and started pecking away. The clip-pad had been a graduation gift from Bala, a special clip-pad, complete with a hidden switch to block the surveillance microphone on the side. Ren leaned toward her co-worker. "What exactly are you doing?"

Ignoring her, Lidya swiped something from her device to Ren's. "Just give me a minute."

All the other plebes crowded toward the front of the office to watch a funny vid about body art mistakes and the stupid alterations people had made to themselves. Ren didn't like those vids. After three days of trying to fit in and watching their mean screeners, she finally settled into hanging back with Lidya and getting educated on the Protectorate party scene.

Despite being two years younger, Lidya had more world experience than most of the plebes combined. She'd graduated from the raising home at fourteen, moved up from the floor below to this workroom last year, and had already made four matchments. Plus, the guy she crushed on now was a Viand and a secret forbidden. Ren didn't know what that meant exactly, but it sounded interesting.

"Here." Lidya handed the clip-pad back and, with a giggle, whispered. "What do you think?"

Ren opened the device to see Overseer Whitler's handsome face staring back at her. "Um ... what did you do?"

She leaned over. "He's the perfect screensaver. Those eyes. That hair." A sigh escaped her smiling lips as she took a long look at their boss sitting in his office on the far side of the work floor. "Perfection."

Whitler had the looks. Ren wouldn't argue with that. And this matchment-watching made more sense than experimenting with the smokes, blades, and bashes most of the plebes her age gravitated to. With her aberration, she didn't need anything else playing with her mind or helping her "escape."

Still, Ren hesitated to go for a matchment and put her profile in the blender. Lidya swore by the app. She said the guardians had perfected it. That was the wrong argument to use. Anything the guardians pushed as "good" was probably the opposite of helpful.

Bala had let Ren skip all the matchment requirements in the raising home, even the mandatory matchment required to graduate. The nanny had said there was more to relationships than what the guardians pushed in the vids. People were designed for a connection of hearts and minds before all that other stuff.

"Thanks." Ren slid the cover over Whitler's face. "He is kinda cute."

"Kinda? He's the cutest. And he's not above gracing one of us with his charms. I've heard he's already matched with two or three of his plebes. No one here, though. At least, I don't think so." She eyed the others and shook her head.

Owen and his assistant, Nil, exited the conference room where they'd been for most of the lunchtime. "Are those two matching?" Ren nodded toward the pair.

Lidya let out a cackle that attracted a few eyes. "Gats, no. Who would ever match with Nil. She's like a robot. No emotion, except she seems a little happier when she's writing someone up. And Owen." She looked him up and down. "He's got potential, but his social skills are lacking, if you know what I mean."

Owen's eyes met Ren's, and the corners of his mouth turned up. His social skills weren't all that bad. If anything, he seemed a little unsure of himself. Unsure and masking it with talking incessantly.

Ren smiled back, then turned her attention to the stack of assignments on her desk. This topside community wasn't so scary. She had a new friend who wasn't over forty, and she had her own place, her own little corner of the world where she could hide away and run to if the aberration showed up.

Maybe the Protectorate would work for her. No one, besides Owen, even seemed to know about the nasty interrogation when she first arrived, not even Lidya, who knew just about everything else.

Things were definitely turning out better than she could have hoped.

Owen scanned his notes. He hadn't made any strides in figuring out which plebe to transfer, and his progress with Ren had been painfully slow. Hopefully, this next assignment would be of some help, not with Ren, just with figuring out who to cut loose.

So far it seemed clear Ren shouldn't be the one to go. Besides with the Superintendre wanting her here, and Maxey, the guardian, investigating something, Ren already seemed to be an asset to the team. She was a mixture of smarts, experience, and somehow complete innocence. One minute she'd offer a strategy for a project, and the next she'd comment on the puffiness of the clouds. She had no clue about the merit system, always seemed to forget to respond properly to the mantra, and evidently had no idea when a man was showing interest in her.

It baffled him and somehow attracted him. Even if Maxey hadn't given him a spy assignment, he would have taken an interest in this strange girl.

"Back to your seats, everyone." Nil raised her voice. The woman sounded like a man who'd spent too much time at the smoke shack. "Before you begin your afternoon assignments, Master Owen has a challenge for you."

The side conversations died off as Nil finished her call to action and landed by Owen's side. He surveyed the room, lingering for a second on Ren. She tapped away at her pad, concentrating and serious.

Every conversation with her usually ended with him feeling like she'd just broken a guideline. But she hadn't. She'd say the right words, but her tone or the look in her eyes would convey the opposite. When she said the mantra, it was almost like she was making a statement against the whole goodness for all, which made little sense. Out of everyone he knew, she was the most giving. She helped those below her, didn't partake in the cruel screeners, and she treated Lidya like an actual friend instead of the target of shame that the other girls did.

He just hadn't been able to gain her confidence at all. At this rate, he'd have nothing to offer Maxey. And he needed to come up with something or Jasper was going to try his hand at Ren. The whole thing twisted his stomach in knots. Plus, he still needed to eliminate someone. The entire situation felt impossible and like any success would still be a failure.

He cleared his throat and focused on the task at hand. Time to separate the haves from the have nots.

"As you know, the Plateau wants to do some rearranging. I will conduct an array of challenges to better discern each of your gifts and abilities." He left off the part about needing to eliminate one of them.

"Yesterday afternoon's group escape exercise was a warmup." A group of guys near the front gave one another nods. They ignored Ren, who'd been instrumental in the win. "These challenges may seem like games, but I assure you they are not. You should approach them with the gravity you would a tier-deciding project." That had their attention.

"I'll read through the problem once, and then you will have thirty minutes to find the best solution. Write your solutions on your clip-pad and submit before the deadline. Any questions?"

The usual plebes piped up with their usual questions. Owen let Nil field them before he gave his final warning.

"At first glance, this challenge may seem like a gimme, but it's not, and I daresay not one of you will figure it out. Good luck and may the best plebe win."

Whitler graced the doorway of his office and listened. Owen nodded to him. The overseer probably didn't even know the answer to this one.

Owen scanned the anxious faces. "Your challenge is—you have a major assignment given by order of the Plateau to complete. A hard copy of the assignment must be delivered to the sentry post at the transport station no later than noon, and it must be delivered by you, in person. No one else. The time is currently ten a.m., and you are here in the workroom.

"You are on target to finish by the deadline when a sentry-issued proclamation is given to everyone in this workroom. The proclamation states:

> *All citizens of the Protectorate are hereby ordered to work only in their assigned divisions. No fraternizing with other workers within a given building will be permitted. In addition, no citizen of the Plateau is allowed to walk anywhere outside of their current building.*

"Your assignment must be delivered no later than the deadline. What do you do?"

A few hands went up immediately, but Nil stepped in. "No more questions. You have thirty minutes."

The heads went down, and the room was silent.

Owen settled at his desk and set the timer on his clip-pad. A message popped up. Ren had turned in her answer. *What?*

She sat at her terminal, staring out the window like she didn't have a care in the world. *Great.* So far, her work had been good, maybe even above average, but this shallow attempt at the challenge just highlighted her newness. Maybe he could offer again to tutor her or even require it. That might work.

"Sir?" Nil stood in front of Owen's desk looking, grumpier than usual. "423B7 turned in her answer."

"Yes, I noticed." He glanced back at Ren. She was talking to A-2. "No talking." It came out louder than he meant, but between having to get information for the guardian and needing to eliminate one of his team, he was a bit stressed.

Ren met his stern look, and Owen thought he saw a sparkle in her eyes before she looked away.

"Sir?" Nil hadn't moved.

Owen rubbed his temples. "What is it?"

His assistant leaned uncomfortably close and whispered, "She got it right."

CHAPTER 8

THE GIRL

The air vent was nearly as big as Dart's shower. She shimmied across the fortified metal toward the voices and held her breath.

Gander, the ex-sentry, sounded more like thunder when he talked than an actual person. His deep voice rumbled through the air duct. Something about safety and not trusting guardians. Same old, same old.

Dart rolled her eyes and moved closer. Altrist had arrived at Snowshoe Falls sometime last night and called a meeting. She wasn't invited. Not a problem, though. The air vents in their underground palace were as big as some tunnels. They'd never know she was here.

All the principals in both camps gathered below, plus their assistants. It seemed like they all had some special gift. Everyone except for Thim. Dart figured his gift might be his being okay with not having a gift. Nothing seemed to rattle him.

Altrist sat at the head of the room, glowing and giving Gander his full attention. The ex-sentry stood a foot taller than any of the others and a good two feet over Altrist. "You can't go to the Protectorate." The steel duct vibrated as he spoke.

"I know." Altrist looked away. "But I'm hoping I won't have to. If this villager found me once, maybe she can do it again."

"And we just wait?" One of the Pocket dwellers questioned from the other side of the map room.

"We've waited this long, haven't we?" Altrist always seemed calm and in control. A glow hung to his white skin. The very sight of him made Dart want to smile, even if she felt terrible. His kind voice, glowy presence, and intuition into her heart drew her.

He was her one connection with their leader. Altrist had been there right before she felt the leader's presence. She never saw their mysterious leader, man–or messenger, or whatever he was, but she'd heard his voice. It resonated in her heart, and she felt him take her hand in his, kiss her palm, and tell her he loved her.

Just thinking about it put a lump in her throat.

"Who is this girl anyway, and what does she have to do with us?" Gander thundered again.

"I don't know." Altrist ignored the mumbling in the back of the room. "But I think she was going to the Protectorate, and she has a gift." Dart recoiled. A gift? Village bait with a gift? How could that even happen? The murmuring got louder.

This time Anna spoke. Older than most, she brought years of village experience with her. She'd gone through the whole gambit. Bought it all until they refused to let her see her son. Then she broke. "Villagers have deviations." She spoke in a low tone, like it hurt to talk about it. "They don't call them gifts. They're considered aberrations. I never thought their abilities came from the Leader." A husband and wife across the long table agreed, but others looked confused.

Anna continued, "Most go for adjustment or accomplishment before they ever leave the raising home. It's a miracle she's even gotten this far. Aberrants do not live free."

"Well, this one does." Altrist sounded tired. "At least for now."

That's what he was doing in the woods, looking for some village girl. Dart's pulse picked up steam. Six short cycles ago, she had been the one Altrist found in the woods. He'd brought her back here and given her a home. She shouldn't be upset if he wanted to do that for someone else. Still, a villager with a gift wasn't fair.

Altrist's calm voice broke the rising angst in the room. "I don't know why I saw her or what exactly her gift is. I do know that it wasn't a coincidence. I was in the woods at that moment, and she found me. No coincidences. The Leader is in this, and I mean to see it through."

The room hushed, and then Gander took up his cause. "But you can't go to the Protectorate. We can't risk it."

"He can't, but I can." Olivope spoke. Dart scooted closer. She'd only seen the female messenger twice, and only from afar. "I can go. I have a better chance of not being noticed."

The grumbling started again, and Dart repositioned herself to get a better look at Olivope. The beautiful messenger sat opposite Altrist. Her skin glowed too, more pink than white. Tall and slim, she looked older, maybe twenty to Altrist's twelve. Both were ageless, though. Like the leader, time did not affect them.

"We can't risk you being caught either. Tatief hasn't given up the search. It's too dangerous." Pander argued this time. He did the patrols. He knew how dangerous it was out there. "Why is this girl so important? So, she has a gift. We have gifts too. We don't need her."

Altrist stood. "This isn't a question of needing her. It's a question of helping her. Do we just live in the caves and in Pocket using our gifts and keeping to ourselves? Is that what we're here for?"

No one answered, and Dart held her breath. For a brief flash, she felt like she might be intruding, but she pushed the thought away.

"We owe it to our camps to care for our own." Frish stood when he spoke. An ex-sentry like Gander, he was older than most and stronger.

"If we stick to ourselves and don't make a difference, then we're no better than the packs. Those sick, sad people care for no one but themselves. Their hatred controls them. They're just as imprisoned by Tatief's lies as those in the villages. Their exile did not enlighten them to the truth. Reality stares them in the face, and they deny it."

Shame snaked its way into the air vent and curled around Dart. It wrapped its guilty thickness around her heart and made it hard to breathe. She was a wild born, a pack dweller. Not exactly exiled, but about the same. The exiled didn't have gifts or aberrations or whatever they called them.

Images from her past skittered across her mind. Ugly pictures, painful ones. And things she'd done, bad, awful things.

Altrist kept talking, but Dart scooted back. She didn't want to hear anymore. Some things were better left in the dark, unsaid and unseen. Life in the packs was bad. They didn't have to tell her. She knew firsthand. Every day here in their underground sanctuary reminded her of how far she'd come from that night in the woods, wanting to die while she fought to live.

The woods always filled up Dart's senses and helped her thoughts not go negative. She plopped down at the crest of the hill and faced the stream below. No matter how much they told her she would get a gift, it didn't matter. She didn't have one, and something inside told her she would never get one.

Maybe the differences between her and them were just too great. No pack-born person had ever left that world for theirs. Most never lived long enough, but still. Maybe the villages had one thing right. Bad genetics can't be overcome. The only hope is elimination—eradicating the culprits and cleaning the gene pool.

Leaning back, she rested her head on her hands and closed her eyes. A crow cawed to her left, and a squirrel scampered through the brush behind her. This made her happy—being out here where the world kind of stops and time slows down. The afternoon sunshine filtered through the trees and kissed her cheek.

A breeze brought a fresh dose of blossoms to her nose, just as a twig snapped to her left. Her eyes flew open, and she reached for her skeer which she'd left at the cave. *Shikes!*

Someone moved on her left with clumsy feet. Rising, she turned and waited for him to show himself.

An arrow struck the ground by her right leg. She shrugged and tried her best to look bored, though the adrenalin pumped double time. Two exiles way outside their territory.

A skinny redhead carrying a bow jumped down from a tree. "Sully sent us to gives you a message."

Next, the clumsy one on the left stepped into view. She recognized him. "Hey, Cable, still running with Sully's posse?" He nodded and didn't seem as confident as the other guy.

"Sully says you got two choices." Arrow man held up three fingers. "You come backs or we drag you backs."

Dart inched her foot backward. She might not fit in Altrist's world, but there was no way she'd ever go back to Sully's.

"You hear me." The freckled spokesman pulled out another arrow and nocked it to his bow. His hands shook like crazy. "Don't make this any harder than it needs to be. We can all still be friends."

"Friends?" Dart drew in a deep breath and steadied herself. "I'll die before I go with you."

Arrow man chuckled and licked his lips. "Have it your way."

A light flashed behind her, and Dart's heart jumped at the sound of Altrist's voice.

"Maybe there's another option." The messenger's childlike voice didn't fit the scene.

An arrow flew, but Altrist deflected it with a wave of his hand. He stepped beside Dart and gave her a smile. "How ya doing?"

"I've been better." She checked the woods for other exiles. They were like vultures. Where there was one, another wasn't far behind. "We should maybe go."

The guy with the arrow took another hopeless shot, then yelled to his counterpart, and they retreated, yelling something about freaks and magic.

Altrist squeezed Dart's hand. "You sure you're okay?"

She wanted to hug him, but instead she nodded. "They wanted me to go back."

"But you don't want to go back." Altrist's statement hung in the air.

"No, I don't."

"But something's bothering you." He led her back to the trail toward the falls. "You can talk to me about it, if you want. You're not alone anymore."

She smiled and looked at her hand in his. His white skin glowed against her tanned fingers. There was dirt under her fingernails, and she wondered if he noticed how sweaty her palms were.

So much had changed for her over the last six cycles. Life with Altrist and the others had delivered her from night to brilliant day. Yet, she still felt like she needed to shield her eyes and hide away. Like she should watch them from the shadows for just a little while longer to make sure they didn't vanish like a dream or stab her in the back like everyone else she'd ever known.

"I'm fine." She lied. Altrist didn't press her. His deep blue eyes only held love.

They walked back in silence, and Dart let her mind wander to the girl from the Protectorate. Would she struggle as much to fit into their world, or would it all feel like she was waking up and coming home?

CHAPTER 9

THE "SORT OF" DATE

Lights twinkled in the homes below. Owen loved the view of the Vantages from the lookout. As the shadows swept in, each magnificent home came to life, readying itself for its master's return.

"Amazing," Ren whispered from her spot beside him. Owen had almost forgotten she was there. They'd spent the last two hours together, and all he'd heard from her was a word here and there. He'd used his best stuff, too. The story about how he'd graduated early. How he owned the prestige of being the second youngest guide in the Protectorate. And he even shared about his struggle to be relatable. That part was meant to make her feel sorry for him, but so far, it wasn't working.

She'd hardly noticed any of it. The three butterflies they'd passed had gotten more of a reaction out of her.

He leaned forward on the railing of the overlook. "Yes, it is amazing." Maglium orbs came on in another house, sending a spray of light up into the trees. "Look at that. One of these days, I'm going to be there." The wind danced across the leaves, and the silver outlines of the homes glistened in the pinks of the sunset.

"What?" Ren looked at him straight on for what felt like the first time. Finally, some interest.

"I'm going to live in one of those luxurious homes one day."

She glared. At least, he thought it was a glare. And then, she returned her attention to the treetops, speaking under her breath. "You've got to be kidding."

Owen pulled back. "What did you say to me?" He wasn't entirely sure whether to be indignant at her tone or encouraged that she had spoken more than two words to him.

If she'd been anyone else, he would have given her a demerit for disrespecting authority. But this called for more care. They were over a week into his month deadline from Maxey, and this was the first sentence Ren had actually spoken to him since he'd escorted her home her first day.

He stood straight and waited. She glanced up once, but her lips didn't budge. Taking a breath, he softened his approach. "What did you mean? I'd like to know."

She gazed back toward the view and took a good minute to speak. "I just thought it was strange for you to be enamored with the beauty of the buildings when there's all this to see." She waved her hand toward the treetops, dusty purple sky, and darkening mountains.

Owen took in the view. A deep ribbon of purple reached down toward the horizon where the last pinks of sunlight dipped beyond the Silver Rim. Fireflies flashed in the trees and across the valley. And street orbs popped on as the shadows reached the roads of the Protectorate. If there'd been music playing, it would have been a symphony. She was right.

He nodded, and a calm quiet settled between them. Owen welcomed the silence. He needed to think. No one below his station had ever reprimanded him before, and he was pretty sure no one above him had ever been right.

"It's spectacular." Ren broke the quiet. "Even if it is mostly cloudy." Eight words. She gave him eight words. He needed to respond, say something to carry the conversation forward, but his injured ego muzzled him for the moment.

A breeze blew up from below, carrying the scent of someone's dinner, and Owen's stomach growled. Then the words he needed popped out. "Are you hungry? There's a great place for sandwiches near the park." Not exactly an on-topic response, but what says "let's be friends" and "you tell me what you saw" better than buying someone food?

She didn't respond, and the awkwardness got louder.

Now what? Should he ignore that he just invited her on a date, sort of? This whole thing was exhausting. The transitory matchment service and Blender app seemed seriously brilliant right now. No wondering about what's going on or what to say, just straight up clarity about what's expected and where it would go.

"Okay." Ren spoke so quietly it almost didn't register. "Really?"

She smiled, and Owen didn't wait for more affirmation. Evidently the secret to getting her to talk was to be quiet and not easily offended.

Shaking his stave on, he held the light up and led the way down Overlook Road. He talked less on the way down, and Ren pointed out all kinds of things he hadn't noticed or thought about before, like the way the trees created a tunnel for the road and the sweet scent of the blossoms.

The crowds in town had thinned by the time they reached the restaurant, a tiny hut nestled among the trees in the park by the river. Decorated with old-timey stuff, the restaurant didn't use solar orbs. Candles lit the tables, casting a warm light between them.

Owen ordered for them once it was clear Ren had never seen a menu before. Of course, there weren't any restaurants at the raising homes, but they trained people for the topside culture, didn't they? After the server set down silverware and took their orders, he attempted to launch into an actual conversation.

"So." Owen paused until she looked at him. The radiant look in her eyes took him a second to process. She caught him off guard—a plebe with a bunch of paradoxes. The way she stood tall and sure of herself, but then appeared to recoil when you addressed her directly. Being shy and restrained, but not caving when questioned by a superior, and then, just now, taking him to task for not appreciating nature. She apparently couldn't graduate on time, but had no problem solving the last challenge he gave.

"Tell me about yourself." He leaned forward. "What raising home were you in? Any hobbies? What do you want to share about Ren?"

Her eyes widened a bit, but she didn't look away this time. "Um, I don't know." She fidgeted with her hands. "I was in the Castle Home ... for most of the time." Her voice trailed off.

Most of the time. That normally would merit a few more questions, but Owen let it go. He knew why she had moved.

There's no going back once you leave for adjustment, even if they don't scramble your brain.

He moved on. "No sunsets or butterflies in the raising home."

"No, but Bala and I used to go to the observation deck and watch the colors in the sky change."

"Bala?"

The server dropped off their fizwater, and Owen shot her a look. Ren was talking, and he didn't want anything to stop that.

This time Ren waited to speak as the tier-five worker padded away. "My nanny."

"A companion nanny?" Owen thought back over her file. Bala had been around Ren for a while, longer than a normal companion nanny.

"I guess you could say that. I'm not sure how it worked, but Bala has always been there." The candlelight flickered in Ren's eyes.

"Do you miss her?" Owen had grieved his companion nanny when he'd come above. "They become such a part of your life, and then they're gone, and you never seen them again. It's weird when you think about it."

"I do miss her." A heaviness carried Ren's words. "A lot. But I don't miss the raising home and being monitored all the time and the constant indoctrination of Tatief worship and guardian perfection."

She did it again. The words weren't infractions, but they were so close to the edge that Owen checked the room for sentries. Still, he needed to gain her trust, and what better way to gain trust than to join in on the rebellion. It wasn't so hard, anyway. He had his own beef with the powers that be, making him eliminate someone from his team.

"I know what you mean." He leaned forward and lowered his voice. "But it's not all rainbows out here. I recently got an order from the Plateau to eliminate one of our team." Better to not mention the elimination was because of her being added.

Ren moved closer. "What do you mean?"

"They say I have to transfer someone. Only twelve to a team." Their faces were so close he could smell her coconut shampoo. "That's why I've been giving those challenges. I'm trying to figure out who should go."

"That's terrible." She sounded like she meant it. Unlike most people who breezed across the surface of a bad situation with fake platitudes, Ren took off her shoes and jumped in. No breezing by. It was full submersion or nothing at all with her. "Wait a minute." She drew back. "You can only have twelve. It's because of me? You have to eliminate someone because I'm here?"

Owen hadn't thought his spiel all the way through. She was a quick one.

"I don't even want to be here. I was supposed to go to the Viand. And then ..." Her voice trailed off.

"I know." He grappled for a way back to a positive place to gain her trust. "The Superintendre wants you here, and that's how it's got to be. It's not on you, and it's not on me."

She looked like she'd just gotten a demerit and been told she'd be going to the center for a revision. "It's not fair." Her words barely made it to him.

He couldn't argue with her. As much as he wanted to be an actual guardian, live in a fancy house, and go to the Plateau, some of this stuff made him sick. He couldn't swallow the idea the balance of their world relied on good people going away forever. He'd fallen for all that once, and now he knew the cost of it—what it would do to the inside of you, how it hollows you out and makes you more of a robot than a person.

"I don't know what I'm going to do." He put aside his task from Maxey for a moment. "I've thought about petitioning for a difference, but I'm not even sure where to start, and Whitler's no help."

"Of course, he wouldn't help you." Ren snapped, then caught herself. "I mean ... he's just ... you know ... he pretty much can't think of anyone beyond himself."

Owen smiled. A real-bonding-over-Whitler-dislike smile. "You've got that right." His eyes met hers, and she broke into a slight grin. A weird and unfamiliar feeling ran through his heart. A light, happy sensation. Like the world wasn't messed up, and he wasn't here to trick her into talking. It was just him and her by candlelight, sharing bits of truth and being real.

"One thing's for certain." Owen paused while the server set their sandwiches down. "I'm glad you're here, Ren-423B7."

"Oh, I hate the number." She brushed off his compliment and picked up her sandwich.

His eyes lingered on her a second longer. He meant it. He was glad she was here.

CHAPTER 10

THE SECRET FORBIDDEN

This was a stupid idea. Ren leaned against the concrete back wall of the pavilion and glared at Lidya. Her new friend poked her head around the side toward the park. "He said to meet him at *our* place. He'll be here."

The river flowed in front of them, and Ren picked up a rock and tossed it at the water. She liked the water, but it made her uneasy. All those failed swimming lessons with Bala stayed close to the surface. "Behind the old pavilion near the river is your *place*? That sounds really romantic."

"And you would know about romance, how?" Lidya came back around and gave Ren a look. "The cameras back here don't work. It's the only place besides the woods where we can be free of the compliance regulators."

Meeting Lidya's "secret forbidden" wasn't at the top of Ren's fun list, but friends know stuff about you, and this is what Lidya wanted to share. Ren pulled open her messenger bag and rummaged for a snack. "You know, he doesn't have to be a secret. You could just submit a ticket. It's a few keystrokes, and it's registered. They don't really care, right?"

"What fun is there in that? And yes, they do care." Lidya returned to watching for her mystery guy. "They care about it all. You don't walk into the Sharp Complex without them measuring your temperature and checking your vitals. It's all great. I know. For our own good, but sometimes it just feels a little claustrophobic."

Ren couldn't argue with her. All the boundary lines and guidelines and curfews felt restrictive instead of freeing. She pulled out a nuggetbar and the map Bala gave her. The river was the only identifiable landmark she'd noticed so far.

"What's that?" Lidya had left her post.

Ren held up her nuggetbar and crumpled the map. "Salted caramel, apple, and nut."

"Not that. The dirty cloth in your hand." A mixed expression of curiosity and accusation punctuated Lidya's perfect eyebrows.

A man's voice broke the tension. "Well, who do we have here?" Lidya's secret forbidden jumped from the other side of the river to a large rock protruding from the water.

Lidya hopped and clapped. "This is Ren, the new one." She turned back to Ren. "That's him. So cool, right?"

Cool? He was blatantly breaking a major guideline. Ren checked the dangling cameras again.

"Ren, this is Pandon. He works in delivery." The unshaven tallish guy leapt over two more rocks and then to the bank.

A hint of beef jerky and sweat drifted from the rugged lover boy. "The new one, eh?" He slid his arm around Lidya's bare shoulders.

Ren could hear Bala in her head saying it might be permissible, but that doesn't make it beneficial. "Were you just outside the boundary?" She sounded like a nanny.

Pandon grinned. "Maybe." He didn't carry himself like most of the Viand workers. A black, long-sleeved shirt peeked out from under his green coverup, and he spoke more assertively than any five tier Ren had ever seen.

White teeth capped his smile. "So, what do you think of the great Protectorate—the place where beauty and brains make guides and guardians?" He pulled Lidya closer, and she giggled.

"It's fine. I guess." A warm breeze blew up from down the river, wisping Ren's hair around her face.

"Oh, it's more than fine. This is greatness." His tanned skin complimented his dirty blond hair.

"That's right." Lidya piped in. "The Protectorate is where we pro-practice it until we pro-perfect it and move to the pro-plush Plateau."

Ren shook her head. Pro-propaganda was more like it.

Pulling his arm from Lidya's shoulder, Pandon leaned forward. "Take it. You deserve it. It's what you make of it. If you want it, it's yours."

Ren shifted backward, and Pandon eyed her like a cat about to pounce.

"You've got to play the game, Ren." He acted like he knew her. "Use whatever you can for an advantage. C'mon, what do you say?"

Lidya pushed his shoulder. "Stop playing with her, Pandy."

He ignored her. "It's all about what you can do. What can you do, Ren? What do you have to offer that's brought you here?"

Ren swallowed, and the pressure of a vision waved through her head. Who was this guy? She pushed back. "Well, I guess I could ask you the same thing." He had the smugness of a guardian and the force of a sentry all rolled into his low-tier green coverup. "From the looks of your Viand placement, I suppose you've not been so successful at navigating the demands of the contribution expected by our great guardians."

Lidya got quiet, and Ren regretted her big mouth.

But Pandon didn't miss a beat. "Well done." He clapped his hands. "She's everything you said, Lid. Smart, blunt, and beautiful."

Ren broke free from his eyes.

Pandon held out a hand. "Lidya told me about your winning the challenge and being super mysterious. I just thought I'd see if you're a newbie shooting for the Plateau or if you're normal like the rest of us."

Ren shook his hand and felt a tingle up her arm. Nothing seemed normal about Pandon. Out of the corner of her eye, something flashed across the river. Shadows settled in the trees, and the water took on a dark hue. "Did you see that?"

Pandon chuckled. "That's the mazar. It's a kind of laser fencing to protect the boundary."

A tiny blue light shone midway up a tree. It brightened every few seconds, then went off before building back up. At its brightest, Ren could make out thin lines strung from tree to tree. "A fence to keep us in?"

"Or to keep what's out there from getting in here." Pandon unhinged himself from Lidya and got in Ren's bubble. "It's all for our good, remember?"

Ren nodded. "What's out there?"

"There's all kinds of stuff out there."

Lidya moved between them, but Pandon kept his focus on Ren. "I can take you out there sometime."

Lidya hmphed.

"Both of you." Pandon smiled, but Lidya stayed cold and grabbed the map from Ren.

"Maybe you could use this." She unfurled Bala's map.

Pandon plucked it from her hand. "Well, how did you get this?"

"Give it back." Ren reached, but he deflected her. A surge of fret sent a spray of tingles into her chest. "That's just a memento."

"No, my dear. It's a map. And a very old one, too. Some of these roads don't even exist anymore. And this ... what is this?" He pointed to the cabin Bala had marked.

Ren stayed silent.

"Well, if you ever do want to go out there, let me know. I'll take you and have you back in no time."

"What about the fence?" The blue light flickered again.

Pandon held up a small black box. "There are ways around the fences."

Ren snagged the map from his hand and slid it into a side pocket of her bag. "I thought it was dangerous. You know, the untamed wild."

"It's only dangerous if you're not careful and can't handle yourself." He grabbed Lidya and spun her around. The attention doused the embers flickering behind her dark eyes. When he let go of her hand, he snatched at Ren's, but she averted him and put some distance between them. Surprise registered on his dark face.

"I gotta go." Ren left the two of them snickering behind her. She needed some space and maybe a shower to get rid of the icky feeling Lidya's Pandy gave her. He was the exact stereotype Bala had described for wannabe guardian alpha males pandering to the hearts of smitten plebes.

Off the main road and on a back path to her shanty, she veered away from the trail and pulled out her clip-pad to check for messages. There were still a few hours before all-in, and she hadn't seen Owen since she'd left work. They'd had dinner three nights ago, taken a cart out to the Silver Rim viewing station two nights ago, and worked late last night. Three hours in the office, just him, her, and their shared desire to keep everyone on Owen's team safe and sound.

They hadn't solved that problem. One answer seemed painfully obvious—to send her away. She shouldn't be here anyway, but for the Superintendre butting in. Owen ignored her suggestion, though, and she was glad for it.

Two messages popped up. One from Owen. "Trail by your shanty, 22:30. No shoes and the moon." Ren smiled. She mentioned walking barefoot in the moonlight once to him, and he hadn't forgotten.

The second message was from Bala. Ren's heart soared. They hadn't talked yet, and only communicating via messages was not enough. Especially not these messages. Everything in code and short.

Bala wrote, "Take deep breaths when you need to. And treat everyone like you would Nanny Skelt." Her mails were mostly reminders. Take deep breaths to keep the visions under control, and don't trust anyone. Got it.

The visions hadn't been a problem. Except for battling them through the interrogation and the charge she'd just felt with Pandon, she'd not had any actual threats. Of course, she hadn't used the aberration either. Not even for the challenges Owen gave.

Closing her eyes, she took a deep breath. The cool twilight air rustled the leaves in the trees nearby. With one thought, the aberration pulsed through her. It was a feeling and an awareness that joined to form a picture in her head. And for once, it felt like an old friend, and not something to be hated. She'd missed it.

The thought went to Owen, and in a flash, the picture took form, and she saw him setting out a blanket in a field, a picnic basket by his side, lit candles, and the purples of night settling around him. It made her smile. The vision dissolved, and another surged into view.

This time she didn't see anything—only light, and an overwhelming sense of peace settled in her chest. Almost like it was stepping into her. She had the sensation of falling backward, but instead of trying to catch herself, she let go, and joy rushed through.

Then, the light drizzled away, and the boy she'd seen from the transport came into view. He sat around a fire talking to a group of people. Midway through a sentence, the boy looked her way.

"Hi, there." He spoke to her. "I'm Altrist, and you are?"

Ren shook her head. "You can see me?"

He smiled. "It would appear so."

"How?" It felt like a dream, but it was all much clearer than any dream she'd ever had.

"I suppose there are a lot of things about your gift you don't understand. I can help you with that." He used the word gift. "I can teach you and show you how to use it."

"Who are you?" Ren's heartbeat thudded in her ears.

"Altrist. And what is your name?"

"Ren." The answer popped out before she could stop it.

"I can help you, Ren." Altrist stood and held his hand out like he was bidding her to come. "There's another way." The words echoed through her head. Altrist's face glowed brighter. "There's more. More hope. More freedom. And more truth. There is a better way. I can help you."

Ren shook her head and pushed at the vision, but it stayed.

"Ren, let me help you." Altrist whispered in her ear.

Forcing the vision off, she threw herself back and landed hard on the ground. The scene flashed away, and the night air blew across Ren's sweaty face.

"What in the world?"

CHAPTER 11

THE GLOWING GIRL

Cold, wet feet and the best night of Owen's life. Well, maybe not the best, but it wasn't over yet.

Ren leaned back and gazed at the sky. "It's beautiful."

Owen agreed. "Like a bunch of sparkling diamonds on a deep blue velvet backdrop."

"Leave it to you to bring something rich into the moment." She giggled and tapped his shoulder.

He was long past getting offended at her jabs. Now, it felt weird if she didn't poke fun. He appreciated her wit and could tell she respected him, despite her strong dislike for most leadership.

"You okay?" He sat up. The blanket he'd brought to the field was damp with dew. "You seemed out of it when you first got here. Did something happen with Lidya?"

Ren rolled to her side. In the darkening night, her face had a softness to it. "Her secret forbidden's a real piece of work." She cleared her throat and sat up. "Oh, I shouldn't have said that."

Owen waved her off. "Don't worry, everyone knows about him. Of course, the guy's a bit of a mystery. I don't think he's from the Viand like he says. He doesn't seem like a Wall guy, and he's not from here. Maybe a Progenate with connections."

"Yeah, I think he's been around. He even offered to take us beyond the boundary if we wanted some *real* fun."

Owen lowered his voice. "You maybe shouldn't talk about *that* too loud."

"Don't worry. I think we're safe out here." She lowered hers also and pulled on her socks. Owen hoped that didn't mean she was about to leave.

As she slipped on her shoe, Owen realized this was the first natural opportunity he'd had to dive into his assignment from Maxey. His last report to the guardian hadn't gone well. She'd mentioned Jasper's tactics and moving up his deadline.

"Did your transport ride here show you any of the great wild?" A cloud drifted in front of the glowing moon and sent a massive shadow across the field.

Ren slipped on her other shoe. "It was incredible."

"Oh, what did you see?" His voice cracked a little at the end. Finding out what she saw was his assignment, yet it didn't feel like the right thing to do.

Ren quieted and pulled her knees to her chest. Owen knew her well enough now to give her room to think. Silence always brought her around.

After another minute, she looked his way. "What do you think about people with aberrations?"

That took a weird turn. "What?"

"I was just thinking about how incredible the world is—the trees, sky, birds, grass, flowers—all of it. And how maybe when the first squirrel popped onto the scene someone might have thought it was an ugly, deformed bird, but it wasn't. It was just something new. Maybe the aberrants are just something new." Her rabbit trails had taken them down a thousand different conversational paths, but this one was the first to make him squirm.

He stayed focused on his task. "Did you see an aberrant out there in the wild?"

"No." Frustration pinged her tone. "I was just wondering. That's all. Have you ever known an aberrant?"

Owen cut from her eyes. Slivers of silver peeked through cracks in the clouds. And the details of his past pressed in on him. "Yes." The word slipped out before he could sensor it.

Ren leaned toward him and waited.

"My best friend was an aberrant. Tylon. We used to do everything together. Like what I think brothers would be. And then one day, they came and took him away."

She squeezed his hand. "Doesn't it seem strange that some people get eliminated because they're different?

What if the aberrant ones could help people? What was Tylon's aberration?"

The sad memory crept into Owen's reach, and for the first time, he spoke it out loud.

"Tylon was the smartest person I knew. He challenged me to be better. But then things changed. He became distant and moody. I skipped class one day to check on him and found him crying.

"He didn't want to tell me. But I reminded him that friends share stuff. We were partners through and through. We had a plan. He was going to be the Superintendre, and I was going to be a Master Guardian.

"He made me promise not to tell anyone, and then he showed the aberration to me. He pulled information from his clip-pad and hung the words in the air. He could take anything—any device, cam, bean, or whatever, and tap into it, pull out the information, and display it. He could tap into anything, even files at the Plateau."

"Whoa, that is weird—and very interesting." Ren accompanied him down memory lane. "What happened to him?"

"They found out. They always find out, and they took him. I never saw him again." His voice caught. How had his interrogation of Ren's strange sighting landed him back in this pool of guilt? He took a deep breath and forced his attention to the present. "That's how it works. That's why *this* works."

He waved his hand at the open field and then pointed to the shimmering of the Silver Rim peeking over the trees in the distance. "Master Tatief and the guardians set up the rim and created the guidelines to protect our society from the destructive forces on the outside and the deceptive differences on the inside." The rhetoric sounded right, but it didn't satisfy Owen's heart like it used to.

"Is that what you really believe?" Ren turned back toward the field, and Owen felt a bit of a loss from the redirection of her eyes.

Maybe a more direct approach would get her talking. "It doesn't matter what I believe. It's how it is. We live inside the rim, safe from the outer annihilation and dependent on the science and wisdom of eliminating defects and protecting life."

"What if that's a lie, though?" She whispered. "What if they got it wrong? You wouldn't need to eliminate anyone from our team. Your friend Tylon could be here. The squirrel could be the squirrel, and the world would be better for it."

Owen's brain stuttered over Ren's questions and metaphor, so he let the silence respond to her words. The same quiet blanketed their walk back to her shanty until they reached her front pathway. He paused and looked into her sweet blue eyes. "Thanks for coming tonight." The porch orb popped on.

"Thank you." Ren's smile lit up her face. "The moon was beautiful."

A whippoorwill sung in a tree nearby. Owen wouldn't have known that except Ren had pointed the sound out last night when he walked her home.

He followed her to the porch. As she waved her hand over the entry pad, the door slid open. She paused and turned to him. The blue in her eyes caught the light.

"You know, I didn't want to come to the Protectorate. I thought the Viand was where I should go. But I'm glad—" she took a deep breath as if to gather courage "—I'm glad I'm here. Bala says real friends are scarce. I'm not positive about you, but barefoot in the moonlight and you not scolding me for my squirrel tangent seems like friend material to me."

Happy concern ricocheted around Owen's head. Happy because she was beautiful standing under the light, a near equal who challenged him and made him better. But concern because she emphasized friend more than he wanted. He also wasn't ready to say goodnight, and then there was the thing with Maxey hanging over him.

Unfazed by his silence, Ren tapped his arm, bid him farewell, and disappeared into her shanty. He waited a few seconds, then left.

The wind carried a chill, and Owen cut through the woods behind Ren's shanty. With the moonlight, he could just make out the slender path, snaking its way to the service road near his neighborhood.

He and Ren lived in plat 3 in the Sharp Borough. In the raising home, the plats are said to be the building blocks of community. Each is divided into zones of homes where everyone knows everyone, at least for a while. It's like small towns from long ago. Except people don't grow old and settle down. They either move tiers, retire to the Plantanate, or get accomplished, whatever seems most prudent for the good of all.

A flash of white in the woods caught Owen's attention. He stopped and listened for sentry footsteps, but only the whippoorwill filled the night. The light flashed again and then settled into a steady pink glow.

"What the heck?"

He left the path and using his outstretched arms inched toward the glow. "Who's there?" he whispered.

The light brightened, and a person came into view, smiling and looking him full in the eye. A girl. A striking, shining girl.

A soft haze surrounded her white skin as flickers of light zipped around her long, white braid. *Hello.* The greeting rang in Owen's head.

He checked the woods behind him. All seemed normal and quiet.

The rational side of Owen's brain stayed close to the guidelines, but the other part kept pointing out the obvious. This girl wasn't a plebe, a guide, or a guardian. She was something else altogether. And she glowed.

Ren's supposed sighting of someone from the transport jumped to mind. If some guy outside the Protectorate worried the guardians, then a glowy girl trespassing within their borders might cause a total panic.

The glow dampened, but her smile stayed. *What is your name?* Again, the voice sounded inside his head.

"Owen." He blurted out. Thoughts of him being the one in the interrogation room made his heart race.

"Owen." She spoke the word out loud this time. "I think we shall be friends."

"Who …" Owen's dry throat struggled. "Who are you?"

She lifted her arms, and the sheer material of her long tog blew in the growing breeze. A circle of light grew from her middle until it reached the top of her head.

"Who are you?" Owen called louder this time.

The brightness flashed, then the woods returned to filtering the pale moonlight. A low hum remained, though, and Owen heard her voice in his head one last time, like a card left behind.

Just a whisper. *Olivope.*

CHAPTER 12

THE QUESTION

A guy walked by carrying a glowing ball of energy. Dart tried not to stare, but this was a gift she hadn't seen before.

"That's Buddy." Thim slid next to her on the large rock. "He and his brother put up the shield around the camp. It keeps us from being seen. That's how the Pocket dwellers survive out in the open like they do."

Dart nodded, as if this were a normal thing. The sun's warm rays peaked across the treetops as at least fifty people milled around the campsite having breakfast and visiting. "I've never seen this many people in one place." Sully's pack had gotten up to fifteen once. "Look." A girl shook her arm as her palm went from blue to green to purple to pink. "Do they all have gifts?" Dart balled her hand with the faded sunburst into a fist.

"Most of them, I guess." Thim munched on an apple, unfazed. A light flashed, and Liza appeared behind him. She waved at Dart and then headed toward a table set with tasty cakes, eggs, and fruit.

A guy strummed his guitar, and a group congregated nearby to listen. The soft melody wove its way around the men, women, and children who had gathered. Hands patted their thighs to the beat, and expressions lightened. Music was another strange gift—more beautiful than teleporting or running fast. But not quite as useful.

"So can people in the villages do any of this stuff?"

Thim shrugged. "I don't think it's the same as us. But then again, Altrist said he found a girl from the Protectorate who had a gift, so who knows?" Thim was the opposite of Dart. His eighteen years had only been with this group of loving people, living free, and doing no harm.

He patted his hand on his knee to the beat. "The villages don't do music. Not anymore. My ma told me that. They listen to recordings from long ago, but no one makes music now. Not like this, anyway."

"Don't you think it's weird that a villager would have a gift? I mean you all said the leader gives the gifts, so then how do village bait have them too?" A girl zipped by, followed by a guy whose bottom half was invisible.

Thim didn't seem to notice. "Yeah, I guess it's weird, but Altrist says the Leader's not just here for us. He wants to help everyone. Village bait, exiled bait." He looked at her. "Everyone."

She unrolled her fist and wiped her hand on her brown leggings. That sounded good. So why did she still feel like she didn't belong? "Have you ever seen him?"

Thim looked around. "Who?"

"The Leader."

"No." He took another bite of his apple and chewed it on one side of his mouth. "I mean a couple of times I felt like he was around. Close, but I've never seen him. How about you?"

Dart crossed her arms. "No, not really. I sort of thought I heard his voice in my head, and then this showed up." She held up her sunburst smudged hand. "It sort of seems like a dream now."

He took another bite and chewed it before he spoke. "Did you really never hear about the Leader when you were out there?"

She pushed back. "Does that surprise you? I mean, no one in the villages knows about him. Why would it be any different for the exiled?"

He shrugged. "I don't know. I guess I figured if you weren't all drugged up and steeped in Tatief's lies, then the truth would be easier to see."

"Truth?" A heavy feeling blanketed Dart's heart.

"Yeah, about the Leader. That there's more."

"It's really hard to think of anything else when you're in the packs." A squirrel ran by, clutching a piece of tasty cake. "Out there, there's no one coming to the rescue. You're on your own."

68

He put his hand over hers. "I'm sorry that you had to live that way."

"Me too."

"But someone did come to the rescue. Altrist found you, and you're here now." He spoke as if every crummy thing she'd ever been through—all the pain, the scars under her coverup; the loss, watching her mother die; and the fear, never knowing which day would be the last—somehow magically disappeared the day they brought her here.

It didn't work that way. Some of being here brought more questions than answers.

"I wish he could have found me sooner." She mumbled the words.

Thim sighed in agreement. "We're trying. It's just slow, and a lot of people don't want to reach out to the villages or the exiled. They're content to stay here. Leave them alone, and maybe they'll leave us alone."

She got all that. People were people. In the end, they would always do what served them best. "But what about the leader?

"What do you mean?"

"Well, he's supposed to be this great savior, right? Then where is he? Why isn't he here doing something about all this bad stuff? If he cares so much, then why let us suffer?" Her heart beat fast.

Thim's eyebrows creased downward. "I don't know." His answer didn't surprise her, but it did let her down. "We have Altrist and Olivope. They're here."

"Yeah, and Tatief's here too." She turned to face Thim and lowered her voice. "Do you ever wonder if the Leader is real? Maybe they just made him up to keep us from feeling hopeless."

Everything around them blurred, and Dart hung, waiting for Thim's answer. He didn't have a gift either—he, like her, had no tangible proof of the Leader's touch. Her weird, fading body art didn't count. If anyone else in their happy little world might have doubts, it would be him.

"I guess you have lots of reasons to think he's not real." Thim's blue eyes seemed to look inside her, and she turned to face the campsite. He continued, "It sounds kind of crazy. Some powerful Leader who's going to come and set things right. What's he waiting for?"

A burst of music swallowed the question. Thim drew her eyes to his. "Before she died, my mom told me we see only a little of this world. That there's more. Maybe I believe all this stuff about the Leader because all these people do, but I hope when the time comes, I'll see the more she told me about, and it will all make sense."

Dart hadn't heard the story of Thim's ma. But no matter what, she couldn't bring hope and death together in her head. She whispered, "Your ma is dead." A cold fact that made its own statement.

Thim understood. He nodded and a glaze of tears touched his eyes. "Yes. And because I saw her die, I have hope that there really is more."

That didn't make sense. Dart had seen death. The empty look in her ma's eyes, the stiff coldness to the skin, the shell testifying to no more. There was no hope in death.

Thim continued, "One flash she was there, sick and struggling to breathe, and the next she was gone. And I knew, there had to be more. She was gone from her body, but she wasn't gone." His eyes held a question, not for him, but for Dart. "Do you see what I mean? There's life here like we experience it, and then there's life—more, deeper life, and that's where the Leader is." It felt like he was tossing her a rope and trying to reel her in.

Dart swallowed and nodded. She didn't get it, but she didn't want to disappoint him. It all sounded good. She wanted it to be real.

But then there was the matter of what she'd actually seen and the things she'd done. Those were real too. Ugly, awful, and damaging. Maybe the good things in life were only for people like this—gifted, pretty, and put together.

The music stopped, and Altrist motioned for everyone to join him. "Please gather around. Olivope's got news, and we have some decisions to make."

Thim jumped up to join them and held out a hand for her, but Dart waved him on. "You go. I'm fine here." He gave her a look but let her be. There was an innocence about him she didn't have. A kindness. Everyone here seemed to have it, even the reformed sentries who had probably done far worse than she had.

They huddled around Altrist and Olivope in the shade of the trees. Families stood together. Matchments grouped in twos. Somehow even the people who were standing alone stood united with the assembly.

Dart swallowed hard. She stood on the outside, looking in. The leader had whispered in her ear, and for the last six cycles, these kind people had welcomed her. But it hadn't stuck. The lines of the sunburst faded more every day, and with them dwindled her feelings of belonging.

They all thought her some poor orphaned girl, beaten by the exiled and left for dead. And she'd let them. When they shared stories of the depravity in the packs, she'd not let them know about her part in any of it.

They said the leader would give her a gift. She just needed to trust him. Everything would be okay. They didn't seem to realize that sometimes things don't work out. Sometimes people die, lies win, and the innocent do bad things.

Dart pushed up from the warm rock just as Olivope spoke. The messenger's sweet voice sounded like a song on the breeze. She said something about the Protectorate and choices to make, but Dart didn't listen. She needed a break from their goodness.

CHAPTER 13

THE VERY BAD DAY

No one teaches you what you really need to know about making it above ground. Like how not to worry about what everyone else thinks or how to tell when someone likes you or doesn't. The nannies didn't touch on any of that.

Ren stared at the blank screen suspended on the divider wall of her workstation. Every few seconds a series of blue, purple, and green circles floated across the black monitor like bubbles. She'd finished her work for the day and couldn't shake the feeling she'd done something wrong.

Lidya had been quiet. Almost like they weren't even friends. And Owen ... he'd kept to himself too. Ren pulled her collar and sniffed. She didn't smell bad. At least not that she could tell.

"Here's the assignment vids. I watched them last night. B-o-r-i-n-g." Lidya held out three cracker-sized vids. "Sorry I didn't wait for you, but I couldn't sleep, so I popped them in. Did the trick in no time."

A warm sensation ran from Ren's shoulders and through her head. She drew in a deep breath. The feeling dissipated as she exhaled. "No worries." She slid the vids into her messenger bag. "I got nothing else to do tonight." That sounded pathetic. She glanced at Owen. He hadn't stopped by her station or suggested a walk or anything. Last night had been fun, but maybe he'd decided her talk about aberrations was a little too racy.

Lidya packed her clip-pad and iridescent notebook into her messenger bag. "Why don't you come with me?

Cara and some new girls are going to the body art studio. I'm thinking about getting my leg done."

"Oh, I don't know." A flicker of light crossed Ren's eye. The vision visit with Altrist yesterday had awakened the aberration in full force. She took a deep breath and pushed it back.

"Come on. You really need to loosen up. You know, Pandy was a little hurt by how you just ran off." Lidya flashed her big eyes. Sometimes the gulf between her and Ren seemed far greater than their taste in men.

Ren stood and looped the bag strap over her head. "I thought you two probably wanted to be alone."

A sneaky grin lit Lidya's face. "Well, you're right about that. What do you say? Come have a little fun with the girls?"

It felt good to be wanted again. Strange how she could go most of her life content to avoid people, but after making a few friends here, she couldn't help but fold under the silence. "Okay, but just for a little bit, and I'm not going to get any Protectorate hotties painted on my leg."

Lidya bounced and clapped. "We'll see about that."

"Maybe a butterfly right here." Ren pointed behind her ear. "Where no one will notice."

"Unless they get super close." Lidya giggled in Owen's direction. "How are things with you and Guide O going, anyway?"

Heat rushed into Ren's cheeks, and this time it wasn't from the aberration. "We did some moon gazing last night." She wanted to take the words back even before she'd finished saying them. Confiding in people wasn't a strength, and no telling what Lidya's loose lips would do.

"That's three times in one week. I'd say things are kind of promising."

Ren didn't want to have this conversation. As much as she needed boy advice from someone, Lidya wasn't the person. "You ready to go?"

"Ren, may I speak with you." Owen stood by the conference room door. The sound of his voice did something to her insides.

Lidya gave Ren a look and grinned. "We'll wait for you outside."

Owen led her into the conference room, almost as if she were in trouble. He'd rolled up his blue sleeves and the scent of something clean with a touch of something rich wafted over Ren as she followed.

A few degrees cooler than the outer office, the room reminded her of a Castle classroom. No windows, white furniture, and red cushions. The counters and tabletop were black marbled granite.

"I want to talk to you about something." Before she could respond, he turned to a panel in the wall and punched in a code. "That gives us a minute before the system resets and starts recording again."

Ren checked the symbols flickering across the tiny screen. It was more like ninety seconds, but she wouldn't correct him.

"Can you maybe meet me in the park? I've got to finish up something for Whitler, but then I'm free."

She wanted to ask him why he'd been so standoffish all day, but his deep brown eyes made the quiet not seem so bad. "I'm going to the body art studio with Lidya, but after that I'll be free. Ping my clip-pad when you're ready, and I'll get away."

"Body art?" He gave her a look that said he wasn't mad at her at all.

"Yeah, I'm thinking about getting a maglium globe painted on my neck. What do you think?"

He leaned close. "Something so beautiful should be left just as it is."

With all his talk about the Vantages and their beauty, she wasn't sure which way he was going.

"I'm talking about you, not the globe." A sweet smile pulled at his lips, and he shook his head. "You really don't need any body art."

Ren's insides did a somersault. "I better go. Talk to you soon." She left just as the symbols flashed to numbers and the powers that be could hear them again.

By the time she exited the building, the sun had dipped below the mountains. A familiar giggle drew her attention to the shaved ice stand in the middle of the plaza between her building and the rest of the Protectorate.

Ren headed for the gaggle of girls, but then stopped. One of the new girls was from Castle Raising Home. Three weeks and Ren hadn't seen either of Castle's plebes anywhere—something she'd celebrated.

Lidya's friend, Cara, nodded toward Ren and said something to the group. Five sets of eyes looked her way— not friendly looks either. The whole thing felt far too familiar. This was why having a nanny as a best friend made adolescence much easier.

Lidya broke eye contact and looked down. No telling what the girl from Castle had said. Words like freak, weirdo, and loner came to mind. Another wave of tingles crashed through Ren's body, a precursor to a vision. She shook her head. They could have their laughs.

Cutting from the plaza, she aimed for the park. Orbs strung along the boardwalk swayed in the breeze as if everything was pleasant and fine. Ren glanced down at her clip-pad, but no messages popped up. Stupid girls. Bala said most girls can't break free from the pack. It's their safe place. The numbers make them bigger, smarter, prettier.

Ren slid onto a park bench and stared at the calm river. It's not like girls hadn't been mean to her before. But always before, she'd had Bala, and none of them had been a friend to start with. Lidya wasn't perfect, but she had helped make those first new days not so scary.

A couple walked by on the boardwalk and peeled off to the hidden area behind the pavilion. Ren checked the clip-pad again. Maybe it was better to keep her distance. If you didn't get close to people, then you couldn't be sad when they let you down.

She missed Bala. This is the longest she'd gone without talking to her friend. They had another week before they were supposed to have their first call, but who made up that rule anyway? Bala wanted to play it safe, but things weren't as bad as she'd said they'd be. There hadn't been any sentries lurking around, no guardians pulling her aside, nothing. Just a bunch of smarmy girls acting like they're better than anyone else.

"Maybe just one brief chat wouldn't be bad." Ren awakened the screen and pulled up the calling code. Bala should be free this late in the day, unless she'd found another protégé to teach Aikido to. The screen pulsed to green waves as the code went through.

Waiting for Bala to answer felt like that moment right before the transport pulled out into the above-ground world for the first time. The new friendship with Lidya didn't come close to all that Bala was.

The screen flashed to black, and then a face popped into view. Nanny Skelt. Ren's heart stopped.

"423B7? Is that you, Ren?" Skelt's harsh voice seized the clip-pad.

Ren considered punching the out button, but the damage had already been done. "Yes, ma'am. How are you?" *Good grief. How are you?*

"I'm fine. What can I do for one of our fine Protectorate grads?"

Ren wondered if the nanny knew about the Superintendre's order and that she wasn't really a Protectorate plebe at all. Just an imposter with a huge secret and no friends. "Um, I was actually trying to reach Nanny Bala."

"Oh?" Skelt's bushy eyebrows looked even bigger on the tiny screen.

Ren fumbled for a good excuse. "Yes, I wanted to tell her thank you. Things are going wonderfully, and she had a lot to do with preparing me."

Someone called to the nanny from offscreen. "I'll be there in a moment. I'm sorry, B7, but Bala isn't with us any longer."

"What?" Ren leaned closer to the clip-pad. "Where is she?"

"I can't really say. She left here shortly after your departure. Now, I've got to go. For the good of all." Skelt waited.

"We give ourselves." Ren said the words as she hit the out button. The world had just shifted. A tectonic plate had just jutted out of place, leaving a gaping hole where normalcy should be.

"Hey, Spunky." Pandon plunked down next to Ren on the bench as if he were welcome. "Who ya talking to?"

Ren slid the cover over her clip-pad. "No one." It felt like her body wasn't connected to her brain anymore. Bala hadn't said anything about leaving the raising home. They had a plan. If she'd changed it, she would have said something.

"Whoa, you don't look so good. What's wrong?" The Romeo actually looked concerned. "Did you get bad news?"

"My friend, Bala, is gone."

"Bala? I don't know a Bala, and I know everybody. Tell me all about her. Maybe I can help. I have connections, you know." Pandon turned toward her and waited.

As the numbness of shock faded from Ren's senses, adrenalin took its place. Something awful had happened to Bala. The picture of Nanny Reece waiting for the guards flitted across Ren's memory. Bala wouldn't have gone with them as easily. Something was terribly wrong.

CHAPTER 14

THE WARRIOR

Owen pecked out a quick message to Ren. *Can't meet. Something came up. Chime you later.* That was a colossal understatement. Something came up. More like the pendulum had swung, and the guardian was back.

Maxey had pinged him moments after Ren left. "Meet at your cabin. 19:30." She wanted her update in person this time, and he had little to offer.

His encounter with Olivope had changed the field for him. He'd even considered telling Ren about the strange girl dressed in glowing white. He didn't want to go there yet, though. As far as he knew, the mysterious boy sighting hadn't involved any communications. And he really didn't want anyone to know about Olivope. For once in his life, he ignored what had happened and hoped it would go away.

The pathway toward his bungalow lit as he passed under the plasma lanterns suspended overhead. With each one, a camera came to life, recording his coming and going and keeping the world safe for the good of all.

Owen slowed his step as he approached his house. Two sentry guards stood like statues in the dark at the end of his walkway. One of them moved, and the lanterns flashed on.

"Hello, sirs." Owen scanned the woods for any strange glowy people.

"Come with me." The guard on the right marched toward the door and spoke into a device on his wrist.

"427M8 has arrived." The door opened, and another sentry blocked the contents of the house from view.

"427M8?" The other sentry filled the entire doorway.

"Yes."

"Do not speak unless you are asked a question. Do not sit unless you are invited to sit. Do not make any sudden movements. And do not, under any circumstances, share with anyone the subject of this meeting or that it even occurred. Do you understand?"

"Y-y-yes, sir." Owen forced a deep breath.

The guard stepped aside, revealing more sentries, Maxey and another woman. The stranger was far more beautiful than anyone Owen had ever seen, and somehow fiercer than any sentry he'd ever encountered.

Maxey sat in his leather wing chair and didn't look up. She was the complete opposite of the powerful guardian he'd met a few weeks ago.

The fierce lady rose and met Owen eye to eye. "Do you understand who I am?" Dressed in guardian black, she wore a golden sash around her waist. Ruby jewels, punctuated by a black diamond, outlined the revealing cut of her top. Bright red lips heightened her tanned face, and her eyes caught the orange light of the solar orbs, making them look almost red.

Owen did not know who she was, but the force of her presence sent him to his knees. Sheer power, a guardian of the highest order. He cast his gaze downward.

She stepped closer, and the blue light of her scinter winked from where it lay on her side, under her cape. "Rise, Master Owen. We have much to discuss."

Owen backed away as he stood, but the woman motioned, and a sentry brought a kitchen chair for him to sit. "I am Eviah, the Warrior, second to Tatief and an enforcer for the good of all."

"We give ourselves." The sentries spoke the mantra with force. Maxey whimpered it out, and Owen just moved his lips.

Eviah's eyes narrowed. "I also serve as the Superintendre."

That caught Owen by surprise.

She looked at her nails as if she were talking about what to eat for dinner. "The former owner of the title failed the master. Seems the poor fool had gotten attached to a certain overseer and mixed up his priorities."

Sweat trickled down Owen's neck, and his mind raced. It didn't make sense why someone so powerful would visit him, in his home, unannounced, and at night. He dared another look into the woman's cold eyes. Something about her felt familiar—the way her mouth curved and the slant of her nose, but he'd never seen her before. He would have remembered it.

There'd been no education that included a warrior or a second to Tatief, either. Of course, he had only ever seen what they had wanted him to see. The guardians limited his education on Tatief and the upper echelon. They were too great to be known. Too powerful to be understood.

"My assistant has tasked you with the girl. What do you have to say?" Eviah's eyes cut to Maxey, then back to Owen.

A clear picture of Ren's sweet face flashed into Owen's head. He chose his words with care. "I have developed a strong rapport with Ren. She's beginning to trust me."

The report fell flat. Displeasure crossed Eviah's perfect face. "Master Tatief demands the location of the boy, and he will sacrifice this girl to get it."

A crazy fear grabbed Owen's heart. "But what if she doesn't know where the boy is?" The sentry on his left smacked Owen out of his chair.

Eviah offered an approving nod to the guard but raised her hand to stop his next punch. "Then we'll have to find out from another source."

Owen wiped blood from his mouth. "And Ren?"

"She will serve the master through accomplishment." She said the words as if they didn't matter. Owen shook his head, and Eviah's tone softened. "If you have a fondness for the girl, then get her to tell you what she knows. It's the only way you'll save her." Fondness. If they'd really been watching these last few weeks, they'd have seen more than fondness.

Eviah flicked her wrist, and the sentries grabbed Owen and put him back in his chair. "Getting the location of the boy is all that matters." The words didn't sound so sure, but the Warrior's fierceness returned. "The boy is a threat. His existence pulls at the seams of society. He is an enemy to Tatief, and he endangers all for which we stand."

A chill ran up Owen's sweaty back. Who was this kid they were so desperate to locate? Tatief had put up the wall, saved humankind, created this world. What could a boy do to him? Owen kept his questions to himself and turned his focus to saving Ren.

"I am here to serve my master." His lie met Eviah's sharp eyes.

"Then find out what she knows." She believed him. "It seems you've been an asset to us before." Guardian power charged the warm room. "Master Tatief rewards devotion, like what you did with Tylon."

The mention of Tylon pinched Owen's heart, but the Warrior didn't notice. "The girl's survival is in your hands. Use whatever charms you have to find out what she knows and hope beyond measure it will lead to the boy."

Owen couldn't maintain her gaze. "I will not disappoint." His voice caught.

She leaned close and whispered in his ear. "You better not or Jasper will have his go at her." Her hand landed lightly on his shoulder, not matching the threat she'd just delivered.

"You have twenty-four hours." And then she left.

Maxey popped up from her seat and followed. And within a few seconds, his little home was his again.

But the intrusion remained, and the number of questions pecking at the foundation of his world outnumbered the answers.

CHAPTER 15

THE DREAM OF A CRAZY IDEA

Ren paced the expanse of her shanty. That wasn't saying much. Ten steps crossed the length of it but multiply that by an hour and a half of fretting, and she was tired.

Not being able to reach Bala felt as bad as the week-long solitary restriction after she ignored a junior guardian's order so he wouldn't see her eyes all glowy. Even then, Bala had sent her little messages on her food tray. And now, nothing. Not a word.

"Where are you?" She grabbed her clip-pad. Bala's last message had been two days ago, but Skelt had said Bala left the home weeks ago.

Ren checked the time stamp and info marker on the last message. It looked different. Numbers she didn't recognize ran where the words Castle Raising Home used to be.

Returning to the mailbox, she pecked out a new message. No secret code this time, just her own words and frustration, "Where are you?" She pressed "Send," and a familiar zipper sound tweeted from the device.

She plunked the pad onto her unmade bed and started the pacing again. Getting mocked by Lidya's girl posse was nothing compared to not knowing where Bala was. Now, she really was alone. The thought stopped her in the middle of the one-room shanty. Without the tether line to Bala, this new existence of hers would completely unravel.

If Bala had been taken, then they'd probably come here soon. She didn't want to be accomplished, even if it was supposed to be the best thing for society. Deep breath. Reel it back. Maybe Bala had taken a long-needed holiday. The woman never went anywhere. Her whole life had been spent keeping an eye on Ren.

With another breath, Ren closed her eyes and summoned the aberration. Four attempts already had turned up empty. Two took her to the past—sweet memories of Bala. Another landed her in the raising home watching Nanny Skelt's skin care routine, and the fourth brought the glowy Altrist into view, waving and looking happy to see her. She shut that one down fast.

The stupid ability did nothing except leave her body all tingly and her brain numb. She exhaled and took up pacing again, catching a cool, night breeze from the window.

The clip-pad dinged, and Ren ran to the bed and swiped the screen.

A message from Owen. *Sorry I had to cancel. I missed seeing you.* The white letters pulsed at her, and for the first time in her life, the thought crossed her mind to trust someone else other than Bala. It felt a little like betrayal, but what if? What if someone else knew her real self— what if they knew about the aberration, adjustment, and everything? A flit of excitement tinged with terror took a flying leap into her heart and bounced into the realistic pit of her stomach. That was a crazy idea.

Another message popped up. *Did you get a maglium globe painted anywhere?* She climbed into bed with the clip-pad, a smile pushing her worry to the side. *Or a picture of me plastered to your leg?* With that one, she burst out. She thought about saying she had Whitler sketched on her calf but thought better of it.

Instead, she pecked out a two-sentence message about her awful evening, mean girls, and Bala's disappearance. And Owen jumped into her worry pit and sent a barrage of messages with possible reasons why Bala was gone. She typed out her worries, and he met each one and somehow made her laugh in the midst of it.

By two o'clock, they called it a night with the promise of meeting for breakfast and watching vids together after work. All the Bala worrying had faded into the bright light of Owen's friendship. And as she fell to sleep, the dream of the crazy idea returned. What if she could trust him? What if she could tell him the truth?

CHAPTER 16

THE DECISION TO TRUST

Owen could have kicked himself as he and Ren approached her shanty. They'd met for breakfast, teamed up for a project at work, and he'd taken her to the screening of *The Plantanate Promised Land* vid, all without once bringing up anything about the mysterious boy she saw on her first day.

Getting to the topic never fit into normal conversation. *Seen any glowing people lately? Anybody ever talk into your thoughts? Anything weird happen since you left Castle?* Well, he did actually try that last one, but she smartly worked around it. With less than six hours before the Warrior's deadline, he needed to up his game.

Ren's hand bumped his while they walked, but he didn't let on how being close to her made him feel. *Focus, man, focus.* In the dusky twilight, she looked even more beautiful.

"Tatief looked different from what I remembered." She interrupted his thoughts. "For some reason, I pictured an old man."

Owen thought back to the vid. He'd seen it so many times he hadn't thought much about it. "Yeah, I guess so."

"How does that even work? Isn't he like hundreds of years old? How can he look no older than my nanny?" Street orbs popped on as they walked down the lane.

"That's what makes him so amazing, right?" Owen searched for an opening to bring up the sighting. "I wonder what he looked like as a kid or as a new plebe."

A dirt trail broke off from the lane and led into the woods, and a crazy idea took root into Owen's head. His first reflex was to shake it off, but he didn't. Instead, he let it settle inside of him and light up his insides. Telling the truth. It didn't make sense, but it felt right.

He slowed the pace and put a finger to his lips. Everything moved in slow motion, except for his heart. Was he really going to do this? She questioned him with her eyes but didn't speak. Motioning to the narrow path, he grabbed her hand and led her onto the trail.

It surprised him how easily she followed and how good it felt to hold her hand. The lane petered out, and he forged onward through the unkempt foliage of the woods ending at the edge of the field—the field where they'd walked barefoot under the moonlight. He didn't want to be out in the open, though, not for this. He skirted the brush and found a huge old tree leaning into the field. No cameras out here.

"What are we doing?" she whispered.

"I wanted to talk to you. Just you."

Her eyes said she understood.

"I need to tell you something, and you have to promise not to tell anyone. I know that's a lot to ask." He searched her face.

She didn't give much away, but she did nod.

Owen ran through his options again. This wasn't just about Maxey's assignment anymore or getting a promotion. It was about not being on the wrong side of the interrogation glass—for both of them. He needed to know what Ren knew.

He let go of her hand and swallowed. "I know you saw something on your first day here. It's in your file, and I wasn't going to press you about it. I figured you'd tell me when you wanted to, but something happened the other night, and I think it's connected to your sighting."

The air felt electric. He checked again for cameras, then pressed on. "I saw someone."

"The boy?"

"No, I saw a girl. She looked to be twenty maybe, but if I had to guess, I'd say she's a lot older than that."

Ren's eyes held his, and for the first time in maybe ever, he felt like he didn't have to dumb anything down, although the next part of his little story might need more explaining. "And there's something else." He was really doing this—jumping in with everything. Well, not everything. That would mean telling her about Maxey and the Superintendre. He wasn't ready to be that honest yet.

"This mystery girl glowed and spoke into my head. She said we'd be friends." Ren didn't look surprised or like she was going to call a sentry, so he continued. "Did that happen with you?"

She shook her head, but something about the look she gave him told him she wanted to talk. He took a breath and waited. The silence always coaxed her out.

A breeze blew strands of hair across her face. She started to speak, but then backed off. He waited. He'd just given her major leverage. If she told anyone, his hope of ever being a guardian would evaporate into nothingness.

"Owen." She stared into his eyes like she'd asked a question and the answer was hidden there.

Holding her hand again crossed his mind, but he didn't move.

"I don't know if I should tell you."

He reached for her now, his hand touching her arm. She trembled, and he pulled her to him. A response, without thought or motive. An embrace, and her arms slipped around him as she rested her head on his chest.

"It's okay," he whispered. For once, he couldn't think of anything else to say. "I know there's something that you're not saying. I've noticed for a while. You can tell me. You can trust me." He meant it, too. No matter what he, wouldn't let anything happen to her.

No one had ever held her like this. Ren melted into Owen's embrace. He'd just told her the truth. A truth that could lead to his adjustment if anyone found out.

And here she stood, a liar. He only knew the shell, not the real her. The real her was an aberrant. What would he do if he knew her secret? His mystery girl would pale in comparison.

"It's okay," he whispered, his breath warm on her ear. "You can tell me about the boy."

She pulled back. "It's not okay." Silence, and then she met his eyes. The deepening shadows ate them up. Here they stood, two rebels, beyond the reach of compliance regulators or snooping guardians, and she held back her truth. Bala barked in her head. Don't trust anyone. But Bala had left without a word.

Ren's heart beat so fast she thought it might fly out of her chest. "I think I want to tell you." The breeze stopped, and the trees held their breath. "I've seen the boy. From the transport ... and then here."

"Did he say anything to you?"

Ren nodded. "He said he would show me how to use my gift."

Owen leaned closer. "What do you think he meant by that?"

It was now or never. If she took this leap, she wouldn't be able to return.

He ran his hand down her arm and pulled her hand into his. "We're in this together." His voice was husky with heart.

Stilling the torrent of reasons to stay silent, Ren closed her eyes and summoned the ability. "It's not just about the boy." The tingles flooded her body, and the darkening night lit as she opened her eyes. "It's me too."

The moment felt holy. Different. For just a second, Owen stood in a free world where truth triumphed and love meant more than a fleeting feeling. A hundred fireflies danced in Ren's eyes. It reminded him of their first real conversation at the Overlook. And then, reality snapped the truth into focus.

An aberrant. She was an aberrant.

Five years ago, he would have used this to his advantage, but not now. His heart was too disconnected from his cold head. This person standing in front of him didn't deserve to be accomplished. Neither of them did.

"It's okay. I won't tell." The thick feeling in his throat made it hard to speak. He'd never cried in his life, but he thought this might be what it feels like before you start.

Calmer now, Ren turned toward the field. The hazy light from her eyes cast an eerie glow on the grass. "She's here."

Owen followed Ren's gaze, and off in the distance stood Olivope. He couldn't see her face from so far away, but he knew. He felt her—a fullness in his chest. Then her voice echoed in his head. *Tread carefully, Master Owen. The choices you make will affect far more than you know.*

The glow from Ren's eyes faded. "What do they want with us?" The normal Ren came back, and Owen didn't have an answer for her.

The world was not as it ought to be, and he had just opened a door that couldn't be closed. They both had their secrets. Granted, hers were far worse than his, but still, neither of them would ever be the same.

CHAPTER 17

THE SULLY

Sneaking out wasn't so hard with everyone busy with the reunion. The folks from Pocket stayed above ground. They didn't like the tunnels. Dart slipped from her chamber without seeing a single person. She had forgone breakfast to sleep late and ignored the knock when Liza came looking for someone to help decorate tables for the banquet.

The reunion of the two camps drained her already lagging optimism. Everyone had a gift and an opinion about Altrist and Olivope's push to fish people out of the villages. She sided with those against it. She had nothing against helping the masses, but rescuing a bunch of guardian-loving robots seemed counter-productive to the loving, kind society they had built here.

Moon orbs cast a blue hue in the quiet tunnels. Dart padded along without a sound. Everyone had gone topside for more conferencing. In addition to the reunion festivities, they also had classes on all sorts of things. *How to Put Village Life Behind You. Practicing and Perfecting the Gift. When to Talk and When to Run.* The last one cracked Dart up. She could tell them when to talk to an exiled. Never. And they should always run.

Pushing open an access panel in the tunnel, she slipped into the narrow passageway weaving away from the underground living quarters. Dart's sight adjusted to the darkness. It couldn't be too much farther now. If it hadn't been for two of the friends from Pocket, she could've just gone out via the normal exits. But their special forcefield gift set a vim around the camp that made it particularly hard to sneak away for some me-time.

A ladder ended the passageway, and Dart started the lengthy climb. Visiting her old woods would clear her head. She'd not been back since Altrist had scooped her up and brought her here. By now it was probably just a bunch of empty campsites and burned out firepits. Sully's clan and the others wouldn't be there. They never stayed in one place too long.

Pushing the circular metal door open, she shielded her eyes. The sun beat full force down on the clearing. She had never come up from the tunnels this way. With a few sweeps of her foot, she replaced the grass and hid the metal door.

A short hike brought out the familiar scent of pine, honeysuckle, and weary firepits. An old campsite lay deserted on her right. A clump of cedar trees to her left. Both brought back memories. She jogged toward the campsite. It wasn't like she remembered. Another pack had probably been here since then. The lay of the logs and the sagging clothesline reminded her of her mama, and she didn't stop the memory from creeping back into her heart.

Six years ago, when her mama had been killed, there'd been no time for goodbyes or anything.

Turned out from the village, her mama had survived the hunt from the sentries and used her tailoring skills to make friends with the packs of undesirables. They left her alone, mostly. She would make them clothes or mend their old ones, and they'd throw her some food and give her a place to hide when she needed it. Dart was like a pet to the packs. They taught her how to fight, and she'd do their chores.

The sentries weren't even looking for them when they stumbled on their little camp. Three armed sentries to two of them. The packs had all moved closer to the wall to keep warm during the cold season.

Mama had tried to reason with them, barter, but the men had other plans. When Mama said the code word, Dart scrambled for something to use as a weapon.

Mama gave the first blow, taking down one of the sentries with a pot of boiling water and club across the head. Dart took out another by stealing his skeer and leading him to the snag trap.

That's when the final sentry grabbed Mama. He held his scinter to her throat and said someone would have to pay.

Mama just laid there, still. She didn't fight back. Dart screamed and ran to her, but she held up a hand as if to stop her. "I love you, Dart. You are my sunshine."

The sentry sneered and pressed the scinter closer. "Love. What a joke. You animals make the world a weaker place." And then he slid the glowing shaft across Mama's throat and said, "For the good of all." Mama didn't say another word.

Dart fell to her knees. A pain like nothing she'd ever felt seized her chest.

Mama's body fell limp next to the monster. Then he spoke to Dart as if he were some kind of teacher. "Did you know, the people in the villages have no concept of death? They believe their sick and old go off to the Plantanate to retire and live happy little lives. They have no idea what the Plantanate actually is." He nudged Mama's body with his boot. "And death—they call death an accomplishment. It's some grand thing they can do for the good of all."

He leaned down and tilted Dart's chin so her eyes met his. "You understand all about death, don't you?" He whispered. "You see what the thousands in the villages have no clue about. You're a feral little animal." He chuckled.

Dart slid her hand to the skeer. The sentry didn't notice. He was so full of himself—so sure. He continued to explain the goodness of knowing the truth about life and death instead of living in oblivion like the people in the village.

Pacing while he spoke, he finally stopped in front of Mama's still form. "What will I say about this?" He swiveled on his heel and faced her. "The Superintendre will not be pleased with two of his finest succumbing to some woman and her little one." He leaned forward. "Of course, you can help me. I imagine they'd find you very fascinating." He lit up his scinter again and came at her.

Without a thought, Dart zapped the skeer to life and swung hard. The sentry fell back, dropping his weapon and bleeding from his shoulder. Running to him, she kicked him in the head.

"That's for coming here. And ..." She lifted the weapon over her head. "... this is for Mama." With all her strength, she plunged the glowing end into the sentry's stomach. He groaned, then fell silent.

Sunbeams streamed through the treetops, sending shafts of light across the pine-needled floor. Dart shook the memory away. She ran her hand through the ray of light. The sunburst, glistening on her palm, would be totally gone soon. "Where are you?" She whispered to the air.

An oriole chirped to her left, and a bunny scooted by, but all she got from the leader was silence. If she hadn't felt his presence that one time and seen the sunburst on her palm, she'd never have fallen for all their talk about this leader.

She forced the sad thoughts from her head and picked her way down an old trail leading to a stream below. Two boulders lined the way. As she rounded the bend, she stopped. A young girl, no more than six or seven, was lying on the pebbly beach.

Dart eased toward the girl with caution. "You okay?" The girl didn't move. Leaning down, Dart checked the kid's pulse. Good and strong. Dart's hand went to the knife strapped to her side, and she stood. She'd seen this trick before. "Naptime's over, kid." She tapped the child.

"Still using little ones to do your dirty work, Sully? I thought you gave up on that after I gave you some perspective."

An arrow whizzed by Dart's head and clunked against the boulder behind her. The fellow from the other day stepped out of the shadows on the other side of the stream and waved.

Five others joined him, and two stood on the boulders behind her. Ahead and to the right, another man moved among the trees, watching. His blue-green clothes didn't match the dirty rags of Sully's pack. He stood there, unengaged, observing. Dart couldn't make out his face.

"I see you, Dart." Sully's voice came from farther downstream. He stepped out from behind a massive rhododendron. "I see you trying to figure out how to get out of this."

Dart glared. There was no way to scowl enough to display how much she despised that man. "What do you want, Sully?"

He leered. "Not much, just to talk."

"I think our talking days are over." The little girl in front of Dart sat up and looked at her master. Dart's heart hurt for the kid. "I see you have a new pet."

"Jealous?" The smug look on his face hadn't changed from the last time Dart saw him, right before she shoved a scinter into his leg.

She groaned. "What do you want? I have better things to do than reminisce about old times." Taking another survey, Dart noted the strange observer among the trees was gone.

"I can't tell you. I have to show you." Sweat dripped down Sully's unshaven face.

Despite the distance between them, she could smell the mixture of body odor, last roll's dinner, and sassafras on him.

He took another step toward her and held his leg where she'd stabbed him. "I was very disappointed about how things went when my boys came to visit you the other roll. You wasn't very hospitable. You and your freak new friend."

Dart fake-smiled. Her heart thudded in her ears.

"But here you are all by yourself. No freaks. Just you. And all's forgiven. You're back where you belong."

She met his cold eyes. Everything she hated about her life stood right in front of her.

"You know what your problem is, Dart. You don't consider all your options."

An image of her hands around Sully's neck made it a little easier to hear him speak. She hated how he made her feel, the sound of his voice, how his eyes were set too close.

Sully strolled to about three meters from the little one. "Did you think we wouldn't want you back? That you didn't matter?"

"I'm not coming back." Crazy fear surged through Dart like lightning filling her veins. But she couldn't move.

Sully took another step and balled his left hand into a fist. "Oh, I think we can persuade you." He brought his fist up fast as if he were catching a gnat. A trigger, a sign.

And then a thousand volts poured through her body, and Dart staggered backward. Hot pain raged up her right leg. "What?" Her tongue curled in her mouth as the heat tore through every cell, and she fell to her knees. Her eyes locked with the little girl's as the child withdrew the scinter from Dart's leg and smiled triumphantly.

CHAPTER 18

THE BETRAYAL

The girl in the bathroom mirror looked the same, but she wasn't.

Hiding in the bathroom. Ren had excused herself from her workstation to regroup. Owen had just arrived. He'd rolled in late, not looking his normal put together perfectedness. His trimmed brown hair, not quite as sharp, and his coverup suspiciously resembling yesterday's.

Last night, they had walked hand and hand to her shanty, lingered on her porch, and he'd held her close. She could still smell him and feel his warm breath on her neck and the sound of his voice in her ear as he said goodnight.

She'd done it. She'd actually told someone about herself—about the aberration. It didn't seem real now. Someone knew. He knew, and it was okay. More than okay. He'd held her in his arms and understood.

It felt like a dream, and now she stood here, staring at her reflection—the face of someone who'd faced down a fear and triumphed.

The bathroom door swished open, and Lidya entered. "Nil sent me to check on you."

Ren took a beat before responding. She and Lidya hadn't spoken since the other day, and she wasn't ready to be all chummy again. "I'm fine."

The flowery scent of Lidya's perfume invaded the room. Ren washed her hands and reached for the dryer. She didn't know a lot about friendship, but she did know she wanted friends who wouldn't mock her and desert her when things got tough.

Lidya had failed. She should have at least said she was sorry or something, not ignored the snub. "I'll be out in a minute." Ren dismissed her.

"I ..." The traitor bit her lip. "I, uh ... I think Master Owen wants you too."

Ren stopped her fiddling. "What makes you think that?"

"He just keeps looking at the doorway like a puppy waiting for its master." A small grin relaxed Lidya's worried face.

On a different day, this might have been an opportunity for girl talk, but not yet. The image of Lidya with the mean girls was still too fresh. Without another word, Ren marched out. She glanced Owen's direction as she returned to her seat. He caught her eye. The quick connection spun her insides with bliss.

A message blinked on her clip-pad. But it wasn't from Owen.

Owen and Ren, come to my office ASAP. W

Master Whitler? What did he want? Owen rose from his desk and crossed to the area between Whitler's office and the conference room. He waited. For her.

As she stood, Lidya cleared her throat and held up her clip-pad. The bright fuchsia screen offered the words "I'm sorry" in a curvy, dark blue font. Ren couldn't deal with her right now. She offered Lidya a nod and left it at that.

Owen took a step toward her as she approached and redirected her into the conference room. As the door slid shut, he waved his hand over the panel on the wall and punched in his secret code.

"You look good." He sounded sincere, but something was bothering him. Circles betrayed his tired eyes, and the hint of hesitation lingered in his voice. A thread of worry tugged on Ren's joy, but she took a breath, caught his vanilla clean scent, and renewed her hopes of him putting those strong arms around her.

He must have sensed her heart because he took a beat, then enveloped her in his arms. She hugged him back. His chest warmed her cheek, and she wanted to slow down time and explore the feelings consuming her.

Pulling away, he cupped her face in his hands. "We need to talk." He sounded heavy, like he hadn't slept. "After Whitler gets finished with whatever this is about, take a break and meet me at the shaved ice stand in the courtyard."

Ren managed a nod, "Is everything okay?"

"I think it will be. I just need to tell you some things, and it's hard to have a safe conversation around here. We can't run off into the woods whenever we want."

They seemed connected somehow, like they were caught in a bubble of happiness together. Ren touched his stubbly cheek, and her fingers grazed his warm lips. His face brightened, and he leaned toward her mouth, but the panel dinged, breaking the spell. He drew back. "Thank you, 423B7. That will be all." He winked.

Whitler popped up from his desk as they entered. "Good. Thank you both for coming so quickly. Something's come up." He ushered them to two large brown chairs and motioned for them to sit.

"The Superintendre assigned a project." He tapped at the keyboard built onto the top of his desk. An image of a girl flashed on the wall to their right. Ren caught her breath. It was the girl from the interrogation room, the one who pretended to be from the Protectorate. Now, instead of blue, she wore guardian black and a smug expression of authority. Whitler tapped his desk again, and the image dissolved. A bunch of words took its place.

"I'll get to her in a minute. First, I need you both to see these orders."

"Both of us, sir?" Owen leaned forward. "Ren is a new plebe. Should she be on assignment so soon?"

Irritation flickered across Whitler's normal arrogance. "I received this order from the Superintendre about fifteen minutes ago. Don't ask me why the Superintendre requested Ren—or you—for that matter. This seems like something I should be in charge of, but we can't contest the Superintendre." He nodded toward the screen.

"You will conduct a census which includes this questionnaire." A list of twenty questions filled the wall. "Perhaps the reasoning behind Ren's being assigned is that a new plebe will be less intimidating. Of course, that doesn't explain you being recommended." His egotistical eyes locked with Owen's.

Ren read the questions to herself. *Has any person been found to possess any extraordinary skill or attribute? Does anyone in your area, workplace, or social circle appear to not fully engage? Have you noticed any unusual absences or unaccounted time missed from anyone?*

Owen stopped her at the third question with one of his own. "What is this about? Who are they looking for?"

"I don't know." Whitler leaned forward. "I've not seen anything this aggressive in a while. The last time was when a Viand guy kept saying stuff about the Plantanate not being real and people living outside the boundary. They tracked him and everyone he'd talked with down."

"Everyone he'd talked with? Why would they do that?" Ren broke her silence without being invited to speak.

"That's what they do." Whitler ignored the infraction. "Breaking a guideline, especially something like spreading rumors that might affect the safety of others, isn't merely about the offender. The effects of something like this can be far-reaching. Can't they, Owen?"

Owen took two seconds to respond. "Yeah, I guess."

"Well, wasn't that the case with your friend? What was his name? Tylon? Didn't they accomplish his nanny and a few others after you turned him in?"

Owen looked down and nodded.

Ren couldn't pull her eyes from him. He'd lied. He'd told her his friend had an aberration and how awful it was when they took him away, but he'd left out the part where he had been the one to turn Tylon in.

Owen's jaw twitched, and his eyes stayed fixed on the desk. Part of her wanted to call him out right there, and the other part wanted to run. The whole thing about hating what they did to people with aberrations—had he made it all up?

"Maybe that's why you're on this project." Whitler didn't notice the raging bundle of emotions sitting in front of him. Ren burned, and Owen sat there as if he hadn't just played her like a guardian would have. "Owen, you have more knowledge about this sort of thing than any of us." The overseer sat back in his chair. "Now I'm feeling a little better. I've been racking my brain for the last ten minutes trying to figure out why I wasn't chosen for this job."

Ren spoke up. "You can take my place. I don't want to be part of this."

The two men stared at her, then Whitler cleared his throat and gave her the kind of expression someone gives you right before they put you back in place. "No, Ren. This isn't up for discussion. You don't have a choice. It's your duty for the good of all." He paused while she and Owen mumbled back the mantra.

"They're going to have a lot of work to narrow down their search," Whitler continued.

Owen glanced her way, and she knew exactly how long it would take. Not long at all. Not now. A wave of nausea washed over her.

"I've sent the questions and full assignment to both of your inboxes. I'll let you read it over and get started. I'm here if you need me. Now get to it." Whitler pushed up from his desk. "Oh, and Owen, I think it's time you briefed me on what's going on with this." The overseer pecked his desk, and the female's face popped back up on the wall. "I hear you've been working with a guardian."

Ren could feel Owen looking at her, but she didn't respond. A strange numbness engulfed her. It doused the flare of anger and set her into motion—a series of steps, the door, the workroom, and as far away from Whitler's suffocating office as she could get.

Owen had lied. Why would he lie except to trick her? And it had worked. She had fallen for it completely. His charm, his stories, his listening, and his arms around her. Bala had been right. No one could be trusted.

CHAPTER 19

THE MAZAR

What a colossal idiot. Ren threw another rock into the placid river. She'd been so stupid.

Owen had lied. All of it had a been a lie. Every conversation, every look, every act of concern. The whole time he had been working for that imposter guardian interrogator. Of course, he had been on their side. He knew from the start. He'd walked her to her shanty that first day. He'd been playing their game the whole time.

She leaned forward. How could she have believed him? Bala had said trust no one. Ren's head throbbed. Not from a vision, the pain came from too much crying.

She'd left the Sharp Complex without a word. Grabbed her things and gone. Nil had called after her, but Ren kept moving.

She wouldn't wait around while Owen figured out the best time to expose her and claim whatever prize they'd promised him for his wicked devotion. He wouldn't get that satisfaction. Let them question him about the whereabouts of his plebe. Let him feel what it's like to be on the wrong side of the table for once.

Of course, eventually they'd come for her. There was no place to hide in this blasted village. She could hold up in her shanty until then, but why not just stay out here and enjoy the sunshine as long as she could?

Her clip-pad pinged. *Where are you? Let me explain?* She swiped Owen's message away without a response and flipped the device over. Bala's special clip-pad came complete with an on/off switch that would prevent anyone from tracking her. She pressed the button to off. "I guess there's no worry now about who on the team should go." Her throat got tight.

Footsteps came up beside her. "We've got to stop meeting like this." Pandon pushed his cart alongside the bench. "Or maybe we don't." He grinned.

Ren wiped her eyes and jammed the clip-pad back in her bag.

"You still upset about your missing friend?" He clicked the cart to off. "I did some checking and so far, nothing. Castle Raising Home is in the middle of nowhere. Have you heard from her?"

"No." Ren shielded her eyes from the sun. "Thanks for checking." It didn't really matter now, anyway. Soon she would be the one who was missing.

Pandon lowered his voice and leaned toward her. "Say, some of us are going to take a trip out tonight. You want to come?"

"Out?"

"Over there." He nodded toward the other side of the river. "Just a little wiladash."

"Wiladash?"

"Wild lands bash." A gold chain dangled from his neck as he leaned. "It will help take your mind off your blues. What do you say?"

For the first time since she'd met lover boy, she was actually considering taking him up on something. Out there was where Bala's map said to go. For all she knew, maybe Bala was at the cabin now.

"Yeah, maybe I will."

Pandon settled next to her. "You won't be sorry. There's some trippy stuff out there." A horn sounded behind him, and they both turned. A squad of ten sentries zipped up to the Sharp Complex. Pandon stood. "Whoa, what's going on over there?"

"What are they riding on?" The cycles had wheels and hover drones attached to a square platform with handles.

"Drespins. Special sentry stuff. They don't let us normal people have 'em. Us nobodies have to move about the old-fashioned way." He hopped onto his cart. "We'll have to wait until the commotion dies down. I'll meet you out by the pavilion around sunset. It's going to be great."

The cart's motor whizzed, and Pandon pulled back and headed in the opposite direction of the sentries.

Ren focused on the group and called on the aberration through her stuffy head. Nil met the guards. Owen and Whitler joined them. The entire gang was there. Owen kept his gaze aimed at the park. He would know where to find her.

She slinked from her perch and padded across the boardwalk toward the pavilion. It was still hours before sundown, but with any luck, she could hang there until Pandon showed up.

The cameras at the corners of the pavilion dangled by wires, lifeless and dead. She just needed to wait here. The sentries would go to her shanty first, anyway. By the time they looked here, she'd be off wiladashing it up beyond the boundary.

Three large rocks protruded from the water, spaced within leaping distance of one another. Pandon had used them to cross the other day.

She peeked around the corner. The group of sentries dispersed. Two broke away with Owen treading between them. The prideful guide held his head up and almost looked like a sentry himself. Straight back, purposeful stride, and no hesitation. She wanted to hate him.

Three other sentries split across the open park—one heading her direction. Jumping, she swung around and slammed her back into the wall. The river glistened in the late afternoon sun. They were going to find her. This would be her last real day.

What would Bala do?

Ren closed her eyes, took a deep breath, and reached for something from all of Bala's instructions to help her. There were times to fight and times to run. That's all she had to go on. She knew that gem already. Bala had taught her to fight, but not a squadron of sentries. And running was also familiar. She dismissed both and turned to the only other thing that might offer some guidance.

Closing her eyes, Ren reached for the aberration. The vision pulsed through her head and a rainbow of brilliance flooded her senses, erupting into one simple face. The boy.

The vision raced through trees, over hills, and then ducked underground. It flooded tunnels, then hallways, and ended in a grand open room. And there he was, laughing and standing with the girl from the field. He grabbed the girl's hand and turned toward Ren. They glowed, and their white hair glistened.

"She's back," he whispered, and the girl smiled. They both could see her. Ren froze. She couldn't get her words out. What was she supposed to say? Help me? She leaned forward and swallowed. The vision pulsed through her, as if it were a simulator turning the simulation into reality.

The words finally came. "I need help." Tears trickled down her hot cheeks.

Altrist reached out his hand. "It will be okay. He will help you. Don't be afraid to jump."

Jump.

The vision evaporated in a flash, and Ren stood next to the river. Men's voices called from behind her, and without hesitation, she grabbed her pack and took a running jump onto the first rock in the river. The clear water flowed around the rock with no fuss, and Ren held her breath and jumped onto the second rock, her arms flailing to give her balance. She glanced back to check for sentries.

The third rock had a flatter surface than the others, and she hopped to it with no problem, except that the distance to the bank from where she stood was much farther than she'd anticipated. A light flickered in the woods on the other side of the river. The mazar fence. *Great.*

She checked the distance again. It was too far. She'd never make it onto the bank and to the trees. And as soon as the mazar fence triggered, they'd be on her. Slinging her pack into a bush on the far bank, she did the only thing she could. She stooped down, slid one foot into the water, and then another. The cold felt like a thousand prickles all over her body.

Her feet barely touched the bottom. Sloping down, the rock offered her only a few slippery crevices to grip. She pressed as close as she could and held her breath.

"Ain't nothing back here." A man called from the bank. "I don't get what the big deal is. If she's a runner, then they should just let us have a go."

"Orders are orders. Now scout the boardwalk. Last ping on her device was around here."

Ren waited several seconds after their last comment before checking to see if they were gone. As she moved, her foot slipped, and she fell under the cold water.

Flapping her arms, she sank fast, her feet squishing into the river bottom. Pushing up, she reached for the surface and got a gulp of air before ducking under again. Every awful swim lesson rushed through her, and an urgent tingling raged into her head, blocking out the haze of water with brilliant light.

Her feet touched bottom, and she pushed off. The white light of the vision poured through her and sent a jolt of tingling to the tips of her fingers and toes.

She chopped her legs like scissors and brought her hands together then back, cutting through the current, one arm and then the next as her legs pumped beneath her. Two more pumps and her foot met squishy ground. Three steps, and she grabbed the grassy slope and pulled herself onto the bank.

The tingling still pulsed through her head, outlining the world with silvery threads. Even the leaves on the trees were trimmed with a silver lining. The glistening strands pulsated, getting super bright then fading to nothing. Over and over.

Ren counted the flashes between the brightest pulse to the dark outline, then ten flashes until it started again. The brightest point of light emitted from a small box fastened to the side of a tree. White threads of light connected box to box, all pulsating to the same rhythm. The mazar fence.

Bright, and then dimmer, until almost ten flashes of darkness gave way to the building light again. Ten flashes. She could get through there in ten flashes.

Ripples of electric energy coursed through her body. This would be it. Taking a resolute breath, Ren grabbed her pack and hunched down like a runner about to take off, counting the flashes until the silvery thread went dark. Three-two-one, and she let the aberration guide her through the trees.

CHAPTER 20

THE SENTRY

The metallic taste of blood greeted Dart as she stirred to consciousness.

"I didn't do it." Sully leaned against the tent pole and scowled. "It was one of the other guys. I told them it wouldn't be proper to smack you around while you were out cold, but I think they're scared to try it while you're awake. You do have a bit of a reputation."

Dart wiped her face with her sleeve and winced as congealed blood tore away from a cut on her lip. Sully tossed her a cold press, and she put it to her face.

"I really am sorry. But you weren't going to come easy, and I wanted you to come. There's something you need to see." He pulled a card-sized image taker from a pack next to Dart's cot. The exile's accommodations had taken a step up from a blanket on the ground next to a dying fire. The tall tent gave Sully plenty room to stand, and it came equipped with three cots, a table, chairs, and a case filled with provisions.

"So, you've made a new place for yourself. I can respect that." Her old pack-mate sounded sincere, but lying was his first language, so Dart kept her focus and played along with a small nod. He continued, "I can't say we didn't miss you, though. We took down Bido's pack. Caton didn't join us. Silly old man. You'd think by now he'd get who to trust."

Dart coughed phlegm from her throat, moving the cold compress to her temple. Sitting up made her head throb. "I think Caton knows exactly what he's doing."

"He's an idiot. You can't trust the sentries. They're worse than me."

She nodded. Laughter from outside the tent sounded familiar. The same old gang, sans a few who couldn't keep up. "You got anything to drink?"

Sully opened a green box with a white lid. Bottles nestled in ice filled the crate. "Here." He tossed one to her.

"You've been raiding the Viand Village, have you?" She popped the top and tried to take a swig. Her swollen lip didn't cooperate, but she managed a few swallows of the sweet liquid.

"Yeah, it was pretty bad. Five plebes goofing off past curfew had decided to swipe some snacks. You should have seen their faces when we told them everything they'd been believing was a bunch of lies. You'd have been proud of me. I actually tried to help 'em."

A wave of sadness rippled through her. "Poor kids."

He nodded but then lit up his scinter and waved the weapon in the air. "I felt some bad, but we got two of 'em in our pack, so I guess it worked out for them."

"And the other three?" She didn't need him to answer. The sentries would have taken care of them like they did their old and sick and troubled ones.

Sully wagged his head. "They made a big sport of it, you know."

She set the cold pack aside. Thinking about what the sentries could do wasn't her favorite subject. How did people ever get like that—so far gone they make a game of hunting down their own? A familiar rage dulled the throbbing in her head.

Sully leaned forward, his hushed scinter back in place and the image card in his hand. "There you are. I knew you hadn't gone and forgotten everything." He almost whispered the words. "You can run off with those freaks, but you can't run away from who you are, can you?"

She met his sure eyes and swallowed. Every awful thing about her life was here. "How's the leg?" Her gaze fell to where she'd struck him the last time she saw him. She hadn't struck to kill that time—just to escape.

"It's fine." His hand went to the spot. "It's in the past." He lied. Letting go of something like her getting away wasn't just a blow to his midsection. It messed with his ego.

Sitting all the way up, Dart checked the exit and put her bare feet on the dirt floor. Four silhouettes stood guard by the tent flap.

"You can go back to your bunch of freaks, if you want." Sully had never met any of the leader's people. He only knew not to mess with them. "Look, you're free to go. We didn't tie you up or anything."

"How generous of you." Her shoes were missing. Going barefoot would make a quick getaway unlikely.

"But first, I need to show you something." He held out the image card, then pecked a button at the top. The screen lit up, and Dart froze. The last face she ever wanted to see stared back at her.

"No." Trembling, she grabbed the card. "He's alive?" The image held mostly the sentry's face and not enough of his surroundings to identify where he was. "How?"

A half-empty smile filled Sully's unshaven cheeks. "Two rolls ago. See. I told you you'd want to know about this. A scout saw him out near Ogden Bluff. Him and his goons are looking for something."

"And they haven't raided any camps?" She handed the screen back; if she held it much longer, she'd put a fist through it.

Sully shook his head. "Mostly only patrolling. His troop does split apart and pick up trails here and there. Don't worry. They haven't got near your precious new pack. Not that I know. Those freaks are the hardest group of people to track. We haven't seen anything of them for a few rolls."

Buddy's shield. That was good. But the knowledge of her friends' safety didn't assuage the building fury inside of her. He was back. The monster. The last time she'd seen those eyes, he was holding a scinter to her mama's throat.

"So, what do you say?" Sully pulled her back to the present. "Are you in?"

"What?" She knew what he meant, but she didn't want to. She wanted to forget and move on and be all those things Altrist said she could be, but how could she? "I don't know." The tent swallowed the words.

"What's not to know, Dart? I would do it myself, but I knew you'd want to. Being with those happy nut jobs hasn't corrupted you enough to let him get away with what he did, has it?" He looked her in the eye for a flash. "No, it hasn't. I see you. I know you. And you want to end him more than any of us do."

"How did he live? I skewered him. It's not possible." Grabbing the image card, she examined the man's face. It had filled out from when she'd seen him—a grown man now more than a young sentry guard.

Sully sneered. "Maybe you should ask your new friends." His cold eyes said he knew more.

"What? What do they have to do with this?" Even as she asked the question, she knew. She'd heard the story. Liza had found a sentry near dead. She and Anna had saved him. Thim had told her Jasper had been injured. They saved him, and then, when Liza didn't return his affection, he turned on them all and ran off, back to the villages.

Her heart raced. Confirming her thoughts, Sully's lips curled upward. Her new pack had saved the sentry who killed her mama.

Puffed up and sure of himself, Sully held out a scinter. "So, are you in?" His cold eyes warmed. "You know what you're getting with us. We've got your back, and there's no way that shiker is going to see another roll."

Dart pulled warm air into her lungs and opened her palm. Nothing more than a smudge, the sunburst didn't protest. Moving back in with Sully's pack would fit. She knew it. Everything would come back to her like she'd never been gone.

Maybe this was always where she was supposed to be. After all, the leader hadn't given her a gift. He'd not given her anything more than some lame body art and a bunch of words from Altrist and the others. The ones who'd embraced a murderer. Had they told the sentry the same stories they told her, given him promises of a better life, made him feel wanted and loved?

She shook the thoughts away. Was there no one she could trust? Altrist would be off looking for his new girl project, and Sully would take what he wanted and stick a scinter in her back when he was done.

What did any of it matter? The sentry's face flashed into her mind. At least the scoundrel would pay for what he did. She grabbed the scinter. "I'm in."

CHAPTER 21

THE HUNT

The contents of the bag covered the tall grass. "Where is it?" Ren rifled through the pack for a third time.

"I put it in the side pocket." Easing back, she examined the contents of her bag and ignored the lump forming in her throat. "I had it with Pandon and Lidya by the river and put it in the side pocket."

The sun dipped below the tree line, and the damp spots on her leggings seeped their coolness into her bones. Night would be here soon. The darkness and no cabin did not mix well.

Six hours had passed since she had learned the awful truth about Owen. Five since she'd made it across the river and past the mazar. In none of that time had she seen a single cabin, shanty, or anything. Even now, the dirt road mocked her. Some great wild place to sneak away to. It might be beautiful and woodsy, but there was nothing wiladashing about it.

"What have I done?" She settled on the grass and rested her head in her hands. Owen knew. He knew her secret. She'd blabbed it like a lovesick match with hearts in her eyes and the Blender app for a brain. So stupid.

If she'd kept her mouth shut, she'd be sipping a caftewater and scrolling through her clip-pad—deleting every single one of Owen's messages.

Her head tingled as if on cue. She drew in a breath and aimed the ability at her new enemy, then stopped. Instead, she forced Owen out of her head, took another breath, and focused. Perhaps the aberration could show her the cabin and what she should do next. It had shown her the boy and helped her with the mazar.

A spray of tingles rushed up her spine, and white light eclipsed the green world around her. *The cabin. Where's the cabin?* Through the mist of white, a small shanty came into view. A man was frying eggs in a large black pan over an open flame in the kitchen, and a woman set the table with chipped stoneware and a smile on her face.

The picture swirled together, and screams tore across Ren's head. "Run, Bala, go." *Bala.* With the mention of her friend, Ren lost her grip on the vision, and the hazy white melted into the dusky purples of twilight.

Men's voices carried through the trees. For a second, Ren thought it was part of the vision, but then the world flashed back to normal, and she jumped to her feet. Sentries were coming.

The sentries already knew the location of Ren's shanty, so Owen followed in silence. Her disappearance had rocked Whitler's elite agency. *Plebes do as they are told. They don't leave without a word in the middle of the day.* What had she been thinking? Why didn't she let him explain things?

As the door to the shanty slid open, Owen paused. He'd never been inside, but Ren's presence filled up the small room. Some wildflowers sat in a jar on her table. A line of rocks graced her countertop. Blue coverups draped the only chair, and leggings lay in a pile nearby. The trashcan held the remains of her burnt raising home uniform.

He should've told her the truth last night, but he needed space to process and figure out what to tell the Warrior. By the time he'd crafted the perfect message to delay her deadline and gotten the approval to meet tonight, it was too late. Ren hadn't given him a chance to explain. He would have told her everything.

His arms could still feel the embrace of her little body. Somewhere between their questions by candlelight and confessions in the moonlight, he had surrendered his heart to this strange plebe with soft skin, blue eyes, and a bossy streak.

"Look, it's on a loop." One sentry stood on a chair with the side panel to the monitoring device open. "She's probably messed with the transmitter bean too." The other sentry checked the panel behind the refrigerator, then barked some orders over his comm.

They went back and forth on their comms, yelling orders and getting more and more worked up—their enjoyment of the chase grossly apparent. To them, this was a game. At one time, it might have been all play for Owen, too. But not now. His view of the world had changed. The Vantages, with their fancy lights, glass, and gold, rewarded the devoted, but at what cost? To get there required the subjugation of goodness and truth. Nothing about this place was for the good of all.

"What are you looking so smug for?" The shorter of the two sentries turned his aim on Owen. "All of this certainly makes one question why her guide knew nothing of her character."

"Character?" The word seemed in juxtaposition with everything the sentries stood for. Owen swallowed the rest of his response and forced a smile.

The other sentry finished the conversation over his comm and joined them. "Looks like the guide's gotten himself into trouble." He held his clip-pad up for his partner to see.

The short one guffawed, spit flying in all directions. "Well, I guess he won't be so high and mighty after that, will he?"

The two witless imbeciles exchanged a few more jabs in Owen's direction before Owen guessed at the purpose for their taunting. "Is it the Superintendre? It's about time she sent word for me."

The tall sentry tapped the clip-pad and cleared his throat. "Is that so, smart guy? Well, you're on your own. The Superintendre awaits you at the Transport Sentry Base." He nodded to his partner. "He will show you the way."

The short sentry's laugh sputtered to a stop. "No, I won't." He stepped away from them, shaking his head and looking more like a fat mouse than a snake.

"It's okay, guys. I know my way. I've been there before." Owen swiveled on his heel and left them there.

Halfway down the lane from Ren's shanty, another sentry met him. This guy looked like a Jasper protégé. He didn't say anything, but his purpose was plain. The Superintendre had sent an escort to ensure Owen's arrival.

As they climbed into the cart, Owen filed through his options. The first and most obvious one was to divulge everything he knew about Ren. The tidbit about her aberration should be enough to deflate any questions about his loyalty. It might even secure him a sweet promotion to guardianship.

It took him all but five seconds to move on to option number two. He could play dumb, say she duped him as much as everyone else. That would still paint Ren in a bad light, but at least he wouldn't be going back on the promise he'd made to himself after Tylon.

Neither of those options made it past his heart. As much as his sense of self-preservation and personal grit told him to seize the moment, he knew he couldn't. Not yet, anyway. Maybe in another day he would be able to turn on Ren, but not right now. Right now, his heart directed the show, and his heart told him to protect the strange girl and keep hidden what he knew.

The sentry led him into the sentry post and escorted him down several hallways, stopping at two tall black doors.

As Owen waved the doors open, a flowery mist accosted him. The scent attacked his senses, and the room blurred. Something significant had just happened, but he didn't know what.

Blurry and beautiful, the Superintendre rose from behind an oversized desk. "Owen, thank you for coming." Her voice echoed in his head. She motioned for him to sit. "Do tell me what you've discovered."

Owen settled onto the red leather sofa and tried to think. A fire crackled to his right in a massive fireplace, and sweet-smelling candles surrounded the sitting area. He swallowed the fragrant air and turned his attention from the fire to the beautiful Warrior seated across from him.

He still had no plan, but he couldn't refuse the Superintendre's gaze. The heat, the smell, her eyes. Altogether, they clouded his mind. What could he say to fix this? Perhaps the truth? He shook the thought away, but it slid into an image of Olivope and then one of Ren's glowing eyes. *Did he say that out loud? No. Say something. Anything.* "I had thought Ren trusted me." The words tumbled out, nearly slurring as they went.

The Warrior's lips curled up on the edges, but it wasn't a smile. "Yes, I understand there's been quite a stir around the girl at the moment." She crossed her legs and her long jacket fell back, revealing the scinter strapped to her side.

She continued, "And I believe you were supposed to deliver something to me, except now the person in question appears to be missing—and crafty. How do you suppose a new plebe ever knew how to put the monitoring devices on a loop and link the transmitter to a recording?"

Owen wagged his head. "I don't know" The heat from the fire suffocated him. He checked the room. No one else seemed to struggle. The two guards by the door blurred and then came back into focus.

The Superintendre looked tall, towering. "You don't know. Hmmm, well, I don't believe you." Her silky voice snaked around him, sparking something inside. He wanted to please her. She pulled at his resolve—his non-plan. What did he hope to accomplish by evading her questions? Was he truly willing to exchange his lifelong dream for some girl who ran off, giving no thought to those it might affect?

Understanding flickered in the Superintendre's eyes, as if she knew the effect she was having. She poured him a glass of something brown. "The girl's betrayed you, hasn't she?"

Owen's eyes drooped shut and then batted back open. The drink spilled a little as he attempted a sip.

"I've seen it happen before," she continued. "You think you're making progress. You think you're actually getting somewhere with someone, and what happens? They take off and leave you."

Now the entire room blurred, and Owen couldn't shake it back into focus. The Warrior kept on, her smooth voice drawing him into the deep. Ren. Betrayer. Lost.

"She's lost, Owen. But you don't need to be. Do you have what it takes to be a guardian? Think. You know something. You can tell me." Whispers of words floated toward him, cooling him with each breath. "Think, Owen. What is it? What did the girl say to you? Did she tell you her secrets? Where's the boy?"

A fresh breeze blew away the edges of the darkness weighing down Owen's thoughts. For a flash, he saw Ren's face, smiling in the moonlight. Not a betrayer. A girl, simple and kind, with a secret. "The choices you make affect far more than you know." Ren's mouth moved, but it didn't sound like her. Another puff of air cleared the cobwebs, and Owen pointed at the darkness staring back at him. "She's there?"

"Who?" The voice crackled with the fire. "Who's there?"

Taking a long drink of the tainted air, Owen slid down onto the soft ground. "Olivope. It's Olivope."

CHAPTER 22

THE GUARDIAN-IN-TRAINING

Moonlight poured through a circular window in the ceiling, and a ghostly white light greeted Owen as he stirred awake. His head pounded, and the dark room blurred in and out of focus. Where was he?

Rolling over, he tried to sit up. A burst of cool air kissed his flushed face. The air vent in the wall next to his bed blew straight at him. Four walls, a bed, a table, and a chair. The tiny cell held nothing more.

The door slid open, and a woman clipped into the room, making way too much noise in her high heels. "Oh, good. You're finally awake." The voice sounded familiar.

Two solar orbs warmed the darkness, and Owen shielded his eyes as Maxey, the Superintendre's faltering assistant, strutted closer.

"Eviah wants you in the transport before sunup, so pull yourself together."

"What's going on?" Owen swayed as he stood. He still wore yesterday's coverup and pants. "Where am I?" The room swirled, and he leaned back on the bed.

"Here." Maxey tossed a black top and trousers to him. "Put these on. Seems you just got promoted." She turned to leave.

"Wait. Tell me what's going on. What happened?" The words stumbled over his swollen tongue.

The young woman twirled to face him. "You giving me orders now? Barely a guardian-in-training, and you're already bossing people around." She tossed the last few words over her shoulder to the outer room, and a few chuckles told Owen they weren't alone. "Listen, do what I tell you and maybe you'll make it out of this without getting adjusted." The smug person who had interrogated Ren had returned.

"Don't you mean both of us?" Owen forced himself to stand straight. The wooziness from getting up too fast had lessened. "I don't think I'm the only one who needs to worry."

Maxey narrowed her eyes and pushed the door wide open to reveal three armed sentries. "Are you sure about that?"

The challenge slowed him for a second, but he regrouped and took a step toward her. "I won't be the only one laid out on an operating table if they don't get what they want from me." He wasn't entirely sure they hadn't already, but the statement got the reaction he sought.

Fear flickered in her eyes, but her tone stayed steady. "There's no need for a power play, Master Owen. The Superintendre will have you returned, whether or not you come with me. Besides, isn't this what you wanted? Guardian black and everything you deserve."

Owen's heart raced. What had he told them? Did they know about Ren … about Olivope? Everything was a sick blur. From entering the Warrior's office until now, he hadn't been in control. And right now was debatable. He returned his focus to Maxey. "Can't you just tell me what's going on? It's to both of our benefits."

The smugness faded, and Maxey closed the door and lowered her voice. "Your plebe has crossed the boundary."

"Ren?"

Maxey smirked. "Oh, is this going to mess with your matchment plans?"

"You really have no friends, do you?" Owen countered.

The jab hit its mark, and Maxey sobered up. "Well, if you want to find out anything about your *friend*, you'll have to come with me, won't you?"

"I'll come, but I just want to understand what's going on." Desperation swung from the edges of Owen's heart. "Forget about the plebe. Just tell me how one flash, I'm sitting in the Superintendre's fancy chambers, and the next, I'm waking up in something that looks way too much like a prison cell."

Maxey sighed and took a seat in the chair. He could tell part of her wanted to divulge everything she knew. "Evidently you proved to be more important than anyone thought."

"Uh ... thanks." He cracked a smile to lighten the mood.

"Once the cambian took effect, you provided Eviah with a piece of valuable intel."

Cambian. That explained the blackout and the hangover. "Intel? What did I tell her?"

Maxey paused. "I don't know, but she's taking you to *him*. Now get ready."

"Him?" Owen knew what she meant and wished he hadn't asked the question.

"Tatief." The name filled up the quiet, and Owen couldn't hold on to the strength he had mustered. He slumped back to the bed. What had he done?

Maxey leaned toward him. "I've caught enough flack for turning the assignment over to you. Don't mess this up."

Owen stared at her and then to the black clothes in his hands. There was no way out.

"If you ask me, we should have cambianed your plebe up and sicced Jasper on her." Maxey stood. "But the Warrior wanted a gentle touch. Her orders, but I'm the one blamed for this disaster." She headed for the door and barked back. "We leave in five minutes. Get ready."

Owen ran his hands through his hair. The throbbing in his head couldn't compete with the dread filling up the rest of him. What had he done?

CHAPTER 23

THE SILVER RIM

"The Silver Rim." The massive wall protecting their world caught Ren by surprise. She'd crested the hill just as the morning sun cleared the treetops, and there it stood.

Tall columns pulsed with light, and the rim's mirrored panels reached up into the pale blue sky at least fifteen meters. At the top, a sheen stretched into the clouds. As the dome reached farther from the wall, the sheer ceiling became invisible. There it stood, Tatief's magnificent wall forged to create a sanctuary for the good of all. Mostly all, anyway.

All those childhood vids and stories about the barrier had failed to capture its grandeur. The words of one rhyme flooded to mind. "To keep us safe, he braved the heights. And built a wall to stop the carrier. It holds back the bad for the good of all. His gift to us—the Silver Barrier."

When she was four, that rhyme was a favorite. Little ones believe just about anything. She hadn't believed for long, though, thanks to Bala. Bala's education about the state of reality had started early. And when the aberration appeared, and Ren's eyes started glowing, Bala ramped up the lessons.

Ren stretched her back. The warm sunshine overtook the chill in the air, and the day stretched out with nowhere to go. With a quick look around, she retreated off the path to the glen behind her. Best to stay out of open areas. Even out here, a few cams and beans had dotted well-traveled areas like a crossroads or near transport lanes.

She used the aberration to scan the trees. No cams nearby, but a device clutched a branch closer to the wall. It probably caught her. It was only a matter of time before she messed up and walked into a mazar or didn't notice a cam next to her head.

Instead of moving on, she slid down the side of a Lina Maple and fished through her bag for a nutibar. Part of her didn't care if they found her. Her life had revolved around hiding the aberration. It had been one long reaction to a guideline that was wrong to begin with, and she grew weary of it all.

In a flash, she saw her six-year-old self, playing with the aberration in the wrong place at the wrong time. Bala had been so upset when the nanny turned Ren in. No one goes for adjustment and comes back. But she did.

The Plateau guardians and medics had poked and tested her. They'd run scans and asked a ton of questions, and Ren had followed Bala's instructions to the letter, crying on cue, laughing at their jokes, teasing, fretting, and even showing her smarts.

"You're a special little one, aren't you?" That's what the lady Master Guardian had said. She had opposed the testers with certainty, her course of action different from theirs. "This child has more to give. It would be a tragedy to adjust her. No more tests are necessary. Put her back in play." And she'd knelt before Ren and taken her hands. "Do you understand, Ren?"

Ren nodded, though this didn't fall under any of Bala's directions. Bala had said the guardians would adjust her. How much they meddled with Ren's little brain depended on how well Ren could win them over, but it never even came to that. The Guardian Master had stopped them and bestowed kind words—words unexpected and significant to a six-year-old's ears.

A smile lit up the woman's sharp features, and her eyes glossed. "You will do great things." She tapped Ren's nose. "Be strong."

And they sent her back to Bala's waiting arms and a new raising home. So far, that master guardian had been very wrong. No great things had been done, just running and hiding and making mistake after mistake. Even worse than that, Ren wondered if her presence hurt the world more than helped it. People of difference weakened society. They required more than the fragile system could bear.

Still, the aberration had pulled her out of a few jams. In twenty-four hours, it had taught her how to swim, guided her through the mazar, kept her away from sentries, and given her a safe place to lay her head and get some sleep. It might not be useful to the rest of the world, but it was helping her out.

Leaves rustled behind her, and she sprang to her feet, her ability ramped up just enough to see the woods in silvery threads of light. A man stepped out from the trees and shuffled toward her.

His greasy hair stuck to his head. "The rim's pretty, but it hurts." He waved the nub of an arm on his left side. "The wall's got a power all its own. It'll blow yous in two if you lean on it."

Ren glanced at the wall, but mostly kept her eyes on the stranger.

His dirty face creased into a tooth-challenged grin. "My name's Caton. Caton 14266. Where're yous from?"

Ren hesitated. "Back there." Nutibar stuck in dry throat. "Where are you from?"

His grin turned dark. "Back theres." The guy smelled like the garbage hull and the sewage center mixed together with a sprinkling of sweat. "What you doin' way out here?"

"I'm headed to meet up with friends." It was a crazy lie in many ways, but she didn't like the idea of this guy knowing she was alone.

"Nobody comes out this far to party. What yous really lookin' for?"

"Just getting out to see some friends." Her voice shook. "Away from all the rules, you know? Wiladashing." She should stop talking. Every word sounded forced and fearful.

He chuckled.

She took a step upwind. "Well, I better go before they come looking for me."

"No." His dirty paw reached for her, but she averted his grasp. "Don't. Maybe I can help yous. We could be—fri—frienndsssss." His lack of familiarity with the word *friends* didn't help. "How's about I walks you to your pals?"

A crack split through the quiet woods, and Caton jumped, alternating on each foot. "Oh, shikes! They's coming."

Ren took another step, but the crazy little man held up his nub. "They'll get yous. Yous better hide, over there." He pointed with his good arm toward a thick clump of trees and bushes. "Those ain't the bad briars. Yous goes right there, and I'll fetch yous back. Go!"

Ren didn't need to be told twice. She took three steps before turning, then darted for the thicket just as a squad of five sentries crossed over the hill.

"Sixty-six, stop?" A tall sentry led the group.

As the squad approached on drespins, Caton rocked from foot to foot and kept his head down.

"Stop jumping, scrap." The shortest of the sentries pulled out his scinter and flicked it on. Caton settled down.

"You got anything for us?" This time the biggest one spoke. "Anything new?"

Caton straightened up. "I got news, Master Jasper. I got news."

The sentries shielded their faces from Caton's stench. "Well, let's have it."

"Theys on the move."

"Who?" Jasper jerked Caton up by his collar.

"Da ones from Pocket Wilderness. Theys all left."

"The boy with them?"

"I ain't seen da boy. Nobody sees da boy, and da girl's gone too."

Jasper threw the man to the ground, and another guard kicked poor Caton in the stomach.

Tingles pricked suddenly at the back of Ren's head, and the scene in front of her morphed into something else. Instead of sentries, she saw men with gaunt, ashen faces. The spectacle sickened her, and she turned away from it. A shimmering blanket fell across the trees behind her with a silver cord winding its way through the thick woods, its path unobstructed and open.

Caton whimpered as the sentries punched him again. Ren couldn't look back. She couldn't help him, but she wanted to. She wanted to scream and force them to stop. But she waited, listening to their abuse and waiting for the vision to subside.

The crazy little man screamed again, begging for mercy. Then it got quiet, and Caton sputtered, almost a whisper, but she still heard him.

"Over there. She's over there." He repeated it getting, louder each time. Ren popped up and, without looking, took off chasing the silver cord of her vision as it led her through the trees.

CHAPTER 24

THE LOST GIRL

Being on hunt returned without a hitch. Dart followed Sully, and three pack members trailed them.

With the full moon brushing the treetops, the woods looked gray and weathered. The small band had headed out after supper when a scout reported a sentry troop sighting near the wall. It probably wasn't Dart's sentry—she hated that term—but she went anyway. It got some shoes on her feet and distance from Sully's camp.

The quiet forest offered Dart a reprieve from the cussing and craziness of the pack. After living at Snowshoe for six cycles, the exiles seemed even more ridiculous. Their fun consisted of cutting each other down or beating something to a pulp. Their anger was like another person in the camp.

And the smokes and blades had everyone hooked. The whole camp smelled like a skunk that had vomited a rotten cantemelon. How they didn't all walk around gagging escaped Dart.

A whistle in the dark brought Dart's scinter from its strap. Two exiles jogged toward them. The tall one addressed Sully. "Caton said the sentries have been after some girl since this morning."

Dart slid the scinter back into its place and shook her head. Poor kid.

"She's giving them a good run." The guys laughed. "If they don't nab her, we ought to give it a try."

Sully split the men into two groups. One would circle around, following the sentries' trail. The others would head northwest for higher ground. Dart stayed with that group and Sully.

Halfway to the bluff, he pulled her aside. "You sure you're ready? I mean, you are kind of out of practice."

"I'm fine." She tilted her head upwind. His breath smelled like ripe trash.

"Here, take this." He pulled out his scinter. "It's better than yours."

Dart hesitated. Sharing wasn't Sully's thing. "You sure?"

"Yeah." He grinned. "And don't say I never did nothing for you."

"Thanks." Dart exchanged his scinter for hers.

They resumed walking single file and not talking until they got to the bluff. From the high vantage, the trails lined up like a web leading to the boundary lines.

"Look." One of the guys pointed to a sprinkling of lights in the trees. Sentries on drespins. Dart's stomach tightened. "And there." Another group hiked down a path from the rock field near the wall.

A gray cloud crossed in front of the full moon, sending a shadow over the valley. Dart's gaze shot to the trees below. Something moved.

Sully and the others took turns with the ocular, checking out the two groups. They hadn't noticed Dart's shift of focus. She scanned the trees until she saw it. A girl, thirty meters down, scrambled up a rocky trail and hid between two enormous boulders.

Dart shifted to block the guys' view. She reached for the ocular and played her discovery off. "What do you see?"

Sully let loose of the device. "I think we found him."

The news grabbed at Dart like frozen fingers on cold flesh. Her mama's killer led the troop coming from the wall. The two packs would meet up soon, doubling their forces.

"We have the element of surprise, but they're heavily armed." Sully crouched by Dart. What do you think?"

A wave of nausea squeezed at Dart's stomach. She breathed in, counted to four, then exhaled. "I think we wait and see what happens when they meet up. If they don't join forces, then it's not a question." A cool breeze swept across the bluff, shaking the tree tops like applause.

"Sounds good." Sully tapped the guy closest to him. "You got the plan. Get in position and be ready for my signal."

He nodded and grabbed his cohort's shirt. "Sure thing, boss." They left.

"Looks like it's you and me for a bit." Sully settled on the rock and patted the ground.

Dart slid next to him. In a flash, her other life was back. The hurt little girl sat next to her master and hated the world.

Sully knew about her past, and he used it every chance he got, keeping her right where he wanted her. His pet. His trainee. Forever in his debt.

"Feels good, huh." He bumped her shoulder. In the moonlight, his face looked older. Dart swallowed and played her part.

"Yeah."

But things were different. Knowing Altrist had changed her. She couldn't return to this life. Not like when she was ten and scared. She knew better now. Of course, sitting on a bluff waiting to kill someone didn't reflect that very well.

"Those freaks didn't mottle you up too much." He pulled out a wad and lit it, pulling in a drag.

When she first told Sully about Altrist, the pack master didn't believe her. The exiled didn't talk to those weirdos. They were dangerous, unpredictable. Exiles don't talk, anyway. They attack first. Talk later.

Then, Sully pretended he wanted to see the kid in white. She knew it was a lie, but what if? Maybe things could change? It was possible.

They left in the morning while the others slept. Dart figured Sully wanted to keep quiet until he had checked it out. But the truth was, he didn't want anyone to see him kill the girl they'd poured all their training into. Being an ugly, heartless beast was one thing; killing one of their own was another. The thugs had some sense of decency.

The first blow of his fist against her jaw surprised her. She didn't even try to run. Somehow, dying didn't feel like the worst thing that could happen.

"You're doing this to yourself. What did I tell you about those freaks? They're crazy—worse than sentries." He kicked her in the side. "You disappoint me, kid."

Lighting up his scinter, he held it to her throat like the sentry had done her ma so long ago. "You going to stop this nonsense?"

She knew the right answer, but she pressed her lips together. He smacked her with his free hand. "You want to rethink that?"

Closing her eyes, she waited for the piercing touch of the scinter, but it didn't come. Instead, peace settled over her. Fearless peace, the kind of dreams coming from places on the other side of understanding pain and loss.

Sully crouched next to her and slid the hot scinter across her arm.

She screamed, and that got him going.

"That's right." He shoved her and stood tall like her cries powered him somehow. Dart seized the moment, wrapped a leg around his foot, and kicked hard with the other one, sending Sully to his butt. Then, she snatched the scinter and tapped the end to Sully's leg just enough to slow him. He yelped, and she ran and didn't look back.

Sully shifted next to her, jarring her back to the present. "It's time." The sentry troops had gone separate ways. The one with her sentry came toward them, heading toward the girl as if they knew exactly where she was. "If you need help, I'll be here." He put his paw on her shoulder. "Just remember you deserve this."

"Thanks." She pulled his hand off and retreated into the cover of the trees.

The sentries fanned out, combing the woods. Dart slinked toward them, then thought of the girl. They'd find her for sure. Even if Dart got her sentry, the others would find her, or Sully would.

Backtracking, she negotiated the large rocks to approach the girl. "Pssst, hey you." Leafy shrubbery covered the villager. Dart moved closer, and the girl peeked out. She started to speak, but Dart put a finger to her lips and whispered, "Follow me, if you don't want to be sentry bait."

They skirted the rocks and walked parallel with the road.

Dressed in village blue, the girl definitely didn't belong here. Dart wanted to question her, but the sentries were too close.

Pulling out Sully's scinter, she slowed. Something wasn't right. To her left, a form came toward them—a lone sentry, scinter glowing. He was young and wiry—not the sentry she'd come for.

She told the girl to hide and pressed stun on Sully's weapon, but nothing happened. She tried again. The sentry faced her now, the glow from his weapon lighting up his ugly face.

"Something wrong, Git? Is your toy not working?"

Dart threw it down. Sully had tricked her.

"Where'd the other one go?" He looked past Dart, but the girl was gone. Her hiding skills had improved.

Dart shrugged. "I don't think she's your type."

"I don't think your crazy is my type." He reached for his com strapped on his shoulder.

Dart made a move for his scinter, but in the same moment, a shadowy figure knocked the sentry across the head. The scinter fell to the ground and went out.

Dart grabbed the weapon and aimed it at the shadowy figure. The girl stood over the unconscious sentry, holding a very large stick in her hand.

"Will he be okay?" The weak village bait had attacked the sentry.

If they weren't still in danger, Dart would've laughed. "Who are you?"

The girl dropped the stick. "Ren. And you?"

Dart grabbed her hand and pulled her away. "An exile with an identity crisis."

CHAPTER 25

THE MASTER

Two servants watched Owen's every move. If he even looked at the mini-bar, they jumped into motion.

Maxey had snubbed his attempts for information and brought him to the master's quarters of the Golden Horizon. The place was a fortress. Nestled somewhere in the wilds between the Protectorate and the Plateau, the Golden Horizon housed the second residences for any and everyone who mattered most. Tatief, Master Guardians, the Superintendre, they all graced the GH at one time or another. It was state of the art and opulent to the max. A transport station with a castle on top of it.

A horn sounded, and eight sentries filed into the large room. Maxey and Owen jumped to attention. This would be it. His lifelong goal of getting to the top had arrived. It lacked the thrill he thought it would have. The sick feeling teasing his stomach bubbled up to his chest.

Eviah glided to a spot under a massive chandelier with dragon heads clutching the light orbs in their mouths. Decked in a shear black gown with scinter and a skeer strapped to her, the Warrior accessorized her fierceness well. "Owen, I hope you don't disappoint me." She ignored Maxey. "May I present, Lord Tatief. The one who sacrifices for the good of all."

Everyone chimed the mantra. "We give ourselves." Owen came in on the last word.

Five seconds passed, and then he appeared. Dressed in clothes from older times, the master wore black pants and a jacket with a white shirt and paisley scarf. Power graced his square jaw, and his black eyes gleamed toward Eviah first, then came to rest on Owen.

Owen couldn't move. His mouth had morphed into an arid wasteland. Where was that servant with vitawater? Should he bow? Smile? He didn't know, so he stood still and focused on the decorative rug by the sofa.

Tatief clapped twice, and the sentries dispersed around the room. "Come let us sit." He took Eviah's hand and guided her to the chairs opposite where Owen had been sitting. "We have things to discuss."

"I suppose I should start." Eviah crossed her perfect legs, and the black teasing dress she wore fell open up to her thigh.

"No, my dear. I think we need to get acquainted first. Owen?" Tatief's deep voice sounded like it was inside Owen's head. Owen risked a look into the master's eyes, and Tatief's face warmed. "There. That's better. I want you to know, this world has survived because of people like you—people willing to count the cost and do what's right."

Owen balled his hands into fists, so the shaking wouldn't be as noticeable.

"Let me tell you a secret, Owen." Tatief motioned to a map over the fireplace. "It's taken me nearly a thousand years to create this paradise." His gaze intensified. "You've heard stories. The destruction on the outside, the need for the Silver Rim, and then the rebuilding."

Owen knew the history. He managed a nod.

Tatief continued. "The stories don't share the treachery. My brothers and sisters did nothing to help me when the attack came. Three remained outside the wall, their uncertainty securing their fate. The other two hid here, but their allegiance has always been to themselves and never to me. Despite my efforts to repair the brokenness in our relationship, they have refused me.

"In rebellion, they raise up a civilization of their own based on lies and preying on the weak-minded. I didn't mind as long as they kept it outside our boundary, but they've become bolder. Within the last few months, they've sought to destroy the fabric of our world by enticing our strongest and smartest. We believe one of them may have contacted your plebe."

"Ren." It pinched Owen to say her name.

Tatief's mouth curved upward. "Yes."

No one spoke. Maxey had probably shared her theory of Owen hoping for a matchment. Unballing his fists, he wiped his palms on his pants and tried to picture himself in control instead of shaking and unsure.

This was it. The crossroads he'd dreaded. It didn't immobilize him like he thought it would. He still had no plan, but one word popped into his head. Honesty. Not the plan of action he wanted, but until something better formed, he'd go with it.

Tatief stood. "That's enough talk. Shall we discover what you're made of?" The air around Tatief glowed like embers around a fire. "We plan on appointing a full-fledged guardian today." For the first time, he noted Maxey's presence. "We're on the brink of something entirely new. It will require fresh leadership, the kind that can seize a moment." His eyes locked with Owen's. "The kind willing to do the thing required because he knows he's worthy. He knows he deserves to be at the top."

Tatief captivated them. His presence was like a drug. It drew you in, clouded your thinking, and shaved off your sharp edges. Owen tried to hang on to his heart and not betray Ren, but the more Tatief spoke, the more he wanted to please him.

"Both of you have worked hard. It would be an honor to have either of you." He paused letting out a sigh. "But that's not how it's done. Like any privilege, you must prove yourself. You earn it."

He took deliberate steps to the end of the red carpet where a large circle of black with a red T painted in the middle broke up the checkerboard pattern of the floor. Tatief stood at one end of the top of the T, and Eviah took her place at the other.

"Come, Maxey. Stand." He pointed to the tip of the T. The gangplank. "In order to earn your place as guardian, you each must offer something to persuade us."

Owen wasn't sure if he should stand or stay put. He opted to stand. It felt like the right thing to do.

"Eviah." Tatief deferred to the Superintendre.

She radiated power and poured it all at Maxey.

"Maxey, I had expectations for you." The more she spoke, the scarier she sounded. "And I thought we had an understanding. You failed me. Jasper should have interrogated the girl. But that's not what you opted to do. Instead, you put *him* into play." She nodded toward Owen. "And look where it's gotten you. Do you remember the first thing I taught you?"

Maxey swallowed. "Trust no one." She spoke louder than Owen expected.

"Yes, such a simple rule. Yet, you trusted him to do your job." The Warrior's accusation had holes to it, but Owen stayed quiet.

Tatief took aim at Maxey now. "Can you say anything, Maxey, anything at all to dissuade us from accomplishing you here and now?"

At the mention of accomplishment, Owen's legs buckled. This would be it. He'd known it was a possibility, even tried to expect it, but hadn't thought it would come to this. As much as he didn't care for Maxey, he'd rather neither of them be accomplished. And as much as he hated himself for thinking it, if it came right down to it, he'd rather it be her than him.

Tatief caught his eye, and Owen got the distinct impression their leader knew what he was thinking, and it pleased him. Owen looked away. Think. He would be next, and he needed an answer.

Maxey's shaking voice tore him back to the matter of her well-being. "What can I say? You've already made your choice." She got stronger as she spoke. "I have information on this girl, Ren, incriminating information for someone among our ranks." Her teary eyes locked with Eviah's black glare.

"Go on. I've made no decision yet, my child." Tatief motioned for her to continue.

"I did my homework, and the girl is missing something that she shouldn't." Maxey paused. "A birth order. It would seem Ren arrived at the raising home by unconventional means. No one ordained her. Her genetics are unknown. I think there's more to her than just being a pawn in a power play between you and your siblings. Someone manipulated our system."

"How interesting and pathetically weak." Eviah sneered and aimed her awfulness toward Owen. "Shall we hear from you now?" She dismissed Maxey from the gangplank with a flick of her wrist.

Tatief stayed silent.

Owen took his place. No super strategy had come to him. Just the word *honesty*, and he wasn't sure what to do with that. Telling Ren's secret might help him, but he couldn't do it. He wouldn't do it.

Sweat dripped down the side of his face, and he wiped it with his black, silk sleeve. He was a pawn in their cosmic game, and now, he had the chance to exchange his piece for something better. No, not better, more powerful maybe, but not better.

He took a deep breath and raced through his options. The matter of the master's siblings jumped out, and some of the pieces fell into place. The boy Ren saw, and the girl who had approached him. They started this. "Olivope."

Tatief's face lit. "Yes. Go on. What of Olivope's attempts to entice Ren away?"

"It wasn't Ren she was after. It was me." Owen's body shook with the truth. "It was me, and I can trap her for you. I can get Olivope."

This time Tatief flicked his wrist toward Maxey. A thud sounded behind Owen. He didn't look back. Better to continue thinking accomplishment might be good than to know for sure it wasn't.

"Well done." Tatief applauded and then put an arm around Owen. "I believe you have the makings of a Master Guardian."

Owen let the leader of their world guide him out of the awful room. Platitudes of praise buoyed him along. They would go to the Plateau. He would become a guardian, and with each step, a piece of him fell away. Olivope's kind face kept coming to his mind and her words hung in the air, "The choices you make affect far more than you know."

CHAPTER 26

THE SON

"What were you thinking?" Gander towered over Dart. The bear of a man had never spoken harshly to her before.

"I was thinking you guys help people who need it, or did I miss something somewhere." She pressed her back to her chair and kept her eyes on the grain of wood in the kitchen table.

"We help them, but we don't bring them here. Not until we're positive we can trust them." The chandelier trembled as he spoke, making the kitchen shimmer. "Why were you even out there anyway?"

Anna handed Dart a cold cloth for the bruise on her face. They all figured her injuries came from the sentry. "I was just exploring." She lied.

"It's too dangerous out there, especially if you don't have a gift." Anna ran her motherly hand down Dart's arm. "And you'll get your gift. You'll see."

Dart shook her head and rubbed her face. It was late, and she'd not slept in a real bed in a few days. With everyone freaking out, it was hard to concentrate. Maybe bringing the village girl here was a big mistake. "Look, I'm sorry I didn't realize I was breaking some rule. I figured you would want her. And if I'd left her out there ..."

Everyone filled in the blank with their own variation of the evils outside their safe haven. Dart looked around the table. Gander, Anna, Thim, and Liza nursed their cooling caftewaters and picked over their slices of apple loaf. She knew they meant well, but the adrenalin from the chase had burned off, and now she just wanted to stretch out, close her eyes, and pretend she hadn't been planning to kill someone a few hours ago.

She shrugged and pushed her empty cup away. "Altrist brought me here after only a week, and I'm not from a trustworthy bunch."

Gander softened his bear voice. "*Altrist* brought you here. That's different. No offense, but I think we all trust Altrist's judgment better than yours." He had a point there, but what was done was done. Blaming her wasn't going to change the fact that some village runaway was three tunnels down, sleeping in her room.

"It's not that we don't trust you." Thim chimed in. A young voice of understanding amid a bunch of worried faces.

Anna cleared the plates. "It's just that we've seen this before. Poor village girl runs away and says she needs help, when she's really a spy for Tatief."

"Well, I don't think you have to worry about this girl." As she spoke, the picture of Ren standing over the sentry with a club in her hand crossed Dart's mind. "Of course, I guess we can't be too careful."

Gander rumbled out a story about a guardian who posed as an exile once. Dart looked at her friends. The yellow orb in the middle of the table cast a warm glow on their faces. They chatted and made their points and offered a comforting word here and there. They all knew one another and held each other up. But they didn't know her, and if they did, they wouldn't hold her up.

She rubbed the spot on her leg where the scinter had pinched her. No one had pieced together that she'd been gone for two days already. They were all so busy with their own stuff.

Besides, talking about the pack might bring up the sentry, Jasper. A tightness gripped her chest and made it hard to breath. Her hate for him pressed in on her. But it wasn't just him. It was the whole awful irony of him getting rescued and her falling into Sully's hands. And these people being the ones who brought him back from the edge of death.

They would say the leader saved him and never realize that in the same breath they were saying the leader hadn't saved her. He had let the worst of life inflict its best on her, and now, she was here sitting amid his loving throng feeling more betrayed and hurt than ever before. If they told her one more time that the leader cared about her, she might scream.

"I'm tired. I think I'm going to go sleep by the falls tonight." She grabbed a blanket off a hook by the door just as Elias bounded into the kitchen.

"What are you still doing up?" Anna scolded the ten-year-old.

"We're playing century poser in the big room, but I needed a snack." The kid headed for the apple loaf.

"Don't worry about the girl, Dart. We'll work it out." Gander sent a wave of assurance her way. "She's only seen the entrance you brought her through, and there doesn't appear to be any tracker in her things." He nodded toward Ren's bag on the counter. Elias fiddled with the girl's clip-pad and crammed a slice of bread in his mouth.

"Cool." He held up the device. A white swirl danced on the screen and then twisted and moved as the picture of a man appeared. "Look!"

"Elias, turn it off," Gander called.

Anna dropped a plate to the table. The color drained from her face.

"Don't worry, Anna. The vim will block the signal." Thim chimed in. "They won't track it here."

Anna tore from the group and snatched the clip-pad from Elias's sticky fingers. "It's him." She held the picture up again. "It's him. I would recognize that face anywhere."

"Who?" Everyone spoke at once.

"My son." The focus shifted to Anna, and the others crowded around her. Dart backed away. She'd had enough of them for a while. Gander caught her before she could make a clean break.

"I didn't mean to be hard on you. The girl's probably fine." A wash of peace took the prickles off Dart's raw emotions. Gander's strange gift. Besides being super strong, he could help a person feel better or worse, though she'd never seen him make anyone feel worse.

"Thanks. I needed that." She let him wash the bad away. It would be back soon enough, but for now she needed a break from feeling so miserable.

"You sleeping by the falls?"

She nodded.

"I locked our little visitor in your room." He held up a thin card with a track pad and three buttons. "So, don't go letting her out until we've gotten the okay from Altrist."

"You did what?" Dart raised her voice.

Anna stopped her story about her kid and how she'd never forget him even though he was three when she last saw him. All eyes focused on Dart.

The ex-sentry tried his gift again, but Dart wouldn't have it. "I can't believe you. I told her you guys would help her, not lock her up. And when did you put a lock on my door?"

"It's always been there. You just have always had permission to enter it. The Leader designed it." He slid the card back into his pocket like mentioning the leader made everything okay. "I'll do what it takes to keep us safe."

Dart shook her head. No telling what Ren would think when she woke up and realized they'd trapped her in a bedroom. That could wait until morning, though. For now, a little peace and quiet was needed to clear away the yucky feeling creeping into Dart's heart. She left them there and headed for the falls.

The water roared with numbing power. The hidden world of Snowshoe spanned for miles with tunnels shooting upward creating access points in a variety of places. Dart's favorite entrance to their underground fortress was by the falls.

Hundreds of gallons of white water poured over the bluff and slammed down a slippery slope of rock. Behind the water, hidden from the outside world, a twenty-foot crevice opened into a cozy cave. A thick rug and an old sofa graced the back of the crevice. Dart liked it because it was usually vacant, and the crashing water always helped her think.

She snuggled up on the couch and watched the torrents fall. A tear slipped down her cheek. Maybe more than any pain she'd ever felt was the fact that the leader had saved her enemy. He had pulled that monster out of certain death and brought him back, for what? So he could hunt someone else down?

Not just that, but at the same time, the leader had left her to Sully. For six years, she had suffered, been beaten, and molded into an exile. Six years. It felt like a lifetime. And now, he teased her again, bringing her here, giving her the sunburst and these friends, and then deserting her. That seemed wrong in so many ways. If he were real, she would tell him just what she thought of how he cared for some and left others to fight for themselves.

It wasn't fair. Jasper shouldn't have gotten to live. Her mother shouldn't have died so senselessly. The world shouldn't be like this.

More tears joined Dart's wet cheeks, and she fell asleep playing out every awful thing she would tell the leader if he ever dared to show his face.

CHAPTER 27

THE SQUIRREL

Ren rolled over and closed her eyes. The covers of Dart's bed felt like butter, and she wanted to burrow down and not come out. The silence comforted her. In the dark, she could pretend nothing had changed. She was still a new plebe, acing the challenges, and making new friends. Or better yet, she was in the archive waiting for Bala and sipping caftewater.

She pulled her knees to her chest and made herself into a ball. If only she could disappear. No more hiding the aberration or worrying about being discovered.

Her throat tightened. Fits of crying and restless sleep took turns through the night, reminding her of everything. She would wake up, cry, and then fall back to sleep. It wasn't the best cycle, but it lightened the weight sitting on her chest.

Dart had given her a box of tissues and a nightgown when they first arrived. The strange girl had led Ren through a web of tunnels and offered her a room for the night. The niceness could have been a trap, but Ren didn't care. She'd spent the last two days running and hiding. She was tired, needed a shower, and wanted space to think.

The soft glow of an orbitt lit the hallway leading to the bathroom and closet. Ren drew in a quiet breath and concentrated. The room glistened and sparkled as her aberration warmed up. Her mind drifted to Owen, and the vision faltered.

It was naïve to have trusted him. Three weeks. She'd not even known him a month. Maybe Bala had caught wind of Owen and saw it coming. Poor little lonely Ren couldn't keep her secret. Still, his betrayal didn't make sense. He had given her some leverage. She could have reported him.

None of it made sense. Not one thing about reporting people for their aberrations or differing opinions or dislike of Tatief made any sense. It pitted friend against friend and kept people from ever building any trust. Perhaps that was the point. No lasting attachments. No trust, and people are forever bound to the guardians to tell them what to think and who they are.

Ren turned and sat up. Dart's room succumbed under a flurry of swirling light, and a pool of white engulfed Ren. The whir from the air vent, the drip from the faucet, the hum of the orbitt, each sound blended then dissolved into the vision.

"Owen." Ren whispered his name.

An image flashed into her mind. His cabin. Empty. Then the workroom in the Sharp Complex blurred into focus. Whitler stood with Nil. The plebes all stared at them, even Lidya who usually had her nose stuck in her clip-pad, but there was no Owen.

A wave of sadness washed the images away. But sadness for what? Not seeing him, knowing her only attempt at close friendship had failed, or everything else that had happened over the last two days. She wasn't sure.

Ren let go of the scene and returned to reality, waving her hand by the globe on the table. A warm glow filled the room, and the light from the vision drizzled to the floor.

Dart's room was nicer than the shanty. Wooden furniture, rugs, and pictures reminded Ren of the rooms in the old tunnels at Castle.

She checked herself in the mirror. Her eyes weren't glowing, not even sparkling. Somehow the last few weeks had changed the aberration. She'd only had one wild vision, and even that had left little behind in her eyes to give her away.

All that time she and Bala had spent trying to hide the visions and subdue them had perhaps missed the point. Maybe instead, they should have been trying to learn more about it and how to use it. Maybe they should have let her be a squirrel instead of trying to make her into a bird.

That would have never worked, though. Not in their world. People don't get to be different, at least not different from what *they* say is okay. There are no squirrels. There are only healthy, happy birds flitting around like all is fine, and the only thing that matters is retiring to the Plantanate to live out their days in jolly oblivion.

Bala had said it. The aberration wasn't the enemy. The world was. Yet even Bala had tried to put the anomaly in a box and shove it away, so no one would know.

Ren slid from the bed and changed from her sleeping gown into the black leggings and cream coverup top Dart had left. This was not the world of the villages. That was for sure. She checked herself in the mirror. Not once in seventeen years had she ever seen anyone wearing black and white together.

"What is this place?" She reached for her messenger bag under her dirty clothes, but it wasn't there. Her food, her notes, her clip-pad from Bala. It was all gone. "Oh, that's just great."

Using her ability, she perused the room. No cameras and no clip-pad. She tried the door. Locked. "You've got to be kidding me."

The aberration highlighted the room and showed the doorway outlined in green with a rectangular panel beside it. A soft green handprint pulsed in the rectangle. Ren pushed the vision away, and the panel disappeared. Then an idea went through her mind, and with the aberration's help, she found the handprint and placed hers over it. The door dinged and slid open.

Soft orbs hanging from sconces on the walls lit the hallway. A dozen rooms lined the carpeted corridor, and Ren snuck by them. The air smelled of cake, cinnamon, and burning wood.

The muffled conversation of two men wafted from around the corner. Ren took cautious steps when the carpet ran out.

"I don't think it's anything but a big reminder that we need each other."

Ren peeked around the corner. The men stood by a workbench, their backs to her.

"Maybe, but it seems like there's more to it. All this talk about making us ready and someone coming from the village. I'm not sure I like it. Things have been good the way they are."

"Here, lift it up." The man stepped away from the workbench as the other one tilted a large plank of wood with the words "The truth will" burned into the surface. "Good. This will go nicely over Olivope's cabin door."

"If they have their way with things, she won't go back to her cabin."

"Where else is there? Why would we want to leave? Things are good. With the vim and so many gifts, we could probably give the Plateau a good run for it."

Ren swallowed. It was one thing for her and Bala to bash the Plateau. They were just two nobodies hiding away in an old library. It was quite another to talk where anyone could hear.

The one holding up the wood chuckled. "Maybe one day Altrist will let us stick it to them."

Altrist. Ren's heart jumped to her throat.

"Hold it steady." The other fellow pointed at the wood, and a stream of fire shot from his index finger burning the letter *s* into the plank.

An aberration. He had an aberration, and he was using it as if it were a normal everyday thing. Easing away from the doorway, Ren held her breath and pressed herself to the wall.

She didn't mean to freak out by the guy's aberration, but it was the first time she'd actually seen anyone else exhibit anything abnormal. The irony of her reaction wasn't lost. They had something in common, this rebel with a weaponized index finger and her and her weird visions. They shared a common freakishness, yet her first thought was to get as far away from the aberrant as she could.

"Who are you?" A deep voice filled the hallway. The large man with the laser finger took a step toward Ren.

She put her hands up. "Dart brought me here. I'm just visiting. I'm nobody."

The other guy, short and chubby, joined them. "How did she get in here?

Ren froze. For all of her averting danger over the last two days, she had no clue how to get out of this or what laser-finger guy would do if she tried to run.

CHAPTER 28

THE OLD FRIEND

The stout little man flicked his wrist, and the boy ran to the table and got another swath of cloth. Owen rolled his eyes and yawned.

"I think ten outfits will be fine." That was something he never thought he would say.

Hillton stood as straight as his enormous belly would let him. "Clothes are everything." He pursed his lips. "The clothes make a statement before you ever open your mouth." His serious face underscored his opinion, but his patchwork jacket, pink leggings, black shorts, and aqua heeled boots failed to bring his diatribe full circle.

Owen forced a smile and slipped his new black loafers on. His stomach growled. Earlier, he had given up the fight for the lunch tray to Hillton and his fashion team.

As he picked through the remains, the double doors to the round fitting room flew open. Two sentries filed in, followed by Tatief.

"Well done, Hillton. He looks like he belongs."

Hillton bowed as far as he could and came up with a smile. "Thank you, Master."

"What do you think, Owen? Is it you?" Somehow Tatief filled up every mirror in the room. He lifted his arms "My god, it's good to be the maker of our own futures."

Tatief put an arm around Owen like an old chum. "Are you ready for the grand tour?" He pulled a purple piece of cloth from Owen's shoulder. "Never purple, Hillton. Never purple." Tossing the swath behind him, he guided Owen toward the door.

A rush of cool air kissed Owen's face as they marched into the depths of the Plateau. People darted to the side, heads down and hands clasped in front of them. Tatief bolted on, pointing out everything from architecture to pretty girls.

Owen's blurry mind couldn't take it all in. Nothing in the last twenty-four hours had gone the way he thought it would. He'd gone deeper into the belly of the guardians. Guilt, loss, and every opulent, expensive, chic thing he'd ever wanted came along with the journey.

"This is the Kirkenwall." Tatief waved his black tog-sheathed arm, and a bronze door swung open. An empty room with three walls of screens awakened when they entered. The monitors covered one wall completely, then dwindled down on each of the other walls.

"What is this?" A screen near Owen cycled through a series of pictures. The face of a male from birth to adulthood.

"This is the wall of accomplishment." Reflections of the faces danced in Tatief's eyes.

Accomplishment. Owen took a step back. The faces of those who had been accomplished. He swallowed. Any guilt he had stuffed away forced its way through the door and propped up its feet.

Tatief observed him. "What do you think?"

Owen shook his head. "It's too much for words."

"Yes, it is." The master flew to the wall on the right to the very last screen. "And here's our Maxey."

Owen forced himself to watch the images cycle through the screen. Her birth, the curls of a five-year-old, awkward glasses at twelve, her appointment to Eviah, her standing defiant at the top of the T. Everything in him wanted to run or scream or do something, but he stood there, forced a smile, and nodded.

Tatief clapped him on the back and whispered, "It will get easier. Eventually you'll find this room calms you. Give it time." The smell of mint with a hint of smoke added to the churning in Owen's stomach.

"C'mon, there's still much to see." Tatief swiveled and moved on.

Owen took one last look at Maxey's face and hoped beyond measure this room would never get easier to see.

By the time they stepped onto a waiting transit box, Owen had stifled his stomach. A dull melody played in the background, and a woman's breathy voice lilted through the speaker.

"Take it. You deserve it. It's what you make of it. If you want it, it's yours." Over and over. Tatief swiped at a miniature clip-pad, engrossed and hopefully oblivious to Owen's unsettledness.

"Take it. You deserve it. It's what you make of it. If you want it, it's yours." Owen craved some space to think. Except for a quick rest when he arrived, he hadn't stopped or been alone to work through everything that had happened.

As the doors pinged open, Tatief snapped his clip-pad shut. "Sorry, Owen. I've got something I need to attend to." He whistled, and a girl wearing a tight-fitting, short, black jumper and a low-cut top lined with jewels came running from a reception area. "Show him the overlook."

Without a word, the girl took Owen's hand and led him up a spiraling walkway. Something about her made it hard to think—the perfume, the way she moved, her hand pulling at his. taking up the space in his head. He could only focus on her. Body art extended from her chin around the back of her neck and beneath her jeweled top.

She stopped on a balcony and announced, "The Plateau."

A city of glass, steel, and black onyx stretched out before him. Not entire buildings, only the tops of them. A few spires reached up into the sky, and some of the roofs went higher than Owen's entire cabin. In between each, shiny streets of black shown like cooled, polished igneous.

The girl giggled. She leaned toward him, blew into his face, and an enticing thickness crowded Owen's already cluttered mind.

He shook his head. "What are you doing?"

She shrugged and held his gaze, like a snake charmer, moving ever closer.

"Sir." A guardian sentry stepped between them and cast a dismissive glance to the girl. She slithered away, and Owen drew in a deep breath of air and tried to shake off the heaviness.

"Master Tatief requests your presence in the Lower Room."

Owen followed, feeling like he'd just been rescued from something.

The sentry stopped at the transit box. "Just put your hand to the screen. It will take you to the correct floor."

As Owen entered, the recording lilted again. "Take it. You deserve it. It's what you make of it. If you want it, it's yours." *Ugh.*

The door opened to the sound of a thousand muted conversations and a narrow, dark hallway. It sounded like a bunch of listening beans thrown into a pot and echoing off each other. Shiny and black, the glass walls gave Owen the impression whoever was on the other side could see him.

A gray door at the end of the hallway glowed. No handle, no entry cards, nothing offered any direction, so Owen stood in the glow and waited. After a few minutes, the door slid open, revealing a white room with just one man seated at a desk. He faced images sectioned off into sixteen squares and hanging in the air. No monitors, devices, anything. The man tapped the air, and the images dissolved.

Owen couldn't move. He'd only ever seen one other person do that.

The man touched another, and the pixels dripped away. A turn of his hand and a new image hovered in the air. This one showed Ren at the Silver Rim. The picture was from a distance, but Owen could tell it was her.

"It's your girlfriend." The man spoke, and Owen's heart traveled back in time to two ten-year old boys, a shared love of winning, and dreams of grandeur.

"Tylon?"

The man spun around. "Hi, old friend." Tylon labored at the word friend.

"You're here." The images behind Tylon flickered with Owen and Ren huddled together at work, laughing at dinner, and strolling through the park. Owen tried to focus. So much had happened, and his head felt full and empty all at the same time.

"Same old Owen. By the book and off the hook." Black body art lines ran up Tylon's arms and neck stopping at his chin in jagged points like spikes. "It's always been so hard for you to think outside your box, hasn't it?"

Owen shook his head. He needed a minute to process. "You're alive."

Rolling his liner-doused eyes, Tylon spun, tossed another vid into the air, and narrated as it filled the space between him and Owen. "I came here, like everyone who has a—gift." He smirked. "Of course, not everyone makes out as well as I did, but one does what one must to survive."

With a wave of his hand, the vid of Maxey and Owen at the Golden Horizon played out in front of them. Tylon let the whole ugly scene finish before he continued.

"I suppose you understand that. Don't you, Owen?" He blew, and the images dissolved. "Lucky for me, I have a very useful skill set.

A chime sounded, and the Superintendre strode in with three sentries. Five seconds later, Tatief paraded in. Tylon sat up a little straighter but didn't stand.

"So, they have her?" Tatief's square jaw flexed.

Tylon waved his hand, and the picture of a sentry with an ice pack on his head hovered in the air. The vid came from the Superior's body cam. The injured sentry cowered. "I saw her, but then a stupid exile got in the way."

The superior spoke, and Owen recognized the voice. "And the exiles attacked you?" Jasper.

Tylon tossed another image up as if he were pitching a ball. This one had no picture, just audio lines and sound.

"Where'd the other one go?" The same sentry spoke.

A girl answered. "I don't think she's your type."

"I don't think your crazy is my type."

Some scuffling and a thunk, then Owen heard her. Ren. "Will he be okay?"

"Who are you?"

"Ren."

The recording stopped. Owen needed something to lean on.

"You know, I'm not the expert, but it sounds to me like your little plebe isn't like other plebes." Tylon leaned back in his chair. "I mean what new plebe would plaster a sentry over the head?"

A low growl sounded from Tatief. "One educated by a nanny trained in the special guard."

Tylon whistled. "That's some nanny."

"I told you I'm taking care of it." Eviah spoke over Tylon's commentary. Everyone in the room seemed to be in on the same secret. All Owen could think of was that Ren was still out there on the run.

Fuming, Tatief ignored them all. "Where is she now?" He growled in Tylon's direction.

"No idea. She disappeared with the exile chickie."

"She's with them." Embers smoldered in Tatief's dark eyes. "This is ridiculous." His tanned skin flushed with red. It almost glowed red. "You knew she'd seen the messenger and yet, instead of Jasper taking a turn, you just let her go." He directed his tirade at Eviah. "You thought she would just tell him what she saw? What kind of plan was that?" His shiny shoes clacked on the floor as he paced.

The Warrior stood straight, but her eyes gave away some of her worry. "It was Maxey's call. I trusted her judgment. I shouldn't have."

"No. You shouldn't have." Tatief turned his attention to Owen, as if he just realized the guide was there. "Well, it looks like you're up. You get us Olivope like you promised, and maybe this won't be a total failure."

Owen snapped to attention. He didn't want to think about his promise to deliver Olivope, but now wasn't the time to deny the master what he wanted.

"Sir, I'll have the mission director compile the plan." The Warrior took the lead.

"Very good." Tatief stepped away from the others. "I will check on your progress later." A dull white light grew and enveloped Tatief, and then the master disappeared.

"Owen, come with me." Eviah took off for the door. "It's time you got a crash course on messengers."

Owen put his hesitation aside and followed.

Tylon tossed images from their childhood at him all the way to the door. "Bye, old friend."

CHAPTER 29

THE HOME FOR ABERRANTS

A series of stupid mistakes. If they ever wrote a life plate to describe Ren's life, she was sure it would start with the fact that toward the end, she made a series of stupid mistakes.

The big guy waited for an answer, but she didn't have one. She figured she could get away from both men if they tried anything, but where would she go? She didn't know.

"There you are." Dart stood a few doors down with her hands on her hips. Ren wanted to lunge toward her with huggy arms, but she played it cool. Dart met her halfway. "Sorry about the locking-you-in-my-room thing. I didn't do that, and boy, did I let Gander have it. That's no way to treat a guest. How did you get out?"

Ren waved off the apology and the explanation about her escape. "Do you know those guys?"

Dart looked past her. "I met the chubby one once. The big guy is from Pocket. Why?"

"The big one has an aberration." Ren whispered the last word.

Dart cocked an eyebrow. "A what?"

The chubby guy cleared his throat. "An aberration. It's village talk for a gift."

Laser-finger-guy grinned, but he looked more annoyed than happy.

"Makes it not sound like such a good thing." Dart moved between Ren and the two men. "Don't worry, guys. She's just visiting for a few rolls."

Strained smiles stretched the men's faces, and they nodded. Ren watched the aberrant's hand. The world was much bigger than she'd thought. People lived free lives with their aberrations. Whole underground villages existed apart from Tatief's touch.

"Don't worry. They're fine," Dart whispered. "We just don't get many visitors down here."

"She needs to go to Altrist." The large one growled, then went back into the workroom. The other guy shot a glare and followed. Neither fazed Dart. She looped her arm around Ren's and directed her through an archway toward a moving staircase.

"They're worried you're some kind of spy, but I know that's not true." Dart talked a lot like Bala, straight with an aftertaste that left you wondering whether you should laugh or worry.

Ren looked over her shoulder. "I don't think they liked me."

"They don't like Tatief, and you look a lot like someone who does like Tatief."

"Well, I don't." The words zinged out. "I just mean there are some things about the guardians that don't seem to be for the good of all, like some of their rules."

"Oh, there are lots of things about them that aren't for the good of all. Their rules are like the least of their wrongness." The moving stairway took them up three stories. This underground world was a city, not a revamped raising home.

The stairway spit them out into a huge foyer with other hallways splitting off from it. A large fountain sat in the middle with a skylight overhead. They were still underground, but the place was magnificently underground. No wet tunnels or foggy skylights. The architecture spoke of years dedicated to precision and elegance. It was beautiful and bright.

Dart headed toward the fountain, nodding to the few people who passed them. Everyone seemed to be on their way somewhere. A woman scooped a small boy into her arms and gave Ren a worried look.

"Who are all these people?" No one wore the normal village colors. It was a rainbow of outfits. Parents with their children and no divisions. "Where did they come from? How did they get here?"

Dart stopped in front of the fountain. Water shot up toward the skylight, splashed into an oval mirror with crystal orbs framing it, and then sprayed downward. The light, water, and crystals created an array of colors in the mist.

"I love this fountain. Rainbows and promise." Dart smiled and stared up at the colors. Ren checked a passing guy whose legs were invisible.

Dart smiled upward. "The villages."

"What?"

"You asked where they all came from." Dart waved her hand through the spray, then gave Ren a no-nonsense look. "Most of them were rescued from the villages. The Viand, Wall, and some from the Protectorate."

"What? How?" The insulation of her life had never felt so pronounced. Sure, everything was hand fed to her by nannies and guardians who told her what to think and why, but this had never occurred to her. People escaping the villages? Living outside the boundary? This wasn't some wiladash for fun or a jaunt to a cabin for a little while. These people would all be accomplished if apprehended. This was treason.

She and Bala had talked about how the guardians didn't always know best and that there had to be a better way to treat people of difference, but they'd never once talked about living outside the villages—not until Bala produced the map and dropped the bomb about her father. He had lived outside the villages in some cabin in the middle of nowhere. Or was it nowhere? Maybe it was more here than nowhere.

Dart continued, "Some of them crossed the boundary like you did, some got away from the hunt, and a bunch were rescued by a bandy." Dart delivered her world altering news as if she were explaining the history of the Silver Rim.

Ren's legs felt wobbly. She needed to sit down. "Bandy?"

Dart dried her hand on her leggings. "A small group who go in after a specific person. A lot of times it's someone they worked with in the village. They go in, explain things to them, and then get them out. If the village bait will come, that is. Some people don't want to leave."

A tingly ringing played in Ren's ears. It wasn't the aberration. It was her world opening up.

"Hey, Dart." A sandy-haired boy came up from nowhere and pulled on Dart's arm. "They want you to bring her to the Point."

Dart pried his grubby fingers from her elbow and introduced him. "This is Elias. He has a very special aberration. It's aberration thievery, actually."

He giggled and then moved past Ren. "Oh, is that Simper." Elias snuck toward a man who was carrying boxes without actually touching them.

"Does everyone here have an aberration?" Ren surveyed the people passing by. "Is that why you live down here, to hide the aberrations from the guardians?"

"No, not everyone has one." Dart cleared her throat. "Come on. I need to take you to the others."

Ren's legs still felt unsure, but she followed Dart anyway. "Are you taking me to Altrist?" For some reason, the thought of meeting the strange boy in person, instead of in a vision, felt like an anchor—a tether between two worlds, the village and here.

"Yes, I am. He needs to approve of your being here before everyone else will stop looking at you like you have a third eye." They headed down the largest walkway, which led to another downward staircase. "Altrist is the kindest person you'll ever meet. Don't worry about him."

"I'm not worried about him." Moments from their last meeting flashed through Ren's head. "We've met before."

"Wait a minute. You know Altrist? How is that?" Dart stopped fast and whipped her head to face Ren.

"I saw him from my transport my first day in the Protectorate, which got me in big trouble, by the way. And then I saw him again a few nights ago when I was out for a walk. He said he was trying to help me, but I think he was mostly just pointing out how much I need help." Ren left off the bit about her aberration.

"Hmmm, well that's an interesting development." Dart took off again, then paused at the entrance to a large room with beautiful banners, a burning fire, and about twenty people gathered around food tables. "Say, would you mind waiting here, I want to get Gander. I don't want him to miss this."

Ren didn't answer, but she stayed put when Dart took off into the room, heading straight for a group gathered around what looked like a table spread with sandwiches, fruit, and cakes. The banners reminded Ren of the ones she'd found in the library at Castle. The abundance of food made her stomach growl.

Everyone looked normal—normal people, living free. A tall, thin man sat at a grand piano and played. Ren pulled up the aberration and took in the scene. Everyone's skin had a pale glow to it. Each glow was a different color, like the many facets of a prism. The room looked much brighter through the eyes of her gift.

"What are you seeing, my dear?" Altrist stood beside her. A huge smile filled his white face.

Ren sucked in a breath and tucked the aberration away. "Nothing."

"I'm so glad you're here." The strange boy took her hand. "I knew the Leader would guide you here. I just thought I would be the one who would bring you."

Altrist stood in front of her, her hand in his, and a soft white glow clinging to his pale skin. He looked the same as the other times she'd seen him—about half a foot shorter than her with spiky white hair, big blue eyes, and an air about him that seemed filled with experience and knowledge.

When he released her hand, a warm tingling went up her arm. "Tell me, Ren. How did you get away? You were in the Protectorate, correct?"

It was a long story she didn't want to share. She shook her head. "Yes. I crossed the river."

"That was brave. Are you alone?"

Ren shifted from one foot to the other. She couldn't read him. He seemed sincere, but he also knew stuff. Stuff she didn't want him to know. "Yes." She broke away from his deep blue eyes. "Dart brought me here. She saved me from the sentries."

Altrist nodded, then smiled and looked past Ren. "Olivope, come join us. It is her. The one I told you about."

A beautiful girl joined them. Ren recognized her from her vision in the field with Owen. A flush of heat rose in Ren's cheeks.

"Welcome, Ren. It's nice to meet the ghost in Altrist's head. Is your friend with you?" Olivope smelled like fresh air and flowers.

"My friend?" Ren felt like a five tier, standing next to two master guardians.

"Owen." Olivope's voice sounded like a song. "Did Owen make it out, as well?"

At the mention of his name, a wave of tingles rushed up Ren's chest and to her head. The burst came from nowhere and caught her unprepared. She closed her eyes. The edges of the wild vision spread across her mind.

"Are you okay, dear?" A gentle hand tapped her arm, and a thousand prickles of warmth rushed through her, like a herd of friendly fireflies darting from her arm to her chest.

Before she could answer, someone slammed into her side. "Oh, sorry." Elias, the kid she'd met earlier, stumbled away from Ren, then hovered his hand over three apples, coaxing them off the floor and into the air. As he juggled away, a wave of sparkles chased after him.

Ren took the distraction as her opportunity. "I'm sorry. I'm not feeling well." Without waiting for a reply, she tore away and headed for Dart's room—or at least the direction she thought was Dart's room.

CHAPTER 30

THE STRANGER

"That went well." Dart brushed leftover tasty cake crumbs from her coverup. "I just want to point out that Ren had already been vetted by Altrist." She shot a look to Gander.

"Hey, guys." Elias stumbled toward them, waving his hands. "Something's wrong with me."

Anna rushed to his side. "Are you okay? You ran into Ren pretty hard." She checked the boy over, then stopped. "Oh, dear—Altrist."

Elias grinned from ear to ear, his eyes shining like little solar orbs inside his head. "This is so cool."

Altrist and Olivope laughed. But they were the only ones.

"Uh, kid. That's kind of creepy." Dart looked back and forth from Elias to Altrist. "What's going on?"

"Elias touched Ren when her gift was active." Altrist spoke between laughs. A few others laughed too, but not everyone. Concern creased some faces. "What do you see, Elias?"

"You're all glowing."

The sweetness of the tasty cake soured in Dart's mouth as she pieced together the scene. The kid had pawned off Ren's gift. Ren was the person Altrist had been talking about. That's how they knew each other. And somehow, Dart was in the woods at the exact time Ren needed someone to help her and bring her here.

No coincidences. Evidently, the leader made sure everyone else in the world was safe and got their gift. Just not Dart.

"That's just great." No one heard her. A group of five broke away from the levity, saying words like *dangerous*, *spy*, and *deception* as they passed Dart. She took advantage of everyone's distraction and made a clean exit.

When she got to her room, the door was locked, and Ren wasn't answering. Dart knocked harder. Ren, the gifted wonder, could find another room to sleep in. Let Altrist give her his room since she's so special. Still no answer, so Dart pressed her thumb to the keypad, and the door slid open to a dark room with a huddled form on the bed, swathed with a blanket.

Dart's anger dissolved. "Are you okay?"

A quiet sniffle sounded in the blanket cave. "I'm fine. Just not feeling so great." She wiped her nose on her sleeve.

Dart considered ignoring the woes of the poor villager, but she just couldn't do it. Maybe some of Altrist's love stuff had rubbed off over the last six cycles. "It's okay you have a gift. Pretty much everyone does. It's actually a bigger deal if you don't have one."

Ren didn't respond, and Dart tapped the globe on her dresser. The warm light revealed Ren's long fingers pressed against her closed eyes.

"You're safe here." Dart pushed through the quiet. "No one's going to hurt you."

Ren lowered her hands and opened her eyes. Tiny flecks of light danced in her blue irises. "How did you know? Was I that obvious?"

"Not at all. I totally thought you were going to toss your tasty cakes or something, but Elias, the kid who 'borrows' gifts, evidently got a good dose of whatever it is you've got going on. His eyes were glowing up the room after you left."

Ren's mouth dropped open. "Does everyone know?"

"Yep. It's really hard to keep a secret around here." Dart jumped on the bed. "You want to go for a walk? Get some fresh air?"

Ren brightened, and in less than a flash, the two had wound their way topside to the bank, looking down at the falls.

"It's beautiful."

Dart threw a rock into the falling water. "It's Snowshoe. You can't see the shoe shape right now because it hasn't rained, but when the water's really falling, it looks like a big white boot when it hits the rocks below."

Ren's eyes flickered. "Oh, I see." She used her gift.

Dart rolled her eyes and headed for the trail away from the falls. Ren followed. The two walked in silence except for Ren oohing and ahhing over every flower, bug, bird, and leaf. It might have been cute, but Dart couldn't shake her annoyed feeling. Life was just one big irony piled on top of another. Acceptance of that fact did nothing to erase the pain of the past or the uncertainty of her future.

There was only one person she could aim her angst at. The mysterious leader. The more she mulled it over, the more she realized he was to blame. If he could work it so Dart would find Ren in the middle of nowhere, then he could have fixed it so none of the awful stuff in her life had happened. Ma wouldn't have died. Sully wouldn't have taken her, and the world wouldn't be so grim.

Dart clenched her jaw. Just let the leader come back and whisper in her ear again. She'd ball up her faded-sunburst fist and hit him with it.

Ren left the trail for a patch of wildflowers, and Dart followed. In the shade of the trees, a light flashed. Altrist's little voice called from the shadows. "You two are near the vim." As he stepped into view, his glowy whiteness competed with the afternoon sun. "Dart, if it's okay, I'd like to speak with Ren."

Dart glanced at Ren, who seemed to have fully recovered from her gift trauma. Ren nodded, and Dart peeled off. "Sure, I'll just wander over here for a bit." Altrist said something about not taking long, but Dart didn't wait. Let him have his little powwow with his new pet project.

The trail wound uphill, then petered out, and the trees gave way to rocks leading to the bluffs. Dart slowed. The dazzling shimmer of Buddy's vim force field separated her from the beautiful view of the bluffs. When she tapped it, the shield flickered with rings of energy. Warm tingles ran up her arm.

"Weird." Everyone's talk about the vim hadn't done it justice. She pushed on the invisible field, but it didn't budge. "That's an impressive gift," she muttered. The owners of the gift, Buddy and Buck, projected the vim from some place closer to the falls. "This gift would have been very helpful in the packs." A sparrow swooped down and bumped into the shield. The energy field caught the little guy, pulled him back like a gentle slingshot, and sent him on his way.

The bird flapped like mad toward the bluff. As he darted to the brush, a whistle sounded from the rocks, and a man pulled himself up over the edge. Dart ducked down. The vim should hide her from his view, but she didn't want to risk it, so she crouched by a butterfly bush.

Tall and tanned, the brown-haired man took a long draw from his canteen. His white shirt and black shorts resembled the ones from her mama's history books. He dug in his pack and pulled out a blue-green hooded coverup. Dart had seen that color before, in the woods before Sully's attack.

"It's really rude to stare." The man spoke matter-of-factly.

Dart tapped the vim. Rings pulsated from her touch. The force field remained, but it wasn't working very well.

Grinning, the stranger covered half the space between them faster than ungiftedly possible. Dart slid farther behind the bush.

His eyes sought her out. "You got a name?"

The bush was no help, and neither was the vim. She took a step back as she stood. "You can see me?"

"It would appear so." Tall like Gander, the guy looked twice her age. His brown hair had golden flecks that matched his eyes.

"You were in the woods with Sully's pack." Dart checked behind her for Altrist and Ren. They hadn't followed. She and the stranger were alone with only a faulty vim separating them. "What are you? A spy or something?" She stood straight and met his warm gaze.

He didn't have the desperate, lost look of an exile. And his speedy gift recommended him as someone who knew the leader, unless he was like Ren. Village bait with a gift.

"None of the above, Dart." His firm voice quieted the woods. He knew her name. But it wasn't just that he said her name. It was how he said it—like a warm blanket wrapping around her chilled body or a soft pillow holding her head after a long, hard day.

Her eyes met his again, and this time she felt like she knew him, or more like he knew her—and more than just her name.

Soft lines framed his mouth as he spoke. "Is there something you want to say to me?"

She shook her head. "I don't know you." The air grew warm. "Maybe you shouldn't hang around with Sully, though."

He nodded. "Yeah, I could say that to you, too."

"I'm not with Sully."

"And neither am I." The vim shimmered as he spoke. His breath created rainbows across the glossy surface.

Something about the guy endeared him to her, but Dart kept her distance. Any friend of Sully's was not a friend of hers. "Then why were you skulking around the woods during his little ambush?"

"I was there for you." The stranger stepped through the vim. Ripples of color pulled at him from the broken shield, but the vim didn't stop him. As he cleared its hold, he grabbed Dart's wrists. She pulled, but he held her in place with a strong careful grip—the way a mother does to calm her child.

Dart considered kicking him, but the kindness in his eyes kept her foot in place. "What? How did you? You don't know me."

He relaxed his hold. "I know all about you, Dart. And you do know me." Warm sunshine broke from the clouds and glistened in the sheen of the vim behind him.

The hairs on Dart's arm stood at attention, as she searched the stranger's face. "I've never met you before in my life." The words hung in the air the way a warning call does right before the first arrow lands.

He released her wrists but stayed close, the scent of fresh air and pine hovering between them. A smile lit his lips, and the sun shone brighter. Dart considered running, but the stranger's kind seriousness captivated her.

Soft and stern, he whispered, "I see you, Dart." Love glistened in his eyes. Dart knew the look. She had seen it in her ma's eyes and even in Altrist's. The stranger continued, "I was there—with you—huddled in the wet leaves crying, shaking by the rocks, praying for a way out, hiding under the taxar, looking through the ocular."

As he spoke, every image from her awful past crossed her memory. Her heart pounded to her throat. "Stop." She couldn't breathe. Hot air filled her lungs.

He whispered, "I saw you then, and I see you now, and I won't leave you."

The memories played in her head. She couldn't stop them. Sully beating her senseless. Being stripped and forced to serve. The sentry holding her mom's head back.

Tears streamed down Dart's face, and her body shook. The stranger reached to embrace her, but she pushed him away. "No. You don't know me." Turning, she ran. She ran from the lie she'd just spat at him and clung to what she knew. No one had been there. She was alone. No one cared. No one.

CHAPTER 31

THE CABIN

For the first time in Ren's life, her aberration hadn't backed her into a corner. Instead, it took center stage, beckoning her to come and join the show. And she did. She embraced the daylight and conversed with Altrist about her gift.

A butterfly landed on Altrist's white tog, and its black-and-orange wings glowed for a flash before it lifted off. Altrist didn't notice. The strange boy had not stopped talking since Dart left. He replayed the story about Elias, then dove into the wonder of gifts and how to develop them. Ren listened and nodded. Her deepest, darkest secret was now conversational fodder. The unfamiliar territory made her insides jitter.

"Is that why you ran away?" Altrist's soft blue eyes met hers. His face was full, like he hadn't lost all his baby fat. "Was it because of your gift?"

Ren hesitated. Fear and excitement colored the butterflies flitting around on the inside of her. When she'd seen Altrist in the Protectorate, he had offered to help her with the gift, teach her about it. Back then, the idea seemed crazy, but now she wasn't so sure. These people knew all about aberrations. Maybe if Bala had known all of this, things could have been different.

Bala had known more, though. She'd had been outside the boundary. She knew about people living out here. The thought struck a negative beat inside of Ren. Bala had kept so many secrets. She should have explained some of this.

Altrist took Ren's hand, and his glowing warmth rushed up her arm. "Your life hasn't been easy. Not many people ever make it out of the raising home. Is that why you left?"

Ren pulled her hand away. A few lies popped into her head. The whole wiladashing thing, getting lost, or just saying she didn't like the villages, but none of it was even close to true.

As she dismissed each lie, she realized she didn't want to lie. She just wanted to be herself, her weird, aberrant, selfish self. Too many people had lied to her already, and it didn't feel good. Owen. Bala. Her entire life so far had been a lie—always careful to do poorly on tests, faking illnesses when the visions came, and acting like she was okay with it.

A breeze rustled the flowers around her ankles, and she drew in a full breath of free air. "I had to run away." Altrist stayed quiet, so she continued. "They were going to find out about my aberration. I told the wrong person." The words came out faster. "I just couldn't stay there and let them take me away. And Bala had said if there was a problem I should run to the cabin, so I ran."

It kind of felt like she'd thrown up words all over him. Altrist didn't seem to mind. He took a breath and then responded. "What cabin? Who's Bala?"

Ren glanced at another butterfly vying for attention. "Bala is—was my nanny. She's been with me as long as I can remember. She gave me a map to a cabin beyond the boundary. She said if I needed to get away, I could go there."

"Hmmm, interesting." Altrist's white hair stood at attention on top of his little head. Dart had said he was older and not to let his looks make you think otherwise, but it was hard. His cute kid features detracted from the wisdom in his words. "Can I see the map?"

"I lost it." Ren remembered she wanted her bag back.

Altrist teetered to his tippy toes. "I have an idea. Come with me." He grabbed her hand and headed for the trail. Even though he was a foot shorter, he moved fast, and Ren had a hard time keeping up.

"Dart. Hey, Dart, come on." Altrist surveyed the empty woods. "We're going back to Snowshoe."

Dart crested the hill, her face white and her eyes looking like she'd just seen the guardian master. Altrist left Ren and went to her. "You okay?"

"I don't want to talk about it." She sidled up to Ren, and Altrist took off again.

Ren stayed close to Dart. "You sure you're okay. You look kind of pale."

Sweat dampened Dart's hairline. "I don't want to talk about it."

The three of them went down into the lower tunnels. As they entered a large room, orbitts warmed to a golden glow. It was a map room—a magical map room. Topographical representations of mountains, valleys, forests, and villages covered three of the four walls of the room.

Ren stood in the center and scanned the maps, starting with the left wall and ending with the right. Cottony clouds hovered over the scenes, and the pink hints of sunset played across the raised mountains. A spray of water showered one area in the far corner.

"What is this?" It almost looked like a vision.

Dart blew a puffy cloud and pointed to a village. "This is the Protectorate." Then, she traced a line to a grove of trees near a waterfall. "And this is where we are."

Altrist lifted his arms in the air, and as he brought them down, the walls changed. Roads moved. Some buildings disappeared and others popped up.

"Whoa." Dart twirled around. "What are you doing?"

"I'm taking us back a few years." The scenes stopped changing, and Altrist reviewed the walls before he spoke. "Ren, do you think you could find the cabin from the map Bala gave you?"

Ren ran her finger over the thatched roof of a shanty in the Protectorate and then followed the river. "There." She pointed. "That's it."

The glow dampened from Altrist's face. "How did your nanny know about this cabin?"

"Bala said the cabin was my father's." Saying father didn't feel as weird anymore. "She told me if I got in trouble and needed a place to run and hide to go to the cabin—that my father's people would protect me."

"Your father's?" Altrist paced and mumbled to himself. Dart laughed at the little guy, and it felt like the roots of friendship were finding their soil.

Altrist stopped between them like he'd just gotten smacked in the face. "How old are you? Fifteen? You just got your assignment, right?"

Ren cleared her throat. "I'm seventeen." Would the raising home humiliations never end?

Altrist's eyes got huge. "Oh. Oh my. I never knew." The pacing took off again. "Seventeen. That would mean…" And then the mumbling started.

Dart threw up her arms. "I don't know what's up with him." She seemed to have gotten over her funk from the woods.

Ren returned to the map. The Silver Rim glowed. And in a few places, she could see beyond the rim. Just trees and grass, but not the abysmal destruction they taught about in the raising home.

"What's over here?" She pointed to one of the larger patches showing a field and trees beyond the Silver Rim. "I thought it was all blackened magma and radioactive fallout."

Altrist slowed his step. "What? Oh no, dear one. No magma. No radiation. Just a world much like what's on the inside. Now, have you been to the cabin?"

His fixation with the cabin was a little worrisome. "No. I couldn't find it. And from the looks of it, even if I'd had the map, all the roads have changed. Who lived there?" Her insides tensed. Was she really asking about her father?

Altrist stood in front of the cabin on the wall. "Use your gift, Ren. As I tell the story, use your gift."

She didn't understand, but she closed her eyes and pulled on the ability. The sluggish tingles ran up her arms and legs and picked up speed as Altrist spoke.

"A long time ago—eighteen or so years—to be precise, two young women were found close to where that cabin stands. One of them, Balandria, was taken in by the Bluffs clan. Fourteen wonderful, kind, loving people. The other, Eve, matched with one of our lookouts. His name was Wood. He sent word of the matchment just a few months after they met. It was fast, but who can argue with love?"

As he spoke, random scenes played out in the vision. A man and a woman holding hands. A group embracing a young girl. Then sentries tracking through the woods.

"Balandria and Eve were spies. They led sentries to Wood and the others." Altrist's voice quieted. "No one survived."

Ren closed her eyes and pushed the ugly images from her mind. Faint echoes of screams lingered. She shook her head. "It wasn't Bala." She hadn't seen the women's faces, but she knew it wasn't Bala. It couldn't have been. "It's not her. She never would have hurt innocent people."

Altrist shook his head. He faced Ren, and for the first time she saw him for what he was, her elder. If he were in the villages, he would be a guardian master or more. Except, he was the opposite of a guardian. His strength took arms with kindness. His commands were founded in trust. He patted her arm. "People are not always as they seem."

Dart broke the thick emotion. "That's for sure."

Ren pushed back. "No, Bala wouldn't have done those things." But even as she spoke, she could see Bala teaching the finer points of combat and walking her through how to handle an interrogation.

Altrist pulled her into a hug. "It's no mistake you are here." When he released her, tears perched in his blue eyes. "I know it's hard."

She refused to agree with him. For now, though, she would return to faking it and hoped he couldn't see her thoughts. And once she got some time to herself, she would ramp up her ability and search for Bala and the truth.

CHAPTER 32

THE CALL TO ACTION

A large man named Frish slammed his fist on the table. "We can't trust her. It's a trap." Dart jumped at the outburst. The group's reaction to the news of Ren's cabin had been way worse than Altrist's.

Their fear took lead of their mouths, ugly and controlling.

Most masked it quickly with anger, but it was clear. Their first reaction had been to throw up the fences and pull out the artillery. No telling what they would do if Dart told them about the stranger who could see through the vim. She said nothing, though. She didn't want to think about him.

Thankful not to be listening while wedged in the air duct this time, Dart stood in the corner of the granden room. She'd deposited a shaken Ren in her room and come straight here at Altrist's personal request. Ten people sat around the long oval table with Altrist and Olivope at the far end.

Altrist held up his hand, and the discord quieted. "You're right. It could very well be a trap." Sharp whispers dwindled to silence. "If so, we're already compromised."

Dart pressed against the stone wall. She'd brought Ren here. This was her fault.

"I don't think that's the case, though. Ren's nothing like Tatief's spies." Altrist's voice caught. Dart wanted to ask more about the women, but she stayed quiet.

Olivope nodded in agreement and placed her ivory hand on his shoulder.

Frish grunted. "She knows about Snowshoe. What's stopping her from bringing sentries back here."

"And what if they have a tracker on her?" A guy next to Gander chimed in.

"Trackers don't get through Buddy's vim." Anna spoke up.

Altrist continued, "And Dart brought the girl in through the old tunnels from the northern hatch. We've already shut those down. We'll be safe for now." Dart didn't bring up Ren's familiarity with their Snowshoe entrance.

"Listen to yourselves." Olivope stood. The light hugging her skin reflected off the shiny table. "Fear controls you, and that's not who we are. We've become comfortable and complacent, and even before Ren showed up, we knew things needed to change.

"Don't deceive yourselves into thinking Tatief's lies haven't already made their way into our world. We've grown lazy. This place and Pocket—they suit us fine. Our people go about life and have forgotten there's a war going on.

"You know the truth, and yet one strange girl with a gift, who knows about a cabin she shouldn't, has you plotting to do what? Drop her in the woods or enslave her—or worse? That is not who we are."

"And what about what they did to us?" The tracker guy stood, his voice husky with emotion. "Balandria and that evil witch friend of hers slaughtered fifteen of our own. They led the sentries right to them." Gander put a hand on the guy's shoulder and guided him back to his seat. The room stayed silent, and Dart held her breath. She'd been in meetings like this with Sully and the pack, but those usually ended with someone needing stitches or worse.

Altrist met the man's pain with care. "Ren isn't Balandria, and there's a lot we don't know. Let's stick to the facts. It was no coincidence my path crossed with Ren's. No accident Dart found Ren and brought her here. Our enemy couldn't have orchestrated those events. We've learned from the past. We won't make the same mistakes again."

A rosy flush filled Olivope's creamy cheeks. "There are hundreds and hundreds of people in the villages who've never heard of the Leader or if they have, it's been told to them like a fairytale. They see Tatief as their savior. What have we done to help them?"

"Our recovery missions have been successful." Liza spoke this time, her effervescence never dimming. "We save a few every month from the hunts, and several of our village attempts have worked."

"It's not enough. We've scaled way back since we lost Wood and the others." Olivope stood her ground. "We've become satisfied with the status quo. Your gifts provide you with a buffer from the evil out there, but you can't escape it. Whether it's a spy of Tatief's, taking advantage of kindness or subtle contentment lulling us into quiet lives, both roads lead away from the Leader, not toward him."

Tension filled the room. Dart had never seen these people so at odds. For all their love and caring, the disagreements were few. Until now.

"What about us? What about our safety? We can't just open ourselves up to them." A woman spoke this time.

"Safety?" Altrist leaned toward her. His question felt full—not a challenge, leading, like a mother taking her child by the hand. "This isn't about safety. We're here for a purpose. A journey that encompasses everyone—our people, the villagers, and the exiled. We did not build this community in the name of safety. We don't live for some present paradise. Our hope is yet to come."

He paused, and his voice took on a more tender tone. "All of you have experienced hurt." His gaze met every pair of eyes, even Dart's. "And you've also experienced healing. The question is not one of safety, but of how you are going to live out these things we have said we believe?"

"What are you saying?" The woman's voice shook.

"I'm saying we've had our time of peace. Perhaps now is the time to push back and make our hope known. It's time to take risks. I will take responsibility for Ren."

Protests started with Gander and rumbled through the room. Olivope raised her voice over them.

"And I will take a bandy to the Protectorate to rescue Anna's son." Olivope spoke like a warrior. "Our simple attempts to save a few are not enough. We must do more."

The woman who had talked about safety stood. Dart didn't remember her name, just that she was from the exiled, and she had been rescued from one of the bluff packs. A pan pipe dangled from a leather strap around her neck. "What if Tatief captures one of you? You risk yourselves, but without you, we will all be lost."

The words charged the room. Dart fisted her hands.

Altrist shook his head. "No matter what, your trust in the Leader must never waver. We are not the answer. He is. He is coming back." Altrist's deep gaze drifted to Dart. In all her talk about not belonging and them not really wanting her, she'd suppressed something very important. She'd not fully voiced how desperately she wanted to be here, in this world, with them. More than anything, her heart and mind yearned for it. She reached for it as if it were just out of reach, and something blocked the way.

Altrist's sure voice quieted the rising panic in the room. "He calls each of you to himself, not to me or to Olivope. And he is going to put an end to Tatief." The glow clinging to his skin grew brighter. "Will you stay and follow him, or will you hide and hope you're never found?"

He spoke to everyone, but Dart wondered if he meant the words just for her. She wanted to stay. This place, these people, were oxygen to her. She'd never considered there being no Altrist or Thim or Anna. No rainbow fountain or tunneled sanctuary. She could take leaving if all of this still remained. Just knowing these people lived in peace somewhere gave her strength, but if this world fell apart, then what hope was there for any of them?

Frish challenged Altrist. "If you leave us, then you're practically giving us over to the guardians."

Anna countered, "That's not true. We are not alone. The Leader has gifted us. He will help us."

Frish ignored her. "What if Tatief captures one of you?" Frish aimed his anger at Altrist and Olivope. "What will happen then?" The messengers stayed silent, and the man commanded the room. "I'll tell you what will happen. Tatief will grow even stronger. He will dominate all of what's inside the rim. There will be no place we can hide. No tunnel or vim strong enough. He will hunt us down. Every last one of us."

Dart waited for Altrist to refute him, but the messenger stayed silent. He and Olivope had said their part. They stepped away and let the accusations fly. The room exploded and sides were drawn. Fear, anger, helplessness, and even revenge spewed from their mouths. Not everyone joined in. Anna, Gander, Thim, and Liza sided with the messenger's silence.

Tears perched in Dart's eyes. They had a point. Without Altrist and Olivope, what hope did they have? The leader wasn't going to help them.

"Don't cry, Dart." Altrist whispered in her head, and she closed her eyes. For once, she welcomed the intrusion into her spiraling thoughts. His calm voice didn't reflect the hot emotions flying around the room. "Some things must break, so they can become stronger."

Dart shook her head. "Or so they can be shown for what they are." She whispered back. He sighed in sad agreement. Things were changing, and the leader seemed farther away than ever.

The sunburst on Dart's palm was all but gone now. Another reminder that nothing good lasts. Everything breaks eventually.

CHAPTER 33

THE FIELD OF FLOWERS

Ren pressed her hand to the hidden keypad, and Dart's door slid open for the tenth time. She checked the hallway again. Still no Dart.

"Ugh. Where is she?" Stepping back into the bedroom, she waited until the door locked shut before plopping onto the bed. Dart hadn't come back after Altrist had his big meeting last night, and so far, only Altrist had visited her. He brought her breakfast and offered to give her a little training with her gift.

The training was mostly her explaining what she knew about the gift, and Altrist nodding his head and asking a question here and there. It probably would have been refreshing, but Ren had other things on her mind.

After being sent to her room yesterday, she'd used the aberration to look for Bala. The search came up empty. No matter how many times she tried, she couldn't go back into the raising home or the transport or even the Protectorate. Nothing. Mostly what she saw consisted of some misty light, a city built into a mountain, and another female messenger, taller and even more beautiful than Olivope. Nothing she'd ever seen before.

After a few hours of trying, her head pounded, and the tingles numbed the rest of her body. That's when she finally landed on something helpful. The cabin.

The vision took her to the cabin, and this time, the scene wasn't from the past, but from the present. Rundown boards and a sagging porch suggested years of neglect.

And then a light came on inside. It flickered through the window—a soft blue light, and the sounds of someone walking.

Ren urged the ability forward, but it wouldn't move, and whoever was on the inside stayed there. It was a start, though, and something in her heart told her this might be some sign of Bala. Now, if Dart would just show up, Ren could get a little closer to an answer.

Pushing off the bed, she marched to the door again, pressed her hand to the key, and poked her head into the hallway. A bright light greeted her, and Altrist's little face appeared with the rest of him not far behind.

"Going somewhere?" He held a brown sack in his hand. "I brought you a sandwich and a tasty cake."

"Thanks." Ren swiped the sack. "Do you know where Dart is? I wanted to ask her something."

"No. I haven't seen her since last night. I think the meeting shook her up a bit." He escorted Ren back into the bedroom.

Ren didn't say anything. She knew the meeting had been about her, and that some people didn't want her here, hence the being "locked" in a room for most of the morning.

Altrist got straight to the point. "I was wondering if you might like to get out for a bit." The messenger's glow had a happy feeling. Not that lights or colors have feelings, but the soft light that surrounded him gave Ren a giddy joy whenever he was near.

"Yes." She set the bag on the bed. "I'm ready when you are."

He held out his hand. "I have an idea about your ability, and I wanted to give it a go." The glow around him grew brighter. "Take my hand, please." Ren put her hand in his, and he pulled her closer. "This might feel weird."

The light engulfed them, and in the next flash, she let out a breath and heard a loud roar. Torrents of water poured down in front of her. An old sofa on a rug with a table by its side sat toward the back of the cave. "Cool."

"We're behind the falls. You okay? Sometimes the journey makes one sick." Altrist released her hand and gave her some space.

"I'm fine. It feels good to be out of that room." She held her face up to the mist coming off the falls. "I was feeling like a prisoner."

"Yeah, sorry about that. Until things settle down, it's best you keep a low profile."

The weight of everyone's assumptions about Bala strained Ren's hope. Being here and living free from Tatief felt like the perfect answer to all her societal woes, but she couldn't reconcile their judgment of Bala with what she knew of her friend. "My Bala isn't the person who did all that awful stuff."

A sad smile underlined Altrist's kind face. "I hope not. I hope she's everything you believe her to be." He held the moment for a beat, then moved on. "You know, we've talked about Bala and your father, but you've not asked anything about your mother."

If she could have pulled a door shut between them, she would have. Instead, she just shook her head and deflected. "What's to say? Mother's not a word anyone uses for anything." But she didn't mean it. Maybe a month ago, when Bala first used that word—when the world hadn't opened up to her and she hadn't seen mothers with their children and families together. Now, it hurt, like a loss, but a loss of what she didn't know. How can you feel a loss for something you never even knew existed?

The real truth was, she didn't want to know the truth. It might hurt worse than simply letting the whole thing fade away.

Altrist's glow dimmed. "I'm sorry. I didn't mean to bring up something painful."

Ren shrugged and faced the furious water again. Finding Bala might help. If anyone could fill in some gaps, Bala could. And that led Ren back to wondering about Dart's whereabouts.

Altrist walked about ten steps back. "Okay. You ready for some gift practice. I wanted to try something."

Sucking in the cool air, Ren faced the bright-eyed little guy.

He had a determined look on his face. "I want you to pull me into a vision."

"What?" The roar made it harder to hear. She thought he'd said to pull him into a vision. "I don't think you understand how this works."

"No, I don't think you understand how this works." He spoke the words into her head. "Just try it. Use the ability to see some place else. Let's say the field with the flowers where we were yesterday. Then, I want you to draw me into the same picture."

She shook her head. "Okay." Two deep breaths, and the familiar spray of energy coursed through her body. When she opened her eyes, the field lay before her, washed in sunlight and smelling like wildflowers.

"Now, bring me into the picture," Altrist whispered to her thoughts.

Ren reached for Altrist. The power coursing through her wrapped around him, and then he stood in front of her in the field. "I see you here," she whispered.

"And I see you." He smiled and looked around. "And the field, with the sun, and the scent of flowers, and a pesky butterfly. Nice touch."

"How am I doing this?" It all looked so real.

"Hey you guys? What are you doing?" Dart's voice cut through the scene, and it fell away like raindrops.

"Whoa, I couldn't hold on to it." Ren stumbled forward, and Altrist rushed to her.

"You did it. I thought you could do it, but I wasn't sure."

"What did I do? What was that?" The heat from the vision flushed her cheeks. "It felt so real."

"It was totally real." Altrist beamed. "I probably could have picked a flower."

"What are you guys talking about?" Dart stepped between them. "You were just standing there looking at each other. It was like the great Snowshoe Stare-Off or something."

Altrist smacked his hands together. "I've got to tell Olivope before she leaves." He took a step back and began to glow. "Dart, will you help Ren get back to your room without any trouble?" His voice faded away as he disappeared from view.

"What did I miss?" Dart dropped on the couch and pulled her legs to her chin.

"I don't know." Ren eased to a cushion, the tingles still somersaulting through her brain. "I had a vision, and I pulled Altrist into it. It was weird."

"The curse of the gifted." Her voice had more snark in it than usual.

Ren caught that Dart didn't have a gift, so she put hers aside and changed the subject. "Where have you been all morning?"

Dart shrugged. "Just walking out in the woods and thinking."

"I missed you. I've been locked in your room."

"I would have taken you with me, but you were supposed to be locked in my room. Speaking of which, we'd better get back down there. I don't want to be the one who started a riot at Snowshoe."

Ren grabbed Dart's arm. "Wait."

Dart gave her a look but stayed seated.

"Are you up for some adventure?" Ren lowered her voice. "I want to go to the cabin. Can you take me there?"

Dart shook her head. "No way. I'd get in huge trouble. Plus, it's dangerous. And nearly twenty kilometers away. Your little village feet would never make it."

"C'mon, Dart. We'd be back before too late. I'll keep up. I promise." Ren put on her most sincere face. "And how dangerous can it be? You know the woods like the back of your hand, and we'll travel during the daylight. Please?"

Dart rubbed her face, and Ren could feel the wild girl's resolve weakening. "Please, Dart. No one will ever find out. They'll think I'm in your room, and they never know where you are. Please?"

"Why? Why do you want to go there? It's not a cheerful place." She had a point. Still, the vision showed someone at the cabin. Ren held back that bit of info, though, and opted for an appeal to emotion. She sniffled and worked on a tear or two.

"I just can't stay cooped up all day, and I came from that cabin. I just want to see it." A tear escaped her eye.

"Oh, stop it. I know you're faking." Dart shook her head. "I'll take you. What else do I have to do today? I don't enjoy being around here with everyone angry all the time, anyway." She jumped up. "But we're going to need some snacks first. Why don't you ramp up your vision thing and make sure the coast is clear for a kitchen run?"

"Sure thing." Ren let the tingles flow. The day was looking up.

CHAPTER 34

THE TRAP

Owen stared out the window of his cabin. The trees swayed in the warm breeze untouched by all he had discovered at the Plateau. He'd been back in the village for two days with no sign of Olivope. Not that he had tried too hard to find her. Every walk near the woods brought up thoughts of Ren and his guilt, so his walks had been short and halfhearted.

He let out a heavy sigh and grabbed his jacket and satchel. The schedule and village might look like old times, but nothing else was. He kept up the pretense of serving as a guide, but it was all just motions. Being at the Plateau had changed him and made it hard to focus on anything besides the task at hand. Find the messenger. Bring her to Tatief.

Messengers were powerful and not to be trusted. Except for Tatief, of course. He was to be trusted above all others. He saved humanity. Even with the haze perverting his thoughts, Owen didn't believe all the rhetoric. Olivope didn't seem dangerous. If anything, she seemed good, full, kind. Still, she posed a threat to the master and needed to be apprehended.

Eviah said Tatief would reason with Olivope, show her the villages he had built, and try to help her understand the good he had achieved. Owen chose to believe that's what would happen. He couldn't face the alternative.

Coming back reminded him of what he'd done and what Ren probably thought of him. The last time he saw her, the look in her eyes said everything. Disbelief, anger, fear. He should have forced her to listen to him. Maybe then she'd still be here, and they'd be working on the project in the best place to keep her secret safe.

He shook the pointless thought from his clouded head and tried to focus on his current situation. No one had questioned his absence. Evidently Whitler knew it had been guardian sanctioned and left it alone. Ren's disappearance had all the workers worried, towing the line and getting their assignments done early. At least, the pressing need to remove someone from his team was now moot.

Take it. You deserve it. It's what you make of it.

Owen pressed a finger to the dull ache in his temple. He almost had everything he'd ever wanted, but somehow, it didn't feel as good as it ought. Ren had changed his perspective. That and Maxey's demise and the Plateau and being so close to it all. Everything looked different from this view.

As Owen approached the Sharp Complex, Whitler exited with an older woman Owen didn't recognize. Both walked fast, deep in conversation. Owen avoided eye contact and kept his heavy heart aimed at making it through another day of work.

He had done everything Eviah had said to do. She and the guardian mission director had laid out the plan. Tatief had approved it, and now Owen dangled out in the open as much as he could, hoping the strange, sweet Olivope would venture back and take the bait.

He eased into his chair, did his work, and watched as the day rolled by like every other one before it, but different. Before the evening chime could sound, Owen aimed for the door. Warm air hit him as he exited the building.

It was hard to stay still. Hard to string together more than a few thoughts. Seven days ago, he would have never guessed he'd be a full-fledged guardian, crushing on a plebe with an aberration, and on a mission from the master. He'd gone from walks with Ren to lurking around the trees hoping Olivope would show up.

As he wound his way to the field where Ren had shared her squirrel theory, the shadowed trees swayed in the breeze and contrasted with the orange late-day sky. Ren would have liked the colors. The thought squeezed his heart. Then, from the corner of his eye, he saw it—a flash of white. Owen held his breath. *Please.*

The fluttering glow moved toward him. By the edge of the field, the glow faded to a dusky light, and Olivope stepped into view. The sight of her took his breath away. Stunning. She was the opposite of Tatief. White hair to his jet black. Pale skin to his tanned perfection. And radiant joy sparkling in her eyes to the penetrating, hungry look that dominated the master's.

"You're here." Her smile grew. "I wasn't sure I'd find you as easily during the daylight."

Owen checked the trees for cameras. Tylon had been expanding his digital reach, but as far as Owen could tell, no cameras had been added this far back.

"You're inside the boundary." To be the first thing he said to her, that probably wasn't the best choice.

She narrowed her eyes and tilted her head. Several seconds ticked by until she spoke. She took slow steps toward him. "Yes." The joy in her demeanor faded. "I see. He knows, doesn't he?"

Owen swallowed the little bit of spit collecting in his dry mouth and tried to manage his expression. The word *honesty* popped into his head. He should tell her the entire story, but before he could gather the pieces together, his thoughts clouded again, and he faltered. "What? I don't understand what you mean."

"The choices you make affect far more than you know."

The scene of Ren sharing her secret and the first time he heard those words jumped to his heart. It stopped him. Then, in the heavy fog that was now his mind, he heard the chant of the Plateau. *Take it. You deserve it. It's what you make of it.* And his resolve returned.

Olivope reached out her hand. "Will you come with me?"

Owen tapped his collar where the listening bean was. "Um, where?" He stalled and listened for sentry footsteps.

"Outside the boundary." She smiled, and then, in the shadow of a heartbeat, she closed the distance between them, cradled his face in her soft hands, and looked him straight in the eyes. It made him think of the moon for some reason.

"I want to help you. Do you understand?"

He nodded, even though he didn't know what she was talking about.

"This is going to feel weird," she whispered. "Hold on."

A flash of white enveloped them, and Owen felt pressed in. The air rushed from his lungs as if knocked away, and a spray of colors showered down around him, blocking out the trees and the ground.

The next thing he knew, he was standing on a dirt road in the middle of nowhere. Olivope, looking a little windblown, stood in front of him. She released his arm and gave it a pat.

"You okay? Sometimes it makes a person queasy."

Owen shook his head. His stomach was fine, but his eyes couldn't comprehend their surroundings. "Where are we? How did you do that?"

"We're beyond the boundary, and you wouldn't understand if I told you. Now, come with me." Her slender form took off down the road. Owen followed.

A narrow path snaked between the bushes, and Olivope moved like a cat on the prowl. Owen didn't see any cameras here either. He tapped the bean.

The path ran down a hill, threaded between giant boulders. On the other side of the rocks, Olivope slowed her gait.

"Come out. We've no time to lose." She shout-whispered the words, and murmurs and footsteps came from the rocks. A large man squeezed through a narrow crevice.

Olivope waved. "Gander, come quickly." Others followed.

Owen was about to ask who they were when he saw Whitler's lanky frame pop out. "Whitler?"

Olivope shushed him. "We'll explain later." Then she addressed Gander. "They know, and they're coming."

A shower of questions and fear poured from the group.

Olivope cast a sad glance toward Owen and brushed off their queries. "It doesn't matter how. It just matters the worst is coming. I'm sorry. I fear I may have led us all into danger."

"We should split up. We'll have a better chance." Gander barked orders to the others.

Olivope touched his arm. "There's only one way."

"We can't leave you. You're more valuable than any of us." The large man was like a child before her.

"No, dear Gander." She looked at the others, as well. "This is my road. Not yours. You must go, and I'll try to delay them as much as I can."

Owen felt like he was watching one of Tylon's vids. It was almost like he wasn't even there. No one noticed him. They were all wrapped up in their impending demise.

"But before you leave, Anna, come—" Olivope grabbed Owen's hands. The older woman Owen had seen with Whitler in the village ran to his side. Olivope pulled Owen in with her sweet gaze. "This is all I can do for you. I pray it will be enough."

As she spoke, a needled warmth crept up his arms from where she held him. The lady, Anna, put her hands on Owen's head.

Owen closed his eyes and stood still. The thickness that had been slowing his thoughts dissipated, and he took a deep breath. Fresh air flooded his body, and the cobwebs cleared from the corners of his mind.

"Owen, we can't clean all of their poisons away." Olivope spoke into his thoughts. "You must want them to go. Do you want them to go?" She spoke the question out loud.

"Yes." The little she'd done felt like waking up. He wanted more. More room in his head to think.

He heard her smile. "Good, but I must warn you. If you do not trust the truth, then the next time it will be harder to clear the fog away." Emotion choked her words. "The deception is deep, and you must fight it."

"Honesty." This time he spoke the word, knocking at his thoughts. "I want the truth." He meant it too.

Her hands warmed his head, and she blew into his face. It sounded like happiness and felt like an airy kiss. *The truth has already found you, dear one. He will not let you go. Trust him.*

When Owen opened his eyes, he saw tears in Olivope's.

"What did you do to me?"

"All that I could. They drugged you. Poison in a variety of forms. We cleared much of it away. The rest is up to you." She dismissed Anna back to Whitler. "You must go. All of you. Now."

The group hesitated, but then split off in two directions. Olivope watched them go, and Owen took his place next to her still unsure of what was going on.

He was just about to ask when a loud whoosh kicked up the dirt behind them, sending a hazy cloud brushing by. Olivope took Owen's hand. A low growl, like a sick laugh, rumbled at their backs, and they turned together.

Tatief flanked by six sentries, the Warrior, and Jasper blocked the path.

The master took a calculated step toward them. "Hello, sister."

CHAPTER 35

THE SECRET GUARDIAN

"Can we stop for five minutes?" Two hours of walking had left Ren with aching feet and the annoying feeling she'd made a mistake.

Dart slowed her pace. "Okay, but if we're going to get there and back before sundown, we can't take long. Something tells me the walk back will go slower than the walk there."

"Ya think?" Ren took her brown flat off and rubbed her foot. She had been unable to keep pace with the wild girl for the last thirty minutes.

"Here." Dart held out a bottle of vitawater. "We haven't got much farther. Maybe another half hour is all. You've done pretty well for village bait."

Ren caught the jab and nodded. She'd own it. "Being raised underground makes one appreciate the wonder of the great outside, trees, and sky."

"That's so weird." A breeze blew Dart's crazy hair around her face. "I can't imagine growing up underground. It just seems unnatural."

"Yeah, the guardians do it for control. It's impossible to escape, and it breaks you." A chill snaked up Ren's spine. Bala had said even though the guardians made it look like it was for the good of all, keeping little ones locked underground really only served Tatief and his agenda.

Dart took a slower pace when they headed back out. "And you never met your parents? How does that work? I didn't meet my dad, but my mama said that was for the best. He died when I was two. An exile territory war or something."

Altrist's poking around about Ren's mother had her on edge about the parent topic, but there was one kind of family she could relate to. "I had someone with me. Bala. She had been with me since I was a baby." Ren's voice trailed off. Her knowing Bala wasn't a positive with Altrist's folks.

Dart shrugged. "Is that why you wanted to see this cabin? Because it's part of your past? Do you think seeing it will help, because I gotta tell you, I think it will hurt more than help."

Trees shielded them from the late afternoon sun, but sweat still trickled down Ren's forehead. Maybe it was time to fess up about the vision. "Not exactly." She searched for the right words to tell Dart she'd left out an important detail in her begging to go to the cabin. "Bala didn't do those things. She was a nanny, not a guardian."

Dart didn't respond, so Ren continued. "I saw something in a vision that makes me think there's someone at the cabin." She said it all in one breath.

"What?" Dart stopped on the rocky trail. "You saw what?"

"I used the ability to look at the cabin, and I think someone's there. I couldn't get a look at them, though. But I saw a light, and I heard steps." It sounded crazy. They'd just spent a few hours walking in the woods because she saw a vision of something that may or may not be there.

"Your ability?" Dart heavy sighed. "You should have told me this." Hurt, not anger, tinged the wild girl's tone.

"I'm sorry." Now, who was being sneaky and not being fair to their friend? "I didn't think you'd bring me if you knew, but I should have told you."

"Yes, you should have told me. This could be dangerous." Dart sounded older than she looked. Her years out here in the scary beyond showed. "When we get there, if someone is in the cabin, let me do the talking."

Ren didn't respond. Responding would have made it seem like Bala wouldn't be there, and she hoped beyond measure her friend would come running to meet her.

The cabin stood at the edge of a small, overgrown field. A shed with two walls caved in sat to the right, and a row of cedar trees puffed up to its left. The front door hung open, held in place by a rusty hinge.

Dart pulled Ren down in the tall grass. "I'll go up first and see. You stay here." She didn't wait for Ren's consent, but took off tracking back into the woods toward the cedars. Before she reached the cabin, a man came out and threw a bucket of dirty water over the bannister of the porch, then went back inside.

Ren sat up. "Pandon?" She crouched in the grass and moved closer.

The guy came out again. This time, he draped a worn rug over a banister and smacked it with a broom. It was Pandon. His face was even more unshaven, but she recognized his walk and the green coverup.

She stood. "Pandon?"

The man stopped. "Ren." He ran down the steps and met her in the grass. "Finally, I've been trying to find you."

"What are you doing here?" For some weird reason, it was good to see someone from home, even if it wasn't Bala.

Before he could respond, Dart joined them, her eyes lethal and her stance wary. "Hey, do you two know each other?"

"Yeah, this is Pandon. He's from the Protectorate." Ren put a friendly hand on Dart's shoulder. "And Pandon, this is Dart. She's helped me stay safe out here. Wow, it's so weird that you're here. How did you find this place?"

Digging into his pocket, Pandon pulled out Bala's map. "I found this, and when you went missing, I guessed you might have gone wiladashing alone."

Ren snatched it. "My map."

"So, you're Dart, eh?" Pandon aimed his charm at Dart's icicles. "Interesting name. Like the things you throw?"

"You can think that, if you want, Pandon." Her use of his name sounded more like a curse word.

He returned to Ren. Nothing seemed to faze him. "That's not all, Ren. I've got news about your friend. The one you wanted me to look for."

"Bala?" Ren gripped the map like it was her ticket to hope.

Pandon took a step closer and lowered his voice. "They've taken her. I think she's supposed to go to the

Plateau, but they're holding her at the Golden Horizon for a day or two." Ren's heart stopped for a second.

Pandon continued, "I can take you to the GH. We might even be able to get her out. I can't promise, but if she's in the lower level, we should be able to sneak in and out without being seen. You could at least talk to her. They've been rounding up all your contacts for questioning, but your Bala friend gave them some trouble."

Ren turned away and pulled up her ability. The late sun sent long shadows across the field, and all she could see through her vision eyes was Bala's face bidding her farewell in the archive at Castle.

"How do you know all that?" Dart stepped between Ren and Pandon. "I mean, that's guardian stuff, right? How do you know it?"

Pandon didn't miss a beat. "I'm a traveler. I get around. I might not be a tier 3, but I get to move about, and I go through the GH all the time. Plus, they already asked me what I knew. It wasn't a big deal. They know about the occasional wiladash. They just didn't like Bala's answers."

"And you get to come all the way out here? I thought they kept a pretty tight rein on everybody." Dart kept on, and Ren took another deep breath. *Come on vision. Is Bala okay?* But nothing came to mind.

She turned back before Pandon could answer. "I've got to go to her."

"What?" Dart grabbed Ren's arm and pulled her away from Pandon. "Are you crazy? That guy has guardian written all over him. This whole thing stinks of trap."

Ren pulled free. "I've got to go. Bala's the closest thing I've ever had to a mother. If you were me, you would go."

"Yeah, but I can handle myself on my own. No offense, but you're not used to this stuff."

"Bala made me ready. She trained me. I can take care of myself."

"Oh, the nanny who isn't a guardian spy? She's the one who trained you?" A breeze kicked up the hot air between them. Dart softened her tone. "I get it. You're worried about her, but running off with him isn't the brightest idea. Let's go back and tell Altrist." She lowered her voice at the mention of the messenger. "He can help."

That all sounded fine, but they didn't have a lot of time. "I'll be careful. I'm not going up against any sentries on my own. At least, not without a club in my hand." She tried to lighten Dart's seriousness. "I'll be okay. If there's a chance to get her out, I've got to do this. She was like a mother to me." The word mother lingered in the air between them, and Dart relented.

Pandon broke in. "If we're going to go, we need to leave soon. It's too dangerous to travel after dark."

Ren grabbed Dart's hands. "Please tell Altrist what's happened. Bala isn't what they think she is, and if she needs me, I've got to do this."

Dart followed at a distance. Everything about the guy reeked of lies and guardian stuff.

Night settled in around them. The cool air licked at Dart's face. This was her favorite time of the day, but not so much right now. Pandon knew the woods well and made it hard to keep up without giving herself away.

She lost sight of them when they veered off the worn path and descended an incline. Holding her breath, she listened, but nothing. Another step and then a furious burst flooded her abdomen. As she turned, Pandon caught her and guided her to the ground.

"Don't worry, honey. It's just on stun. I couldn't have you following me now."

Dart's legs wouldn't move, and she felt like a hundred marbles were crammed in her mouth.

"Here, take this." He dropped a beeping device onto her chest. "Just a little something to ensure the sentries don't pass you by." He grinned and ran a finger down her cheek. "I think they're going to have some fun talking to you."

She shook her head and grunted. Only once before had she ever wanted to hurt someone, and this almost rivaled that moment.

"Well, I've got to go. Ren thinks I'm erasing our tracks so the sentries can't follow." With that, he tapped his scinter to her cheek, and the world brightened to white before all went black.

Light from a stave lit up the sentry's ugly chops. "Hey, sir, I found one of them." He pointed his skeer at Dart's face.

Footsteps sounded to her left. A man barked orders. She knew the voice. The tone. The sureness. Jasper.

Recognition registered in his eyes as he towered over her, glowing staves all around lighting the night into day. "Well, who do we have here?" He hoisted her to her feet with no effort. "I thought you'd have been dead by now." More sentries joined him.

She was alone with a troop of sentries.

CHAPTER 36

THE GOLDEN HORIZON

Pandon held up his lit stave and smiled. "Not too much farther now."

Ren didn't reply. The dusky walk with Pandon had brought up all kinds of thoughts. And not just about how hungry she was or how much her feet hurt.

In the last few days, the world had swung from the home of backstabbing, conniving, and lying guardian wannabes to the friendship, kindness, and acceptance of some underground radicals. And in some ways, it felt like coming alive. Dart, Altrist, Olivope had something Ren had never seen before—a kind of freeing acceptance and respect, in spite of locking her in the room.

Parts of their underground world reminded Ren of Bala. How these new friends said what they meant. Their devotion to each other, and the way the mothers looked at their little ones. Ren's throat got tight. If Bala had been with them so long ago, why wouldn't she have stayed? If Ren's father had been one of their group, then why not bring her here to live with them? Life could have been so different.

Ren clenched her teeth and focused on Pandon's sure steps. Bala couldn't be their Balandria. She couldn't.

Pandon slowed his pace and walked beside her. The stave cast creepy shadows on his face. "You doing okay?"

She nodded, but her feet cramped with every step, and she regretted not bringing the sack of food Altrist had brought her.

FOR THE GOOD OF ALL

"Lidya told me what happened. She thought that might be why you ran away. If it helps, it bothered her for a bit when the other girls called you names."

It took Ren a second to remember Lidya's infraction. "A bit?"

He grinned. "Well, come on. She wasn't bred for empathy."

"Shouldn't empathy be a part of everyone's breeding?" Ren pulled her hair back into a ponytail. "It's not rocket science to treat a fellow human being with a little respect."

The light from the stave dimmed, and Pandon shook the device. "Who are you kidding, the only ones worthy of respect are the guardians." The stave brightened.

"What?" After meeting Altrist and Olivope, Ren's estimation of the guardians was even lower.

"The guardians, and master Tatief, of course. No one else really matters. Just the means to an end—born and bred to serve, for the good of all." He touted the rhetoric like a guardian master of the highest tier. Ren couldn't believe it.

"What?" Pandon aimed the stave toward her face. "You know it's true. Don't let your little jaunt out here pollute your thinking. You've got one chance, Ren. Don't blow it. Take it. You deserve it."

It was good Dart didn't come. She would not have gotten along with Pandon. Ren let it drop. He could believe whatever he wanted. The world had gotten bigger for her. She wouldn't let it return to pleasing guardians worshiping Tatief.

A few minutes later, Pandon took her hand and pulled her off the road into the bushes. A golden light shone from the crest of the hill in front of them.

"What is it?" she whispered.

He sucked in a happy breath. "It's the Golden Horizon."

"The transport station?"

He nodded, but his face lit with excitement and said there was more to it than a bunch of transits and moving people around. They took light steps forward until the station came into view.

Tall, white columns with sheets of light running between them lined a sunken garden with a golden walkway down the center. Sentries marched back and forth around the perimeter of the garden in front of the columns.

"Is that actually gold?"

Pandon shushed her.

The columns framed two massive rectangles of empty field on either side of the sunken garden. The transport station lay at the other end. It was huge too—tons bigger than the one in the Protectorate. A balcony came out over the entryway, and lines of gold graced the rest of the structure all the way to the shiny black roof.

Pandon directed her to a spot behind a bush. "Wait here." Then he cut back and out of sight.

She scooted into the bush and peered over the hill. The pale moonlight had nothing on the glowing pylons and sheets of light.

"Amazing."

A familiar tingling rippled up through her arms and shoulders to the back of her head. Tired and weak, she didn't fight it. Maybe the vision would come and be gone before Pandon returned. Maybe it would finally show her Bala.

A black mist snaked its way down the stairway, leading from the hilltop to the garden. The white columns glowed red now with fire shooting out the top. Between the columns, a sheer, red haze hung like a fence panel, and behind it, in the massive walled-off rectangle, something moved.

Ren scooted closer. Brown creatures with ribbed black armor scampered over one another, watching the sentries who patrolled the garden. The bug-eyed things reflected the red of the columns, making their eyes look even more eerie. Whatever the haze between the columns was, it held them back. The buggy creatures never passed beyond the pylons.

"A ruby balustrade." The vision flashed to black, and then everything became normal again. No creatures. Just tall, white columns and empty fields of green sheathed behind panels of white light.

"Spunky," Pandon whispered, then waved for her to come to him. He took her hand and led her down a narrow path to a service door in the side of the hill. They didn't speak until they'd made it down the skinny staircase and into a tunnel leading toward the transport.

"You okay?" Pandon smelled like beef jerky and reminded her she was hungry.

"Yeah." Her stomach growled, and Pandon chuckled.

"I'll see if I can find you something to eat." Back to his flirty self, he tapped her nose and grabbed her hand, leading her deeper into the tunnel system. "This was far easier than I thought it would be."

"What?" Ren wasn't sure they should talk above a whisper.

"Getting down here." He slowed his pace but kept her hand in his. "I must say, I impressed myself."

Ren didn't respond. An awful feeling stifled her thoughts. In the warm glow of the tunnel, Pandon looked older, even more sure of himself than he normally did.

"I am good." He pulled Ren close, then twirled her around. "Oh, yeah."

Yanking her hand from his, she gave him a Bala glare. "Listen, I'm not here for some fun. This isn't one of those wiladashing things. My friend is in serious trouble."

Her anger didn't faze him. "There's that spunk." Two steps and he had her backed against the wall with an arm on each side, corralling her in. "You look pretty when you're angry."

She pushed at his chest. "What's wrong with you?" In three seconds, he'd gone completely nuts. "This isn't a game." He didn't budge.

A grin spread across his face. "Well, it sort of was for me." Backing off, he grabbed her hand again. "C'mon, Ren. I'll take you to your friend. And we'll see if you don't thank me and tell me I'm wonderful."

He practically dragged her down the tunnel. Two turns, through a circular doorway, and then they stood on a blue carpet with golden stars woven into it. This place rivaled Altrist's underground palace.

"We're almost there." With a broad smile, Pandon crossed the carpeted foyer and waited for her to join him. Then, he swiveled on his heel and pushed open a set of double doors.

Women's voices poured out from the room, and Ren got a strange feeling one of them sounded familiar.

"Ladies, I hope you can fully appreciate the ease with which I have accomplished my task." He glanced at Ren, who stood frozen in place.

"Oh, stop it already, Pandon. You missed one important piece." The silky voice sounded commanding, like she wasn't impressed at all.

"What?" Pandon reached for Ren and pulled her through the doorway. "I got her and entered the depths of the Golden Horizon with nobody noticing. What are you training the sentries these days, anyway?"

Ren couldn't move. A scary, tall woman stood in the center of the room, decked in sentry leather, with a black top, body armor, and a scinter strapped to her side. Her cold eyes landed on Ren, then darted back to Pandon.

"You didn't get the messenger." She leveled her fierceness at Pandon.

"The messenger wasn't my assignment." Pandon pushed Ren farther into the room. "She was."

The woman's face softened. "Well, you can tell that to *him*, can't you?"

Ren figured the *him* was Tatief, but it didn't matter right now. All she could think of was the other woman in the room—sitting there, dressed in guardian black, and looking happier than Ren had ever seen her.

"Bala?"

CHAPTER 37

An Unlikely Confidante

Soft ticks and a buzzing hum propped up the quiet moans from the inner room. Owen had only glimpsed Olivope once since Tatief had taken her away. And now, standing behind a partition, fear held his feet in place. He couldn't look at her full on but only took quick glimpses through the monitors.

Two sentries manned a button-littered control panel. Four more stood at either end of the partition, and even more framed the table where Olivope lay. Wires snaked from her arms and legs and connected her to a large pulsing machine.

Owen wanted to see her face, but his feet wouldn't move. She'd helped him, and he'd betrayed her. Ever since she and Anna cleared his head, he'd wanted to ask a thousand questions, but there had been no time.

After Tatief arrived, everything went crazy. Eviah stunned him with a scinter. The next thing he knew, he was waking up at the Plateau with a guard posted at his door.

And now he stood five meters from Olivope's limp form, frozen, wanting to say something to make the crazy pain inside him stop. He'd caused this.

The door behind him swished open, and more sentries entered the outer room. Then, another set of footsteps.

"Hello, Owen." Tatief's heavy hand landed on his shoulder. Tall and commanding, the powerful leader looked straight ahead, as if he could see through the partition. "How is she?"

Still no words. Just a feeble shake of the head.

Tatief gripped his shoulder, then released him. "I hate it had to be this way."

Owen clenched his teeth and focused on the drab wall separating them from the sad spectacle on the other side. Tatief had called Olivope *sister*. A strange term to use in a world where there are no families, just children cooked up in a lab and raised by nannies. It was supposed to mean someone close to you—someone you would stand by and care for.

"She brought this on herself. If she'd just let me help her, I would have. None of this needed to happen." He sounded sad, but Owen knew it was an act.

"What's wrong with her?" His eyes ventured to a monitor, but Tatief hooked an arm around his shoulder and guided him into Olivope's room. Her still body lay motionless except for a slight lifting in her chest. Clear wires stuck to her body with long silver needles in her arms, legs, chest, and head. Drips of blood stained her white tog.

"We're relieving her of her energy source." Small beads of light trickled through the wires. "It's the only way to stop her. I've tried reasoning. She will not listen. We'll harvest her energy and then promote her to her own Plantanate." He smiled. "For the good of all."

Owen couldn't bring himself to respond with the surrounding sentries.

"We give ourselves."

His heart raced against his chest. Air seemed scarce.

"I have some news." Tatief led Owen out of the horrible room. "It seems we've located your plebe."

"Ren?" Owen picked up his step to meet the master's.

"Yes, she's chosen to return with one of our own."

"Really?" They stopped by a fountain. A large pool of clear water encircled a male and female statue, half-clothed, standing with water spewing from their mouths. It might have been comical if it didn't have an eerie feel to it.

"You sound surprised." The master drew nearer to Owen, and the guide held his breath and turned his head. Already, his thoughts had lost their edge. Tatief's very presence consumed him. "Why are you surprised? Of course, she would return. She belongs here."

The master's deep eyes bore into Owen's, and he couldn't look away. A softer tone carried Tatief's words. "I think perhaps you need some refreshment to clear your head." He lifted his hand and snapped his fingers.

The girl who'd walked him to the Overlook returned. Her dark eyes stayed on Tatief.

Tatief chuckled and slapped Owen on the back. "Doni will attend to your needs. I don't think you've gotten to enjoy all the pleasures of the Plateau. Drink deeply." He winked at Doni. "Work your magic, my dear."

The girl stood on her tippy toes and grinned at Owen. Puffing her lips, she blew a fragrant breath of air into his face. Owen couldn't take his eyes from hers. Tatief excused himself, but his exit was a blur.

Doni snaked her hand into Owen's and pulled him close. "Let's go for a walk."

Any attempt at stringing together a reply gave up to Owen's beating heart pounding in his ears. He wanted the clarity he'd had in the forest with Olivope, but he couldn't hold on to it.

The girl pulled his arm close to her warm body and guided him toward his apartment. She hummed as they walked, and the sound of it kept him from concentrating. All he could think of was the sound of her voice, her scent, her skin.

As they reached the transit box, she twirled around, dancing to the button and looking more beautiful than any woman ever could. Sliding inside the box, she motioned for him to come, and he floated to her.

Just as he reached the door, a hand pulled him back. "Not today." Eviah jerked him to her side. "Snap out of it." She smacked his face. A gush of adrenalin freed Owen from his stupor.

Doni ran to his side and pulled out her colorful vocabulary.

Eviah backhanded the girl and sent her flying to the floor. "Slither off and find someone else to sink your venom into." Then, she grabbed Owen and headed in the opposite direction. "C'mon." They worked their way through the crowded underground walkways to a skinny alley. Halfway down, Eviah pulled open a door and pushed Owen inside.

She led him through several more doorways before they entered what appeared to be a bedroom. Pulling up a carpet, she opened a circular hatch with a ladder leading downward.

"Where are we?" The farther they'd gone, the more Owen's mind had cleared.

"I needed to get you some place free and safe from all the muck." She led him into a cozy room complete with chairs, a sofa, and a large picture window with a vid of a park scene giving the impression they weren't hundreds of meters below the ground. She motioned for him to sit, then poured a glass of water. "Want some?"

Owen nodded and guzzled it down.

"We can't stay long. I wanted some place where they wouldn't hear." She nodded toward a short, silver disc on the table next to him. "That little charm will jam any listening frequency trying to home in on our voices." She settled in a chair opposite him, another disc next to her. "I'm curious."

She paused so long; he thought he should say something. "Curious?"

"I just ... I've had my doubts."

"Doubts?" He'd work his way up to a whole sentence soon.

Eviah shrugged. "Part of it's the drugs."

Owen held up his glass of water.

"No, not the water. I didn't drug you, you moron." She chuckled. "Well, not this time. No, you're drugged and deceived. Classic Tatief style. Usually, he doesn't need the drugs. He's enough. He gets in your head and before you know it, you're slithering away with that skank Doni or another one just like her." It seemed both strange and familiar to be sitting on a couch, chatting with the Warrior. Owen wondered how fast she could kill him if she wanted to.

"He lost his grip on you." Her voice cracked. "Olivope cleared the cobwebs. He probably wonders how far you've gone." She paused, and Owen kept quiet. "Anyway, I'm curious about something. I'm going to conduct an experiment, and you are going to be my lab rat."

"What?" Owen sat the glass down.

She ignored him, went to a desk, and opened a small black box. "Have you seen one of these before?" She held up a gold cylinder. He shook his head. It looked like some kind of makeup, but he didn't offer his guess.

Pressing the end of the cylinder to her thumb, she tapped a button on the other end and grimaced. When she pulled her hand away, blood ran from her thumb. She wiped it on her black leggings, then held the cylinder out for Owen. "This is for you."

He slid the hot tube from her hand. "What is it?"

She smirked. "Well, I'm not going to tell you that. It's part of the experiment."

"What experiment?" He raised his voice.

She settled herself across from him again. "I'm putting the Leader to a test."

"What leader?" Owen moved the hot tube to his other hand. "What is this thing?"

"If the Leader wants you to know, he'll tell you."

"What are you talking about? I don't know any leader."

Her cheeks flushed, and her smirk straightened out. "Well, according to Olivope, he knows who you are." She sounded indignant, hurt almost. "I don't suppose he exists. If he did, then how could he allow Tatief to extract Olivope's life away? How could he stand by while I killed his precious few? Where is he?"

Owen stood. She sounded like she'd lost it. She wasn't the confident picture of power he'd encountered earlier. Now, she almost looked normal—like a heartsick woman in the Protectorate, not a cold-blooded killer.

His heart thudded, telling him to run, but making sudden movements didn't feel like the best course of action. Maybe one more question, a redirect. "Why are you doing this? Tatief wouldn't approve, would he? What makes you take the risk?"

Tears filled her fierce eyes. "No one can ever know we met. If you tell anyone, I will end your life so slowly you will beg me to slit your throat."

Despite the threat, Owen stood his ground. "I don't understand what you want me to do."

Her black hair shimmered as she shook her head. "I don't want you to do anything. I hope beyond measure it's not true—that nothing happens except exactly what Tatief has planned, but if it doesn't, if he somehow shows up, then I want him to see I played a part."

"Who? The Leader?" None of this made sense.

"I heard Olivope say it to you in the mic you wore." Eviah looked past Owen. "The choices you make affect far more than you know." A single tear appeared on her cheek, then she snapped back to herself. "We'll see. The Leader is nothing or everything. And we shall see."

She wiped her face. "And one more thing, Owen." She waited until he looked her in the eye. "If you let anything happen to Ren, I'll see my threat through to the very dead end." The Warrior was back.

CHAPTER 38

THE SAVIOR

Dart closed her eyes as Jasper yanked her up. So far, she'd not said anything about Altrist and the others, and she wouldn't. As long as she could hold out, she wouldn't give him anything.

"Altrist left you. That's what they do, you know. They only take care of themselves." He threw her against the steps of the rundown cabin. Ren's stupid cabin. The impact knocked the air from her lungs.

"I wonder if Altrist knows *our* history." Jasper looked her up and down. "Sweet irony. That's what this is."

A sentry opened the door. They'd made the small building into a makeshift post and lit it up in the night with solar orbs. Two troops had already arrived from their rounds.

"Sir, Kelly 5433 is about a click out. Should I tell them to stop here or continue on toward the willows?"

Jasper grunted. "Neither. Send them all toward the Plateau transit stations. With one messenger in hand, the other one will most likely show up there. If we can get them both, then the freaks will be easy to pick off."

"You don't think he'll come for her?" The grunt nodded toward Dart.

"Nah, I doubt that. Ain't nothing here he wants."

His needled words punctured her deflating hope, but Dart controlled her face. He wouldn't get the satisfaction. Four more sentries rounded the building—all with their weapons at the ready.

"And, sir ..." The lower officer hesitated. "Will you be much longer? Master Tatief requires an update."

Jasper got in Dart's face. "Normally, I'd leave the trash to junior recruits, but I don't want to rush things with this one." His eyes narrowed.

"Yes, sir." The sentry retreated into the cabin.

Jasper rallied the small troop left around him. He faced his sick audience. "This one and I go way back, fellas. She knew me before I earned my bars for interrogation and adjustment. Why, if it hadn't been for some luck, she would've ended me. Poor, weak girl. Just couldn't finish the job." He got in her face and lowered his voice. "No one's going to come help you. No one."

Dart twisted from his sick, smug sureness and caught a flicker of movement in the woods. Someone else was here.

Jasper jerked her face. "Look at me when I'm talking." He hauled her up like a rag doll and shoved her into another sentry. The guy gave her a push, sending her flying into another.

Dart let the adrenalin flow. It was now or never. Without thinking, she let her body do what it knew best, and as the third sentry caught her, she landed a crushing blow upside his face, sending him sprawling backward. Her foot caught another in the knee, and he hit the ground—then, she disarmed a third sentry before he could make a move.

As she reached for his scinter, a jab ripped through her shoulder, and she rolled onto the ground.

"Gonna take us all on?" Jasper's boot connected with her side, and she heard the rib crack. "You're going to die out here, and no one cares."

Dart rolled and faced him. "Someone does." She held her fading palm up, but she didn't believe her own words. After the weird encounter in the woods, she thought maybe the leader had been in it—that he'd sent the strange guy to help her, somehow. But when she'd gone back to find him, he was gone, and now, she was here.

Jasper smacked her hand down. "It's a bunch of lies." He pulled her up by her hair and tilted her head back. "You don't have a gift, do you? You don't have a gift and look where they left you? They tell you all that junk to get the gifts. That's all they want. Their building their own little army. There's no leader. No one's coming to help you." He released her with a thud. "They don't care about anybody but themselves. That's not how it is with us. We care about the good of all."

The stupid sentries repeated their stupid mantra.

Dart wiped the blood from her mouth. "You're pathetic."

"What?" He nearly ripped her hair from her head this time. "What did you say?"

"You heard the truth and believed it. You were loved, and you threw it all away because you couldn't have what you wanted."

Jasper's heavy hands went to her throat. "Be very careful what you say next."

Dart pulled at his grip. The suffocating hold didn't budge.

"Not yet," he whispered and loosened his hold. The back of his hand connected with her jaw and sent a spray of lights across her eyes. "Useless, exile trash. You could never make it with them. You know what exiles are good for, don't you? Fence practice."

The other sentries laughed.

"Yeah, we toss 'em at the rim and watch 'em fry or come apart, lose an arm, a leg, whatever. Maybe we should take you there. What do you say, boys? Anyone up for a trip to the wall?"

They cheered.

Jasper gave the order, and two sentries heaved Dart to her feet. Her side burst with pain. Before they could drag her forward, a *thunk* sounded in each of Dart's ears. She knew the sound well. Arrows. The sentries let go as they clutched the arrows sticking from their chests.

A scream from the woods signaled the fight was on. Sully and his goons poured from the trees, yipping like wild animals.

Jasper sent a spray of electricity from the end of his skeer, but he only nipped one exile. Grabbing Dart, he pulled her toward the cabin.

"Oh, no you don't." Sully lit up a scinter and winked at Dart. "Sorry about last time, dearie. Just having fun."

Jasper shoved Dart to the ground, and she crawl-ran for the bushes.

She forced her feet to move away from the light of the glow torches and scinter rods. The woods didn't offer any familiar footing, but she kept going. The fight would end soon, and they would come for her. Jasper or Sully, she didn't care. They were equally bad.

A shaft of moonlight broke through the trees, giving Dart some help. Behind her the sounds of the fight died down. The smell of scinter touching flesh hung in her nostrils.

Her head pounded, and the throbbing in her side made it hard to breathe. Leaning against a tree, she tried to focus. *Keep moving.*

Jasper's angry commands interrupted the surrounding calm. He'd finished the fight. Sliding down the tree, she crawled toward the brush and stopped. A taxar bush. She swallowed. It was her best bet. They wouldn't come in after her; they wouldn't even look.

Moving slowly, she navigated around the prickly leaves. The bush created a canopy over soft ground. She stayed low and kept moving. A sentry shouted off to her left, and she checked the distance to the other side of the bush. The moonlight made the leaves look like spiked ghosts. Just a little farther.

Holding her breath, she wiggled her body out the other side of the bush. The branches hung lower to the ground here, but lying flat, she maneuvered under the deadly spikes. As she turned though, her foot caught, and a hot flash sent jolts up her leg. It went limp.

The throbbing in her head lessened as the edges of the world went black, and she slumped to the ground. Two hands slid under her shoulders and pulled her up.

"That was not the smartest thing I've ever seen." The man lifted her and swung her arm over his shoulder. "You've got to help me some. I can't carry you the whole way."

Dart fought against the cloudy feeling filling her head. She couldn't speak. The man kept talking, quietly urging her on, but the words came and went until finally she fell. Her body tumbled toward the ground, but she never hit. The darkness blanketed her, and the pain ebbed away.

CHAPTER 39

THE PLATEAU

Cinnamon and vanilla, and the strangest dream.

Ren rolled over in the gigantic bed as the misty remnants of the night faded away. In the dream, she'd been taken to the Plateau, but instead of being escorted on a fancy transport, she'd been captured and brought by force.

The scary woman, the Superintendre, stood on a platform next to a man called Hyperion, who looked more like a dragon than a man. It all flooded back like a memory—like an old book she'd lost herself in and thought was real.

At the end of the dream, everyone knew about her aberration, and it was okay. She was free.

She opened her eyes. "Back to reality." But this did not seem like reality. A spacious suite with a huge fake window, a bathroom, a sitting area, and strange art of contorted people and flaming animals surrounded her. A plasma screen sported a fake view from the pseudo window—a countryside and the sun peeking over the trees. The view conflicted with the blacks and reds of the room.

Pulling off the silky covers, Ren grabbed the clothes she had borrowed from Dart and tossed the satiny red lace nightgown on the bed. The Plateau. They'd brought her to the Plateau. The Superintendre, lying Pandon, and Bala had put her on a transport, given her something warm to drink, and brought her here.

They all seemed thrilled to find her. There had been no talk of adjustments or accomplishing.

Pandon had lied. Evidently, Lidya's Pandy was a lying, scheming guardian from the start.

And Bala? Bala had been fine.

Chills ran up from Ren's bare toes and stopped at her neck where a warm sensation stunted them. A spray of lights crossed her vision. Deep breath. No visions. No aberration. Bala hadn't told them about the visions, and evidently neither had Owen. No one knew, at least not yet.

They had to be watching her every move, though. Drawing in another breath, she swallowed, and the tingles dissipated. A dull hum buzzed in the back of her head, and her thoughts couldn't make it past seeing Bala in her fancy guardian clothes next to the Superintendre. The scene haunted her.

A thin white-and-gold door on the other side of the elaborate bedroom slid open. Bala graced the doorway, her black guardian coverup accented with a large, patterned sash. "Are you up?"

Ren pulled on some socks and her shoes. "Yeah." This couldn't be real. The one thing she never thought she would see standing right in front of her was Bala as a guardian.

Bala entered, followed by a servant dressed in gray and pushing a cart laden with pastries, scrambled eggs, fresh fruit, and ham. "Just park it over there by the dinette." Bala pointed to a small table and chairs Ren hadn't noticed before. The servant bowed and scurried out.

"Come. Sit. That stuff Eviah gave you makes you thirsty and hungry. Come on. Get some food in you, and let's catch up." A soft touch of gloss kissed Bala's lips, and her hair was braided and pulled into a decorative bun. She looked like a totally different person. "Come on, now. I need to hear everything." Her voice sounded strange. Not full and sure. Thin and unsettled.

Ren couldn't stop staring. She had a thousand questions. Most of which she wanted to scream, except a dull fog enveloping her thoughts made it hard to speak. When she stood, the buzz in her head took a sharper turn, and she steadied herself with a chair. "What stuff Eviah gave me?"

"Just something to relax you and help you travel. No worries. All is good." This wasn't Bala. Someone else had taken over her body. It couldn't be Bala.

The nanny-turned-guardian poured a cup of frothy caftewater. "Okay, now stop your swaying and come sit. I think we have some catching up to do."

That was an understatement.

Ren eased into the chair and swiped a pastry. "What do you mean all is good? I don't understand any of this." Pastry glaze dripped over Ren's fingers. She shouldn't say anything, but she couldn't stop herself. "What is this? Why am I here? What's going on? And you? A guardian?"

Bala took a sip of her caftewater and cut her eyes around the room. "Everything's going to be fine. Although, I suppose you will have some explaining to do about your escapade outside the boundary. But having friends in high places helps. And if you tell the Superintendre what she wants to know, all will be fine." She smiled, but it wasn't an actual smile.

High-pitched footsteps sounded down the hallway, accented by a man's nasally, overbearing voice. Bala rolled her eyes. "Sounds like you're about to experience a little Hillton."

"What's a Hillton?"

Before the nanny could answer, a man's shrill voice turned both of them toward the open doorway. A fat man with thin legs and a puffy orange hat strode in with another man drafting behind him.

"That's a Hillton." Bala grunted.

"There you are." Hillton grabbed Ren's hand and looked her over.

"Sir, the mistress told us to wait." The tall, thin man grabbed his master just as two sentries entered the room.

"Unhand me, fool. I have much work to do here, and I will not wait around to get permission from the daunting goddess." He smacked at the skinny man with his free paw, then eyed Ren. "Let's see what we have to work with."

Ren attempted to pull her hand free, but he kept his chubby grip. A spray of white shot across her vision. *No. Not now.* She drew in a breath, but the aberration kept coming.

Bala noticed and stepped between them, breaking Hillton's hold. "What is this?" She used her stern voice.

Ren pulled in another breath and kept her gaze on the floor.

"Who are you?" The large man met Bala's fierceness.

"I'm someone who says if the master's Warrior told you to wait, then wait is what you shall do." The ex-nanny forced Hillton to take a step back. Ren stole a look as the threat of a vision subsided.

Hillton straightened his velvety blue coat. "I'm Hillton, and I'm here to make her presentable. The master intends to see her today, and he wants her ready."

"I know who you are." Bala let him retreat. "I thought all you did was plaster some black sequins and lace on and braid her hair. How much more is there to do?"

The sentries chuckled and received a harsh shush from the tall guy.

Somehow, Hillton grew bigger, and his face became a deep shade of cherry. "You have no idea what I do. What are you? A three-tier guardian. Step aside, or I will have you adjusted." He went to swat her, but Bala snatched his hand and twisted his wrist behind his fat back.

"Is that so?" The nanny applied more pressure.

A piercing squeal came from Hillton's painted lips, but no one moved. Ren wasn't sure what Bala's plan was. Beating up some fancy guardian didn't seem like the best course of action.

"Oh, let him go." The order came from beyond the sentries. The daunting goddess was back.

Bala released the cad and stood at attention. The sentries snapped to attention as well.

"Balandria, you said you'd behave." An amused glint flashed in the Superintendre's eyes, then she got serious. "Hillton, take the girl and do whatever it is you do. I'll send someone for her in the afternoon."

Ren stiffened. *Balandria. She called Bala Balandria. No.* Ren's tear-stacked eyes went to her friend. A statue, the nanny didn't look at Ren.

"And Ren," the Superintendre demanded attention. Ren picked up her senses and glared. This woman, who'd already meddled so much in Ren's life, just stood there. Strong, commanding, and indifferent to the weight of her words. "I believe there's someone you'll be happy to see." A tear slid down Ren's face, as the scary woman waved the doorway fully open, and Owen arrived.

Her heart split to pieces.

Dressed in black with a sky-blue tie and shiny shoes, Owen looked right at home. Everything except for his eyes fit perfectly into the picture. His eyes betrayed him, but Ren couldn't place the emotion they held.

His name lodged in her throat. "Owen," she whispered.

He acknowledged her but didn't speak. The gulf between them was so massive, thousands of words would be required to ever cross.

Eviah broke the tension. "Well, it's so good to have everyone reunited. Now, I believe Ren needs some fashion repair, and I have another messenger to capture."

"Another?" Ren's hope crumbled even more. *Please, no.* Bala's eyes stayed on the floor, and Owen couldn't look at her either.

"Why, yes." The Superintendre put her arm around Owen. "You'd be very proud to learn Owen was instrumental in helping capture the female messenger. He's an all-around guardian now."

The pastry and eggs roiled in Ren's stomach and threatened to return.

"Are you familiar with the messengers, Ren?" The Superintendre's eyes narrowed. "Did something happen on your little adventure outside the boundary that we need to know?" She looked at a steely-faced Bala, then back to Ren.

"No, not really." Ren steadied herself. "I hadn't realized there were two." The lie came out easily enough, but then she remembered Owen. He knew she knew. His chocolate eyes didn't give her away, though, so she continued. "I saw the boy from the transport on my first day."

As she spoke, Bala's training played back in her head. The best way to answer the guardian masters is to give them a fraction of truth and color it with a compliment or accolade. "Bravo for you, though. None can stand against Master Tatief." The words tasted bitter and sounded sheer. So, she took a rancid breath and forced herself forward in their sick world. "For the good of all."

"We give ourselves." Everyone returned the mantra, or at least everyone's mouths moved.

The Superintendre didn't look convinced, but she dismissed Ren with a wave of her hand. Hillton marched out, griping under his breath about valuable lost time. Ren followed.

As she passed Owen, she couldn't help but meet his eyes. He hadn't told any of her secrets, and despite his new attire, he didn't seem like the traitor she thought he was. But then she remembered Olivope and turned her gaze away.

CHAPTER 40

THE DEFINING CHOICE

"Wait" The Superintendre's command caught Owen off guard.

The Warrior locked her eyes on Ren. "You will need this." A nod to a sentry brought him forward, holding a small open box. Eviah lifted a leather bracelet with a thin strip of glowing stones across the top and fastened it around Ren's wrist. When the latch caught, the stones pulsed through a rainbow of colors. "Now, go." Her voice softened.

The guards herded Ren out, and the door slid shut.

Owen wanted to follow her, pull her aside, and tell her everything. He wasn't sure what he would say, but somewhere in the torrent of words he'd pour over her, they'd find the truth. She'd point out the holes in his logic, and he'd keep her from falling to that place where everything was upside down. That's what he wanted to do. But instead, he watched her leave, all her horrible thoughts about him still in place.

"What did you find out?" Eviah addressed Bala. "Were you able to do better with the elusive Ren than our newly inducted guardian here?" She shot Owen a look, but he didn't take the bait. He'd already given them far more than he should have.

"Nothing new." Bala sighed. "She's an innocent. She thinks the best of everyone and doesn't have any idea what she's stepped into." The nanny held her own against the Warrior. They had a familiarity between them. Owen liked her. She had the same I-don't-need you air that Ren so adeptly carried.

"And do you have any idea what's at stake?" Eviah dismissed the waiting sentries from the room. "Tatief will get what he wants. It's how his desires are met that we can affect. There is no winning this game." A tiny gold dagger pinned the Warrior's hair up. She still wore her body armor, but a paneled, sheer skirt partially covered her long legs.

Bala didn't back down. "I've never thought it a game."

Eviah's lips looked the shade of shiny blood. "And that's why you've spent the last seventeen years being a babysitter."

"Not a babysitter, not even a nanny—a friend, a confidante, a mother."

The Warrior backhanded Bala across the face. The two seemed oblivious to Owen.

Red flushed Eviah's sharp cheeks. "If she doesn't give what he wants freely, then he will apply Jasper to her. Is that what you want? To watch her suffer?"

Owen tensed, and the Warrior noticed.

"This goes for you too. If you want to help Ren, you'll get her to tell you everything. There has to be a reason the male messenger revealed himself to her. They don't just show up, you know."

"Olivope did." Saying her name brought a thickness to Owen's throat. He swallowed, but it didn't move.

Eviah's dark lips curved. "Yes, she did. Thanks to you."

Owen looked away. The heavy feeling descended into his gut. Guilt, his new comrade.

"Get her to give our master something—a location, names, something. Tatief's maddened by their latest ventures. If we can capture the boy, then we can put an end to what's going on outside the boundary. And then you and you ..." She cut to Owen. "can have your precious Ren."

"What do you mean 'what's going on outside the boundary'?" Bala met the Warrior eye to eye. "You speak of them as if they're a disease."

"Just do it." Eviah glared, but she didn't look as fierce. "And bring her to Tatief's private residence when Hillton is finished. He wants to meet the plebe who's been causing so much trouble." With that, she exited.

Owen wrapped his hand around the tube in his pocket. What kind of weird game was the Superintendre playing? One second, she acted like she wanted to help, and the next, she spewed threats.

Bala grumbled and headed for the door.

"Wait." The word caught in Owen's throat. He hadn't used his voice in a while. "Can we talk?"

The nanny's cheek still bore Eviah's handprint. "I don't think we have anything to say to one another."

"Maybe." Owen looked for an avenue to help Ren. "Or maybe we have more in common than you think. Maybe we both want the same thing for Ren." He chose his words with care. Bala hadn't told anyone about Ren's aberration. For now, she might be Ren's only chance to get out with her brain still intact.

Bala's eyes glanced behind him, and he knew they were listening. Tylon probably had his gift fixed on them right now. Cameras rolling and beans picking up every sound. But maybe not everything would be heard.

He motioned for Bala to follow him to the couch. She didn't, but she didn't leave either. He took out the silver disc he'd swiped from Eviah's hideaway. The light wasn't blinking anymore, so he shook it.

Bala ran to him and took it. Flipping it over, she popped open a door and held down two buttons. The light revved up, and she replaced the door and gave it back to him.

"It needed to be recalibrated. Where did you get that?" She sat down.

The word *honesty* popped into his head. "I swiped it from Eviah's hideaway. She said it would keep them from hearing us. I was hoping to use it when I talked to Ren."

"When you talk to Ren?" The nanny looked as if she wanted to rip his arms off. "Like the way you talked to Olivope?'

Guilt ferried its way from his heart to his head, and words failed him. All he could say was he was sorry, and that seemed like a drop in his ocean of regret.

A sheen of disgust crossed Bala's face. "You got what you wanted. Guardian black and all this." She stood. "You're just another rendition of the same old game. Lie, trick, con. Whatever it takes to get what you want."

She shook her head. "Ren trusted you. She said it in between the lines of her messages." Bala's voice broke. "I told her not to trust anyone."

Owen drew in a breath and focused. He'd deal with his guilt, but right now the goal was to help Ren. "And what about you?" He met the nanny eye-to-eye. "You're looking pretty guardian-like yourself. Should she trust you?"

Bala latched her trained hands around his throat and drove him into the sofa. "You have no idea what I've done for her—what I'll do."

Grabbing at her hands, Owen offered his only proof. "I didn't tell them about the aberration."

Bala relaxed her grip. "How do you know that?" She sat back and checked the blinking disk.

Owen rubbed his neck. "She told me." Emotion choked him now. "And I will never betray her."

"Like you didn't betray Olivope?"

His throat thickened. "If I could take that back, I would."

Bala's rage subsided, and silence settled between them. After a few minutes, she swiped the disk from the table. "How did you get this?"

"From Eviah's hideaway."

Bala leaned forward. "Where?"

"From some room she has outside of ..." He pointed toward the lights. "watchful eyes."

A strange, joyous expression softened the nanny's angry face. "Well, maybe she's not all bad after all."

"She seems pretty bad." The disk blinked, and Owen wondered if the guardians watching were confused about why they couldn't hear anything.

"Well, she took you to her hideaway, and you're still alive. That's gotta mean something. Why would she do that? What does she want from you?"

He shrugged. "I don't know. Some test. Evidently, she has a problem with some leader guy who supposedly is really good, really bad, or nonexistent. I didn't follow her completely."

Bala sat back as if she'd been gently pushed, a smile tugging at one side of her mouth. "The Leader."

Owen used his waiting tactic to see if the nanny would say anything more, but she seemed content to stay in her own thoughts. "So, who is this leader person? Another rendition of Tatief? Someone like Olivope?"

A happy glow glossed Bala's eyes. "He's neither. I don't know much. I was only with them for a few months. They say he's powerful, kind, good, and he's going to put Tatief where he belongs."

It sounded like a fairytale.

She read his thoughts. "I know. Crazy, but you have to see them. These people live like no one else. They care for each other. Everyone is valued. No one is accomplished. Their idea of love is so much more than jumping a tier or finding the right body art to match the latest coverup trend."

"And this leader rules them?" Owen felt an energy in the room as they spoke. Something outside himself. He checked the disk, but it blinked still.

"Not exactly. He doesn't have to rule them. They love him back." The disk blinked to red and back. Bala put her finger to her lips.

Owen snatched the disk up and jammed it into her hands. "Take it. Use it to talk to Ren. Warn her. Help her." Giving Bala the device wasn't part of his plan, but it was the best shot at helping Ren.

Bala nodded, but her face conveyed no hope. "I'll try." She tucked the device in her front pocket and left.

Owen settled his heart. He'd done what he could for Ren. Even if he had time to talk to her, he would probably spend most of it explaining all his lies.

Now, he turned his mind to another, and his resolve guided him. There was someone else he needed to help.

The sureness of his next step took hold like nothing he'd ever faced in his entire life. Even his dreams of guardianship, living in the Vantages, and replacing Whitler as Overseer paled in comparison. This was a grownup purpose—a choice made that would define him, and that he wanted to define him. If no one else ever thought of him again—if all they saw was his face on the Kirkenwall—then maybe they would remember this.

CHAPTER 41

THE REDEEMED

The scent of bacon roused Dart from her sleep. She rolled over. A blurry view of water, haze, and rock reminded her of Snowshoe Falls.

"Bacon," she moaned. The area came into focus. It wasn't Snowshoe, but it was a cave—sort of. Footsteps—and then a man stood over her.

"Did you just say bacon?" A grin spread across his tanned face. He looked familiar. "A girl after my own heart." A tray of eggs, bacon, toast, and juice sat next to her. "Eat up. You'll need to regain your strength."

The man from the bluff served up breakfast like an old pack buddy. A blue-green coverup peeked out from underneath his heavy brown sweater. His happy eyes matched the smile on his face.

As she pushed herself up, Dart remembered her close call. The cabin, sentries, and Jasper. Other than being groggy, her body felt fine. Sluggish and tired, but fine. Her broken ribs didn't even hurt—and the taxar scratch. She pulled her leg out from under the blanket.

"All better." He nodded toward the healed wound, then grabbed a stool and sat. "I told you I wouldn't leave you."

"How did you fix me?" Dart didn't want to sound ungrateful or anything, but even Anna and Liza had a hard time with the taxar poison. Put that on top of the beating she took, and she should at least be feeling some aches. "I mean, thank you."

"You're welcome." He snatched a slice of bacon from her plate. His eyes still had the same effect as when she talked to him by the vim—like he knew her and like he cared.

His little home was more like a crevice in the rocks than a cave—a place where the rocks on top jutted out farther than the rocks on the bottom. An overhang.

She checked behind her and noted a metal doorway. "Where are we?"

Warm sunlight peeked through the crevice and silhouetted the stranger. "Out there is the stream that connects Tidal Creek with the Goneer." Then, he pointed toward the metal door. "And if you follow the tunnels far enough, you can almost make it to the Snowshoe complex. There's a collapsed wall blocking the last connection."

Dart nodded. She knew exactly where they were, and the rocks up the side of the cliff. A perfect place for a secret hideaway, if you can get up there. "Smart."

"Thank you." He took her empty plate and rinsed it in a wash bucket.

"I looked for you." Dart put her bare feet on a dusty rug by the cot. Her shoes were lined up at the end, and her leggings had been cut up to her knees above the taxar wound. She pulled the blanket over her legs. "I looked out near the vim again, but I couldn't find you." He nodded like he already knew. He seemed to know a lot about her—a lot more than she knew about him. "What's your name?"

His dark eyes sparkled. "You can call me Melkin." He moved the stool closer and sat in front of her. Something about him made her feel safe and scared all at the same time. His tone turned serious. "And I think we need to talk."

Dart rubbed her freezing hands together, and he gathered them up in his warm grip, turning her palms toward the rock ceiling. The sunburst teased her like a dirty reminder of her lost promise.

He released them, and the cold came back. "I upset you when we talked the other day."

That wasn't a question, and she didn't want to go back through the things he'd said. What she wanted to know was how he knew that stuff. Her eyes met his, and she felt it again, like coming home.

"Who are you?" She whispered this time, and he reached out. Like a magnet, her hand went to his. Adrenalin shot through her, awakening her like she had been sleeping and someone drenched her with a bucket of cold water.

With gentleness, he brought her palm to his lips and kissed her hand, and the sunburst filled with vibrant color. Dart jerked away and scooted back.

"You can't be." He couldn't be. No one had ever said what the leader really looked like. As far as she knew, he was invisible, some unseen force working in the world, not a man, but supernatural, impersonal. "Is this some kind of trick?" But she knew it wasn't. Melkin was him, and that fact tore through her veins like lightning.

She pulled the blanket up to her chin. She wanted to hide, to fall down and cover her head.

He whispered back. "It's okay."

But it wasn't okay. It didn't make sense he had saved her or that he cared. Not after all she'd done, what she wanted to do, who she was. Colorful, the art on her palm didn't fill her with joy like the first time he'd put it there. This moment should have overflowed with happiness and all things bright. She wanted this—to see him, but something held her back.

Melkin clasped his hands in front of him. "I met your Laura once."

At the mention of her mama's name, Dart tensed. The part of her that refused to take hold of the joy reared back ready to pounce.

"You were a tiny little thing. She said she called you Dart because she knew you would be quick, and because darts add shape to things, and you added a whole new shape to the way she saw the world. She loved you very much."

Grief bubbled up from the darkness inside, and Dart mouthed the weighted word. "Why?"

The shift in his expression said he knew the heat of her question. He took a deep breath and shook his head. "I never meant for it to be this way."

That wasn't good enough. If he were as powerful as Tatief, then he could have stopped it. He could have done something, but he didn't. He let those sentries attack them. He didn't stop Jasper's hand. And instead of Altrist finding her, Sully did.

He didn't save her. For six years, she suffered Sully's abuse, flinching from his hand and doing terrible things just to stay alive. "You could have stopped it, but you didn't. Why?" Dart threw off the blanket and pushed him hard. A crazy sadness controlled her arms. "Why?" He caught her and held her close. She wanted to pound him, to smack him, and pull his hair, but instead she collapsed into him with heaving sobs.

"I didn't stop them. Just like I won't stop you." He stroked her hair. "I never left you. This world will bring you trouble, but this is not where you belong. This world belongs to Tatief."

A mess of snot and tears covered her face. The anger melted down to a manageable pool, and Dart waded through it and climbed onto new ground on the other side. "What do you mean you won't stop me?"

Melkin looked her full in the face. "I won't stop you if you go after Jasper or even if you decide you want to leave."

His announcement stuttered her heart. "I don't want to leave."

"And Jasper?"

Dart touched her side where the monster had kicked her, and Melkin cupped her wet face. "Sully and Jasper can't hurt you anymore."

She wanted to believe him, but even hoping that sort of stuff would set her up for a fall. Besides, if it wasn't Sully or Jasper, it would be someone else, wouldn't it? To live is to hurt. Not even the people at Snowshoe could get along. All things fall apart eventually.

He rubbed the stubble on his chin. "Did Altrist ever tell you how he got his name?" The sun stretched farther into the cavern. "Because in the end, there's one thing everyone must do. It surpasses knowledge and reason and even love."

The answer to his riddle eluded her.

"Trust." He smiled. "In the end, you're going to have to trust me."

"Altrist." Dart perked up. "I'll trust."

"I thought it was clever myself." Melkin baffled her. If she had to pick someone out to be the one to defeat Tatief, he wouldn't have been the first choice. Tall and strong, but he didn't have the fight in him. He was unassuming and kind. Those two things don't win wars.

"And Olivope?" He continued. "Can you guess what her name means?"

Dart rolled the name around in her head. "I'll have hope."

"Good job." He leaned forward fast and grabbed her hands again. "Trust me and have hope. There's a hard road ahead. I won't lie. Things will get worse for you before they get better, but I won't leave you. Remember that. I promise."

Tears crammed her eyes again. "Why?" This time her question had a different turn. Not an angry eruption, but steam dissipating into the air. "Why do you even care? I'm nothing. I'm nobody."

His grip stayed sure. "Not to me."

They sat hand in hand for flashes, and the pain from Dart's past melted under the warmth of love. "I'll trust." She drew in a deep breath. "And I'll have hope."

"That's my girl." He stood up. "Now, to get you home."

Dart slipped on her shoes and followed him to the center of the cavern. "I can get back from here. I know the way, but I'm not sure about leaving. When will I see you again?"

"I don't know." He touched her cheek. "And I'd really rather you not tell anyone you saw me. There's still much to happen before I can finish this war with Tatief, and they don't need any distractions from the things they need to do."

She didn't know what he meant, but she went with it.

"Goodbye, Dart. I'm glad we could talk." He pulled her into a hug—the best hug she'd ever received. His powerful arms engulfed her, and for those few flashes, everything in her world was perfect. "Safe travels." He stepped back, and a huge grin filled his whiskered face.

Before she could respond, a hot feeling filled her middle, and light brightened from her center. "What the ...?" Then, he faded from view, and she was gone.

"Is she okay?"

"Give her room."

"Who would have thought?"

"Just in time."

Dart opened one eye at a time to see all her favorite faces looking down on her. "Hi, guys."

Liza clapped her hands together. "You got your gift, and it's perfect." She giggled. "Altrist, you were right." Altrist's face lit up with a radiant glow.

He held out a hand. "Come now, Dart. We've much to do."

She scrambled up, feeling not so sure of her feet. "What's going on?"

Altrist pulled her to him. Fresh air and radiance swirled around them, and a sneaky grin filled his little face. "We're going to save Olivope and Ren."

CHAPTER 42

THE TRUTH ABOUT BALA

Ren's new getup took her breath away. Diamonds outlined the neckline on the velvety blue top, and colorful jewels cascaded down the chiffon panels billowing around her black leggings. She looked like a wispy, starry night. Even the guardians she'd seen had never dressed like this.

"Magnificent. Your height really helps pull this off." Hillton gave the platform a push, and Ren spun around, the panels flowing from her waist caught in the air. Tears glossed Hillton's eyes. "What do you think?"

The tall skinny assistant opened his mouth, but Hillton raised a hand. "Not you. Her." He stopped the platform with a jerk. "Do you like it?"

A hazy feeling of wonderfulness filled Ren's head. "It's amazing. I've never seen anything like it." It was amazing. The entire day had been like some weird, out-of-focus dream. One minute she felt betrayed and lost, and the next it didn't seem so bad, like the world was just as it should be.

Holding on to her thoughts eluded her. Between Hillton's chattering, the perfumes, and the constant barrage of take-it-you-deserve-it messages, she couldn't remember what had worried her when she left her room earlier.

She took a woozy step down from the platform and checked the mirror. Hillton had swept her hair up with blue and black ribbons intertwined in curls. She looked grown up.

"Have you finished your magic yet?" Bala stood in the doorway. "Whoa."

Hillton put a sentry between him and Bala. "You again. What do you want?"

The nanny ignored him. "Ren? Is that you?" Bala orbited the semi-circle of mirrors. "You look—different."

"Hmmmph. Is that all you can say?" Hillton stepped up on the platform. "She's a work of art, if I do say so myself."

Ren met him eye to eye. "Thank you, Master Hillton. It's all very splendid." *Did she just say splendid?* She'd stepped out of a fairytale and discovered herself a princess.

"Yeah, *splendid.* C'mon, Ren. We've got to go." Bala jerked her toward the door. Two sentries moved to block them. Bala stood her ground. "I have orders from the Warrior to take the girl to the master." The men didn't move. "Check. You'll see." One sentry slipped a slender device from his pocket, swiped a few times, then stepped out of the way.

Ren followed the nanny as Hillton launched into a lecture on how what's on the outside actually is more important than what's on the inside. The door sliding shut behind cut short his diatribe.

Bala rushed down the corridor, and Ren fell into step beside her. "So, this is it? I'm going to Tatief?" The question didn't make her as scared as it should have. Her veins had a dull buzz of happy contentment pulsing through them.

Bala veered away from the fancy entryway and opened a door to a side stairwell. The three flights of stairs weren't so easy in high heels, but Ren managed.

"This way." The stairway emptied into a vacant sidewalk.

Ren pointed toward where the sky should be. "Are we completely underground?"

"Sort of." Bala guided her toward a busy street. Guardians dominated the store fronts, sidewalks, and vendor stands. All were dressed in black with colorful accents added. Many stopped when they saw Ren. Some even bowed.

Maybe Hillton was right. The outside seemed to make quite a statement. And not one person made fun of her, laughed, or gave her the stink eye. They respected her. Honored her.

Bala swung into the park and slowed. "Why don't we take a minute before you meet the master." She led Ren to a secluded bench and pulled a disc from her pocket, tapping the top twice. "We need to talk." She held up the disc. "As long as the yellow light is on, they can't hear us."

Ren heaved a contented smile. A warm wonderfulness flowed through her body. Bala leaned forward and stared into Ren's eyes. "What are you on?" Opening a small satchel attached to her belt, she pulled out a leather pouch with three vials in it. "Let's see." Tiny lettering covered the labels. "Probably not this one, and not this one either. Oh, this might work. Here, drink this." She held up the bottle.

"What? No." Ren pushed it away.

"Listen, Ren, we don't have much time, and I won't talk while you're compromised with that junk in your system. Drink it."

Ren lifted the bottle to her lips and swallowed the salty liquid. "What is it?"

"You know, you really should have asked that before you drank it." Bala put the pouch back in her satchel. "Did you ask that question when Hillton offered you his concoctions?"

"What? How do you know he gave me something?" Ren had forgotten, but when she arrived in the dressing room, he'd practically forced her to drink a glass of their finest. It was sweet and burned her throat. Now, the inside of Ren's mouth tingled, and her thoughts lightened like a hazy fog rising to the sun. "What's happening?"

"They drugged you. It's part of how they get you to do what they want. At first, anyway. After a while, they don't need the drugs anymore. Most people buy into all the 'you-can-have-it, you-deserve-it' junk without the juice, but since you've been with the messengers ..."

Ren slumped down. "I don't feel so good."

"Give it a minute, and you'll be back to your old self in no time. Just don't eat or drink anything—not unless you're sure they haven't tampered with it." The strange disk blinked in Bala's palm. "I need to tell you some things I should have told you long ago."

The angst of the morning returned with force. "Yeah, I have questions for you." The shock of seeing Bala at the Golden Horizon, Altrist's accusations, and the Superintendre calling her by a different name. It flooded back. "Balandria?"

Bala closed her eyes, took a breath, and then spoke. "Yes."

The weight of her acknowledgement broke something inside of Ren. "You tricked me? I was safe with Altrist, and you played like you needed help."

"No." Bala snapped. "That wasn't me. That was Pandon's plan. I didn't know. I was just trying to keep them busy, not help them."

"But you killed those innocent people?" Ren remembered the vision.

Questions rose in the nanny's eyes. "Where did you hear about that?"

"Altrist told me, and the aberration showed me. He warned me about you." Ren wasn't sure what to think. She trusted Altrist, and her trust for Bala waned by the second.

A somber tone shrouded Bala's voice. "I deserve that. He has no reason to trust me. But Ren ..." She grabbed Ren's hands. "I didn't hurt them. I didn't know."

"How can I believe you?" Ren pulled away. "I thought I knew you. I never thought you could hurt innocent people, but I would have never pegged you for a guardian sentry either."

Bala released a heavy sighed. "That was a lifetime ago."

"It doesn't look like it was long ago." Ren waved at Bala's outfit.

"I'm playing the game right now. That's all."

The disk blinked to orange, then back to yellow.

"Altrist said you and another woman betrayed them."

The nanny bit her lip, the rims of her eyes red. "I'd lived with them for ten months. Edel, Rob, Loriee, Marsia, Blackburn, and the Ridge family." Bala stared at the air like she could see their faces. "I'd convinced them to move—to leave, but it was too late. She'd already given the order. She waited until I left. She asked me to find herbs in the valley, said she needed them for the baby. I was always a sucker to do anything for you. I think she knew my heart had changed. By the time I got back, it was over."

The identity of the *she* Bala kept referencing loomed in the front of Ren's mind, but she couldn't bring herself to ask. In this world of perfectly grown people, she failed to meet the standard. Hers was an un-ordained creation. Some nameless female guardian had created a child and used it as leverage.

Ren didn't want to hear any more. The more she knew, the more she couldn't deny.

Bala's voice caught. "Your father was dead. Tortured and left to die." Her hands trembled as she wiped her face. "I heard you crying. She'd left you. I took you, and I ran. I couldn't find Altrist or Olivope. And I didn't figure they would trust me, so I came back to this. I tucked you into the most remote raising home I could find, and I resigned."

Ren's body shook. A freezing chill circulated in her veins. She had been left to die in a room next to her dead father by a female who neither wanted her nor saw any value in her. The facts made for unstable ground. With every heartbeat, she sunk in further. She was the complete opposite of the ideal person allowed to live under Tatief's guiding hand.

Bala leaned forward, oblivious to the turmoil inside of Ren. "You saw them, then? Altrist? You talked to him?"

Ren hesitated to move on, but Bala didn't notice. A new determination replaced the nanny's sadness.

Her face lit with hope. "There is more to this life than what we've seen here." She held up one of Ren's diamond-studded chiffon panels. "Everything here is about living for ourselves. Seizing the moment. Living it up. They say it's for the good of all, but it's really only for the good of those who rule *the all*. But there's more." She let the panel drop. "You see that, don't you?"

Ren wanted to agree, but she hadn't gotten past the awful truth of her origin. It was too much to process. No wonder the folks at Snowshoe locked her in Dart's room.

"Love." Bala continued. "That word means nothing here. We love caftewater and a good vid, but we don't love each other. People are matched based on their genetics and profitability, not love. And even then, it doesn't last. Children don't know the love of a parent. Parents don't grow with their kids. There's no love. But with them, that's all they have. Did they tell you about the Leader?"

Ren shook her head. Bala's words came at her like a tornado sweeping her up and throwing everything into utter chaos.

"I was never sure back then. But now..." The disk blinked to red and back, and Bala reeled in her love talk. "We don't have much time. With Olivope captured, Tatief will want Altrist even more."

Bala talked faster. "I don't know their plan, but they think you have information you're not telling. They said you saw Altrist on your first day?"

Ren dialed her senses back and tried to focus. "Yes, from the transport. I saw him through the gift."

Bala smiled. "The gift." The light on the disk blinked faster. "We've got to go. Let me do the talking in there."

The light on the device went out, and Ren's heart jumped into the swirling mess inside of her. Bala's little confessional may have eased the nanny's conscience, but it splintered Ren's insides into a jumbled mess with words like unwanted, mistake, deviant, and worthless bubbling to the top.

And now, she was about to stand before the master of all and prove her loyalty and worth, but her ability to do that diminished by the second. She couldn't stop thinking about a past she couldn't remember with a father who loved her and a mother who killed him. What did that make her?

CHAPTER 43

THE CYLINDER

The partition didn't slow Owen this time. He strode past the guards and straight to the edge of the metal table where Olivope lay, barely breathing and whiter than he thought possible.

The sight choked him. A thousand *I'm sorries* crammed into his head, but none made it to his lips.

The sentries in the outer room guffawed. They had been playing an RP game when Owen breezed by. Olivope wasn't much of a concern for them. Not in this state, at least.

Pulling a chair close, he reached for her hand. Icy and still. Her glow had died out. Now, she looked like a normal girl. Except for the white hair and clothes, she might have fit right in.

But there was nothing normal about her. She'd helped him. She'd cleared his head and told him the truth, and he betrayed her. Just like he had Tylon.

"What kind of person am I?" He bowed his head and hoped the answer to that question hadn't been settled yet.

His mistakes ran like a highlight reel through his mind. Praise and inward assurances he was doing the right *thing* accompanied most of them.

The right thing looked different to him now. Somewhere between agreeing to spy on Ren and watching Tatief show no mercy to Olivope, Owen's idea of what truly made a good life had changed.

To everyone else, he'd sacrificed for the good of all. But he knew the truth. It burned in the sky with the stars, and it captured his heart one night with Ren in the field as the moon climbed over the trees. It rang in Olivope's entreaty about the truth. His heart felt it, and though his mind couldn't explain it, he knew it was real. Nameless, but real.

"There is more." Saying it out loud relieved the pressure building inside. "I know there is more. There has to be."

He waited, longing to hear Olivope's voice in his head. Was she still there? Had Tatief somehow stolen all of her and left only a shell?

"I'm so sorry, Olivope. I'm so sorry." He couldn't finish. Tears threatened, and the last thing he needed was to be seen crying at the side of the master's enemy.

She looked so cold lying on the table, cuffed to chains. Lamps overhead seemed to be pulling energy instead of giving light. They sucked it from her.

Owen swiped a blanket and spread it across her. Silver cuffs held her hands and feet in place. Each cuff had an oval that glowed a soft red where a key might go. Owen's hand went to the cylinder in his pocket He wondered about Eviah's test.

Another burst of laughter from the guards gave him the boost he needed, and he pulled the cylinder out and twisted the end. The part with Eviah's thumb print popped to the top.

Owen pressed it in the oval, then pushed a button on the other end of the tube. A quiet click told him it worked, and he loosened the cuff just enough. It took him a few seconds to free her from the other cuffs. He couldn't get her out on his own, but this would be a start.

"Are you Owen?" A deep voice called from the partition, and the sound of footsteps echoed in the room.

Owen tucked the cylinder back into his pocket before he turned around. "Yes."

A large sentry held a clip-pad and looked back and forth between the screen and Owen's face. "The Warrior says it's time."

Owen swallowed. "Good. Well, then everything looks good here." He breezed by the guard and the others still playing their cards. "Carry on."

Tatief's private residence looked a lot like the master. Sharp edges, dark wood, and expensive furnishings.

"It's about time you got here." Eviah motioned for Owen from a double doorway "If you'd arrived any later, they would have locked you outside. No one enters after the master. He loves the entrance, you know." She guided Owen down the dimly lit hallway. "Everyone else is already here."

"Everyone else?" He kept step with her.

She ignored his question. "I trust you are ready for what's about to happen."

"And what's that?"

Her hand paused on the golden handle of a shiny black door. "The master's about to get what he wants." She pushed it open before he could respond.

A grand hall swallowed him as he walked across the threshold. Cone-shaped, the ceiling ended in an immense circle of black sky and stars. It wasn't the real sky. Even though they were underground, Owen was certain the day hadn't melted to dark yet.

Two rows of sentries lined the carpeted entryway like they had at the Golden Horizon when Owen first met the master. To the right stood Pandon.

"What's he doing?" Owen dropped his question when his eyes met Ren's. She looked like she belonged in a place like this. Sparkling diamonds sprinkled the top and bottom of her deep blue outfit. Her eyes smiled, though her face looked more serious than he'd seen before. The makeup gave her a guardian-like presence.

Bala didn't acknowledge him, except for a slight softening of her solemn face. If she had warned Ren, he couldn't tell. He joined them as they stood in line waiting for their master.

This might be his only chance to say anything to Ren. It wouldn't take much for them to find out he'd freed Olivope from her restraints. If anyone cared to check the cameras, they'd know. If Tylon happened to look, he could toss the truth into the air for all to see.

The thought didn't scare him. He didn't regret what he'd done, but he would regret not setting the record straight with Ren.

His heart threatened to beat right out of his chest. He glanced at Bala. She seemed to be off in her own contemplation. Ren's eyes caught his, and he couldn't breathe.

The connection boosted him enough to speak. "You didn't have to run away." It was the only thing he could think to say that might convey his loyalty to her.

Pandon slid next to Ren. "Oh, but if she hadn't run away, she probably wouldn't be here." He raised his hands to the glorious room. "And here is much better than what could have happened to her." The snake's lips curled upward.

Owen met Pandon eye to eye. "What are you doing here? Shouldn't you be skulking around an alley or something?"

Bala gripped Owen's arm. "Pandon is not who you believe him to be."

Pandon smirked, and Eviah interrupted their exchange.

"Ladies and gentlemen ..." The Superintendre took her place at the end of a row of sentries. "I present to you our master, the savior of our world as we know it, the Lord Tatief." The lights in the room went up, and Tatief roared through the doorway, his gaze blazing around the room and landing on Ren.

"Thank you for coming." He stopped in the middle. "These are exciting times. Do you feel it? I can feel it." An electricity filled the air. Tatief pumped his charisma into the room with every word. "We are close. Our victory awaits us." The air swirled with rich cologne and power. "We will prove our superiority. Our enemies will bow before us, and the world will recognize who I am."

He owned the room. Even if he weren't the leader of the surviving world, he would be the leader of something. It was hard to even think. His presence filled up every space. Perhaps he, himself, was the drug that clouded the thoughts of men.

Owen remembered Olivope's gentle touch as she cleared the cobwebs away.

Tatief pulled him back. "You've got to see this." He

turned, as if something were behind him. "What? Where is he? Tylon, get in here." A sentry pulled a side door open to reveal Tylon juggling images in the air. He waved his hand, and they dissolved. Tatief growled. "Get in here and show them."

Tylon strolled in, cast a withering eye Owen's way, and then tossed an image into the air. It was Jasper, commanding a squadron of sentries as they attacked an energy field.

"What is it?" Pandon moved closer.

"Well, I can't be sure." A smile carried Tatief's guess. "But I would say it's an aberration from one of the outliers. Some kind of force field that hides them and prevents anyone from getting in or out. Are you familiar with it, dear?" His question fell to Eviah.

"No, master. This must be a new aberration. I've not seen it." A sad sheen crossed her eyes for a second, then melted into nothingness.

"Yes, I imagine this is something they've just cultivated within the last few years. But it's not the Silver Rim. It can be penetrated." His hands clapped together. "We've got them." A sick heat roiled through the room. "And you, Master Owen, you played a huge part in this."

Owen clenched his teeth.

"If not for your deliverance of Olivope, we would need to beat the truth out of someone." His eyes wandered to Ren, and then to Bala. "But now, now we can have some fun."

"Fun, sir?" Eviah sounded like she was ready to leave.

He swirled around her. "Yes, my wonderful Warrior. Fun." With a flourish, he waved his hand in the air and a burst of flames shot out across the floor, revealing the letter T. Scarlet red glossed the shape across the black marble floor. "Let's put them to the test."

Owen's heart dropped. He wouldn't do this again. He couldn't. Let his face glow on the Kirkenwall. He wouldn't betray Ren.

Eviah took slow steps to her spot on the T, while Tatief practically glided to his.

"And now let's hear from the candidates." Pandon and Tylon stood on either side of the gangplank of the T.

"Owen, over here." Tatief put up a hand. "You can stand next to me."

Owen didn't move.

Tatief didn't notice. The mighty despot reveled in his power. "And let's see. I think we should hear from the nanny first. What do you say, Eviah? Which shall it be? The nanny or the runaway?"

CHAPTER 44

THE RESCUE

"It has to be Dart." Altrist hushed the protests. Gander started to speak, but then backed down. Altrist continued. "I can't go. Tatief will sense immediately if I'm on the premises. And Liza isn't the right choice for this. I think we all know that." His eyes connected with Liza's. She nodded and looked down.

"Dart is the only choice." Altrist rested a warm hand on her shoulder. "She's the best choice. With her new gift, I can guide her in, and with her special skill set, she can handle the sentries and navigate the Plateau without being seen."

At that, Dart looked down. The skills he referred to had been nothing to boast about before.

Gander spoke next. His deep voice filled the tiny room they were all crammed into. "You're right. She can handle herself just fine." The ex-sentry patted her head, and a sweet release of courage burst through her. His gift. She drank it up.

"We have to act fast." Altrist paced. "He will drain Olivope, take her gifts, suck her dry. We need to get her away from him, and then, we'll figure out how to restore her."

Dart checked the faces of her friends. She'd been gone for a day, and everything had fallen apart. "I'm sorry about Ren."

Altrist stopped and placed his hands on her shoulders. "No, it is what it is. She made her choice, and if we can help her, we will. We'll trust the Leader on this one."

The mention of the Leader filled Dart with hope.

Thim squeezed into the dank hideaway. "They're gone." Faces fell, and Altrist's glow dimmed. "Frish and his group have hunkered down at Snowshoe, and when the others heard about Ren and Olivope, they left. And they took Buddy and Buck."

"Well, we thought that might happen." The messenger sounded old, weary.

"Why did they leave? I don't get it. The exiled desert their packs. The village bait turn one another in. I thought we all stuck together." Dart's heart thudded in her ears.

Gander heavy sighed. "They're scared, and they can't see past it."

"So, they're just going to hide and do nothing."

Altrist gripped Dart's arm. "We can't make them choose this road. And we don't have time to worry about them." He jerked his head toward Thim. "Any word on Anna and her son?"

"No, they all split up. Two of the groups that went with Olivope made it back, but the third is still missing."

"We'll look for them after Olivope." Altrist jumped back into mission mode, but Dart couldn't quite get there. It hurt to see these people she loved deserting one another.

"Okay. Dart, I'll guide you to the Plateau as best I can. I've been there a few times, but it's been a while. I can get you to Tatief's residence. My guess would be Olivope is there. He would keep her close." Altrist's eyes had a fire to them now.

"How's that going to work?" Dart slumped against the damp wall of the tunnel. She'd only teleported once, and her record of winning at sentry fights was zero for three. "You might be overestimating my abilities."

"I'll bring you back if you get in over your head." Altrist gripped her shoulders and looked her full in the face. She wondered if he was standing on his toes. "What do you say, Dart? Are you up to it?"

The caged moon orb flickered over their heads. She loved these faces. She would do anything for them. With a sigh, she consented. "Why not? Heart of the Plateau, crazy, impossible plan, and a thousand guardians wanting to kill me, what's not to love?"

"Perfect." Altrist smacked his hands together, then reached into a satchel and pulled out something black. "You'll need this."

The silky cloth had a feathery weight to it, like nothing Dart had ever felt.

"And this." Gander held out a silver belt. Not the normal practical belt that she would have worn, but a guardian belt—one that carried with it station and purpose.

"What are these? And how did you get them?"

Liza giggled and led Dart from the group. "Come with me. I'll help you get changed. You're going to be the perfect iteration of a junior guardian."

"Are you ready?" Altrist spoke into Dart's head. It was just the two of them, above ground now in the woods. "I think it's almost time."

"You sure? I don't feel anything. Last time, I felt something before it started." Dart's voice shook.

Altrist grabbed her hand. "It will be okay. I promise." His blue eyes sparkled. She believed him. "I'll have you the entire time. It's like a fishing line, and when it's time, I'll reel you back." He spoke out loud this time.

"I'm trying to believe you. It's just I don't know enough about this gift. What if it doesn't activate itself again?" A breeze swirled around them. Trees hid the sun as it approached the horizon. Soon they'd be in the dark.

"Activate?" Altrist's glow pulsed as he stifled a laugh. "I'm sure everything will *activate* at just the right time." As he spoke, she felt it. Warmth spread across her middle like a wave reaching up to the riverbank.

"It's happening." She closed her eyes.

Altrist hummed in her head. "I'll be here. Waiting. Holding on to you. Now, just be light, and I'll try to guide you to the Plateau." The world fell away, and Dart shot up into the air, but not the air she knew. No, now she slipped between worlds, places, areas. Spread out, but still close. The movement applied pressure to her chest, and she held her breath.

A shot of cool air blew her hair from her shoulders, and she gasped. She screamed for Altrist in her head, but all she could hear now was a faint humming, somewhere far back in her mind. And then falling, and colors, then heat, and something slowed her. The humming slowed and grew faint, then increased with a smash, and she felt solid ground beneath her feet.

As she eased her eyes open, the humming fell away, replaced by a slow melody and someone saying, "If you want it, you can have it." The sound came from a speaker over the doorway. She sat in some sort of classroom. Alone.

"I'm here," she whispered. After she spoke, she realized she wasn't sure if here was actually the destination they'd desired. Taking a breath, she steadied herself, then headed for the doorway.

The door opened into an octagonal room filled with about fifty people dressed in black and all looking like they knew exactly where they were. Dart eased into the crowd. She did not blend in. Everyone here wore more casual clothes, none with a belt, and all looking like they stepped out of some advertisement for a matchment service.

A girl bumped into Dart. "Excuse..." The girl stopped. "Oh, I'm sorry. I didn't realize ...." She ran off before Dart could say anything.

The people closest to her moved away. Not good. Dart spotted the exit.

"Hey, what are you doing here?" A man's voice came from behind her.

Dart's mind raced. This was way beyond anything she'd ever done. Fooling Sully and his goons or even a sentry in a village was one thing. Standing in a den of guardians with nothing but her wits was another.

People are the same. She looked around again. They were all just trying to hide their sadness, ignoring their pain, be better, smarter, more than the next person. *No different.* Same dark hearts. Same lost minds. Turning on her heel, she met her questioner.

A guardian sentry, tall, experienced, and smart. "Aren't you a little out-of-place down here?"

Dart grinned. Not a real grin. The fake one. The act had begun. "I was looking for one of them?"

"Them?" He had the eyes of a sentry—deadened, dark, and blind to anything that might recommend him to something better, brighter, or real.

She met those eyes and smiled again. Let him fill in the blank. She waited.

And then something took hold, and his face lit with purpose. "Yeah, I hear you. They're not here, though." He leaned close. "With the Master."

Dart turned her head from his meaty breath. "Oh."

"But have you seen the other *one*?" He stayed near.

"No."

"Oh, you've got to see the other one. I thought all the junior masters went through today. Weren't you with them?"

"No." It seemed wise to not elaborate.

"Well, then come on. This is better than any new pet project." He led her through the crowd to a doorway she hadn't noticed before. "I mean, it's supposed to be powerful, but there's no way it could ever have been as awesome as him. No way. Still, they keep it heavily guarded. I don't get why. It's practically dead now—sucked its energy or light or whatever it has right out of it."

The more the guy talked, the more Dart wanted to slip her hands around his neck and make him stop, but she didn't. She let him lead, and she followed—followed and hoped.

They traveled a series of black tunnels located underneath the underground fortress. Dart stayed close, throwing in a comment here and there to keep the sentry talking.

He stopped at a doorway. "Do you want to swipe in?"

Her heart jumped to her throat, but she choked out a no.

"Suit yourself. But if you're going to get credit for the observation, then you'll need to sign off somehow. The guys inside won't help you."

The door beeped open, and Dart heard the faintest whisper of hope. Olivope.

CHAPTER 45

THE OFFER TO TRUST

Ren's hands shook. The shaking started as soon as they entered Tatief's private residence and grew progressively worse.

Tatief waited, and her heart pounded. She could almost hear the molecules of blood jostling one another as they fled through her veins. Guardians and sentries surrounded them. She faced Tatief, the Superintendre, and Owen, but they weren't looking at her.

The question had gone to Bala. What do you offer that makes you worthy of life? Bala didn't look like she had any inclination to give them what they wanted.

Tatief towered over her. The build of a sentry and the expert touch of Hillton added to his natural magnetism. His thick brown hair was pulled back. The hint of body art peeked from his collar. The vids hadn't done him justice. Fierce, powerful, and commanding, his handsome face captivated and threatened all at the same time.

"What will it be, nanny?" Tatief's voice echoed off the high ceiling. "What do you offer to prove *your* contribution to society?" A slow grin twitched at his pink lips. "You once were a guardian sentry, but your time outside the boundary tainted you. Such a pity. I hear you had great promise."

Bala stood straight, feet apart, chin up. Her eyes sparkled, not like Ren's but with the strength that comes from knowing who you are and what you believe. Ren expected to see at least some glimmer of fear or anger, but there was none. Bala's voice was sure. "You want us to offer you something that would buy us back from accomplishment. Is that correct?"

Ren's heart dropped. *Accomplishment.*

The Superintendre got in Bala's face. "You don't question the master." Every time that woman spoke, Ren's blood picked up speed like lightning cutting through air, fueled by a mixture of anger and injustice.

Tatief waved his hand and pulled the Warrior back. "Let her speak." His silky command carried a threat—not to the Superintendre, but to Bala. "Yes, that's correct. It's a fair game. Everyone has to walk the plank, eventually."

The sentries chuckled. Owen looked down.

Ren wanted to grab Bala's hand, pull her back. There had to be some way out of this. Bala had said to let her do the talking. Ren wanted to scream, yell, do something, but she didn't. She just stood there. Unsure and weak and falling to pieces.

The nanny marched onward. "And that's what it is to you, isn't it? A game. We're two simple people who, when all is said and done, mean nothing to you. Nothing at all."

Tatief's countenance took a sharper gleam. "Do you have something or not?"

"I do have something." Conviction filled out Bala's words. Ren wanted to shush her. Tell her to lie, make something up. But the nanny kept on. "I have a message for you."

"Message?" The air grew hot and sickly perfumed. Tatief was power. He controlled them all, except for Bala.

"Eighteen years ago, I worshipped you. You were the savior. You protected us from dilution, contamination, and a weak society. With you, we were strong. The world was ours. I accomplished people when the order came." Her voice quivered. "I went on rounds and hunts, and when you needed a spy, I jumped at it."

She took a slow step toward the top of the red T on the floor. Her voice grew softer. "And then everything changed. I saw what being cared for and loved meant."

A spray of hot tingles raged up the back of Ren's head. *Not now. Not here.* Closing her eyes, she took a deep breath. *Exhale. Focus.* Another deep breath and the tingles dampened, but in the darkness of her closed eyes, a light peeked through, and she heard a man's voice.

"Trust me," he whispered. She pulled in a warm breath and exhaled slowly, concentrating and pushing the tingles away.

"Whose are you?" The whisper drowned out Bala and the others. "Trust me, or trust him."

Or trust neither of you.

"Trusting no one is to be his. Relying on yourself is to follow him." The light and tingles subsided, but the threat of more lingered. Ren clutched the jeweled panels of her outfit so tightly the stones pricked her palms.

"Yes, it sounds crazy." Bala's voice drew Ren from the edges of her aberration. The nanny addressed the sneering faces of her audience. "For years after I returned, I wondered the same thing. I doubted it—figured I'd imagined it. How could it possibly be true?"

Her focus landed on Tatief, his arms crossed and death in his eyes. "How could anyone ever be more powerful than the mighty Tatief?"

Another rage of tingles shot up Ren's back and exploded in her head.

Bala continued, "And then the Warrior sent for me to get the truth from the girl. I, of course, came back. Not because of the promise of power, but because of the promise of truth, and I found it."

Cool air whooshed across the seething room. "I found the truth." Bala paused, then picked up speed. "You fear love. The Warrior runs from it. Owen denies it. Others of you laugh, but I can see you're scared. And you—" Her aim fell back on the master. "You hate it. You hate it with more force than anything in the world, and in that hate lies your greatest fear. Love will win. It was always going to win. He gave you room so the world could see how wrong you are."

Ren shivered as Bala charged. The nanny was sealing her own fate, and Ren couldn't stop it. *No. Please no.* But the words stayed silent, ricocheting around the swirl of sparkles in her head. Ren couldn't stop this. She was the same broken Ren she always was—the unsanctioned rendition of what happens when a guardian spy tricks a kindhearted man outside the boundary. Just an aberrant—a useless parasite, weakening society and hurting those closest to her.

This was her fault—the awful retribution for hiding her aberration. And a thousand sprinkles of light exploded across her mind and left her immobile and watching her only friend fight a losing battle. The vision would soon consume her. No amount of concentration would stop it. And they'd both be accomplished before the day was out.

Tatief growled, starting low and growing. His eyes blazed. Ren watched the scene through cascading lights in her mind.

Bala continued, fierce and sure. "Yes, I have a message for you. For all of you. Love is real, and he is coming for you." Before her words left the air, Tatief struck her to the floor, then he kicked her. Ren screamed, and a sentry grabbed her tingling arms.

Owen went to Bala's crumpled form and shielded her with his body. "Sir, please."

Tatief waved his hand, and Owen slid sideways ten meters. "Stay out of this, boy."

Bala coughed blood and pushed herself up, but Tatief put his foot on her back and forced her down. "I think we have a winner, folks. The nanny for accomplishment.

CHAPTER 46

THE SECRET EXPOSED

As Owen got to his feet, an alarm reverberated through Tatief's grand hall. The chaos in the moment disoriented the heartsick guide. Sentries poured into the room. A white light flashed above them, and the siren bounced off the wood and granite. Bala lay still. Ren stood, her eyes closed, with a scinter aimed at her throat.

"Sir." Tylon crossed out of line and tossed images into the air. "The prisoner. Look."

A blonde guardian sat on the floor in a darkened room with Olivope in her arms. She called out to the air, "Now, would be a good time." Three sentries lay nearby, unconscious. "Altrist, come on. I've got Olivope, but I don't know where Ren is." As she spoke, a light grew from her abdomen and engulfed the two, and they vanished into the brightness.

Owen steadied himself. She was free. Olivope was safe. He checked Eviah, but the Warrior stood aloof. A miracle had just occurred, and she didn't flinch. He couldn't do the same. The wonder of it took flight in his head and made him think there might still be hope.

Tatief roared, drowning out the alarm, and the sentries jumped to alert. For a second, the master looked more like an animal than a man. His tanned face flushed with red. "Play it again."

Tylon waved his hand in the air, and the image rewound.

"Altrist, come on. I've got Olivope, but I don't know where Ren is."

"Stop." Tatief turned on Ren. "You." He flicked his wrist, and Ren rose off the floor like a broken marionette. "Do you know who that girl is?"

Tylon's image repeated silently in the air. Owen held his breath, and Ren nodded.

Narrowing his eyes, Tatief pulled her closer. "Why would they want you?"

Ren stayed silent.

Tatief walked around her. "It's not over, you know. I may have underestimated the fighting qualities of his aberrant ones, but I have him on the run, and Olivope will be no help." He paused behind Ren and leaned close to her ear. "But he didn't just want Olivope. He sought to rescue you, as well. What's so special about you?"

Owen inched closer. From a few meters away, he could see Ren shaking. Bala moaned and attempted to stand, but Eviah held her in place with the safe end of her skeer.

The choices you make affect far more than you know.

Olivope's words pushed Owen forward. He needed to think fast and do something or Tatief would flick his wrist and Ren would be gone. Suspended in the air, she hung at the whim of the master, her sweet face tilted downward, eyes closed, and determination creasing the space in between her eyebrows. The alarm still blared through the hall, and Tatief still stalked his prey.

As the master finished circling Ren, he brought her back to the floor. Her legs buckled and a sentry forced her back to her feet. Tatief's voice took a softer turn. "Why do they want you?"

Ren shook her head, and a tear escaped her closed eye. A sparkle faded in the drop as it traced its way down her cheek.

No. The aberration had her, and Owen rushed to her side. "Perhaps I can help."

Tatief smirked. "I think you've exceeded your usefulness." He nodded, and two sentries latched on to Owen.

"Wait, I know why they want Ren." His heart smacked its way into his throat. "I know what they want." The sentries loosened their grip, and Owen clutched Ren's arm and whispered in her ear. "When the order says not to walk, you run." It was cryptic, but he wasn't sure how else to clue her in that he wasn't really giving her up to the monster.

Eviah glared at him, but Owen seized the floor. Drawing on his new reservoir of hope, he gave Tatief what he wanted. "They know her secret."

The room slowed for a beat. For a split second, it seemed even the alarm had stopped.

Tatief leveled his fierceness at Owen. "What secret?" A fire smoldered behind the tyrant's blue eyes.

Owen plunged on like he slept with the guidelines under his pillow. "She is an aberrant. She has a gift." This time the alarm really did stop, and the words echoed in the room. Owen felt Ren move a thousand miles away. He wanted to pull her back like their moment in the field, but he didn't. This was her one shot. Tatief would find out about the gift soon enough. Better it happened with a frame around it and tied neatly into purpose.

Eviah shook her head and glared, but Owen pressed on. "They know about it, and they want it."

"Really?" Tatief smelled of smoke and cologne. "Is that true?" He whipped his attention to Ren. "Do you have an ability?"

Before Ren could respond, Pandon broke ranks. "Wait, she has an aberration?" He gave Ren a look. "That nit has a gift? What can she do? I've seen her. The guide's playing you."

Like a Master Guardian, Owen dismissed him. "Stand down. Not every girl bares it all for you."

"Is that how you came to obtain this information?" Tatief stepped between them. "She trusted you, and now you give her up." A subtle glee tinged Tatief's question.

Owen took aim again. "I'm not giving her up." He could feel Tylon glaring. "I'm not doing anything she hasn't wanted to do all her life—to simply be herself and not hide."

"It's true." Ren's glowing eyes opened, and she took them captive. "I can see things." Her voice trembled, and Owen wished he could harness the energy pumping through his veins and give it to her.

Tatief pulled her closer.

"And what do you see?" The glow from Ren's eyes shown in Tatief's.

"I see Altrist and Olivope mourning for their brother." Her voice grew stronger. "That was long ago. Now, they fight a battle they cannot win."

"Yes." Tatief was so close, Owen wondered if he could see the vision too. "What else do you see?"

"Their victory falls to another." Ren's sureness grew. "He is powerful. Unmatched. And the Silver Rim will break before him that the world might know his incomparable preeminence." Her voice grew stronger with each word.

"Bravo." Tatief slapped his hands together. "Brilliant." The others in the room offered tentative splays of applause. Ren drew in a breath, and her eyes returned to their normal hue. She took a step back like she'd just been hit in the gut.

Eviah moved between Tatief and Ren. "That's why they want her." A tremor replaced the fierceness in the Warrior's voice. "That's why they're willing to risk a rescue." The words weren't exactly what Owen had thought to use, but they would work. He watched Tatief to see if the seed would take root.

Tatief drew back. "They want her." He eyed Ren like she was his new trophy. "Or perhaps they don't want me to have her." His tone shifted back into smooth politician, and he spoke louder.

"These insurgents rebel against what we've built. They try to destroy it with their rejection of the simple plans from which we thrive. They steal from us and hide away in their holes and caves, but that's not even the worst of it. Above everything, they refuse to do what is for the good of all."

And there it was. The lasso he used to pull everyone into his charade. Owen could see it clearer now. The sham of power. The lies.

Tatief led people to where he wanted them to go, which was nowhere at all. He proffered advancement, luxury, and every kind of indulgence requiring only one thing from his followers. Everything. For the good of all, we give ourselves. He twisted what should be a heartfelt gift into an essential obligation. He didn't want people to give themselves. What he wanted was for people never to be themselves.

Owen stayed silent as the others chanted back the expected reply. Tatief didn't notice. He reveled in his ability to pull the strings.

Ren caught Owen's eye. She was a sweet squirrel, and with any luck, her aberration would be her ticket out of the Plateau. He just needed to plant a seed in the ground Eviah had plowed.

"Sir, do you think their failed attempt at a rescue will be the last?" Owen held his breath.

"No." Tatief growled, and the sentries snapped to attention. "No, Altrist won't give up easily, so we'll need to stay ahead of him." His eyes sliced to Ren. "And you're going to help me."

Ren looked as if she'd gotten jolted awake.

"You saw it. There's no hope for them." He grabbed Ren's wrist where Eviah's bracelet still blinked. "You're going to be my spy this time."

Ren shook her head.

Bala made it to her feet. "No." With just one arm, she disarmed a sentry and took his scinter, but Pandon intervened and planted his weapon into Bala's side. The nanny thudded to the floor, motionless and silent.

Ren screamed and ran to her. Limp and lifeless, Bala didn't respond.

Tatief strolled to Ren's side. "I can save her, but you must do something for me first." His words fell like arrows. "It's your choice."

"Please." A spark lit one of Ren's eyes.

Tatief patted her cheek. "Good girl. Now, Eviah, prepare our little spy. And Pandon, come with me. I have an assignment for you."

With that, Tatief bolted from the room. Pandon and Tylon trailed after him as if they were pups, hoping for a treat. Eviah barked at the sentries, sending them in different directions, and then grabbed Owen.

"You better hope this works." Her cold hands twisted his coverup by his neck. "I'll take care of the nanny and see to Ren's assignment, but there's something I need you to do first."

The urge to scream and tell her to do her own work crossed Owen's mind, but he remained compliant. She drew closer, her eyes fierce.

"Promise me you'll do what I ask, and I'll let you say goodbye to her."

Owen drove his own bargain. "You'll get her out of here, right?"

Eviah's face softened, and he *saw*—the familiar curve of the mouth, the nose, and the pushy attitude. His eyes looked between the Warrior and Ren, and he knew Eviah would help Ren. She had to—her heart was invested.

He didn't wait for her to reply. "I'll do what you ask." Whatever she wanted, he would do.

CHAPTER 47

THE UNDOING OF REN

The image of Bala lifeless on the floor appeared every time Ren closed her eyes. The loss of her closest friend changed things.

She didn't care Owen had blabbed her secret at probably the worst time ever. He was right. She was tired of hiding. Tired of everything in her life eventually revolving around the aberration, or gift, or whatever, and keeping it a secret—tired of her being a secret. Her very existence should have never occurred. She didn't belong.

Hillton mussed with her hair, and the rest of her felt frozen, stuck in some alternate reality. A plain gray coverup replaced her beautiful starry night outfit from yesterday.

"You really should drink something." Hillton pinned her poof into a messy bun. Ren eyed the liquid and declined. She could barely think as it was.

One of Tatief's directors, in a black silk coverup and light blue pants, had not left her side. He'd relayed Tatief's plan, but Ren had only half listened. The guy stood near the door now, offering updates in his comms every few seconds. It was a play by play of her deconstruction.

They would dump her somewhere beyond the boundary—somewhere an Altrist follower would find her. She would lure them into trusting her while Tatief and his special guard planned their attack. And all would be well. The master's minion assured her the world would be better for this. And Bala would be okay.

Bala.

The thought brought another lump to Ren's throat. She had stifled the urge to cry and scream a thousand times in the last twenty-four hours.

"I think this is the best I can do." Hillton stepped back and made tsk noises.

The sentry guard put his hand to the device in his ear, then jumped to attention. "Make ready one and all, the master approaches."

Hillton took a guzzle from Ren's full glass then spruced his white wig in the mirror. Swiveling the chair, Ren waited. Mirrors lined the doorway, and she caught her reflection. She almost looked like her old self, but she wasn't. She couldn't go back to that girl again. No matter how much they promised she could. That Ren was dying or dead, a casualty of learning the truth and not being willing to return to the lie.

"Make ready for his incomparable preeminence." The guard picked up on Ren's earlier vision, and two lines of sentries poured in, creating a corridor for their master. The Superintendre and Tylon topped off the line. Then, Tatief strode in, his eyes blazing.

"Well done, Hillton. You never disappoint. Ren, are you ready?" Tatief held his hand out. The owner of their world. The savior who said he'd created the Silver Rim to protect them. The decider of her fate held out his hand as if he were offering her a stroll around the park.

She thought about refusing him, of telling everyone what Altrist had said. Not that they would believe her, but at least truth would have been spoken. And maybe years from now, someone would repeat her words and think they might be true.

Instead, she put her hand in his and met his blue eyes. He led her to the center of the room.

"I appreciate you may have some reservations, but let me assure you. You are doing the right thing." His voice sounded like warm honey. A far cry from the low, harsh tones he growled out the day before.

"Bala?" Ren left Tatief's gaze and looked at the Superintendre.

The Warrior joined them. "Your nanny is awaiting the healing work of our master." Ren understood. *Do what we say, and we'll help her.* That's what she meant.

Tatief held her hand tighter in his hot grasp. "Yes. I will do all I can for her." He lied. He would never save her. Bala had defied him. She'd rejected him. His pride would never forgive such disloyalty.

He snaked onward. "Right now, you need to focus on your mission." He released her and spun her around. "Is she outfitted?"

The director at the door moved forward. "Yes, sir."

"And the tracking device."

"But of course." The Superintendre spoke this time.

"And Tylon?"

Owen's old friend stepped forward. "Yes, master. I see all."

"Well then, most everything appears to be in order." Tatief shifted his eyes, and the Superintendre and director fell back in line. "Just one more thing." His gaze fastened on Ren.

A cool spray of tingles surged up her back, but she held her breath and willed the gift away—the revelation from her last vision still bit like a frigid wind scraping across her bare heart. Any more bad news, and the world might completely cave in.

Tatief leaned a fraction closer. Ren stayed perfectly still, obeying—looking the same, but crumbling inside.

"It's important for you to comprehend the truth." Hearing him proffer truth skewered Ren's foundation. Years with Bala made Tatief's lies easy to see but not easy to process when standing in front of him. He delivered everything with confidence and passion. It was hard not to believe him, even though she knew beyond a doubt she shouldn't.

"And I want everyone to hear this, as well." He surveyed his followers. "These are dangerous people." His force fell on Ren. "You've been with them, and they've told you things and shown you their *gifts*. But they are not what they seem. They want *your* gift, and that is all. They care nothing for you." Concern glossed his smooth face. "They offer you nothing like what we have here. Their world is filled with hiding in holes and stories that will never come true."

Ren's heart pounded. Her brain screamed for her to question him, to point out what she saw at Snowshoe, to be brave like Bala, but she couldn't. That wasn't her. Bala's genetic code had nothing to do with the blood flowing through her veins. Ren's birthright was based on a lie and delivered in violence. Still, one query peeked through the darkness. One name she'd heard Altrist, Dart, and Bala say: "The Leader?"

Tatief pulled her closer like a friend or a father. "The leader is their biggest lie of all." The sureness of his statement dampened her hope. Tatief continued, his voice smooth, like he knew she faltered. "They long for someone to help them, but there is no one. The Leader doesn't exist except in their stories. I am their hope, but they refuse me. I only want to bring them back—to keep them safe."

The Superintendre joined them, her words just as smooth as his. "Incomparable preeminence." Ren flinched. She couldn't look at the Warrior. She couldn't breathe. The tingles ramped up again, and she closed her eyes and fisted her hands.

"Yes." Tatief spoke softer. "And Ren can be a part of my preeminence." He took her fists into his grasp. "Ren, you can help them. Bring them to me, and I will save them. Will you help me?" She swallowed and eased her eyes open. Bala would say no, but Bala wasn't her mother. The words of defiance stuck in Ren's throat.

He pressed on. "Will you take on this challenge? Play your part? Will you help us bring these wayward ones back for the good of all.

The room exploded with the mantra. "We give ourselves."

Ren swayed, lost in his power. All her hopes of figuring out her place in the world, mastering the aberration, and living a simple life succumbed to reality. The real truth—the one where she hurt more than helped. The reality that people can only be what their DNA says they will be, and some people aren't meant to be at all.

Her circle would complete itself here—being led into her mother's footsteps and to Tatief's feet. There was no fighting him. His presence consumed them all. His words were a drug. They captivated and corrupted.

Her body swayed under the force of his request, as if it wasn't connected to her heart. Her head nodded consent, and Tatief smiled.

He cupped her face with his hot hands and whispered into her head. "Do this for me, and I will give you everything." His persuasion was too heavy for her to restrain. "You're mine." His lips stayed still while his voice played her thoughts. "You can try to fight, but in the end, you'll see it's true. This is who you are. Mine."

CHAPTER 48

THE SECRET MISSION

Half past four, and sweat trickled down Owen's forehead. Eviah's little request was impossible.

"Are you still here?" Tylon cracked his neck and acknowledged Owen's presence. "I thought you left when I played the highlights from our raising home days." The tiny room, with just one screen and Tylon's gift filling the air with pictures from around the rim, smelled like a mixture of half-eaten veggie roll, cologne, and a ripened armpit. "I've got work to do. I actually have a job here. The master needs me."

Owen leaned over Tylon's shoulder and tried not to breathe. "What exactly are you doing?"

"I think what I'm doing is above your clearance level." If Tylon's head got any bigger, he wouldn't be able to hold it up on his lanky leather flanked frame. "Shouldn't you be off in guardian training or something?"

This wasn't working. Whatever Eviah had cooked up, she was going to have to achieve it with Tylon staying in the picture. An hour of hanging around feigning interest in his old friend's new life had divested Owen of his optimism. Not that he had much to begin with, but now his glass was drained.

Thirty minutes more, and Ren's transport would depart. If he couldn't convince Tylon to take a walk soon, then she'd be gone, and his last chance to talk to her would be lost.

"You sure you don't want to grab a bite to eat. There's a great place down by the park." Owen gave it one more try.

Tylon rolled back in his chair and tossed an image into the air. Ren. She wore plain clothes and followed a sentry through the transport station. Owen leaned toward the scene. He needed to make some kind of move soon. His hand went to the cylinder Eviah had given him, its multi-purpose usage crucial to the Warrior's little plan.

"There she is." Tylon sang the words out. "Your precious plebe about to bring the freaks or die." The tune ended on a bitter note. Tylon cackled. He was nothing like the boy Owen remembered. Too many years living here, doing Tatief's bidding had twisted his mind.

Owen checked the clock. He still had twenty-eight minutes. "So, you say you can tap into any camera or device, huh?"

The black spider painted on the back of Tylon's neck might be the perfect place to stun him. Owen considered doing the deed here, but his office was too risky. If Tylon were found, they'd have him back up and running in no time. And he would be found—sentries were in and out of here like patrolling nannies. Their presence suggested imprisonment instead of special treatment, but Tylon would never see his existence that way. His opinion of himself blocked any view of reason.

"Yep." He spun his chair around again, and Owen jerked it to a stop. "Well, what if I told you I know a place where your little gift can't reach."

"I'd tell you you're wrong. There's no place in the Plateau that I can't get to." A thin streak of eyeliner ran from each eye to his temple. His whole getup looked ridiculous, but at the Plateau anything goes. "And now, your little peach is going to take me into the hallowed ground of those freaks."

Tylon closed his eyes, shook his head, and then spat out another scene from Ren's point of view. They'd wired her with a camera somehow. "You want to monitor that one for me?" He stretched his black lips upward.

Focus. Owen ignored the scene and stayed on target. "Have you ever seen a little device with a blinking yellow light?"

The gifted guardian flipped a finger up and swiped the images away. "Those stupid, pesky things only work for a few minutes. And if I find one on someone, it's automatic accomplishing." His finger slid across his throat.

Owen stood his ground. This was it. His last play. "What if I told you I know a place that's decked out with those little suckers, insulated from your listening ears, and it's right here in the Plateau?"

"Nice try, baby guardian, but the only places like that are in the master's residence, and you ain't going there." He turned back to his desk.

"No, this is some place different—a hidden sanctuary insulated from your reach." He lowered his voice. "I could show you, if you want, but you'd have to put in a good word for me with the master." Owen wiped his palms on his pants. Adrenalin coursed through him like a current zipping through a diode on the way to deliver life to some dead device.

Tylon smirked. "You don't know any place like that."

Owen whispered, "I'll take you there, and then you can decide if you'll be my greatest fan."

"I'll never be your greatest fan." He stretched up from his chair. "But you can show the place to me, and I'll decide if I'll help you or not."

The two followed the same route Eviah had taken Owen on his second trip to the Plateau. She might flip about him giving up her underground haven, but something told Owen nothing in their lives was going back to the way it used to be. Besides, this was the best bet for getting Tylon incapacitated and tucked away.

When Owen opened the last door, Tylon screeched like a dying wild cat. Not that Owen had ever heard one of those, but the scream sounded like some kind of animal. Evidently, the devices impaired Tylon in a painful way. He went crazy around the room, crushing every device he could find.

"Whose place is this?" He collapsed on the floor and rubbed his temples. His eyeliner smeared on his palms.

Owen eased down next to him. "If I tell you that, I'm a dead man."

"You might be one of those anyway, after this." He chuckled, and then got quiet. After the frenzy of the last few minutes, the silence felt like the room breathing a sigh of relief. Owen pulled the cylinder from his pocket. The time might be now or never.

Before he could make a move, Tylon faced him. "You ever feel bad about it?' His black eyes locked with Owen's, and for a second, they were two boys crying as the sentries pulled Tylon away.

Owen swallowed and gripped the cylinder till his knuckles were white. "Yeah, always. When it first happened, I told myself I had to. That you would have done the same thing. It was for the good of all." The words stuck in Owen's throat. "But that was a lie." His eyes met his old friend's. "I'm sorry."

The moment hung between them, suspended in the air like one of Tylon's scenes. And for a second, Owen doubted carrying out Eviah's order. Perhaps Tylon could be on their side, but then he spoke.

"Don't be an idiot." The look of a master guardian crept its way back into Tylon's softened face. "You made a masterful move. Lies, deception, betrayal are what makes this work. I see it. Every. Single. Day." He moved to get up. "And I'd turn in your sorry butt in a heartbeat if I thought it would get me something good."

Without a word, Owen opened the cylinder and slammed the hot point onto the spider art hugging Tylon's neck. His friend slumped to the couch and rolled over to face him.

"Whoa. Well played. Well ... pla ..."

Owen jammed the cylinder into his pocket and ran. Nine minutes until the transport departed.

CHAPTER 49

THE DYING MESSENGER

Olivope's lifeless body lay in the twilight shade of the weeping willow tree. Liza knelt by her side, her hands moving constantly from Olivope's head to her feet. Dart stood with the small troupe in a semicircle, watching and hoping. Hours of the same had brought no signs of improvement.

With his glow diminished, Altrist scooted from Olivope's milky white feet to Liza and pulled the healer away. Collapsing into him, Liza heaved sobs and shook.

"I can't fix her. I need Anna."

Altrist stroked Liza's hair and looked at the small group of five surrounding them. "I don't think Anna will be enough."

Dart dropped to her knees. "There's got to be something we can do."

He shook his head. "The only ones who can help her now are outside the rim." Tears streamed down their faces. Even Gander cried. Outside the wall. That was a death sentence.

Dart couldn't take it. There had to be another way. She grabbed Altrist's hand. "The Leader. He can help her."

Altrist rubbed a tear from her cheek. "It's not time for him yet."

"But ..." Dart sat up. Melkin could help them. He could save Olivope. "I met him." She grabbed Altrist's hand. "I saw him. He helped me. Look." She held up the starburst.

Altrist shook his head. "No." And in her head, he spoke. "You're not supposed to tell these things, are you?" He pulled her to him. "Shhh, all will be okay."

She didn't care that Melkin had told her to keep their meeting secret. Olivope needed him. That superseded some need for secrecy, right? Dart wrestled free from Altrist's arms. "But he can help her."

The messenger spoke hushed words into her mind. "Yes, he can help her, but the way in which he helps her is not for you to decide. We stay together."

She let it drop, for now.

Altrist brightened and addressed the group. "We will go to the rim."

Grumbles rumbled around the five. Liza went back to working on Olivope. Gander stepped out of the line.

"That's not the best idea. There's not much cover near the rim, and the whole thing is under surveillance." The ex-sentry looked almost bashful, opposing Altrist's directive. His giant form dwarfed little Altrist.

"I know, but we'll need to be close."

"For what?" Gander didn't give up.

"The door to open." Altrist's glow cast a warm light on Gander's face.

"Door? What door?" The others backed Gander up. Dart stayed behind them.

"There is a doorway through the rim. It's hidden. I am familiar with the area where the door is located, near the rocks. I can't get us through it, but at least we'll be close."

The men grumbled their disapproval but didn't refute the messenger. A hidden, locked door no one had ever seen was Olivope's only hope. They had to try.

"What about the others?" Liza sat back and wiped her forehead. Her trusting voice cut through the tension. "The ones at Pocket and Snowshoe. Are we just going to leave them?"

"They left you, didn't they?" Dart's upbringing popped out of her mouth. Altrist shot her a look.

"Once we get settled at the rim, we can send two of you to let the others know the plan." Jahn and Block objected with their crossed arms and tight lips, but they didn't put words to their display. They would do what Altrist wanted, no matter how crazy it sounded.

Dart pushed the sleeves up on the silky guardian coverup and kept her mouth shut, as well. While two went to Pocket and Snowshoe, she would go and find the Leader. He could fix Olivope.

Thim joined Dart and gave her a half hug. "Good job getting Olivope out. That was really brave."

"Thanks." She found reveling in her success hard with Olivope lying motionless and the seven of them about to become sitting ducks. "I couldn't get to Ren, though. I guess we're just going to leave her too?" Altrist knelt by Olivope and didn't take the bait. The others, except for Liza, shot a harsh look Dart's way. Saving Ren wasn't on anyone's priority list.

Thim stuck his hands in his pockets. "I guess she made her choice."

"We need to tend to Olivope for now." Altrist called back to them. "Once we get settled at the rim, we'll figure out what to do about the others, including Ren. As he spoke, the whirring hum of a sentry drespin carried on the wind.

Dart held up her hand to shush him. Before she could explain, she saw the flash through the trees. A sentry pod.

A thousand points of strategy from Sully's talks lined up in Dart's head as she looked at her beloved friends. Exile strategy wasn't needed though, because the warmth of her gift had already spread from her abdomen up and out. The others sprang into action, as well. Altrist wrapped his arms around Olivope, the brightness engulfing them. Liza grabbed Jahn and Thim as the glow in her middle widened. Dart looked at the two big fellas next to her, closed her eyes, and hoped her gift could handle the extra weight.

Shouts and sparks faded into the silent whoosh of the gift, and Dart's insides pressed against her skin to get out. The three of them landed with a thud on the leafy blanket of the bluff.

Gander and Block rolled over and retched for a full minute. Dart put some distance between her and them before she did the same.

Stars peeked through the steel blue sky, and the last bits of the day gave themselves up to night. From the bluff, the world rested, peaceful and promising. The rim glowed in the distance.

"We up on Odgen Bluff?" Gander came alongside Dart. "Too bad that gift of yours can't go where we need it to."

"Yeah." The woods behind them grew darker by the minute. "Too far to walk to the rim in the night. Closer to Pocket than Snowshoe. We could try there."

Gander agreed on Pocket. The three made their way to the trail using Block's stave. The ex-sentries always came prepared. Halfway into the chirping woods, someone shouted. Gander held up a fist, and Block stepped in front of Dart. The first time any man had ever stepped between her and danger.

Another shout, more familiar this time. And the shadows tore apart in the air, revealing smiling faces, a glowing fire, and the vim drawing back like a curtain.

Gander grinned. "I think we found the Pocket group."

CHAPTER 50

THE MOTHER REVEALED

The irony of her situation deflated Ren more than she thought possible. She sat on a transport like the first day with a group of people looking forward to their new life. Fifteen others gabbed around her—transfers to the Plantanate. At least, that's what they were told.

"Where are you coming from?" A woman with a cough jarred Ren from her thoughts.

"Um, the Protectorate." She couldn't say Plateau.

The woman moved to the seat across from Ren. "This is so exciting." She coughed again. "I thought I'd go to the Progenate. I'm from Viand, but the work's gotten harder. I didn't mind getting moved down a tier or anything. Once you get to my age, the tiers don't matter as much."

As the woman rattled on about her medic check and interviews, Ren saw their tiny little world in a whole new light. Five villages, the Protectorate, the Viand, the Wall, the Progenate, and the Plateau. There were only five villages on the map. Only five villages on any map she'd ever seen. There was no Plantanate—no wonderful utopia to retire to and enjoy. The poor woman. Tatief deceived them all.

"Excuse me." A female sentry interrupted and set cool eyes on Ren. "The Superintendre would like to speak with you. Follow me."

Ren hesitated. Next to Tatief, the Superintendre was the last person she wanted to talk to. Saying no wasn't an option, though, so she dragged her hazy body up.

The guard deposited Ren in the doorway of a fancy car, all wood, carpets, red, and brass. The Superintendre motioned for Ren to sit on a red velvet settee by the window.

Hills and trees flew by, and Ren kept her gaze away from the scary goddess. The woman eased into a leather chair and faced Ren. She moved like a big cat, a tiger or lion.

"Do you know who I am?" The Superintendre shifted forward. Her dark eyes trained on Ren's. "I've known Balandria for a very long time."

Ren didn't want to talk about Bala and the good old days. "I knew a different Bala than you."

"Yes, you did." Sunshine filtered through the transport windows and lit up the jeweled bracelets cluttering the Superintendre's arm. "Tell me. What did Balandria teach you?"

Ren stole quick glances at the Warrior. "She taught me how to fight and to not trust guardians." The last statement registered in the Superintendre's eyes, and Ren's heart sped up. Lightning coursed through her like it needed to get out.

"It's good you've learned how to fight." The Superintendre spun the bangles on her arm and offered nothing more. Ren returned her focus to the window.

"We will drop you in a hunt. From there, you will be on your own. With your ability and training, you should be fine. It's the most realistic play we have to gain the insurgents' trust. It's what the master wants."

Ren stayed silent and rubbed her frigid hands together. The insurgents were friends, kind people.

The hum of the transport filled the space between them. The Superintendre moved on. "Will you do as he asks?"

The question drew Ren's eyes from the window. She had mulled its answer over in her head ever since she nodded assent to Tatief's inquiry. She knew the right answer—what they expected, and then she knew the right answer—the one Bala would give—the one Altrist and Dart needed her to say. She cleared the muck in her throat. "I don't know. Is it like I have a choice?"

"The master can be very persuasive." Her voice stayed crisp, but the edges softened. "I once had a choice to make, as well. It was a long time ago, and I believed Tatief." Her eyes went to the window. "He gave me a pep talk like yours, except with a more pointed ultimatum. I think he hated not having his eye on us, out in the wild, far from his influence."

Ren stole another look at the woman. She wore less makeup than before—her hair swept up, her coverup cut high, and her scinter strapped to her leg.

"But he still had me, even from a distance. I mean, we can see Tatief. Talk to him. Experience his magnificence. I just couldn't believe their fairytale—their made-up leader." The words and the expression on the Warrior's face didn't match. Her brokenness peeked through her scary exterior. It was heartsick and shy and wanted to be free.

But then, as if she caught herself, her eyes turned cold, and the curtain closed. "Balandria was always a fool—always looking for more. And why? Look where it's gotten her." Hills gave way to trees, and the sunlight cast shadows across the car.

The sun came back, and the spray of light stirred Ren from her silence. "A baby."

"A what?" The flush paled from the Superintendre's cheeks.

"You asked why she gave up everything, and I answered you. She gave up everything for a baby. For me." The truth settled inside Ren like a magnet drawing all the broken pieces home. "She was a mother to me."

"Mother." A laugh escaped the Warrior's red lips. "That's not a word anybody uses for anything."

Ren sat straighter and met the woman's familiar words. "I thought that too, but now I know better. She loved me, aberration and all. I wouldn't have made it without her."

The hum took hold again, and then the fierce woman leaned forward, a softer touch to her voice. "We've met before, you and me. Once, long ago."

Ren shook her head. Ever since she met the Superintendre, she had been steering clear of placing the daunting goddess anywhere in her past.

"You were six." A sheen touched the Warrior's eyes.

Blurry images jogged Ren's memory. Her sixth year was mostly a jostle of feelings—fear, anger, and relief.

"They'd brought you in for observation. Someone had accused you of an aberration. Tatief likes to gather the gifted ones early, so he can mold them and shape them or accomplish them, if they're not needed." She leaned forward and whispered. "I protected you and had your accusers and testers accomplished. I sent you back, cleared, free—an undocumented aberrant."

A faint image of a woman standing over her skittered through Ren's memory. *You're a special little one.* A strange energy hung between them, and Ren couldn't ignore it any longer. "Why? Why would you help me?"

The force drew them closer. "Because I could." Then, she grabbed Ren's arm and held up the bracelet from her first day at the Plateau. The lights on the metal blinked. "It's beautiful, isn't it?"

Ren studied the Superintendre, letting her mind wander to the place she had avoided ever since Bala first mentioned the word *mother*. The vision she'd seen when Altrist described the cabin cast a familiarity on the moment. The man and the woman. Her father and the one who betrayed him.

The Superintendre ran a finger over the lit beads of the bracelet and smiled. "I have one too." A similar bracelet mixed in with the bangles on the Superintendre's arm.

With the smell of hot metal, the transport slowed, and a sentry came to the door. "It's time."

The Superintendre released Ren with a jolt. "I'll discharge them from the rear." The sentry bowed and left.

"The choice is yours." The Warrior stood and went to the far door. "You can serve at the master's pleasure or not. But either way, he will attempt to use you. You can be sure you're not his only play." She faced Ren, a new resolve coloring her worn face. "You can't waiver. Your choice must be sure."

Ren nodded, but her mind wasn't on the master or Tatief's plans. Only one thought stuck in her head, and she wasn't sure she could leave without voicing it. She breathed in her fear and stood.

"In the raising home, everyone gets introduced to their birth parents." The Suprintendre met Ren's eyes. "It's a simple introduction. They share a meal or play a game. It's supposed to help in the growth process. Everyone wants to see where they came from."

"Yes, I know." She looked away.

"Bala skipped the introduction and faked the forms for me because my genetic donors, of course, were not available."

"Should you be telling me this?" The Warrior's cat-like presence didn't scare Ren now.

"I think you already know all of this." Ren's voice broke and she faltered. She couldn't bring herself to ask flat out, so she let her heart go to another place.

"Superintendre," Ren whispered.

"You can call me Eviah." The sharp beauty remained still.

Ren nodded, then closed her eyes and forced her question out. "Did you kill him?"

Silence.

"No."

Ren's eyes met hers, and for the slightest second, a thin line of light connected them.

Then, the Warrior broke away. "But I didn't stop it either."

A part of Ren wanted to run to her, hug her, forgive her, and the other part wanted to scream and strip off any evidence of this awful woman who had a part in making her so different and awkward and lost.

Eviah took a step toward Ren. "Bala did well with the choices she made. I owe her a debt." A single tear escaped the Superintendre's eye. "I was wrong." She closed the gap between them and took Ren's hand.

The universe stopped in that moment, and Ren's gift exploded a lifetime into her head. Her mother's life, and in that fraction of time, she caught a glimpse of why someone might do such awful things and never see them as evil—not excuses, but the pathway to destruction.

Eviah's whispered words drifted into the vision. "Will you tell him I'm sorry?"

Ren didn't understand who she meant, but she couldn't speak.

"Bala is right. Love will win. He is the only one who can defeat the master." She cupped Ren's cheek with her cold hand. "And you, little one, you will do great things. Be strong."

The electricity pulsing through Ren exploded in her heart, and she threw her arms around her mother and held on tight. The Superintendre curved a stiff arm around Ren, and they stayed in silence. A woman lost to the lies and another freed by an unwanted truth.

Shouts from outside intruded on the moment, and Eviah withdrew. More needed to be said, but the door opened, and two sentries stood at the ready.

Ren had questions. She needed answers, but Eviah was done. She crossed to the sentries. Her fierceness returned.

"It's time for the hunt." She was the Superintendre again. "And Ren, I have a surprise for you." The sentries entered the room, and Owen followed. "You don't have to go alone."

CHAPTER 51

THE APOLOGY

Screams and chaos charged the air. Owen stayed close to Ren as she guided them through the woods. They'd stepped off the transport into *the hunt* and discovered the awful truth about the Plantanate.

A troupe of five sentries gave fifteen unprepared villagers a head start, and then the hunt began. Owen didn't stay behind, but the immediate screams told him the fate of those who'd lingered too long.

Ren ran like a deer through the forest, like she'd grown up here. He couldn't see her eyes, but he guessed her gift was at play. After two hours of winding through the tall trees, traipsing up a shallow creek, and working their way through some thick brush, Ren stopped among another clump of trees.

Strands of hair fell around her flushed face, and she spoke to him for the first time. "You okay?"

"Yeah, you?" Owen looked back and listened. Nothing. "Do you know where the guards are?"

Ren surveyed the area with a strong gaze, like her eyes were lasers piercing through the foliage. "I don't see anything, and the silver thread guiding me ended here."

"Your eyes aren't glowing at all." Owen relaxed his stance.

"Yeah, I spent my entire life trying to hide the stupid aberration, but if I'd just let it go, it would have gotten better on its own." She looked like the Ren he'd whisked into the woods and told his secrets to. Her sweet blue eyes, serious and playful all at the same time. And most importantly, she didn't look like she hated him.

She snuggled up to massive oak and dug a nutibar from a pouch on her waist. Owen joined her. This would be it. The first time since she ran away that he'd actually get a chance to apologize. He'd rehearsed this over and over, but now all his elegant soliloquies felt fake and weren't him.

He kept it simple. "I'm sorry I didn't tell you the whole truth. I was going to."

She didn't respond but turned toward him, so he stumbled onward. "I wouldn't have told them about your gift." Her eyes welcomed his.

"I know." A smile pulled at her lips. "I didn't then, but I do now. I should have talked to you instead of running off. I just reacted and did what I always do. Hide."

"You did the best you could in the moment." Peace settled between them, and he wished she could see herself like he saw her. Strong, smart, and full of life.

A light blue butterfly flitted by, but Ren didn't notice. Something deep was going on in that little head, so Owen kept his mouth shut and waited.

"Why do you suppose she let you go with me?" Her voice sounded different, fuller, deeper. Still the same sweet tone, just with something under it now.

"Who? Eviah? I don't know." That wasn't true. He had a guess, but how do you tell someone their DNA has warrior in it? "I can't figure that woman out."

The joy left Ren's eyes, and she leaned against the tree. A flush of pink tinged her cafte-colored cheeks. "You know, it's weird. I've spent my whole life hiding because of the aberration, the gift. And now everybody knows, and I still feel like I'm hiding—like my life hasn't started yet."

"You don't need to ever hide from me." That sounded cheesier out loud than in his head. "I mean why do you think that?"

"I don't know." Two birds fluttered in the branches above them. "I don't like it, though."

"Well, then change it. It's your life. Change it." Sunlight filtered through the trees, catching dust motes in the air and making them sparkle like fairy dust. Olivope's words came back to Owen: "Your choices affect far more than you know."

"It's not that easy. I'm not like you—ambitious and driven. A person can't go from being one way to being another. I think I'll forever be this broken girl, seeing crazy visions, following silver threads, and never really knowing what any of it means."

"I don't know about your gift. It makes sense that you'd have to learn how to use it. So, practice and give it time. And as far as the other goes—" he took her hand. "The only way to ever go from one place to another is by one step at a time. One choice. One decision. One try."

A smile lit her face, and Owen's insides did a cartwheel.

"I want to show you something." She grabbed his other hand and sat in front of him. "Look at me."

That wasn't a problem. Her icy blue eyes laced their magic around his heart and pulled him like a magnet to the North. A sparkle twinkled in their blue glint, and the world around Owen transformed from sunlit woods to a dark field and the two of them under a full moon. It was just like the night she confided in him about her aberration.

"What is this?" He looked around. It was all there. Just like that night. Are you doing this?"

She giggled. "Yes, Altrist taught me how. Isn't it cool?"

"Can you take us someplace else?"

She gripped his hands tighter, and the field morphed into the workroom. They stood by her workstation. Lidya pecked away at a love note, and Nil patrolled the room.

"Whoa, this is so weird. It's like we're there." Whitler stood in his office looking in a mirror and combing his hair. "Nice touch with Whitler. Oh, I didn't tell you about Whitler." His outburst shook the vision, and the office dripped into the woods again.

"I'm not an expert at it." A tiny sparkle glistened in her right eye. "What about Whitler?"

"He's here, outside the boundary. Turns out his mother was one of the insurgents or something."

"Oh, yeah. She saw his picture on my clip-pad. I heard they were going to go after him."

"Wait, you had Whitler's picture on your clip-pad." He loosened his hold on her hands.

She grinned. "Why? Are you jealous? Lidya put it there. Not me. You know her."

"Oh, yeah." That didn't really make him feel better, though. Ren could have erased it. Put someone else's picture there. He decided to let it go. It was just her and him out here—no Whitler. With her options limited, he wanted to seize the moment.

"Ren." He reached for her hands again. "There's something I want to tell you." She looked into his eyes. With the afternoon sun spilling through the trees, the woods urged him onward. "I've done a lot of thinking, and I've never met anyone like you. This probably isn't the right time, but—"

"She's my mother." Ren interrupted him, her cheeks more flushed.

"What?"

"I just think that before you go on any further, you need to know my mother is the Superintendre—the Warrior. That's what's flowing in my veins."

He ran his hand up her harm and rested it on her shoulder. The sweet innocence in her face shown a light on his world like the sun splitting across the snow. It blinded him to any faults. "I know. I mean I had suspicions." He leaned closer. "It doesn't change how I feel. You are your own person, and I—"

Before he could finish, a shout sliced through the trees, and an arrow landed by Owen's feet. A scraggly group of five skinny men and one woman stood in the shadows.

"We's the welcome party." A lanky fellow pointed a bandaged skeer at them and strolled closer. The others backed him up. These were not sentries.

"What's you got to say for yourself?" Lanky fellow motioned and a guy on the end let another arrow fly. This one landed in the oak tree.

"We don't want any trouble." Owen edged in front of Ren, but she moved to his side.

The group snickered and mocked him. Some wore village colors.

Their spokesperson took another step closer. "If you want to live, you can come with us. If you don't, then we can help with that too." He waved the skeer at them, but then froze. The entire group's eyes got big, and they lowered their weapons.

Owen grabbed Ren's hand. Footsteps sounded behind them, and then a girl's voice called out.

"Go on, and no one will get hurt."

A huge smile washed the worry from Ren's face. Two large men and a blonde stood behind them.

Ren wrenched her hand free and ran to them. "Dart!"

CHAPTER 52

THE GIFT FROM A FATHER

Embers floated up from the fire as Ren surveyed the group who had gathered to discuss what to do next. She and Owen sat outside of the circle. A guy with a skeer guarded them from behind. Whitler, who sat with his mother, kept looking back at them. He'd been like a giddy little one since they'd arrived.

A tall man next to Gander spoke. "We have to go help him. This is Olivope. We've got to do what we can." Sighs of agreement rose from most of the villagers.

One woman called out, directing her concern to Gander. "He really said Olivope needs to get through the rim?"

"Yes, and the longer we wait, the worse it gets. There's only Altrist, Liza, and Thim to protect Olivope, and that's it."

Ren glanced at Owen. His head was downcast. She squeezed his arm. "Olivope will be okay," she whispered. The group's reception of Owen had been mixed. His guardian black didn't help matters. Once he changed clothes, the contrast hadn't been so stark. She spoke up for him, too, and told them Owen had risked himself to free Olivope.

He nodded, but she could tell his heart was hurting. He had encouraged her so much, and she didn't know how to help him through the weeds of his guilt.

"We go at first light." Gander's command boomed like thunder. Some protests started again, but he raised his fist. "No. You've all wasted enough time with your bickering. No more. Buck and Buddy will shroud us with the vim, and we'll send a bandy to Snowshoe to gain their support."

"What about them?" The woman pointed at Ren and Owen.

"They're with us." Dart looked at Gander. "Right?" Ren held her breath.

Gander agreed.

Dart ran to her. "I can't believe you're here. The Leader did this, and he can help Olivope too."

Ren nodded. The Leader seemed to get the credit for the good, and Tatief was blamed for the bad. She didn't argue though. Tatief should be blamed for all the horrible parts of life. She had told Dart and the others about her time with Tatief, and they burned her clothes with the beans and cams. Whatever spell Tatief had cast on her foggy brain at the Plateau was completely broken now. Eviah had helped with that.

Whitler hadn't left Ren's side since they set out in the hazy predawn quiet. Not that it was quiet with his fast-talking recounts of all he'd seen in the last week. He may have gained a new perspective on life, but he hadn't lost any of his old self-centered focus.

The non-stop chatter gave her the opportunity to retreat into her thoughts and only offer an occasional "uh-huh" and "oh, really." Another time, she might have enjoyed his stories, but right now she just wanted to think. She was free, but she felt crummy.

She wondered what Bala would think of her now. And then her thoughts went to Eviah. Ren wanted to talk to Bala about it, unpack the whole conversation. Bala would understand.

"Excuse me." An older woman with dark skin and a kind face tapped Ren on the arm. Whitler kept talking, and Ren left Owen's ear alone in the fray.

The woman held a lit stave between them and walked as she talked. "You're new, right? I noticed your bracelet."

The lights on the thin metal bracelet glowed in the dark. Ren ran her fingers over it. They'd scanned it for a transmitter, but it had come up clean.

A smile warmed the woman's face. "May I?" She examined the bracelet, and her eyes misted over. "It's exactly right."

"What is?"

"It's one of his." She released Ren's arm.

"Whose?"

"My brother's." The wrinkles around her eyes softened. "He would be forty-one." They walked in silence for a minute before Ren could speak over the colliding feelings inside her. Fear, hurt, joy, hope, confusion. They globbed together like a pack of tween girls looking over the matchment list.

"Your brother?" Her hand went to the bracelet. The lights blinked as if they were notes singing out a tune.

Despite her loss, the woman exuded joy. "Woody had many gifts. He was a lookout—keen eyes." Pride lifted her chin. "He was a fixer." She tapped her temple. "He was always working on stuff and fixing it. And ..." She pointed to the bracelet. "he could imbue certain kinds of metal and rock with energy. It's like I have a piece of him with me still." She tugged on her collar revealing a matching necklace.

Tears trickled from the corners of Ren's eyes, and she was grateful for the darkened morning. Her father. Eviah had given her a bracelet from her father.

"Oh, don't cry. It will be okay. The Leader will see to that." She squeezed Ren in a half hug.

"The leader?" It was the first time someone had spoken of the leader connected to something sad.

"We grew up out here. Woody and me. Our mother was from the Viand. She survived a hunt, and Olivope found her. We haven't seen what you've seen—the truth has always been part of our lives, but I once heard someone, fresh from the village, say they'd seen the Leader there too. It didn't make sense to me, but then, after Woody, I thought the Leader must desperately want the villagers to know the truth."

That didn't make sense to Ren. "Why would you think that?"

Light from her necklace blinked from under her coverup. "Because he didn't stop it. And if he didn't stop it, then he can somehow use it. Tatief can never have the last say unless we let him." She patted Ren's cheek. "I'm glad you're here. I'm Awny."

Ren wiped her face. "I'm Ren."

"I know." She winked, then fell in step with her group.

As soon as she left, Ren called up her ability and urged it toward the cabin. She wanted to see his face.

Come to me. I am your father.

The whisper floated on raining lights that cascaded around the others walking the trail. And tiny drops of light fell around them.

"What was that about?" Owen retreated from Whitler, and the vision vanished.

She shrugged. "That lady knew my father." Those were words she never thought she would say.

A call came from the head of the troop. "We wait here." A search party slipped through a narrow opening in the shimmering vim, and the rest of the group congregated at the top of the hill.

An incline of boulders and rocks stretched down the hill all the way to the rim. Mostly dirt and stone, the area looked like a dried-up riverbed. The glow from the wall cast an eerie haze over the scene.

"Whoa. It's huge." Owen stared at the rim.

Ren pulled in a deep breath and focused on the ability to survey the landscape. A soft glow tinted the rocks, and the mirrored panels of the Silver Rim blushed in hues of red. All except for one that stood out with a green rectangle frame encasing a cloudy white panel.

Suddenly, her vision darkened, and Tatief's tall form stood among the rocks. She grabbed Owen's arm. "Do you see him?"

"What? No? Who?"

And then the rocks turned into bodies, and Tatief screamed out in triumph. Ren sank to her knees. It all looked so real. The monster surveyed the dead and laughed.

"Please, no."

And then, she heard it again. The gentlest whisper calling to her. "Ren, come."

CHAPTER 53

THE UNSANCTIONED, GENETICALLY FLAWED DAUGHTER

Dart split from the group and jogged to a cluster of bamboo halfway down the hill. She had caught a glimpse of something and needed to check it out.

Threading her way through the stalks, she popped out on the other side. A path on the left went down to the rock field, and to the right a slight incline led deeper into the woods. The gray, hazy light of dawn chased the shadows through the trees.

At the top of the hill, more woods spread out, but off the trail a swampy area boasted hollowed-out trees with their tops toppled off and high wet grass. It looked like a giant had karate chopped them and sucked out all their innards.

"It's not my favorite place." Melkin's warm voice came up behind her. He had his hands in his pockets and a serious look on his face. "You found me."

Dart ran to him and pulled at his arm. "You have to come. Olivope needs you."

He stayed put. "I know what Olivope needs."

"You can fix her." From the look in his deep eyes, she knew he wasn't going to comply. "Why won't you?"

"There's so much more going on here than you know. You see one piece, not the whole. I come not to save one, but all." Morning sun peeked through the trees. "Walk with me." He looped her arm around his and headed back the way she'd come. "Many things must happen before Tatief is stopped, and today will be but one of the battles you will face."

"Battle?" She gripped his arm. "What battle?"

He stopped and faced her. "You won't have to fight today. You've seen so much already. I've another task for you. But your friends will not be as fortunate." He sighed and the woods sighed with him. "This fight is Ren's to face."

"Ren? She's not a fighter." Dart's thoughts scrambled to keep up. "I'll do it. Whatever it is. I'll do it."

His lips hinted at a smile, and he gripped her shoulder with his strong hand. "I know you would, but for now, she's the only one who can do what needs to be done—the only one who can face him and help the others escape."

Dart grappled to find the right question to reveal what would happen? "How? What? I don't understand."

Now, he faced her with both hands on her shoulders. "I love that you came to find me. You were right to, and I will help, but only as absolutely needed. I've already given you everything you need, and what you don't have, I will provide.

He pulled her into a warm hug, and Dart wondered if this is what it felt like to have a father. Strong protective arms and confusing advice that isn't exactly what you wanted to hear.

"It's time. I need you to go back." A warmth spread through Dart's middle, and her gift took hold. "Tell them. Warn them. Tatief is coming."

Owen shook Ren, and she collapsed into his chest. A concerned group gathered, but he angled her away from their questions. "She's fine. Just getting the hang of her gift." He used their lingo, and it seemed to work.

"Hey, you okay?" He tilted her chin to see her face. Her eyes stayed closed, and her sweaty hair clung to her face. The rock field was empty. "I didn't see anyone. It was just in your vision. What was it?"

She held onto him, and his arms wrapped around her. As much as he wanted to be close to her, he'd rather her not be terrified and in tears every time he hugged her. He rubbed her back and gave her time.

"Hey, guys, what's up?" Whitler nosed into the moment. If there were one person Owen would have rather not seen for the rest of his life, Whitler was it. Yet some twisted irony put them here together. Both vying for the attention of the same girl.

"Nothing." Owen turned away from the nemesis.

The rest of the group moved down the hill toward the rim. Owen moved with them with Ren still nestled under his arm. Whitler sidled up on her left, still talking, still oblivious.

Gander called out orders, and the guys with the shield gift set up a dome halfway through the field of rocks to the tree line. That's when Owen saw her. Olivope lay in the glade. Two women grazed Olivope's head and chest with glowing hands while the crowd gathered closer.

Half the size of Gander, Altrist stayed near Olivope but spoke with the three people who had been most vocal around the fire. Their animated gestures suggested a disagreement. If Whitler hadn't still been yammering, Owen might have picked up a word or two.

Ren hadn't said a word. Her trancelike state was beginning to worry him. "You sure you're okay?"

She moved out from under his arm. "Yeah." Her *yeah* sounded more like a *no*, and her attention homed in on the little messenger. "I just have a bad feeling."

"Another vision." The hazy dawn morning gathered some pinks and reds across the sky. "Like the one at the Plateau?"

"Worse."

What could be worse than Tatief becoming the all-powerful despot of their silver-rimmed little world? He didn't ask.

Dart had Altrist's ear now. People huddled close to the messenger, while one group stayed near Olivope. Within the huddles, children clung to adults, and the stronger ones stood like guards with each pod of people. Altrist jumped onto a large boulder, and the quiet conversations grew still.

"We haven't much time." The messenger's little arms waved at the group. "Dart says Tatief is coming." Owen tensed. These people were no match for Tatief's trained army.

He checked his side, but Ren was gone. She had moved closer to the wall, her eyes fixed on one spot in the mirrored rim.

Tingly energy zipped up Ren's arms and legs filling her chest with warmth. The crowd behind her grew louder, their fear springing them to action.

The mirrored wall reflected the chaos. Ren stood in the middle, wearing borrowed clothes. Her confidence was wilting, useless. She was the same girl who was on the stage at Castle, unable to change Nanny Reece's fate or her own. The same girl who watched the sentries beat the man in the woods and Tatief smack Bala to the floor. All the same, watching and helpless. The unsanctioned, genetically flawed, aberrant daughter of a dead man and the woman who caused his death.

That is not who you are.

She was nobody. If anything, she was her aberration. Her whole life had been about the weird ability, about holding it back and hiding. No other thing defined her more.

The gift controlled her. It made her run from Owen and set her apart in Tatief's eyes. Her existence revolved around it.

It's not about the gift.

"It sure seems like it," she mumbled. Her heart pounded in her ears. "I couldn't have done anything to change any of it." The aberration had always had her. It controlled her steps. It dictated who she was and what she did. If anything, she belonged to the blasted ability, not to herself, not to Tatief, not anything else.

But then, she remembered Nanny Reece making her choice; her father choosing love; Bala standing when silence might have saved her; Owen freeing Olivope, and even her mother, holding on to a bracelet for seventeen years. Each of them did something. In the end, life didn't just happen to them. It happened because of them.

And then she saw it looking back at her in the reflection. Her life had been one long reaction. *You can't waiver. Your choice must be sure.* Eviah had said that, but what choice was there to make? She would go where the aberration told her. She would do what they told her to do.

Lay it down—all of it—the good, the bad, and the gift.

Ren shook her head. She didn't know how.

A light flashed next to her, and Altrist appeared. He turned her away from the wall and cupped her face in his hands. "Stop focusing on yourself, on your past, and even on what's next. Focus on the Leader. He will help you."

Tears streamed down her cheeks. "Where is he?" The void of life stretched out before her without a hint at the Leader's presence. "I see lots of things, and I've never seen him."

"You have seen him, and you will see." He spoke into her head. "But how you will see him next will depend on what you choose."

A crash split through the air above them, and Buddy's vim glowed white then back to clear. Altrist's pale cheeks flared. "Tatief is here."

People ran to Altrist and demanded he take action. Gander shouted orders. Dart ran to Olivope.

Altrist called over the din. "We've got to find the door."

CHAPTER 54

THE DOORWAY

Another blast shook the vim.

A woman, holding a child in her arms, fell to her knees and called out to the Leader. A man used his gift to gather everyone's belongings into a barricade. A few others surrounded Buck and Buddy, bracing their arms.

The choices you make affect far more than you know.

Ren's existential crisis would have to wait.

She reached for her ability and the wall morphed from its mirrored shield to sheer panels, except for one. Her eyes went to it again. The bright green framing of the panel resembled the green from Dart's room, and there to the right was the handkey. It looked like a smudge from a distance, but as she moved closer, it came into focus.

Ren examined the handprint. It was different from the one in Dart's room, not green like the frame, but pulsing and indigo. Pulsing like a heartbeat.

She surveyed the frenzied crowd. Everyone glowed, although some brighter than others. The colors pulsed, and not one was the same. Scanning the group, a flash of indigo caught her eye. A man, standing next to Dart, glowed with the same color as the handkey.

Ren's heart pounded in her chest. This couldn't be right. If she were wrong, it could rip his arm off. There was no way to know for sure. She checked the rim again. But it had to be. Another booming crack hit the vim, and Buddy yelled out in pain.

The panicked crowd surrounded Altrist. Where was their Leader? Why not a whisper in her ear now? Just some assurance that she wasn't about to send a man to his death.

Tatief's jab held her in place. A fairytale. A lie. But then, Altrist, Dart, and Bala each knew him. They trusted him. The journey from their unbelief to trust didn't have a map, at least not one she could follow.

But maybe it didn't need one. Perhaps uncertainty was the point. The action required choice, not certainty. To jump and believe without being sure.

She wasn't sure, and short of the Leader popping into view, she wasn't going to be sure, but she could choose. She could choose to trust.

Jumping up on a rock, she waved her arms. "I think I found it." Part of the trusting and believing in the Leader was believing he could make this work.

Ren scanned the crowd for Owen. A dose of his encouragement would be good right now. He helped the women move Olivope away from the edge of the vim.

The lack of response punctured her resolve. Her unsupportive tongue stuck to the roof of her mouth. Pushing her vocal cords into action, she took a deep breath, and yelled, "I think I know where the door is."

No one listened, so she drew in another lung full and tried again and again, until the group quieted. The attention made her want to hide, but she set the fear aside and focused. Her explanation tumbled out, and when she pointed to the indigo man, Dart yanked her off the rock.

"You better be sure about this or Thim's going to lose an arm." The challenge muted Ren for a flash, but what choice did they have. No one else was the same shade of purple as Thim. He volunteered, anyway, and the matter was settled.

Another crash racked the vim, and then Tatief appeared at the top of the hill, tall and fierce, just like in her vision. "It's over," he yelled. The rim amplified his voice. "I knew I would find you here, groping for a doorway that doesn't exist. Come now, it's only a matter of time before we break the shield, and you're all exposed." His gaze groped for his target, but the vim stilted his view.

Gander jumped into action. "If we're going to do this, now is the time." He waved to Thim and ordered Ren. "Guide him to the key. We don't see a handprint."

Another crash slammed against the vim, and this time bolts of energy slipped through, slamming people to the ground. Whitler fell, and his mother ran to him. Ren searched for Owen. He stood by Olivope.

"The vim's not going to hold." Cries rose up from the group.

"Open the door."

"Oh, Leader, help us."

Ren led Thim to the wall and guided his hand to the handkey. Dart stayed by his side. The group crowded together, putting fragile Olivope in the center.

"Are you sure about this?" Thim half-smiled.

"No." Ren held her hand in front of the handkey. "Not sure at all."

"Okay, then." He closed his eyes and pressed his hand to the pulsing indigo print. The panel in the rim dissolved. "It worked." Thim pulled his hand from the wall, and the panel fell back in place.

Quiet settled among the group, but Thim recovered. "It's okay." He looked to Ren, and she guided his hand back.

Dart wedged next to him. "I won't leave you." Thim smiled and pressed his hand to the wall again. A field of golden grass danced in the wind on the other side. Blue sky, with no dome hazing its perfection. A clean, fresh breeze blew in.

Gander shouted directions, and the people got in order. Some of the wounded were moved to the side where Whitler's mother worked on them. Altrist stood nearby, poised and ready if the vim should fail.

Owen came with the group bringing Olivope. Another streak of energy pounded the vim, sending a spray of sparks through the stony field. Buddy cried out and fell. His brother raised both his arms and poured his gift into the air. The barrier between them and Tatief grew thinner. They weren't all going to make it.

Ren pushed through the crowd toward the edge of the vim. Tatief paced on the other side, as the sentries joined their scinters and skeers together and aimed them at the vim. Another crash split into the shield, and Tatief paused, watching as the crack repaired itself.

Half the people had made it through the doorway, including Olivope, with Owen still by her side. Ren wanted to run to him, but that wasn't the choice she was going to make. That wasn't who she would be.

Her fingers played with her father's bracelet. No wonder Tatief didn't want people to know their parents or fall in love or even care for someone else. There was a strength in it that was beyond him. Bala said it. Love. Love is real, and he is coming. Ren knew what she needed to do.

She waited as the sentries pooled their forces and aimed again. This would be it. The vim would fail. Adrenalin pumped through her, fighting the electric tingles crashing into her chest and head. She could do this.

The soldiers pulled back and the bolt broke through. She concentrated and created the scene Tatief most wanted to see.

CHAPTER 55

THE LEADER

Ren crafted the scene from her vision. The rocks became bodies, broken, cowering, defeated people. The Silver Rim remained intact, no open doorway, no escaping insurgents. She hated the picture, but it served its purpose, and Tatief roared his victory.

The sentries backed away. Ren took slow concentrated breaths. This wasn't like what she'd done before. Taking Altrist to a field of flowers and Owen to their office were tricks. This vision-casting took her to a different level. Her body shook with the crazy tingling of the vision. Each breath brought it back down, and then it would ramp up again.

Tatief finished his victory roar and loomed over her. "Ren, you surprise me." He tilted the hot skeer toward her face, and she leaned away from its heat. "I didn't even think you would make it past the hunt." His white teeth flashed within his grin. "But I supposed I failed to see your potential."

Ren swallowed and kept breathing.

No one saw through the vision. Sentries stood at attention. None gave her away.

"Jasper, come." Tatief waved his hand in the air. "I think we may have a new warrior."

The sentry sneered, but Ren kept her focus. Just a little bit longer until she was sure they had escaped through the wall.

Tatief stroked her cheek with his hot fingers. "I reward all who follow. And I tell you what" He held out his skeer.

"I'll let you do the honors, dear." He turned her around to the façade. The scene ripped at her heart.

Altrist cowered by Olivope. Gander stood by Dart. Thim and the others poked their heads out from behind a boulder.

Tatief leaned close to her ear. "Aim at the boy." He pushed the skeer into her hand. "It won't kill him, but it will set an example, and an example needs to be set."

She swallowed and lifted the heavy skeer. Even if this was just a figment of her vision, she wasn't sure she could point and shoot.

Tatief raised his arms. "Listen to me. You have been deceived. I am your savior. I lifted the rim to protect us all." He turned and pumped up the army. "For the good of all."

"We give ourselves."

"Aim, Ren. Shoot the skeer. Level the boy." Tatief's voice snaked into her head, but she held tight to the Leader. Altrist had said he would help her, and the thought of him did help. Peace washed through her and drowned Tatief's drugging words.

The skeer grew heavy, and she closed her eyes and worked in the vision, drawing the ones in hiding out and bringing them to their knees before Tatief.

He roared. "I am incomparable preeminence." The sentries chanted behind them. "Say it." He yelled to the phantoms cowering in the vision. "Incomparable preeminence."

"Incomparable preeminence."

The words exploded into the scene, and Ren lost it. Instead, the earlier vision flooded in with Olivope and Altrist mourning for their brother. And Ren realized they mourned for Tatief. The victory in the vision was not Tatief's. The words came back, and she spoke them aloud. "He is powerful. Unmatched. And the Silver Rim will break before him that the world might know his incomparable preeminence."

As she spoke, a silver thread glistened into the woods.

The ghastly scene with which she had mesmerized Tatief melted to reveal the open door of the Silver Rim, Dart's glow encasing Thim, and the door closing as they evaporated into the air. Altrist leaned over the injured who remained and enveloped them away.

Everything stopped for a moment, and Ren stood by Tatief's side, the skeer in hand, and his full army behind her.

His face flooded with red, and she seized her opportunity, slamming the hot end of the skeer into the monster's side. He staggered backwards but didn't fall. She ran. With all her might, she ran for the woods, the silver thread tracing a path. A bolt struck a tree as she passed, sending bark flying. She didn't look back.

As soon as she reached the cover of trees, the silver thread curved toward the rim. The hum of drespins spun through the air behind her. Her muscles burned, and she tripped through the brush. A man grabbed her and pulled her deeper into the thicket, putting a finger to his lips. Sentries zipped around them.

Tatief boomed orders, taking frenzied shots at the rim that sent sparks splaying over them. The monster screamed threats. "You're mine, Ren! There's no one to help you. No one."

Ren's heart hammered in her chest, but she stayed still and followed the man's lead. He guided her to a creek, and then angled back toward the rim. She didn't recognize him. "Are you from Snowshoe?"

He shushed her and led her down a steep hill, stopping under the shade of a mimosa tree. The trees and the soft buzz of the Silver Rim dampened the shouts of the sentries.

"No, I'm not from Snowshoe." His kind eyes met hers.

He didn't offer more, and she didn't press. The man had just saved her.

"I have another gift for you." The light followed him. It wasn't a glow like on Altrist, but more like the sun. He turned her toward the right and pointed. A dark-skinned man waved, his navy coverup covered in sawdust and a huge smile on his face.

Ren waved back, and then she noticed the bracelet on the man's wrist. It blinked out a rainbow of colors that matched hers.

"Is that ...?"

Her new friend nodded. "I wanted you to see him, and he asks about you always."

Her father waved again, then the sun brightened, and he was gone. Tears coursed down Ren's face, and the stranger wiped them away. But he wasn't a stranger.

As she looked into his dark brown eyes, she saw him in places she'd not noticed before. Next to a crying baby in a cabin. With a little girl in the corner playing alone. A slighted preteen pretending not to care. On the transport to the Protectorate. Under the moon with Owen. Crying by Bala's side. And in the field just now, facing Tatief.

He knew her thoughts and whispered, "Always with you."

Incomparable Preeminence.

Ren wanted to hide from his eyes, but he took her hand. He was the one who would break the rim and defeat Tatief.

His steady, sure voice comforted her. "I know who you are Ren Lyn Leen." When he said her name, an all-encompassing peace poured through her. It replaced the electricity zipping through her veins and settled her racing heart.

"The gift I gave you has caused you quite the stir, but trust me, and you'll find out what you can do. And remember." He brushed her hair back from her face. "The gift is for you to use. It doesn't define you. I define you."

She wanted to fall to her knees, but he held her up.

"You are mine. No more hiding and lying. I've much better things for you to do."

It was hard to look at him—his perfection and goodness, but there she stood, bare and broken and loved. It didn't make sense.

He gripped her shoulders, firm and sure. "Fearfully and wonderfully made."

Time hung on his words, and the universe leaned toward him.

"I'm proud of you." His words were air. His presence, hope. "That was brave. Crazy, but brave. And now, I have a question for you. Where will you go next?"

She shook her head. Words evaded her. And her mind went to Eviah and Bala. They needed to see him—to know.

"I will let you choose. You can stay here, or I will deposit you beyond the rim. The choice is yours. The squirrel must choose." He grinned.

As the branches of the mimosa stirred in the breeze and shied away from the power of the rim, Ren sorted through the wonder of the last few minutes. "I don't understand."

She really needed to sit down. The Leader caught her, then guided her to the base of the tree and knelt beside her.

"It's okay. I know it's a lot. But we really do need to get you to where you're going to go."

She clutched his arm. She didn't want to leave him.

He patted her hand. "I know. But we both have things we need to do."

"Owen, Dart, Altrist? Where are they?" The words sputtered out.

The Leader leaned back. "Let's see. Dart and Altrist are heading to Snowshoe, and Owen is outside with Olivope, wondering where you are. Bala is resting in a tunnel near Castle Raising Home, and Eviah is disobeying her master and disavowing her claim to warrior.

"Now, do you want to stay here or go outside the rim? I can do either. It's up to you." He pushed off the ground and held out his hand. Grabbing it, she got to her feet. She hadn't said thank you or that she was sorry or anything that needed to be said. But when she opened her mouth, he shook his head.

"Those words can wait. Where do you want to go?"

This time, when she looked into his eyes, she saw hope—her hope and the hint of who she could be. Not an aberrant or a gifted or even a warrior's daughter or a nanny's friend. She was free. She was his. The truth anchored her, and she reached out and fell into his arms.

It was an embrace she didn't deserve—one she couldn't earn and a favor she had never looked for, but it found her. He found her.

His loving question came again. "Where do you want to go?"

She nestled deeper into his arms. "Wherever you want me to go."

His happy smile filled her senses. "I love you, Ren."

She held on as long as she could, but then the green woods gave way to light, and her eyes opened to a place she didn't know.

CHAPTER 56

THE GUARDIAN IN THEIR MIDST

The massive door in the rim shimmered shut, and Owen searched the crowd of escapees for the only face he wanted to see. Ren's. The two-year-old he had carried into the golden field jabbered and fiddled with his collar. He sat her down by her mother and brothers. She put her arms up, but he only patted her on the head.

"Be good for your ma, Lacy." Then, he headed for the doorway. Gander carried Buddy like a baby cradled in his arms. The master of the vim rested his head against Gander's shoulder.

"Where's Ren?" Owen resisted the urge to yell. "She made it through, right?"

The tall oaf shrugged and shook his head. "I didn't see her."

"What do you mean? She was by the door with Dart and Thim. Where did she go?"

Gander didn't answer, but Buddy eked out a reply.

"She went to Tatief just as the vim failed."

Owen's heart fell. "What?" He wanted to rip the shield maker from Gander's arms and shake him. "Why? She would never go back to him."

"She didn't go to him." A woman's voice spoke from behind. Owen had seen the girl, Liza, but hadn't spoken with her yet. "She stopped him." A group formed around them, and others called out agreement.

Liza continued, "She stood in front of him, and it was like he couldn't see us. None of them could—not the sentries, not any of them. I don't know what she did, but she saved us."

"What?" Owen couldn't process the news.

Liza squeezed his arm. "I'm sorry. She didn't make it."

"Where's Thim?" He looked around. "I'll go back and get her."

Gander spoke this time. "No, Thim and Dart didn't make it either. He couldn't go through the door because only his hand on the handkey could keep it open. I saw a flash right before the door shut. Maybe Dart got him out of there."

"And Altrist, Anna, and the others?" Someone else called.

Liza answered. "They didn't make it either."

The group grew quiet. In their joy, they bore a loss—one Owen wasn't sure he could bear. A warm breeze blew up the yellow grass, and it waved at their waists. They were pilgrims, lost in a place they never even knew existed.

As reality set in, so did panic, and the group looked to Gander for direction. Owen faded into the background and retreated to the wall. Ren was inside. Did she think he had deserted her? Did she escape Tatief?

Instead of mirrored panels, steel sections composed the Silver Rim's outside layer. Thick, glowing posts joined the sections, and a thin blue light at the top spread inward over Tatief's prison. Impenetrable and inescapable.

Owen fisted his hands. He should have never left Ren's side. Olivope had plenty of help around her, but he was all Ren had, and he left her. They all left her.

A little hand grabbed his fist, and Lacy's face beamed up at him.

"O—O." She raised her other arm and waited for him to pick her up. The little one had latched on to him when he went to see Olivope, and her mother had been thankful for the help as she herded her four boys out through the doorway.

Owen scooped her up. Detached from his new reality, he held the girl and surveyed the group, but it didn't feel like he was actually there. His body was present, but his heart was not.

Gander took the lead, and other gifted insurgents came forward. Two particularly fast ones scouted out the surrounding area and found a deserted village a few kilometers away. When the group set out, Owen lagged behind. If Ren did somehow make it through, he wanted to be there to greet her, pull her into his arms, and tell her how he felt.

The thought choked him. He couldn't stay, but how could he leave? Lacy clung to him every step. After they got out of the field, a road with two dirt ruts and a weedy middle led them through a grove of prickly trees, finally intersecting with a paved street. It was cracked and overgrown, but a good sign of the village being livable.

No one spoke to Owen—no one that knew more words than coud, tee, and O-O, that is. He didn't mind. Lacy's company was about all he could handle for now. If Ren had been here, it would be different. Everything would be a celebration—a deliverance. They would be free. No more accomplishments or adjustments. No more cams and beans and never knowing who you can trust.

It would be the unraveling of the lie Tatief had spun in their lives. The world on the outside—not destroyed or unlivable—beautiful, clean, free. Owen's heart ached to share it with Ren.

"Oh, sorry." A man bumped into Owen's shoulder as they crested the hill leading down to the town. Little houses lined carved out streets. A park sat on one side of the village, a road leading to a lake on the other side, and then more trees all around.

Owen checked the guy who had bumped him. "No worries."

The guy looked back and grinned. "Whatever you say." It was Pandon, dressed in drab clothes and looking like the others.

"What?" Lacy's presence in Owen's arms made him keep his distance from the snake. "How did you get here?"

Pandon shrugged. "I go where my master sends me. Tell Ren I said hi." He pulled a small drespin from his pack and took off into the woods.

Owen searched for Gander on the road, but most of the group had already descended into town.

"Bad, bad." Lacy waved her fist after Pandon.

Owen agreed. "That's right, Lacy. Very Bad, bad."

"Owen, come quick." Liza shouted from the yard of the first house leading into the village. This whole place looked like a plat from the Protectorate. It was no Vantages, but it showed promise.

"What?" Owen peeled Lacy's hand from his mouth. He'd have to find Gander and tell him about Tatief's minion. "Where's Gander? I need to tell him something."

Liza ran up the lane to meet him. "Never mind Gander. There's something else you need to see."

CHAPTER 57

THE PLAN FOR THE DOOR

Snowshoe didn't look the same. Dart found her room, but it felt empty without Ren around. So many people were gone. It hurt her to think about it.

She didn't question it, though. If her life had taught her anything, it was that she didn't know what good might come from something that seemed really bad.

"Hey, you." Thim stood in her open doorway. "Anna's making tasty cakes."

"Oh, yeah. Nothing like some tasty cakes after kicking Tatief's butt." She followed Thim through the tunnels. His rim-opening hand rested at his side with a fresh bandage. "Is that Whitler guy still talking?"

Thim glanced back and grinned. "What do you think?"

"Good grief. I didn't realize anyone had that many words to say."

Whitler's deep voice greeted them as they entered the kitchen. "There she is. The one who saved the day." At least he was spouting off praise for others instead of himself.

Anna mixed the tasty cake batter. "You hungry?"

It seemed weird to move into normal life stuff when everything normal about their life had just walked out the door into a new world. Dart climbed on a stool. "Where's Altrist?"

"Checking on the injured. The others are sleeping now." She smiled at Whitler. "Not everyone has the constitution of that one."

Whitler ate a sandwich with one hand, his other arm in a sling.

"Did someone call my name" Altrist patted in and gave Dart a hug then settled at the table between Thim and Whitler. "The others are sleeping like babes."

Dart spun around to face him. "Yeah, I had an idea."

Altrist plucked a grape from the fruit bowl in the middle of the table. "What kind of idea?"

"The kind that gets us through the wall."

"No." The messenger popped the grape in his mouth.

"You didn't even hear it."

"It's not worth Thim losing his arm. No. This is where the Leader wants us, so this is where we're going to be."

Dart jumped off the stool. "It doesn't have to be. Not if we can find Ren."

CHAPTER 58

THE BEST IS YET TO COME

The sound of voices moved Ren to the window. Her body still tingled with the memory of the Leader's arms around her.

The love he bestowed on her went beyond power. It was tangible, more real than anything she had ever experienced. Still, even with his love ramping up her hope, she was beginning to falter. Two hours pacing this tiny house had left her wondering if she had made the right choice by letting him send her where he wanted her to go.

The voices grew closer. She wiped the grime from the window with a dish cloth. A flood of people walked down the main street, and Ren's heart jumped into action sending her running to the door.

She searched the crowd for a familiar face, but it didn't worry her that there wasn't one. She knew where she was. Not in a village under Tatief's hand, but somewhere beyond the rim. Then above the din of strangers, Gander's bushy head bobbed up, and she ran to him.

"Gander, we made it." Even though they had hardly talked before, it felt like an old friendship, and the surprised joy on his face blessed her heart. He scooped her up and spun her around.

"Look everyone. It's our hero." He set her back on her feet and patted her head. "We heard what you did, going face to face with the monster."

Ren shook her head. "It wasn't me. It was the Leader."

A broad smile filled his ex-sentry face. "So true, little one. So true."

"How's Olivope?" Ren walked with Gander as people continued to explore the deserted village.

He pointed to a group of women coming down the hill. They surrounded a stretcher. "She's okay for now. Altrist said there are more messengers out here—ones that can help her."

Ren nodded. Before she could ask more, a squeal pealed over them, and a girl shoved a wide-eyed Owen toward Ren. He handed off the child he held, and Ren closed the gap, jumping into his arms.

He nuzzled her hair. "You're here."

She didn't know what to say. Gratitude flooded her senses, and the wonderful gift took hold. The Leader smiled and spoke into the golden sparkles raining across her closed eyes. *This is where you need to be. There's work for you to do, my child. But I'm also glad you like my choice.* Happiness engulfed them.

"I do like it. I do very, very much."

Owen pulled back with a grin. "What do you like?"

Ren hushed the vision and looked up into his perfect face. "I like that I'm here."

He leaned closer. "So do I."

"The Leader put me here," she whispered and checked her skin. It felt like she must be glowing, but without her vision ramped up, her skin looked normal. "We're free."

A misty sheen glazed his eyes. "I thought I'd lost you."

She shook her head and smiled. "Not yet, Guide Owen. We've only just begun."

ABOUT THE AUTHOR

Mary Beth (MB) Dahl is an award-winning, multi-published author who believes in the power of a good story.

Sonfire Media published her first novel, *Through the Balustrade* (2013), under their imprint, Taberah Press. She has authored multiple short stories published in the *Embers Igniting Literary Magazine*, and her essay, 'Little People,' was published in a compilation of essays for teachers in the book *Life Lessons for Teachers*.

When she's not writing, Mary Beth can be found hiking, taking long walks with her husband, or catching up with her two amazing daughters.

Check her out at https://www.marybethdahl.org/ and discover how stories help us become the warriors we're meant to be.

A MESSAGE FROM THE AUTHOR

Hi there,

I've tried to picture you as I've written this story. Your quiet thoughts, the dreams you have, the way you hide part of yourself. I believe stories can help us explore ourselves and the world around us, and I hope as you venture on past these pages, you will see how incredible you are—how you've been chosen, loved, and forgiven. Life will try to tell you otherwise, but hold on to the truth, dear friend. You have a purpose, and figuring that out is part of your adventure.

I would love to hear from you, so write me at mbdahl@marybethdahl.org or check out my website (www.marybethdahl.org) for all my links.

And please take a minute to share part of your journey through the Silver Rim with others. Leave a review on Amazon or Goodreads. It makes a difference!

Take heart, warrior friend. There's more to life—we've only just begun.

Peace!

Mary Beth

CHAPTER 1, BOOK 2 OF THE SILVER RIM SERIES

CHAPTER 1

THE LIAR

Sometimes, when least expected or wanted, the past rushes into the present, and things you buried flare back to life. Ugly, painful, and refusing-to-let-you-go-things. Ren closed her eyes and sucked in a deep breath of mountain air. As the memories of distant screams faded in her head, she swallowed and tried to focus on the indifferent blackberry bush in front of her.

"You finding anything over there?" Owen called from behind. He always seemed to notice every fluctuation in her demeanor, even if she were five meters away with her back to him.

"Yeah, a few." She didn't offer more. Her voice might betray her. Some days it was harder to feign happiness than others. She pushed branches back to make it look like she was actually trying to contribute to the food supply of the camp.

The world felt heavy. She'd only come along with Owen because sitting in her tent one more day would have sucked away the progress she'd made. Plus, she couldn't come up with any more excuses. Staying away to try to "get her gift back" only worked the first month. Now, they expected her to pull her weight, even if all she could offer were some berries and firewood. The lie she carried wore heavy on her.

It had started with a misunderstanding. They'd just assumed the ability hadn't worked, and she let them. It was better than the truth. She didn't want anyone to know the truth.

A twig snapped in the woods beyond the bushes. A heavy snap, the kind a boot makes when it's connected to a sneaky someone. Ren checked Owen. He had his arm snaked between a bunch of thorny vines.

She positioned herself away from the woods and out of Owen's line of sight. Deep breath, and she let the so-called lost ability flow through her with ease. She'd learned a lot while hiding it the last month and a half. Not enough to trust it with someone else's life again, but it would work for this. With a long blink, she saw the perpetrator outlined in silver and peeking out from behind a tree.

He stepped on a pine cone, and she grinned. Ander would never learn. "I hear you, Ander. Face it. You're no match for me." The fifteen year old was up to his pranks again.

Owen stopped picking. His brown hair had grown out over his ears. He still held himself like a guide from the Protectorate even though none of that mattered out here. He smiled, and her insides got all tingly. His eyes stayed warm but didn't convey any acknowledgement of the effect he had on her. His presence sent a safety line into her drowning sadness and kept her steady.

Stop it. Focus. No time to ponder their complicated relationship or what might have been if things had been different. Digging around her basket of overly ripe berries, she pulled out a squishy mersippon fruit. She'd been saving it for such a time as this.

Sticky, pink juice dripped through her fingers as she held the round fruit up. "Whenever you're ready, Ander." Part of her wanted to let Ander have his fun and do whatever prank he'd planned, but something else inside pushed her forward like a little one being shoved out of line. She couldn't stop it. Something in the challenge drew her.

Ander muttered and zipped back toward her right. Ren didn't need a vision to figure he would make his play across the open patch of grass between her and Owen. With his gift of speed, any hesitation would result in her missing and him finally getting a win. She wouldn't hesitate, though. There would be no fear of accidentally plastering Owen with the fruit. She wouldn't miss.

Facing the tiny meadow, she breathed in the warm air. Hot season evenings on the mountain smelled of honeysuckle and distant storms. She didn't close her eyes. That might clue Owen in, and not even he could know the state of her gift. Besides, her eyes wouldn't glow. They almost never did anymore unless she lost it, but she wouldn't do that, not for this.

She saw everything play across her vision a fraction before it started. Her throw as if she were aiming for a can on the fence post; Ander's takeoff, using his gift of speed; and then the fast outcast stopped in his tracks dripping with mersippon juice and his face moving from surprise to frustration.

After the fruit left her hand, she wondered if maybe she should let him have his win. *Too late now*. The speed of his movement blew the strands of hair from around her face.

"You're cheating." He looked to Owen for support, but Owen just laughed and went back to picking.

The adrenalin cooled in Ren's veins. "Nope. You're just predictable." She rubbed the pink stains from her hands and didn't make eye contact. She probably should have let this challenge go.

Ander narrowed his eyes and grumbled. She could tell where his mind was going, and telling more lies about the state of her gift made her stomach knot. Maybe she could head him off.

"Look, Ander. I got lucky. Okay? I just threw it. I had no idea I'd actually hit you." *Dead in the chest like a great big bullseye.* "It's just luck. Nothing more." She bit her lip. "Of course, your clumsy feet did give you away a bit."

That got him. He'd made a fatal error underestimating the noise factor. "Yeah." He nodded. "I knew I should've gone barefoot." His voice still had some question to it, like he wanted to ask if her ability had returned. Poor guy, he just didn't know how to do it without calling her a liar.

Liar.

The word stuck in her head. She grabbed it and shoved it into a back closet in her mind and returned to pretending to be useful.

"Master Owen, Miss Ren, come quick." A voice called from the narrow path leading down the bluff. Elias zipped to them before the "k" sounded from his quick. His bare feet stopped a meter from Ren, and his filthy little face looked as if he'd been hiding in the mud. "You gotta see this. They captured that guy."

Ander folded his arms and gave Elias a dirty look. There were only two people in the camp with the gift of speed, and Elias wasn't one of them. The other one was his pretty sister. Ander would have rather seen her than her pesky little brother whose only gift was the ability to copy other people's abilities for a short while.

"What are you talking about?" Owen left his patch and joined them.

A grim feeling joined the knots in Ren's stomach. "Who? Who did they capture?" These kind people didn't *capture* anyone. Locking people up just wasn't their style.

"You know that guy. The bad one." Elias shook his hand in the air. Whenever he "borrowed" someone's gift, he did it through touch. The touch usually left him feeling numb wherever the transaction took place.

Owen gripped Ren's arm. The look in his eyes sent a chill through her.

"Who's he talking about?" She wasn't sure she wanted the answer.

From the look on Owen's face, he didn't want to tell her, but he did. "Pandon."

Her knees buckled, and he braced her.

"Yeah, that's it. His name's Pannon." Elias looked up from his hand massage with a sigh of relief, oblivious to the world shifting under Ren's feet and the memories of screams returning to her head.